Praise for Andy

"Mesmerizing." ~ Ed Park, *Los Angeles*

"Duncan shows an hallucinatory gr[...] actor's clarity at the rendering of voice.
~ John Clute, *Washington Post Book World*

"There's no good name for what Andy Duncan does. . . . Duncan's imagination runs through that fertile ground previously tilled by artists such as Harlan Ellison, Ray Bradbury, Shirley Jackson and Poe."
~ Mark Hughes Cobb, *The Tuscaloosa News*

"Duncan's short stories are marvels of setting and diction."
~ Michael Berry, *San Francisco Chronicle Book Review*

"Virtually unclassifiable . . . as powerful as any from Richard Powers or Rick Moody, T. C. Boyle or Steve Erickson . . . a bizarre blend of Faulkner and Hemingway with touches of Tennessee Williams and Kurt Vonnegut."
~ Gary S. Potter, *Charleston Post and Courier*

"You're likely to be laughing one moment, in awe the next and perhaps horrified before the tale is done. Few authors can pull off such delicate tonal balances in a short story, although William Faulkner achieved it more than once . . . Will satisfy any reader brave enough to handle the strange places Duncan visits, the places between disturbing fantasy and ruthless reality."
~ John Mark Eberhart, *The Kansas City Star*

"Stunningly beautiful." ~ Sean Melican, *BookPage*

"Duncan is often most comfortable when working in the rich tradition of the American folk tale, crafting shrewd and funny stories of the intersection between the modern world and folk traditions and superstitions, particularly those of Appalachia and the American South, but . . . he also has other strings to his bow, and a surprising depth of range as a stylist. . . . Whichever critical pigeonhole you try to push Andy Duncan into, he remains one of the best and most original writers in the business." ~ Gardner Dozois

"Wonderful." ~ Nancy Kress · "Wonderfully demented." ~ Michael Swanwick · "Excellent." ~ Rich Horton · "Superlative." ~ Paula Guran · "Superb." ~ Jonathan Strahan · Brilliant." ~ Mary Anne Mohanraj · "Genius." ~ Nick Gevers · "Irresistible." ~ Ernest Hogan · "Knockout." ~ Tim Pratt · "Powerful." ~ Fiona Kelleghan · "Amazing." ~ Patrick O'Leary · "Unique." ~ Steven H. Silver

"Duncan has amassed a record of superior work out of all proportion to mere number of pages gathered between boards. He feels like an essential, towering part of the fantastika landscape, his every story eagerly awaited."
~ *Asimov's Science Fiction*

"Fantasist and folklorist, he takes premises that are not made up, or at least are not made up by Andy Duncan . . . and creates new and strange stories out of them, which nevertheless tell the truth about the way things happened."
~ Christopher Cobb, *Strange Horizons*

"Duncan will get you to bust a gut laughing. He'll make you teary, and put a shiver up your spine. But most importantly, his stories ask questions you might not know how to answer, and leave you looking inside yourself long after you've read the last line of his singing prose."
~ Lara Elena Donnelly, author of *Amberlough*

"Andy Duncan's unique voice shines through in his third collection. You've not read him yet? Go out now and buy *An Agent of Utopia*. You'll thank me."
~ Ellen Datlow, award-winning editor

"*An Agent of Utopia* is all the proof you'll need to see that Andy Duncan is one of the very best short story writers in Science Fiction, Fantasy, or anywhere else. It's a sure bet that you're holding in your hand the best story collection of the year." ~ Jeffrey Ford, author of *A Natural History of Hell*

"One of the most hilarious and poignant writers of short stories that we have. He effortlessly forges dreamlike and nightmarish tales with wit and wisdom that rivals Mark Twain."
~ Christopher Barzak, author of *Wonders of the Invisible World*

"Andy Duncan is the Andy Duncan of Andy Duncanland, and we are all lucky to have access to that fabled locale via the portal between his brain and these pages. The stories in this collection drip with magic and mayhem and time and place and personhood, along with the most creative cussing this side of anywhere. Each one is a microcosm, a moment from our own history, real or imagined, passed along to us by a master storyteller."
~ Sarah Pinsker, author of *New Day*

"Duncan gives us the oldest form of fantasy, the legend, or folk tale: not just the childish folk legend of fireside entertainment but the one that has taken on enough mythic resonance to seem real."
~ Sherwood Smith, author of *King's Shield*

An
Agent
of
Utopia

Andy Duncan

An Agent of Utopia

NEW & SELECTED STORIES

Small Beer Press
Easthampton, MA

For Sydney, as always,
and in memory of David G. Hartwell,
whose enthusiasm never flagged.

An Agent of Utopia: New and Selected Stories copyright © 2018 by Andy Duncan. All rights reserved. Page 279 is an extension of the copyright page.

Small Beer Press
150 Pleasant Street #306
Easthampton, MA 01027
smallbeerpress.com
weightlessbooks.com
info@smallbeerpress.com

Distributed to the trade by Consortium.

Library of Congress Cataloging-in-Publication Data

Names: Duncan, Andy, 1964- author.
Title: An agent of utopia : new & selected stories / Andy Duncan.
Description: First edition. | Easthampton, MA : Small Beer Press, [2018]
Identifiers: LCCN 2018029763 (print) | LCCN 2018030637 (ebook) | ISBN 9781618731548 | ISBN 9781618731531 (alk. paper)
Classification: LCC PS3554.U463395 (ebook) | LCC PS3554.U463395 A6 2018 (print) | DDC 813/.54--dc23
LC record available at https://lccn.loc.gov/2018029763
First edition 1 2 3 4 5 6 7 8 9

Set in Centaur 12 pt.

Printed on 50# Natures Natural 30% PCR recycled paper by Versa Press, East Peoria, IL.
Cover art copyright © 2018 by Ann Xu (annixu.com). All rights reserved.
Cover design 2018 by Theo Black (theblackarts.com).

Contents

An Agent of Utopia

To the Prince and Tranibors of our good land, and the offices of the Syphogrants below, and all those families thereof, greetings, from your poor servant in far Albion.

Masters and mistresses, I have failed. All that I append is but paint and chalk 'pon that stark fact. Yet I relate my story in hopes it may be instructive, that any future tools of state be fashioned less rudely than myself.

I will begin as I will end, with her.

Had my intent been to await her, to meet her eye as she emerged into the street, I scarcely could have done better; and yet this was happenstance, as so much else proved to be.

I had no expectation of her; I knew not that she was within; she was not my aim. She was wholly a stranger to me. I would laugh at this now, were I the laughing sort, for of course I learned later that even as I stood there with the crawling river to my back, her name was known to me, as the merest footnote to my researches. So much for researches.

In fact, though I had traveled thousands of leagues, from beyond the reach of the mapmaker's art, to reach this guarded stone archway in a gray-walled keep on a filthy esplanade beside the stinking Thames, I had no reason even for pausing, only feet from my goal. I feared not the guards, resplendent in their red tunics; I doubted not my errand. Yet I had stopped and stood a moment, as one does when about to fulfill a role in a grand design. And so when she emerged from shadows into sun, blinking as if surprised, I found myself looking into her eyes, and that has been the difference in my life: between who I was, and who I am.

Her face was—

No, I dare not, I cannot express't.

To her clothing, then, and her hair. That I'll set down. A framework may suggest a portrait, an embankment acknowledge a sea.

In our homeland, all free citizens, being alike in station, therefore dress alike as well; but in the lady's island nation, all are positioned somewhere above or below, so their habits likewise must be sorted: by adornment, by tailoring, by fineness of cloth. These signs are designed to be read.

She was plainly a gentlewoman, but simply clad. Around her neck was a single silver carcanet like a moon-sliver. Her bosom was but gently embusked, and not overmuch displayed. Her farthingale was modest in size; some could not be wedged through the south gate of London Bridge, but hers was just wider than her shoulders. Her hair was plaited at either temple, so that twin dark falls bordered her lustrous—

Ah! But stop there. I am grown old enough.

I add only that her eyes were red-rimmed with weeping, and in that moment—whatever my obligations to my homeland, to you who sent me—to dry those tears became my true mission.

A moment only I held her gaze, and how did I merit even that?

Then her manservant just behind, finely attired but sleep-eyed and bristle-jowled, did nudge her toward a carriage. As she passed, I dared not turn my head to watch, lest I not achieve my goal at all.

Rather, I walked forward, into the sweet-smelling space the lady had just vacated, and raised both hands as the warders crossed pikes before me.

"Hold, friends," I said. "The gaoler expects me."

"Ah, does he?" asked the elder warder. "What name does he expect, then?"

"The name of Aliquo," I said, and this truly was the name I had affixed to my letter, for it was not mine but anyone's. From my dun-colored wool cloak, I produced another sealed paper. "My credentials," I said. "For the gaoler only," I quickly added, as the elder warder was making as if to break the seal. He eyed me dolefully, then handed the letter to the younger warder, who in turn barked for a third warder, the youngest yet, who conveyed my letter within—doubtless to a boy still younger, his equipment not yet dropped.

As I waited, we all amused ourselves, myself by standing on tiptoe atop each consecutive cobble from east to west beneath the portcullis, the warders by glaring at me.

I knew, as they did not, that my credentials were excellent, consisting as they did only of my signature on a sheet of paper wrapped about some street debris from home.

Soon I was escorted through the gate, onto a walkway across an enclosed green. Sheep cropped the grass. Ravens barked down from the battlements. Huddled in a junction of pockmarked walls was a timbered, steeply thatched, two-story house. Though dwarfed by the lichen-crusted stone all around, it was larger than any home in Aircastle. Through its front door I was marched, and into a small room filled by an immense bearded man with a broken nose. He sat in a heap behind a spindly writing-desk that belonged in a playroom. Sunlight through the latticed window further broke his face into panes of diamond.

"Leave us," he told my escort, who bowed and exited, closing the door behind. The gaoler stared at me, saying nothing, and I replied in kind. He leaned forward and made a show of studying my shoes, then my breeches and cloak, then face again. His own displayed neither interest nor impression.

"You don't dress like a rich man," he said.

"I am no rich man," I replied.

Without turning his gaze from mine, he placed one hairy finger on the packet I had sent him and slid it across the desktop toward me: refolded, the seal broken.

"A thief, then," he said. "We have other prisons for thieves. My men will show you."

"I am no thief," I replied.

He tilted his head. "A Jew?"

"I am but a visitor, and I seek only an audience."

"That you have achieved," he said. "Our audience being concluded, my men will take you now."

"An audience," I said, "with one of your . . . guests."

Without moving, he spat onto the floor and my shoe, as placid as a toad. "And which guest would that be, Sir Jew, Sir Thief?"

I was near him already, the room being so small, and now I stepped closer. Arms at my sides, I leaned across the desk, closing the distance toward the gaoler's motionless, ugly face. I could smell layers of sweat and Southwark dirt, the Scotch egg that had broken his fast, and, all intermixed, the acrid scent of fear, a fear of such long abiding that it marked him, better than any wax-sealed writ of passage, as a resident of this benighted land. When I was close enough for my lips to brush the pig-bristles of his ear, I whispered a single syllable: a lover's plea, a beggar's motto, a word with no counterpart in my native tongue, though one of the commonest words in London, where satisfaction is unknown.

Upon hearing my word, the gaoler jerked as though serpent-bit, but recovered on the instant, so that as I stepped back he assumed once again calm and authority. Only his eyes danced in terror and anticipation.

"Worth my life, Sir Thief, were I caught admitting you to *him*."

I made no reply. No question had been posed, nor information offered that was new or in any way remarkable. He had but stated an irrelevant fact.

He lifted the packet I had delivered and poured the pebbles into his palm. He studied their sparkle, then let them slide back into the paper. His palm remained in place, cupping the air, and he raised his eyebrows at me, like a scarred and shaggy courtesan.

These English. Every clerk, every driver, every drayman and barrelmaker and ale-pourer has his hand out for coins, and doubtless every gaoler and prince, courtier and headsman, as well. They conceive of no superior system, indeed no alternative, anywhere in this world. And so I freely handed them my trash. Some were as grateful as children, while others betrayed no emotion at all, merely pocketing the payment as their due, a gift of nature like birdshit and rain.

I pulled from my pocket a thumb-sized paving stone. I dropped it into the gaoler's palm, where it reflected the sunlight in a dozen directions. His nostrils flared as he drew in a breath.

"God's mercy," he said.

The English routinely invoke their God when startled, or provoked, or overwhelmed by their own natures. They pray without cease, without thought, without result.

"The ninth hour," he told the stone, "at Traitors' Gate."

Traitors' Gate was a floating wooden barrier tapping mindlessly in the night tide across a submerged arch, set low in the fort's Thames-side wall. No two public clocks in England quite chime together, but somewhere during the ninth-hour cacophony, the gate swung open without visible human hand, and an empty punt slid from the shadows, tapping to a halt at my feet. I stepped down and in, half expecting the punt to slide from under me and make its return voyage without my assistance. Instead, after a respectful pause, I picked up the pole that lay in the bottom of the boat and did the work myself, nudge by nudge into the shadows, ducking as I glided beneath the arch. The soggy gate creaked shut behind.

Just inside the fortress, the stone marched upward in steep and narrow steps, at the top of which stood, all in red, my hulking friend the gaoler. He was alone. He silently waited as I climbed the slimy stairs to face him, or more precisely to face the teats that strained his tunic. He reached out both ham-sized hands and kneaded my arms, legs and torso. He found neither what he sought nor what he did not seek, and was quickly satisfied. He stooped, with a grunt, and picked up something from the cobbles.

"You're the ratcatcher, if anyone asks," he said. He handed me a long-handled fork and a pendulous sack. "And there's the rats to prove it," he added. "Wait here. When I cough twice, enter behind me, and keep to the right. Follow my taper, but not too close. If I meet anyone, keep back and flatten yourself against the wall like the damp. You might even kill a rat or two, if you've a mind."

I held the heavy fork loose at my side, where I could drop it on the instant if I needed to kill someone, and watched the gaoler lumber into the wall and vanish, through a previously invisible slot perhaps an inch wider than his shoulders. Finally I heard the double cough, fainter and from much farther away than I expected. I slipped into the door-shaped darkness.

We encountered no one, quickly left any trafficked levels of the vast and ancient keep. The dark corridors and archways we passed through and the stairs we climbed were broad and well-made and perhaps once were grand, but time's ravages were not being repaired. In spots we crunched through fallen mortar and stone. Even the rats were elsewhere. The walls were windowless, save for the occasional slitted cross that traded no light for no view.

Finally we passed through a series of large chambers, in the fourth of which the serpent-fire before me guttered as in a draft. My guide stood before an iron-banded oaken door, its single barred window the size of my head. He gestured me close, relieved me of the rat-sticker and sack, and whispered, as urgently as a lover.

"I'll be watching. You leave in a quarter-hour, and whether you walk or I drag you is no concern of mine. Keep your treasonous voices low. Take nothing he offers, leave no marks on his person, and for the love of God, give him no ink or paper; that's powder and shot to the likes of him." He inserted into the lock an iron key fully as long as the rat-sticker. The gears clanked and ground, and he hauled back the door. "Company for you, sir! Oh, Christ, not again. Whyn't he just pull his gentles, like the others do?"

The room was larger than I expected, and more finely appointed. The chairs, tables, washbasin, and chamber-pot were old but finely made; the twin windows were grated but high, deep-set and arched; a river breeze stirred faded tapestries that covered the walls with the rose that was the sigil of the ruling house. In the far corner was a makeshift altar, a cross of two bound candlesticks atop a stool, and before it, in a pool of shadow, knelt a naked man with a bloody back, who slowly gave himself one, two, three fresh strokes across the shoulders with a knotted rope. Judging from the fresh wounds amid the scarring, he had been at this for some time.

As I walked forward, the door thudded shut behind. "My good sir," I said.

The kneeling figure paused a few seconds before flogging himself again, and again, and a sixth time, each impact a dull wet smack. As I drew close enough to smell him, I saw the shadow on the flagstones was in fact a broad spatter of blood.

The prisoner spoke without turning. "You've made me lose count. Well, no matter. I can start over from One, as must we all, each day." He flexed the rope, as if to resume.

"Good sir, please. My time is short."

His laugh, as he turned, was a joyless bark. "Your time?" The engravings I had studied were good likenesses. The Roman features were intact on his blunt, handsome face, but his jawline was hidden by a fresh grey curtain of beard that ill became him. "May I assume, sir, given your evident longing for conversation, that you are not here to murder me?"

"No, indeed."

"Ah," he said. He brought one foot beneath him and stood, slowly but with no evident need for support. "One can imagine worse fates, my good Sir Interruptus, than to be murdered in the act of prayer." Something passed over his eyes then, perhaps only the sting of the wounds as he donned, without flinching, the robe that hung on the bedpost. "Ay, much worse. The killers of Thomas Becket, even as they hacked away, did the work of God in making the saint's most heartfelt desire manifest. They delivered him sinless unto his Maker." He glanced at his blood on the floor as he cinched his belt. "I fear for his shrine at Canterbury, and for his relics. In these fell days, it is not only the living who suffer. A good even to you, Master Jenkins!"

After a long pause, the shadow beyond the window in the door replied, "And a good even to you, sir."

"As for you," the prisoner said, smiling, "we reach an even footing. You impeded my task; I impeded yours. State your business, please, sir, and your name. I have not so many visitors that they grow interchangeable to me."

"I call myself Aliquo," I replied, "and I bring greetings to you, Thomas More, from your old friend Raphael Hythlodaye, and from my homeland of Utopia."

I bowed low before him.

"Please give my Utopian friends my best regards," More said, "and tell them my answer is no."

The next afternoon, moments after I stepped from the inn where I had broken my fast, a man planted himself before me on the street, so that I would have to go around him, or stop. I chose to stop.

"You have seen me before, I believe," said the man.

I peered into his bearded face. "I have," I said. "You were outside the Tower yesterday. You were with . . . the lady."

"I was," he said, "and I am, and I am here on her account only. I am to bring you to her."

"That is quite impossible," I said. "Who is this lady, who makes such demands of strangers?"

"You are a stranger to her, but not to her father, I believe. Her name is Margaret Roper, born Margaret More." He studied my face. "This changes your resolve, I believe."

"Yes," I said, though I had resolved to accompany him the moment I recognized him, in hopes I might see his mistress again— even if he led me straight to the chopping-block on Tower Hill.

Where he led me, instead, without further speech, was to the city's largest temple, dedicated to the name of a first-century per-secutor of the enemies of Rome, who reversed himself to aid those enemies, but remained, throughout his life, in the service of a more perfect, more organized world. A thousand years later, his temple's interior was scarcely less crowded than the streets outside.

At home, upon entering a temple, all men would proceed to the right, all women to the left, and all would maintain their proper places until departing. Here, all was confusion.

"There," said the manservant, stepping aside. "Go to her, and if you speak falsely, then God help you."

Far ahead, across the echoing marble, a line of supplicants, in all modes of clothing, shuffled step by step into an airy chapel, and past a chest-high marble tomb minded by a droning guide. Toward the back of this line was she who had summoned me, she who already had claimed dominion over me with a single glance, though I had yet to realize it.

I went to her.

She watched me approach. She was nearly my height. Her eyes! . . . I dare not describe them. She looked into mine, and then, with-out moving her head or glancing away, she refocused, and looked at me again. I knew in that moment she had seen me more clearly than her father had, than the gaoler had, than anyone had since home. I held my breath, sure she would turn away. Instead she gravely bowed her head, reached for my arm, and guided me into the line at her side. The stooped crone behind her hissed at my insertion, but a steely glance from Madame shushed her.

"Do you speak Latin?" Madame asked me, in that tongue.

"I do, Madame," I replied in kind.

"Do so, in this public place. Here, in this procession, we are pilgrims only, and will draw no attention. You know who I am."

"I do, Madame."

"Have you seen my father?"

"I have, Madame."

"You have an advantage over me, then. How is he? In mind, spirit, and body?"

"In mind, keen. In spirit, resigned, but anxious for you. In body, intact, save for the injuries he inflicts himself."

"God inflicts them," she said. "So he told me, when I was a girl, and saw the bloody linens. A man who would keep secrets from his own household should do his own washing. Now tell me who *you* are."

"Only your servant, Madame," I said.

She blew air from the corner of her mouth. "Please. You are no one's servant, least of all mine. Who are you?"

We neared the tomb and the guide, his pockmarked face, his maimed hands. Many in line had some scar, or limp, or hump.

"Call me Aliquo," I said.

"Your position?"

"In this land, only emissary."

"From whom? What business had you with my father?"

Heeding her manservant's warning, I chose the truth.

"I offered to free him," I said, "and to convey him home in triumph."

Her eyes widened. "You are mad. How? Home to Chelsea? Home to me?"

"No, Madame. To my homeland across the sea."

"The impertinence! What name is given this homeland?"

"It is called Utopia. Your father wrote of it."

She laughed aloud, and a score of heads turned our way in shock as the echoes rained down from the arches above. Beside the tomb, without interrupting his recitation, the guide shook his head, placed the stump of a finger to his chin, and blew.

"He wrote of it, indeed!" she said, in a lower voice. "A fairy-story for his friend Erasmus, invented of whole cloth! A series of japes at the follies of the day."

"Is all this a jape?" I asked, with a gesture at the soaring chapel all around. "Is this statue atop the tomb a jape, because he has a silver head, as the king did not in life? Mere representation is not a jape, Madame. Your father represented us, but we are not his invention."

By now we had reached the tomb. It bore a plaque, in Latin:

Henry, the scourge of France, lies in this tomb.
Virtue subdues all things.
A.D. 1422.

"Above, you see good King Henry's funeral achievements," droned the guide, in nasal English, as he studied Madame for signs of outburst. "His battle helmet, sword, shield, and saddle. Note the dents in the helmet, through which good King Henry's life was spared, glory be to God. . . ."

As she passed, Madame addressed herself to the marble of the tomb. "I have met many scoundrels," she said, "but never one claiming to have stepped from the pages of my father's books. And whom do you claim sent you on this mad errand? King Utopia the Nineteenth?"

"Our king, Madame . . . is not like yours. He is more like the officers of this temple. He has unique responsibilities, yes; he has certain authorities, in certain settings. Yet I was not sent by him, Madame, but by a council of the people."

"An emissary from a headless land. Interesting. But this might explain why, a mere half-day after you stepped ashore at Woolwich, having left your private cabin on the *Lobo Soares,* out of Lisbon, before even buying a meal or engaging rooms, you proceeded not to York

Place but to the Tower, and sought an audience not with the king, but with a condemned prisoner. A strange emissary, indeed."

"Madame is well informed."

"Madame is wholly *uninformed*," she retorted, "on the one subject of any importance. They keep me from my father, and thus I must make do with the world."

"You call your father condemned," I said, "yet you grieve too soon, surely. He is not yet tried, much less convicted and sentenced."

"That is a truth so strictly and carefully laid as to be a lie," she said, "and one more lie to me, however small, will earn you an enemy beside which our present King Henry would seem a stick-puppet. Do you believe me?"

"I do, Madame. Tell me, the man in the tomb . . . he is the current king's grandsire?"

She winced. "No relation. After good King Henry died, his widow married a Tudor. And there Katherine lies, as if in life. So they say."

Only if in life she was drawn, shriveled, and waxen of complexion, I thought, but said nothing. Where one might have expected an effigy lay instead the body, not even shielded but available to all. Katherine was blessedly clothed, arms folded across her sunken breasts. The one-eyed gentleman in line before me, his absurd rapier hilt stuttering along the pedestal as he walked past, half-burst into tears, bowed, and kissed Katherine's face.

"I apologize for my countrymen," said Madame. "They prefer their women venerated and dead. Some attribute miracles to this poor corpse, and seek her elevation by Rome. Humph. 'Twould truly *take* a miracle, now—and our current king has rather discouraged miracles." She had looked almost merry, enjoying my discomfiture at the spectacle before me, but now her face grew taut as Katherine's. She shook her head, and the moment passed. "Tell me, friend Aliquo," she continued. "What becomes of Utopians when they die?"

"Burned to ashes, Madame."

"What, no burial?"

"No room, Madame. Ours is an island nation, at its widest scarcely 200 miles across. We must colonize the mainland as it is."

"And Utopian souls? What becomes of them?"

"They . . . remain. Invisible, but among us still, seeing and hearing all. They observe, are pleased to be addressed and honored, but they cannot participate."

"Interesting. And have your dead ones traveled with you, here to *our* island nation?"

"I hope not, Madame. This place would be most . . . distressing to them."

"I know how they feel. My father refused you, of course."

"Yes, Madame. Doubtless you'd have thought him mad, otherwise."

"No. But I know that even locked in that fortress, he is the king's servant and God's, and if it's the will of both that he—that he—" She faltered. "He would have refused you, had you come at the head of a legion. My father is the best man in the kingdom, and how I have prayed he were otherwise."

We had left the chapel and entered the cathedral's main chamber, where the line of supplicants broke apart and flowed into the larger crowd. We walked slowly together toward the west door, where her manservant stood, his gaze intent upon us, poised as if to spring.

"Madame, I have told you what you wanted, and I have only troubled you with my tidings. I am sorry for that. I pray you grant me leave."

"Stay a moment, friend Aliquo. I am told that earlier today, two cutpurses were found dead in a rain-barrel in Woolwich, a quarter-hour after you set foot on the dock. Their necks were broken. Does this news surprise you?"

"No, Madame. Many rough men meet such fates."

"Oh, indeed. Tell me, why did you *not* bring a legion? Why did your headless land send only you, alone?"

"My people have faith in me, Madame."

"I think it's because you didn't need a legion. I think you could have brought my father out of the Tower unscathed and single-handed, had he but said the word."

"You think me a wizard, Madame."

"No. I think you're a killer, and I have a job for you. I want his head."

"The king's head? Now *you* are talking madness, Madame."

"Henry? Fie! What need would I have for that? Not Henry's head. My father's. More's. You have told me something of your land's customs, regarding the dead. Let me now tell you something of ours. When the headsman on Tower Hill separates my father's pate from his shoulders, his poor skull will be taken to London Bridge, impaled on a pike, and mounted atop the Stone Gate, to feed the ravens and remind all Henry's subjects of the fate of traitors. I would spare my father that. I want his head. I want it brought home to his family. I want it brought home to me."

At that moment, I could have turned and walked out of the temple, the city, England, her gaze entire, perhaps even beyond the range of my memory of her. Instead I tarried, forever.

"Do not ask this of me," I said.

"My family is broken," she said. "My friends fear to be seen with me. My servants have multiple employers. My enemies watch me, and all others avert their eyes. I have no one else to ask."

I glanced at he who stood apart, glowering at me. "But your manservant?"

"That is William, my husband," she continued, looking only at me, "and he is a good man, but for this task, Aliquo my killer, my emissary from the land of dreams, I have no need of a good man. I have need of you."

"Ho, you knaves, you fishwives!" bellowed my leather-lunged boat-man as he sculled straight across the paths of threescore other vessels, missing each by the width of a coat of paint. Whenever the river ahead seemed passable, he changed course and sought congestion once more.

London may once have been a great city, but I was privileged to see it too late, in its twenty-sixth year of groan beneath the man Henry. And swirling among all was the reek of the Thames. That foul brown stream flows more thickly above its surface, and knows no channel, but floods all the nostrils of the town.

I had struggled on foot onto the city's single bridge, in hopes of achieving a perspective not granted to the scullers below—only to gain a fine view of the tradesmen's booths that line the thoroughfare on both sides. Each swaybacked roof sprouted a thicket of faded standards that snapped overhead like abandoned washing, their tattiness mocking the very memory of festivity.

Finally, midway along the span, I entered a public garderobe—for which honor I waited a quarter-hour in line, as some men around me gave up and relieved themselves standing—and once inside, I peered through the privy-hole, to obtain a fine round view of the Thames, my only one since setting foot on the bridge. Amid cascades of filth from above, a grimy boy of perhaps ten summers sat, fishing, in a vessel the size of a largish hat.

"Ay, look out there, you swag-bellied antic!"

The boatman's roar returned me to my present sorry state. I was under no obligation to More's daughter, I still told myself; but there was no harm, surely, in seeing whether her task could be quickly discharged, before my departure for home. A Utopian may be forgiven the odd good deed. But I had seen enough already to complicate matters. I had hoped, once having achieved the battlement, to lift down the pike and use it to bridge the gap to the next building; or, failing that, simply to dive over the wall into the water. But the battlement was twice as high as the adjacent roofs—about twelve stories to their six—and as the Stone Gateway perched atop a bridge that was itself eighty feet above the river, any dive from the height would be two hundred feet, and fatal. A head dropped into the river would be lost on the instant, while throwing it onto the adjacent roof would be a desperate move; the twice-unlucky head would roll off, and land who-knew-where.

No, the only feasible way to bring down the head would be to carry it down the stairs and out the front door. And the only feasible way to gain the battlement in the first place was via the same stairs in the reverse direction, up. Neither up nor down looked likely, short of a safe-passage guarantee from Henry himself.

Would Madame recognize her own father's head? Or, more to the point, would she recognize a head not her father's? The thought of substituting a more easily recovered head gave me no pride, but that at least would be feasible, and would give the lady some measure of comfort. Yet I did not wish to see her so easily gulled.

I leaned an elbow on the saxboard, let the river lap my thoughts as the Stone Gateway bobbed before me. Assume, then, that the battlement was impregnable. From execution site to point of display, the head must travel more than a mile through the London streets—the teeming, crime-infested, unpredictable streets.

Why, anything could happen. And only fivescore cutpurses, fishwives, alemongers, soldiers and spies would have to be bribed to look the other way.

And once the display was over, well, the head would have to make its way downstairs again, to clear a space on the battlement for the next statesman.

"What do they do with the heads, after?" I asked the boatman.

His grin had gaps into which a mouse could wriggle. "Into Mother Thames they go, milord—and don't they make a pretty splash!"

So I could just wait beneath the bridge until the head was thrown to me. A tempting plan. A simple plan. A foolish plan. I would gain only an unobstructed view of the thing sinking to the bottom of the river. And this was, of course, the thought with which my musings began; I had rounded the globe and met myself upon return.

"Oh, is that the state of it, y'say?" roared my boatman, in response to the ribald gestures of a passing fisherman. "Ye don't fray me, you cullion! I'll cuff you like Jack of Lent, I will!"

The trial, and the sentence, and the execution, went as Madame had foreseen. One always should trust the natives. By then, I had settled on bribery and substitution. Cross the smallest number of palms with a few paving-stones, replace the head to conceal its absence, and be done.

Utopia borders the land of the savage Zapolets, useful neighbors in that they always are willing, for pay, to perform errands that are too base for Utopians. There is no dishonor in hiring them, as Zapolets are debased already. London, too, has its Zapolets, and so, a week after More's severed head took its place atop the Gateway, I found myself directly beneath, alone in a boat, by midnight, having silently rowed myself into place, awaiting the descent of my package.

Above me, a low whistle—and again.

I crouched in the boat and looked up at the flickering darkness. Sound was magnified beneath the stone arch, and I heard as if in my right ear someone grunting and panting from exertion. In moments, something came into view, swaying in mid-air like a pendulum, ever closer. A heavy sack was being lowered to me.

Just as I reached up and took hold of it, someone on the bridge shrieked. Suddenly the full weight of the sack was in my hands, and I lurched off balance, nearly upset the boat as I sat heavily on the bench amidships. A hot, iron-smelling liquid pelted me from above, and then something plunked into the water beside me. In the torch-light I registered the staring, agape face of the poor Zapolet I had bribed, as his severed head rolled beneath the river's leathery surface. Just before it vanished, I snatched it by the hair, swung it streaming into the floorboards. The act was instinctive; it might come in handy. Then an arrow studded from above into the bench between my thighs. Thus encouraged, I set down the sack and rowed for the far riverbank.

Sounds carry on a river, but I heard none as I reached the stilts of some enterprise built over the water—a tannery, by the smell of it. No voices called after me. I ducked my head and rode the boat into darkness, till it bumped the barrels lashed to the quay. I tied my boat fast, risked a candle, and peeled back the sacking, to see the head for which I had paid a guard's life. I stared into the broad, lumpy face, its cheek triple-scarred long ago, as by a rake.

For my troubles, I now owned two severed heads, neither of them More's.

In mid-climb, my feet against the outer wall of the Gateway, I clutched the rope, straining to hear and see what was happening on the battlement above. Had my hook been noticed? Apparently not. I heard a murmuring conversation among guards, perhaps three men, but they were distant. I pulled myself up to the edge of the wall.

More than once, in my slow progress up the wall—one window level at a time—I had been tempted to let that damned not-More head that weighted my shoulder-sack, and became only heavier each minute, simply drop into the Thames. But no, a substitute head would be useful. With luck, no one would notice that More was missing.

I waited there, just beneath the battlement, for the guards to go below. Possibly they would not, in which case I would have to kill them all quickly and silently. I determined to give them a quarter-hour, and began to mark my heartbeats as I looked out over the nightscape of the city. But sooner, all three voices moved into the stairwell, and I clambered up and over.

I counted my way to the More-pike, hoping the heads had not been rearranged since sunset, easily lifted the heavy pole out of its socket and stepped backward, laying it onto the flagstones as silently as I could. The head end necessarily was heavier, and hit first, bouncing once. I walked up the length of the pike. I reached beneath the iron band—grimacing as my fingers dented the head's tarred surface—and tugged.

The head did not budge.

I put both feet against the severed neck, braced myself, and pushed.

The flesh buckled.

I pushed again, and the head slowly began to stutter up the pike.

I was thus occupied when I heard voices ascending the stairs.

Frantically, I managed to slide the head clear of the pike just as the first guard crested the roof—facing southward and away from me, thank Mithras. The head fell only an inch or two to the roof. I let the pike down quietly and rolled sideways, putting a low wall between myself and the guards. I hoped they were not in the habit of counting the pikes.

I flung a pebble into the far corner of the rooftop, hoping it would make a noise loud enough to draw their attention. I suppose it landed. If so, it made not a sound.

One guard began walking the battlement toward me. His attention was directed outward, however. Sitting with my back to the inner wall, willing myself to disappear into the shadow, I watched him stroll into view. He stopped, still with his back to me, and stared downstream. A few steps, and he'd all but trip over the pike, and More's head.

I risked a glance behind me. One guard was picking his teeth, another leaning on his elbows, both looking across Southwark.

I stood and crossed silently to my guard, swinging the bag with the not-More head. It clouted the guard at the base of the skull. As he dropped, I kicked him between the shoulder blades, and he toppled over the wall. I dived for cover again. Only someone who was listening for it, as I was, would have noticed the splash, far below.

The two remaining guards continued their murmurous conversation on the far side of the platform. I rolled into a crouch, looked over the crenellated wall that sheltered the stairs. My new friends were standing just barely within the torchlight of a taper on the far wall. They stood side by side facing the city, overlooking the rooftops that lined the bridge below. I wished them to separate, willed them to do so, but my will failed. There they would stand, barely a man's width between them, until they registered their companion had not rejoined them, whereupon they would seek and, not finding, sound an alarm. How to separate them sooner?

Water, moaned a voice at my feet.

You scarce will believe, ye who read this letter, that I did not spring backward, though my leg muscles spasmed in that desire; my overriding desire, to produce no noise whatsoever, saved me, I think. I only hopped, once, silently landing in place with my feet planted a bit farther apart, to either side of the lump of darkness I knew to be More's head. I did not cry out. I did not breathe. I only stared down at the darkness between my feet, desperate to resolve a shape that began to move, to rock to and fro, like an inverted turtle, until it tipped and rolled to a stop against my left boot, its staring eyes reflecting the moon as its only movable limb, its long adder-like tongue, probed the air. Of course, I thought with insane clarity, that's how he could roll over. Face down, he pushed away the stone floor with his tongue.

Water, More repeated, more loudly this time.

The guards! They would hear!

With no more thought than this—nay, with no thought at all—still on the keen iron edge of terror, and preferring to be anywhere but against that More-head, I stood and strode forward, fast, noiseless, toward the two guards, who marvelously yet had heard nothing, still had their backs to me. In mid-stride, slacking neither my pace nor my direction, I returned the favor, turned my back to them, walked backward until their faces came into view and my shoulder blades thumped against the wall between them.

"Wha?" said the one on my right.

I smashed the heels of both hands into the guards' noses. As they fell backward I fell forward atop them, rode them down to the floor and crushed their faces with all my weight, my arms locked in place like bars. Out of respect, I did not watch. Instead I looked to the stars, found Ophiuchus beset, the writhing serpent-head and serpent-tail to either side, and the scorpion beneath his feet. The guards made scarcely any noise, only a grunt or two and one gurgle, as a gentlewoman's stomach might have done, and yet after they died, as I relaxed and flexed my cramping arms, the tower was quieter still. I saw the guttering taper, the flailing flags, but their sounds did not register. As I re-crossed the platform in search of More (his eyes! his tongue!), I moved in a silence like that of a dream, or of a daze from a clout on the head. I heard only the blood and snot and eyestuff pattering from my hands, which I held away from my body as if to distance myself from what I'd done.

I had killed before—had, indeed, likely killed the first guard, not five minutes earlier—and I have killed since, but my work atop Stone Gate that night, and as I left that accursed tower, was of another order. I blamed More, at the time. Whatever animated his head, I felt, was animating me. My body would ache for a fortnight.

I rounded the wall. More's head was gone. No—it was there, nose wedged into the join of wall and floor. But surely I had left it over there, beside the pike?

Water, said More's head.

Loath as I was to touch the damned thing (abomination! impossibility!), I wanted nothing from life, at that moment, but to heave More over the parapet, give him all the water he could drink, and to cast myself in after him. Perhaps I should have done those things, or one of them.

"Hush!" I said.

When would the next guards come on duty? When would the absence of tramping footfalls overhead be noticed? What signals, what duties, would be missed? I worked quickly. Ignoring More, I freed not-More from his sack, with some effort—I had to shake it, my assault on the first guard having got head and fabric somewhat intermingled—and it finally rolled onto the floor with a deep groan that made me yelp in horror. But 'twas only More again, complaining. I jammed the pike into not-More's neck, working it in deeper than necessary, wishing it were More. I hoisted the pike with effort, the head now even heavier at the weighted end of a pole, and set the hilt into place with the first sense of relief I had felt in an hour. I stepped back, snatched up the taper, and held it high, to check my handiwork. As he flickered into view, not-More sagged sideways, and I was sure for a moment that its savaged flesh would tear away and drop it into the Thames—but it held, and I foolishly continued to hold aloft the light, in a terrible elation, until a voice from below cried:

"Ho! What's the matter up there? Who's light?"

"No matter," I cried, even as I returned the taper to its sconce—too late. I heard behind me, from the outer wall, a scrape like nails against flint.

"What's this?" said the same voice—no longer loudly, but half to himself, in a sort of wonder, yet distinct for all that. I looked at my grappling hook as it twitched, flexed, skittered sideways, like a crab in lantern-light. He who had yanked it bellowed, "Intruder! Ho, the tower! Hoy!"

I snatched up More. He tried to bite me, the wretch, as I shoved him into my sack. To fling the hook over the wall was the work of a moment. With my snarling burden I strode away from my ruined lifeline, to the head of the wooden stairs, saw no one, and sprinted down, three planks at a time.

I found myself in a narrow stone chamber, barely wider than the flight of stairs. Beneath the stairs were casks and crates, but no guard, and no doors either. The only door faced me, a stone archway that framed a landing and a more substantial set of stone steps headed down. I had just reached the top when I heard a roaring and pounding from below, as if a cohort were charging, and torchlight flared and brightened 'gainst the stone wall visible at the curve.

I dropped my More sack—he squeaked as he hit the floor—and looked about, gauged my position. Above, in the open air, I would gain room to work, but so would they. Here was better. I stepped back three paces, positioned myself, and waited, as that fell force rose within me.

The leader of the party gained the stone landing but stopped at sight of me. I wonder what he saw. I stood unarmed, hands and sleeves besmirched with gore, a twitching sack at my feet. I know that I smiled. But what more did he see? Whatever it was, it stopped him like a barred gate, and the others clustered behind. Five total. One axe; three swords; the fifth, a torch in one hand and a rapier in the other. Fine.

"Which of you," I asked, "is the youngest?"

They said nothing, but two in the back glanced at the torch-bearer, a beardless boy. They all looked wary, but he, terrified.

Their leader looked me up and down. "Who the fuck are you," he snarled, "to question us?"

I smiled even wider. "I'm the ratcatcher," I said, and sprang.

Afterward, I rose from my work on the floor and faced the one I'd left standing. The boy's quaking face was red with blood not his own. His shaking torch cast shadows that rocked the room. He choked back something, and dropped his weapon with a clang. He kept the torch, though. He was a dark-eyed, lovely boy. I have never been partial to boys.

"Your job," I said, "is to run below, and tell the others."

His jaw worked, his throat pulsed. He made no sound.

"That I am coming," I said.

Still he stood, trembling. The room filled with a smell harsher even than blood, and a puddle spread at the boy's boot.

Christ, cried More, muffled by sacking. *Christ!*

I took one step toward the boy, pursed my lips, and blew air into his face.

With a wail, he leapt into the stairwell, somehow kept his footing, and ran downstairs screaming, just ahead of me. Still he held on to the torch. O dutiful boy! Excellent boy! More clamped beneath one arm, my way lighted by the now much older once-boy, I ran in a downward stone spiral, around and down, around and down, past windows of increasing size, around and down, deeper into the swirling river-stench, until I reached a window just large enough, and vaulted through, knowing not whether I was over roofs or over water but hoping I was low enough. I was over water, and low enough. I plunged beneath the surface and sank, afire with sudden cold but glad of the respite from the smell. As I dropped ever deeper, my cheek was brushed by what may have been a kicking rat, my shoulder bumped by what may have been a spiraling turd, my chest gnawed by what was certainly the struggling head of my lady's father, biting at my heart as we descended into the dark peace below London. Ay, low enough!

I dared not return to my inn, in my bedraggled state, with my unpredictable charge. Instead I repaired to a haven I had noted earlier—a nearby plague-house, marked by a bundle of straw on a pole extending from an upper window, and a foot-high cross slapped on the door in red paint. Local gossip said the surviving family members had long decamped, and the neighbors dared not set foot in the place. From the adjoining rooftop, I gained entrance to the house via its upper storey. I made fast the shutters, risked a single lighted candle, and gnawed the bread, cheese, and onion I had stowed there before my assault on the Gateway. Then, somehow, I slept.

I was awakened by More.

Where is the light?

Be silent, I said. The candle is beside you. Look.

I pulled the bedraggled thing from the sack, set it on the table. His neck looked to have been cut clean, but at an angle. The head listed to the right, as if cocked to hear a confidence. The skin puckered on that side, beneath More's weight.

Where is the light? Ay, am I damned? Am I such a sinner as that?

I cannot say, I told him. But you must be quiet, in any case.

God knows, I am no heretic, said More. *I sought out heretics. I had them killed. They put God's word in the English tongue, in the mouths of fishwives. They rejected the Apostle of Rome. They were protestants to God. I was Lord High Chancellor, but I served the Lord who was higher still. They were as bad as Luther, and Luther is the shit-pool of all shit.*

Were they beheaded, too? I asked.

No, burned, said the head. *Purified in the flames, and delivered shriven unto God. It was all I could do for them, poor misguided devils. I hope soon to clasp their hands, my prodigal brothers. And yet.*

Yes, I asked.

Where is the light?

I turned the head to face the candle, my fingers sinking into his temple as into a soft pear. This made the lace atop the table twist into a gyre; it was intimate with More's neck now.

More moaned. *Where is the light? Ah, Christ my Savior, what is this place?*

I believe it's an apothecary's, I said. We are upstairs.

But where?

London, I said, mere rods from the Stone Gate. You've not gone far.

Ah, Christ, I smell it! The Thames!

You'll not smell it long. I'll deliver you to your daughter.

My daughter? Where is she? What business have you with my Meg?

She tasked me with an errand, I said. With the delivery of your head.

He emitted a wail, like a cat that is trod upon.

Ah, you wretch! you cullion! you ass-spreading ingle! You are a worse shit even than Luther. Meg wanted only my head, but you! Pestiferous, stew-dwelling, punk-eating maltworm! You have stolen my soul!

Hush, man. I have only your head. I know naught of your soul.

He wailed the louder, though his lips were closed. I seized his screaming skull two-handed, wrenched at the jaw until, with a tearing sound, it opened a space. I snatched up an onion, wedged it into the opening. The wailing continued. I seized the candlestick, toppling the candle, and smashed the head with the base. I saw only that I had opened a savage dent, as the flame toppled into my wine and went out, leaving me in the dark with this howling dead thing. In despair, I cried:

Shut up! For Meg's sake, shut up!

Meg, it said. *Meg.* And said no more.

At the time arranged, I stood 'midst the merrymakers on the Bank, on the lip of a bear-pit, a laden pouch slung over my shoulder. The bear below was a sleepy-looking fellow that lumbered in circles along the earthen wall and swatted at the refuse hurled down. Its bristly collar was all a-point with spikes. These did little to allay the general impression of boredom. The criers' voices were hoarse and listless, even as they insulted one another and their customers.

"Ale and elderberries!"

"Sweetmeats!"

"Flawn!"

"Here, this Florentine you just sold me—it's all fat in the middle!"

"Well, it suits you then! Out of my way. Florentines!"

Likely customers ogled an oyster-wench's ample bosom and, secondarily, the tray of shellfish her teats partially shaded. A gatherer outside a theatre collected admissions, one clank at a time, in a glazed money-box. At his waist swung the hammer that at day's end would smash open the profit—or the head of any coxcomb who tried to relieve him of it.

"Suckets, Milord?"

"No, no," I said, waving her past.

Suckets, said More.

She showed no sign of hearing it, but I stepped away, pressing the pouch closer 'neath my elbow. *Suckets,* More repeated. Through my sleeve and the fabric of the pouch, I felt something bite at my arm.

"Any ginger-bread?" asked another.

"Alas, no, but some lovely marchpane, me sister's known for it. Melts on your tongue, it does."

"Just like your sister!" Much laughter.

"It's yer fat stewed prune I wants in me mouth, love, if it's not been sucked off by now!" Even more laughter. The bear rumbled and farted, and the air above his pit fairly shimmered with the stink.

Damn you! I cannot eat! cried More. *And yet I starve!*

His was louder than any voice in the crowd, and yet no one reacted. So I did not react, either.

"Oh, you squirtings! Weasel-beak! Get on with your saucy selves. Ah, there's a love," said the hag, curseying to a gentlemen whose brocaded back was to me. "I thank you, sir."

"Away with you, then," he said, turning: William Roper, and alone in the crowd. He met my eye and cocked his head toward the street, then turned and walked away. I followed him across the thoroughfare, his feathered cap my guide through the throng. I followed him into an alley and around a stack of barrels. Madame stood there, her face streaked with tears. She twisted a bit of cloth in her fingers.

Meg, said More.

"It's you!" she said, and took a wild-eyed step toward me—but stopped herself, and so did not rush to me, lay hands upon me, embrace me. "So William was right after all," she said, more calmly. "I was sure you were seized, or dead."

Meg! Ah, Meg! Finish me!

To the horrid voice in my pouch, she reacted not at all.

I bowed low. "Alive, and free to serve Madame," I said.

"Free." She looked all about, at an overhang of verminous thatch above, at a puddle of piss below, at the leaden sky and the barrel-staves, at everything but me and my noisy pouch.

I glanced at her husband, who gave me only the smallest shake of his head in reply.

"Here, Madame," I said, and gestured at the pouch that swung heavily at my side, still wailing and moaning.

Drown me in the river, Meg! I am your father! Burn me in a pyre! Meg, you silly bitch, listen! Meg!

Madame made as if to reach for the flap, then snatched back her hand with such haste I heard it slap against the front of her dress.

Looking neither at him nor at me, she said, flatly, "William."

Roper, sparing me a cold glance, stepped forward and lifted a corner of the flap a few inches. The moment he lifted it, More's puling ceased.

"Why, 'tis not him," Roper said.

"You lie, sir," I said.

Roper's face twisted in anger. "Dare you speak so?"

Madame looked faint. "What wrong have I done thee to warrant such cruelty?"

Roper and I spoke at once.

"Madame, please."

"Silence, dog!"

"See for yourself."

"Meg, let's away."

"I will see," she said, silencing us. She lifted the flap, looked in, and breathed, "Oh."

As I watched her face, her features seemed to smooth. The lines of care and middle years filled in like canals. Her eyes shone.

"That such a small vessel," she murmured, "could contain such a great head."

"Meg! You are mistaken, surely."

"No. Look, William. Do you not see the mole upon his cheek, the cleft in his chin? As a girl I tried to hide flower-petals in there."

Her husband looked again.

"He is much diminished," Roper said. "And yet."

"Enough," Madame said, stepping away. "The task is concluded. Take him."

I thought this meant concealed guards, that the moment had come, and I was ready. But she only watched as Roper gently lifted the satchel off my shoulder.

"When they told me he was gone," she said, half to me and half to no one, "my own head went a-rolling. I had no mind, no purpose. I wanted only to be in the street, in the crowds. In my slippers I walked through the muck, seeing nothing, facing no one, until I was brought up short . . . by whiteness. White on white, like a heap of saint-souls. I stood, marveling, before a shop-window full of Low Country linen. So, so beautiful. Mother used to say, ah, Meg, it's a shame to bring it home, it ne'er can be so pure again. I suddenly had a single thought: a winding-sheet. Father must be wrapped for burial. Of course. But I had no purse. I had left the house in such grief and such haste, I had come away with nothing. Yet I pointlessly, automatically patted the little sewing-pocket of my skirts, and pulled from that pocket three gold sovereigns, which were not there before. And so I came home no longer mad and pitiable, but sensible, and done with my errand, and this winding-sheet was worth two pounds at the most." She flapped at me the bit of cloth she'd been a-worrying. "Just look at it! Little better than dagswain. Such is the world without my father, friend Aliquo: petty miracles, and petty frauds." She shook her head, seemed to focus on me. "But my household will e'er remember your good offices. I pray you, seek your perfect homeland. I hope it exists—but you'll not find it here." Her eyes ceased to see me. "Ay, not here."

She and her man turned and walked away. "We'll pickle him, I think," I heard her say, "with some elderflower."

As that grim burden swung at Roper's hip, down the alley and into the street, her father's not-voice resumed its wailing.

God damn you. God damn you! God damn you ALL!

I stood at the alley's mouth and watched them grow smaller in the distance, the voice diminishing all the while, until they could not be seen, and More could not be heard.

Freed of my burden, freed of my hopes, I walked southward, away from the city, toward the sea. I moved among women and men, but saw no one, heard nothing.

Two days later, I crouched on a quay on the wet lip of England, hidden behind shipping-barrels, and removed from my pouch the not-More head I had carried all that way.

"Farewell, friend Zapolet," I told it, and laid it onto the surface of the water, as gently as More must have laid his firstborn babe, wiggling and shiny, 'pon her coverlet. I watched the Zapolet's staring head roll 'neath the waves, as the babe sinks into the adult. Then it was gone forever.

I re-entered the crowd and found a line to stand in, waiting to book passage. Something tugged at my breeches. A grimy child, of indeterminate sex, holding a tray of sweetmeats.

"Suckets, Milord?"

Suckets, repeated More.

I bellowed and whirled, my feet crushing the scattered sweet-meats as the child fled. I stared into the incredulous faces of strangers jostling to get away from me. Gulls shrieked. The ocean heaved. Ships' colors whipped in the hot wind.

Thou fool, said More. *Whose head do you think I'm in?*

I write this letter in an English inn, a half-day's walk from London.

I said at the outset that I had failed, and so I believed at the time. Perhaps I will believe that again. In the meantime, with every northward step away from home, questions roil in my head—philosophical questions, such as those chewed after dinner, in the refectories of Aircastle. I will pose them to you.

Was I treated well, or ill, when my lover's husband discovered me in the arms of his wife, and assumed the entire fault was mine?

Was I treated well, or ill, when I, a mere girl, was charged with "forbidden embraces," with "defiling the marriage bed"? When my lover was persuaded to swear untruths against me, to save herself?

Was I treated well, or ill, when I was sentenced to slavery? When I was assured my bondage would be temporary if I was good, and if I denied my nature forevermore? When I was told, moreover, that I was fortunate, that voyagers stepped onto our docks daily in hopes of achieving slavery in Utopia, so preferable to freedom elsewhere?

Was I treated well, or ill, when my natural strength and agility placed me in endless daily training, in service to a citizenry that viewed combat and assassination as tasks fit only for mercenaries and slaves?

Was I treated well, or ill, when I was ordered to rescue a half-mythical figure in a faraway land where even my sex must be denied and disguised, if I am to function at all, and promised my freedom if I succeeded?

It is true, my former fellow citizens, my former masters and mistresses, I did not rescue More. He is dead. He reminds me daily of this fact, and of the impossibility of a better world to come, though in an ever fainter voice, one that I am growing used to. Mostly, now, he speaks a single name.

More is unsaved, and yet, I write you today as a free woman, to say farewell.

Our homeland is not perfect. No homeland is. But all lands can be made more perfect—even this England. And all lands have perfection within them: somewhere, sometime, someone.

Thus ends my story and my service, ye Prince and Tranibors of our good land, ye Syphogrants and families thereof. May my example be instructive to you and to your assigns. Though I never return to Utopia, never walk again beside the Waterless Stream, I will feel my people with me always, all those stern and rational generations. I will always be your agent, but I serve another now.

Joe Diabo's Farewell

In April 1926, my gang was working the thirtieth floor of the Fred F. French Building, on 45th Street midtown, where the Church of the Heavenly Rest used to be. It was a Thursday. Joe Diabo was riveter, the best I ever saw. I swear that when Joe had the hammer I could feel it in my knees from ten feet away, and him grinning the whole time. The rest of the gang was Tom Two Ax, who was the sticker-in, and Orvis Goodleaf, who was the bucker-up, and me, Eddie Two Rivers DeLisle, which is too many names for anyone, even a Mohawk, even a Caughnawaga Mohawk. I was the heater, which is why I got to see it when it happened.

Since most of you don't go up high unless our work is done, when you have enclosed elevators and carpets and pretty girls behind desks and thick tinted windows and air-conditioning and can persuade yourselves you're on the ground, nearly, let me explain what our gang was doing that morning.

It all started with me. I plucked out of the coals the reddest rivet I could find. If it made the ends of the tongs red, too, that was about right. I tossed it ten feet across and three feet down right into Tom's bucket, and Tom winked to say, *Good going, Eddie,* so close to the rivet going *plunk* that it was like an iron eyelid slamming down. Tom and I had been practicing on the reservation, standing on slippery rocks in the St. Lawrence, me with the bucket and him with the hammer, and then switching, ever since we were old enough to see the future.

During the *plunk*, Orvis had yanked out the temporary bolt, so when Tom plucked the rivet out of the bucket, there was the hole in the beam, waiting. In went the bolt until the buttonhead was flush with the steel, which meant about an inch of red tip sticking out the other side of the beam, where Joe Diabo was ready with his gun. But he had to wait for Orvis to fit the dolly bar over the buttonhead, brace himself and yell, "OK."

Then Joe Diabo leaned on the hammer until the red tip was smashed out like a second buttonhead. That was what I felt in my knees, what made Joe Diabo grin. He lifted his gun and wiped his forehead. Already the rivet was dulling down to gray.

"That one ain't going noplace," Joe Diabo said.

Then it was time to move to the next hole, but Tom and Orvis waited for Joe Diabo to move first. When he shuffled sideways, they shuffled sideways, too, on the other side of the beam.

The forge and I stayed where we were. You can't just pick up a forge and move it a foot at a time. It's not worth it. I felt comfortable tossing rivets up to about forty feet, which, come to think of it, is about the width of the St. Lawrence at Caughnawaga village. When Tom and his bucket had shuffled forty feet away, it was time to move the forge. That meant time for a break, because we also had to move the planks the forge was sitting on.

I forgot to mention the planks. They were your basic two-by-tens. The forge and I stood on a dozen of them, laid across two beams. The other guys in the gang had to make do with three planks on each side of the beam, less room if they tried to stand parallel to it, and no room to do anything else, like sit, or walk normally. If you wanted to take a stroll, you used one of the beams, which compared to the planks felt like the sidewalk on Fifth Avenue.

As I said, we were working the thirtieth floor. There were other gangs above and below. If I looked up or down, not that I had the time, I saw two dozen men in each direction getting smaller and smaller, like reflections in a department-store mirror, their jackets ballooning out in the wind.

A girl once made me take her to a pirate movie. Those pirates climbing the sails with their shirts rippling, yeah, I told her, that's what my job is like. She popped her gum and said, "They don't make movies about rivet gangs, Eddie Two Rivers DeLisle," and she was right about that.

Joe Diabo lifted the gun and wiped his forehead. "That one ain't going noplace."

They were about forty feet away. Before Joe Diabo could shuffle sideways, I yelled:

"Break time!"

After we moved the platform and the forge, we took five, sitting on the beam and smoking. Tom and Orvis and I let our feet dangle, but Joe Diabo sat with his legs folded, his feet in his lap, like one of the old-timers. Maybe he was pretending he was sitting on the ground, I don't know. We were from the same village, but only Joe Diabo was one of the longhouse people, the followers of the old ways. He didn't talk about it much. We didn't talk about anything much, when we were in high steel, and that was the only place I ever hung out with Joe Diabo. He was older than the rest of us, and had left Caughnawaga when I was a kid, and I don't recall ever having a conversation with him on the ground. Tom was Catholic, and Orvis, well, I don't remember what Orvis was, nothing probably, and us DeLisles were Presbyterian. But I doubt any of us was thinking of religion that morning when Al, the rivet boy, clambered into view, his helmet down over his eyes nearly.

"Get 'em while they're hot, Mr. Eddie," he said. Watching Al trot along the beams, the one-strap sack swaying at his side, you'd think he was delivering the *Times*, not thirty pounds of rivets.

"Thank you, Al," I said, lifting the sack off his shoulder. His jacket was plastered to his thin frame with sweat.

Al turned to Orvis and asked, "Got a smoke?"

Orvis already had three cigarettes in hand. He gave two to Al, who pocketed one and wedged the other into the corner of his mouth, then leaned forward, squinting, for Orvis to light it. It was a ritual. Al hardly flinched at all now, when Orvis's flaring match neared his face.

"You got a big weekend planned, Alphonse?" Orvis asked.

Al winced. He hated his full name, but was too small to fight about it. "Big enough," he said. Coughing, he pulled from another pocket a ragged patch of newsprint. "Papa and I are going to the movie premiere. Here, take a look."

I looked at the advertisement. A spraddle-legged, buckskin-wearing white man with a flamboyant mustache fired his pistols into the letter "O" of

THE FLAMING FRONTIER
Mightiest of thrillers—A Glorious Epic
of America's Last Wilderness
The Last Word in Great Westerns
With This Great Assembly of Stars—HOOT GIBSON
—ANNE CORNWALL
—DUSTIN FARNUM as Custer
Be the First in New York to EXPERIENCE
THE FLAMING FRONTIER
Midnight Saturday, April 3, 1926
Colony Theater

"I don't know, Al," I said, exchanging a look with the others. "That's pretty late for you to be out."

"Says who?" Al snarled, right on cue, and we all laughed. Al *was* older than he looked, I guess, in some ways. We'd all heard Papa DiNunzio was a bad drunk, and mean.

The others passed his paper around.

"Custer, huh?" Tom said.

Joe Diabo pointed to the mighty figure. "Looks like he wins, this time."

"Hoot Gibson," Tom said. "Is he the one who runs up to the back of the horse and jumps on?"

"That's him," Al said. "Papa used to jump onto a horse just like that. So he says. In the old country, before the war."

Orvis laughed. "Not much call for trick riding on a beer wagon, is there, Alphonse?"

Al flushed, and I took the paper out of Orvis's hands. "Don't listen to him, Al," I said. "Here. You go, and you have a good time."

Al shook his head. "You all missed the interesting part. Take another look, Mr. Eddie. Look at the small print."

I looked, and read aloud.

"REAL INDIANS needed for PAYING WORK associated with this premiere. BONUSES paid for authentic clothing, weapons, etc. Contact N. Birnbaum, Colony Theater box office."

"Real Indians," Orvis said. "I'll be damned. What are they gonna do, stage a massacre at intermission?"

Tom looked around at the girders, the forge, the lunch buckets, the skeleton of the Chrysler Building down the way. "Thanks for telling us, Al, but when they say, 'Real Indians,' I don't think they mean us."

Joe Diabo looked thoughtful, but didn't say anything.

I returned Al's paper, and he went on his way, and we went back to work.

"My turn to rivet," Tom said, reaching for the gun.

Joe Diabo sounded startled. "No, no, not yet. Let me. I'm good till lunchtime."

"You sure?"

"Sure I'm sure. Just getting warmed up."

Orvis was trying to look unconcerned, but I knew this was just fine with him. He never wanted to rivet; he'd be the sticker-in all day, if he could. But Tom was more ambitious. Tom looked to me for help, and I disappointed him by saying, "We did have a great rhythm going there."

"Sure we did," Joe Diabo said. "Let's get to it, boys."

"OK," Tom said, and that was it. No big deal. Sometimes we rotated jobs after a break, sometimes we didn't. And in the high steel, what Joe Diabo wanted, Joe Diabo got. So that was that. I keep telling myself.

I said earlier that being the heater gave me the best vantage point. That was because neither Tom nor Orvis could see anything but the top of Joe Diabo's head on the other side of the beam. And their attention was fixed on the rivet anyway. But me, I could see both sides of the beam equally well, with nothing to do but wait for the time to toss the next rivet. Usually I watched Joe Diabo, who was a master, as I said. I watched him flatten the next rivet, and the next, and the next. Then I watched him lift the gun, wipe his forehead, say, "That one ain't—" and step backward off the planks, into the air.

Why? Who knows why? When I was a kid, I heard an old, old man, one of the nail-keg crowd at Montour's store, tell about his son, also a riveter, who fell from the Soo Bridge in 1890. "Who knows why he fell?" the old man said. "It happens. Sometimes you just get in the way of yourself." That old man is gone now, but his successors sit around Montour's to this day, talking about Joe Diabo.

Some of them say he did it on purpose. I guess any sort of notion is interesting to think about, when you have nothing to do but sit on the side of the highway watching the tourists speed past you toward Montreal and hoping your old buddy on the bench next to you hasn't noticed that you've peed your pants again. But I was there. I watched his expression as he realized what he had done, Joe Diabo, who had walked the beams and the planks for thirty years. It was the same expression that Orvis, for Christ's sake, *Orvis* got every Saturday night, when the latest in a long line of bruisers got tired of his lip and proceeded to knock the shit out of him, and Orvis just standing there, watching it come, marveling at his own folly. That's what I saw in Joe Diabo's face, and worse yet, *he saw that I saw it.* As he stepped back, he looked at me, still openmouthed from the "ain't," and without thinking I looked away, looked down, into my pan of hot coals. But not quickly enough. He saw my face, all right. What did he see there, to carry down with him? One of the coals tumbled sideways and flared red as Joe Diabo screamed.

Don't ask me what he said. Oh, sure, those of us in the steel that day were mostly Mohawk, and we recognized Mohawk when we heard it. And make no mistake, *everyone* heard it. In the steel, a scream like that, you halfway listen for it all day, and when it comes, you're ready. But not one of us, it turned out, followed the old ways. We grew up speaking French or English, with some Mohawk thrown in as needed. If you wanted your mother to make you some *kanatarok*, for example, you had to say it in Mohawk; there was no English word, because English folks didn't boil their bread, they baked it. Those everyday Mohawk words, I knew. But whatever Joe Diabo screamed at the end, it was not an everyday word.

Some people want to make a joke of it, say maybe it was an old Mohawk curse word. Horseshit to that.

But Joe Diabo wasn't talking to us, anyway.

We came down, of course. No more work that day. The construction companies are good about that. Also, they think falls might be catching. White people are superstitious that way. Tom and Orvis went ahead, carrying their lunch buckets with the sandwiches that never tasted as good on the ground, but I had to dampen the coals, fasten the cover and the flue for the night, and so on, and I was always more painstaking at these tasks than the others. I mean, Orvis? Forget it. Plus I was slower than usual, on account of not crying. Mohawk men don't cry, but not crying is hard work sometimes. It takes all your concentration. So I thought I was the last one on our level—the tail end of the goat, my grandmother would say, though she would have said it in Mohawk. But as I set foot on the ladder, I saw a figure sitting alone, way on the other side of what *would* be the thirtieth floor, but was now mostly air.

I walked over, afraid that Al would be crying, too, but no, he just sat there, looking out at the city.

I sat, too. My feet dangled alongside his. I asked, "Did you see it?"

He shook his head.

"Me, neither," I said. I would have put my arm around him, but his sack of rivets was in the way. "This happens sometimes," I said. "Not often. Maybe not again for ten years. But it happens."

"Yeah. Got a smoke?" Al asked, his voice shaky.

I didn't smoke, and he knew that. But it was something to say.

"Let's go down now," I said.

"OK," he said.

For the first time since the accident, for the first time in my life, I didn't want to be in the steel. I wanted to be on the ground. The feeling would pass, would rarely come back. But I felt it then.

Al went first, leading the way. I carried the rivets. Without them, Al was so small, the ladder wasn't even vibrating when I took hold of it. It was as if he weren't there.

Rattling down in the elevator, we watched the city rise around us. As we descended into shadow, it got colder. The car shook like a buckboard, so we braced ourselves against the walls.

I turned to Al and said, "Let me see that advertisement again."

He handed it to me, and I read it over.

"Colony Theater," I said. "I know where that is. I saw a pirate movie there, once."

Al sounded excited. "Are you going, Mr. Eddie?"

"Why not?" I said. "They're looking for real Indians, aren't they?" I drew myself up, jabbed my thumb into my chest. "One hundred percent real Indian, that's me."

The Colony Theater was also in midtown, at Broadway and West Fifty-Third, around the corner from the Iceland skating rink and the IRT substation. Still there, too, but it's changed hands, changed names. In those days it was new, half vaudeville and half pictures, and though I hadn't worked on it, I knew guys who had. For some reason there were a lot of garages and car dealerships on that block, and the night of the premiere, the showroom windows were filled not with cars but with displays of Indian jewelry, Indian weapons, and Indian Indians. Well, people dressed like movie Indians, anyway. They had drawn a crowd, too. Just walking that block toward the theater on premiere night was slow going, more than three hours before the show.

Above each window was a sign, in Western-saloon lettering, telling everyone on the sidewalk what was happening.

"Off to the Trading Post." That was two guys in a canoe, paddling. It might have been convincing if I had been as short as Al, but I could look down through the glass and see the canoe was sitting on blue gravel, and rather than disturb the rocks, the Indians were paddling the air.

"Sharing the Peace Pipe." That window was pretty cloudy. The two old guys with the pipe kept rubbing the glass clear with their elbows, but it just clouded up again. They didn't look so peaceful. They looked annoyed. They didn't look Indian, either. No one in the windows did.

The next window was titled "A Helpless Prisoner." A chesty blonde was tied to a stake on top of a crepe-paper fire, and two guys waving tomahawks were dancing around her. Well, I say around. They had no room in the display case to get behind the blonde, so they just danced back and forth on either side of her, fanning their lips like white kids going wah-wah-wah, and the blonde pretended to scream her head off, only silently. This seemed to be the most popular window, judging from the press of the crowd, but looking at the activity behind the glass was strange because I could hear only the noises on the sidewalk, made by the many people jostling to see.

"Look at the lungs on that broad!"

"Pay attention, Billy. This is history!"

"They're gonna kill her!" That was a little kid, pressing herself back against her mom's knees, trying to back away from the glass.

Only the crowd kept pressing her forward. She was shouting her head off. "They're gonna kill her, Ma! They're gonna kill her!"

"It's just pretend, honey," her mother said.

I leaned down, tapped her shoulder. "That's right," I said. "Those tomahawks, see how they flap back and forth? They're made of rubber. Rubber can't hurt you."

The kid stared up at me, sucked in breath that whistled through the gap in her teeth, filled herself up for another bellow.

"Don't talk to niggers, Cordelia," Ma snarled. I registered only a big flowered hat and a frowning set of eyebrows before she whisked her daughter away in the crowd.

I nearly turned around right then, and went home. But I didn't. Some people. What can you do?

The sidewalk clock showed ten minutes to nine, and I needed to get a move on.

Under the Colony Theater marquee, behind a velvet rope, were a few teepees with more Indians milling around, and a calliope mounted on a circus wagon. An old guy in a U.S. Cavalry uniform was pounding the hell out of the keyboard. He was playing "Take Me Out to the Ball Game." I still don't know why. Guys in coveralls crossed my path, toting into the lobby an upright microphone, a folding screen with glossy photos pinned to it, a balsa-wood cutout of Custer. A man's voice yelled, "Aren't you listening? The Indian village sticks out no farther than *here*, otherwise the crowd is filing down a chute like so many goddamn cattle!"

I threaded through and turned into the alley, clutching the paper they'd given me that afternoon, when I registered for the show. It was a lot less crowded and easier to breathe in the alley, but it sure didn't smell so good. I took my place at the end of a short line of guys shuffling single file through the stage door. I had tried to dress up a little, with rosewater and some shine in my hair, but a couple of these men looked as if they'd slept in their clothes, and the guy just ahead smelled worse than the alley. None of them looked Indian, either.

A leathery woman with a gnawed cigar wedged in the corner of her mouth was checking us in on a clipboard. Her first question, when I reached her, was: "Cavalry or Indian?"

I was tempted, and the thought made it hard to keep a straight face, but I finally said, "Indian."

She flipped a sheet. "Name?"

"Eddie DeLisle," I said.

"Eddie *what?*"

"DeLisle," I said. "I talked to Mr. Birnbaum on the phone. He put me down."

Her cigar tacked back and forth in her mouth as she looked and didn't find me.

I added: "Big dee, little eee, big ell, little eye, little ess, little ell, little eee."

"Big enn, little oh," she said. "I got no Eddies here. See for yourself." Her neck wattles shook like a turkey's.

"Hey, there it is," I said, my big finger tapping the smeared page. I forgot I had signed it "E. Two Rivers DeLisle," but my last name was more of a big dee with a tail.

She grunted and used a grease pencil to lay a thick black smear across my name. "Good," she said. "Tell the dressers you're the last member of the welcoming party in the lobby. First door to your right."

The dressers, when I walked in, didn't wait to be told anything. The moment I entered their long, bright room, barely registering the bare skin and sagging bellies and bobbing headdresses, hands were unbuttoning my braces, my shirt, unwrapping my collar. And these were women!

"Raiding party?" one asked, holding up a big fur hat with horns.

"Lobby," I squawked, as my britches fell around my ankles. "The welcoming party."

"Ah," she said, moving so fast that I registered only eyeglasses, a flurry of measuring tape, and a pencil in her red hair. "Take off his shirt, too. Don't worry, you can keep your shorts. This ain't that kind of theater."

She turned to a clothes rack sagging beneath the weight of buckskin and feathers and started yanking down items, leaving the wire hangers to dance naked. In moments, those clothes were on me, in layers. I could barely move.

"Well well," she said, stepping back with her arms folded. "*You*, at least, look good. *You*, I can believe in." She was pretty, I now could see, and her eyes looked pinched in the corners. I think that meant she was smiling, but before I could smile back, someone dropped a sweaty band of cloth across my eyes. I yanked it up by instinct and turned to see, in a full-length mirror, an Indian chief peering out from under a feathered headdress so long that it dragged the floor behind. I wore fringed buckskin trousers, moccasins, a leather belt with turquoise braided in, and a white fur vest that left my arms and chest bare. I was impressed.

Then the woman's hands were rubbing all my bare skin she could see and reach, smearing on makeup, striping me like a tiger. "The others were too hairy for this," she said, "but you'll look just fine." I thought she looked just fine, too, as she wiped her hands on the tail of her smock, shoved my street clothes into a cubby, and tossed me a wooden number, like in a deli. "You're in Seventy-Six. Don't lose this, because it's your pay chit, too. You'll be naked and poor. Hey, Hilda. Hilda! Show the Chief here to the lobby, will you?"

A kneeling older woman with safety pins in her mouth looked up from an Indian princess's hem. "Mhm-MHM-mhmmhm," Hilda said. "Mhm-MHM."

"Oh, fine, then. Follow me, Chief—well, what *is* your name?"

"I'm Eddie," I said.

"I'm Millie," she said, over her shoulder. "Pleased to meetcha."

We had plunged into a series of narrow corridors full of people on the move—the ones in costume mostly headed in our direction, the stagehands mostly shouldering past in the other.

I asked, "What does the welcoming party do?"

She laughed. "At a guess, I'd say you welcome people. Impressive, ain't I? That's what three years in New York does for an Iowa girl. Makes you smart." She flung open a shabby door, and before us was the Colony Theater lobby. Marble floors, gold-leaf cornices, red velvet curtains, a chandelier wider than my gang's platform, and, in the middle of it, an Indian village. Not like Caughnawaga village, though. Those lobby teepees wouldn't have lasted five minutes during winter on the St. Lawrence. We build our houses right, up there. A dozen Indians and a dozen soldiers in Cavalry uniform were being herded into groups by a yelling bald guy in riding breeches, waving a clipboard.

"See the Kaiser there? Do what he says. Within reason. OK? Break a leg, Eddie." She was already halfway down the corridor.

"Hey, wait a sec," I said.

She turned, one eyebrow arched.

"You gonna undress me later?" I asked.

She laughed out loud. "Oh, someone can help you with that, if I'm busy." She turned away but kept turning as she walked, so she now was walking backward looking at me. Her hands were stuck deep in the pockets of her smock, which she flapped like wings, her tape measure fluttering. "But who knows, Eddie? I mean, who the hell can say? It's Saturday night on Broadway, the avenue where dreams come true."

Laughing, I stepped into the lobby, feeling better than I had in a while, and was nearly run over by a giant squeaky-wheeled platform being shoved past the door. On the platform, rolling in reverse, was a stuffed buffalo, a massive thing, shaggy and awe-inspiring. It nearly ran over some loafing soldiers, too, but the Cavalry scattered in panic as the buffalo slid to a stop, its beard swaying, its beady eyes staring right at me.

———

The welcoming party's job turned out to be greeting the dignitaries who entered the lobby on the red carpet. Just before they reached the radio microphone, we were supposed to raise our right hands, just like swearing on the Bible, and say, "Hail, Great Chief!" No, I am not kidding. Or "Hail, Great Mother!" Those moving-picture gals in their little dresses didn't look like Great Mothers to me, but they sure as hell didn't look like Great Fathers, either.

"Yes, ladies and gentlemen, it's the exclusive Universal Pictures contract beauty, Alice Joyce! Co-star of that terrific new Ronald Colman picture, *Beau Geste!* From P. C. Wren's electrifying best seller! . . . Fresh from his latest sellout show at the Winter Garden, here's everyone's favorite singer, Al Jolson! . . . Here's top producer Samuel Goldwyn, whose new sensation is *The Winning of Barbara Worth!* Starring Ronald Colman, Gary Cooper, and Vilma Banky, the Hungarian Rhapsody! . . . Here's George Jessel, star of Broadway's hit play, *The Jazz Singer.* . . . And look out, everyone! Here are the stars of that wacky new Broadway sensation, *The Cocoanuts.* Yes, it's Groucho Marx, Harpo Marx, Chico Marx, and Zeppo Marx."

"Hey, are you guys related?" asked the one in the painted mustache.

Most of the dignitaries were there because they worked for the studio, or had a new picture coming out, or a show on Broadway, or were just there because that's what famous people have to do, show up to fill seats at things like this—though at least two of the Marxes, I noticed, went out the side door the moment the announcer was done with them, and I didn't see them come back.

One dignitary was different, a white-mustached old man in a Cavalry uniform that was not a costume. He walked with a cane. Everybody else, when we said, "Hail, Great Father," laughed and hailed us back, or in one case honked a horn. This old man just looked thoughtful. For a second I expected him to salute.

"And now, ladies and gentlemen, a very special guest, retired Brigadier General Edward S. Godfrey. General Godfrey, welcome. Please tell our listeners where you were on June 25, 1876."

"I was in command of K Company at the Little Bighorn."

"Remarkable. So you served under Custer himself?"

"I did, yes. Though in that battle, my column was separate from his."

"And how did you survive, sir?"

"We suffered losses, of course, but with the aid of Providence, my men held off the enemy until General Terry arrived, two days later. Whereupon, as the world knows, I learned the sad news that General Custer and the men who rode with him—six company commanders included, and three of Custer's own closest kin—had been slain, victims of an overwhelming enemy force. I know, for I was in charge of the identification and the burial of the honored dead. An awesome duty, a terrible duty, and yet a sadly necessary duty, for—"

"Thank you, General, and enjoy the show. Here she is, ladies and gentlemen, the radiant Clara Kimball Young!"

Finally the parade of dignitaries was over, and almost everyone with a ticket had filed into the auditorium. Only some stragglers were left, and the big crowd outside—the people who had no tickets, but were just enjoying the free stuff—were still standing there looking in. The boss-man shook hands with us, thanked us for being excellent scenery, and said we were welcome to stay for the movie on Universal's nickel, though we might have to stand up in the back of the house. The show was a sellout, seventeen hundred seats full. Most of the Cavalry took this as their cue to leave—in hopes of avoiding the massacre, maybe—but most of the Indians decided to stay, and began filing through the auditorium doors, still in costume because they were afraid if they went back to the dressing room, they'd miss something. The orchestra already was playing the overture. I was about to join them when I realized one of those figures out on the sidewalk looked familiar.

I trotted outside for a closer look. It was Al, his chin just above the velvet rope.

"Look at you, Mr. Eddie," he said. "You got paint all over and feathers like a pigeon."

Al was more dressed up than I'd ever seen, in knickers and a buttoned blue shirt, with his hair oiled and parted in the middle.

"Al, you're missing the movie. Where's your papa?"

Then I was sorry for asking. He sagged worse than if I'd handed him a 30-pound sack of rivets. He looked like he was carrying two floors at once.

"Papa couldn't make it, Mr. Eddie," he said, avoiding my gaze. "He took sick, and I guess he forgot to buy the tickets. But hey, I was all dressed up anyhow. So I been watching everything out here. It's like a free show, Mr. Eddie."

I had an idea. "Stay here, Al. Stay close to the rope."

I went back to the teepees. Most of the Indians had gone inside, but one of the braves who had threatened the blonde in the window was sitting on a stool behind the biggest teepee. He was having a smoke, not such a good idea with that headdress on. "How you doing?" he said, with a nod.

"You using that blanket?" I pointed to a big colorful rumple in front of the teepee flap like a welcome mat, then picked it up without waiting for an answer. "Thanks. Let's see." I patted myself down, but came up short of accessories. "How many necklaces you wearing, buddy? Three at least. Lend me one, will you?"

He wedged the cigarette into the corner of his mouth and stared at me as he slowly unclasped the beads and held them close to his chest. "Say, what's the story?" he asked.

"Just trying to be a good Indian," I said as I tugged the beads from his clenched hand, one at a time. "There's a pal."

Just then, his window buddy crawled out of the teepee, struggled to his feet. He was a little unsteady, his big belly swaying. He'd lost his headdress someplace. Then the teepee flap opened again, and the Helpless Prisoner crawled out, a flask rolling onto the pavement beside her knee. It sounded empty. The headdress was too big on her blonde head, and as she stood, it angled over one eye like a flapper's hat.

"Hiya," she said as she finished buttoning her blouse. She had started at the bottom. "Jeez, that pallet is hard," she said. "How'd they ever make so many Indians, I wonder, lying on the ground like that? I ask you."

As she gave her skirt a straightening tug across her hips, I said, "Hold still a sec, ma'am." As the Prisoner held still, eyes big and smile tentative, I reached up and plucked three feathers from the side of the headdress. They came off easy. "Thank you, ma'am. Good evening to you. Gentlemen."

I carried my trade goods back to where Al stood, solemnly waiting. I wrapped the blanket several times around his narrow shoulders, fastened the bead necklace around his neck, smeared greasepaint from my chest and cheeks onto his face, and planted the feathers in his pomaded hair. Still kneeling, I turned my back to him and said, "Hop on."

"Drop me and I'll bust you one," he grumbled, but he did what I said. I was surprised how little he weighed.

I attracted barely a glance from the scattered smokers and loungers and hat-check girls as I walked through the Colony Theater lobby with an unlikely papoose on my back. I pushed through the auditorium doors and carried the next generation into the dark, into 1875.

I guess it was pretty good, as pictures go. Hoot Gibson jumped on and off his horse a lot, and whenever he did, everyone cheered. Anne Cornwall was good-looking but didn't have much to do. I wondered if the real General Custer had a mustache as big as Dustin Farnum's. It didn't look regulation.

The picture explained that Custer was a friend of the Indians, until they got tricked, by some sharp traders, into going on the warpath. Now, I didn't know much about the West, but I knew better than that. I knew the Indians were fighting because the white people kept taking their land. I knew that Custer, like a lot of other Cavalry officers, probably General Godfrey too, had killed a lot of Indian women and children. I knew that at the Little Bighorn, Custer and his men pretty much got what was coming to them.

None of this was in the picture.

Frankly, I got fidgety in the middle. I work a day on my feet, no problem, but I had been standing for hours, and standing isn't working.

Plus, something about the big black-and-white figures on the screen, fighting and falling and dying, got me to thinking of Joe Diabo, and Joe Diabo wasn't so good to think about at that time, in that place. I mean, what would he have thought of me right then, in my silly outfit, hailing the Great Fathers of Broadway?

So that was my mood when a man slowly came huffing and puffing up the auditorium steps, clanked past me, and pushed open the door. In the light from the lobby I saw it was the old general. The clanking had been his sword and medals.

I had an impulse then, and I glanced at Al, who was standing on the base of a column next to me, so that he could see over the heads of everyone in the back row. He had eyes only for the frantic giants on the screen. So I slipped away, followed the old man into the lobby.

He hadn't made it far. He stood about a yard away from me, his reflection shiny in the marble floor. The lobby looked much bigger empty. Only two other people were in sight. The hat-check girl was leaning against her counter, wearing an abbreviated Pocahontas outfit. She had her arms folded and was shivering a little, like she was cold, and no wonder. Another employee, a guy, was lounging in the ticket booth, reading a racing form. His only concession to the theme was a big gray Cavalry hat that rode his ears.

"Excuse me," the general called out. "Can you direct me to the facilities?"

The ticket guy squinted at him. "The what?"

"The facilities!" the general repeated. "For God's sake, man. The latrine. The privy."

"Oh," the ticket guy said. "The Gents is down the stairs on the left. The Indian will take you."

The hell I will, I nearly said, but the ticket guy was buried in his racing form again, and the general already was hobbling downstairs. He held on to the bannister with both hands and swung his right leg wide on each step, as if his knee no longer bent so well.

I don't know why I followed him, but I did. I waited until he was out of sight, though. My moccasins were quiet on the stairs, and I felt like some treacherous movie Indian, following the hero, and up to no good. I reached the foot of the stairs just in time to see the general shouldering through a swinging door marked GENTS. I padded across a checkerboard tile floor, past armchairs, potted plants, and spittoons, and into the washroom.

The general stood before a urinal, fumbling with his many buttons and his multiple belts. A colored attendant, a bald man in a red jacket, was trying to help. It was taking a while.

I just stood there, not even watching the ordeal, with the strangest thought in my head. What I wanted to do was walk up to the general, cock my index finger like it was a gun, touch my barrel finger to his temple and say, "Bang," the way you do when you're young, and playing cowboys.

The attendant glanced up and saw me.

"Sir," he called, "can you please help us? We can't unfasten his sword belt, and the general is in need."

"Oh, Jesus, hurry!" the general groaned, his eyes screwed shut. "I can't stand it!"

The attendant looked at me again. "Sir, did you hear me? Please, give us a hand here."

"No," I said, loudly and distinctly. I turned my back on them, left the washroom. Halfway across the checkerboard, I could hear behind me, through the closed door, the two of them loudly moaning together, probably in dismay. I ignored them, and walked calmly up the stairs.

What a thing to tell people. Am I ashamed? Yeah, probably. But am I sorry? No, I am not sorry. There's a difference.

As I reached the landing, the muffled orchestra music got suddenly louder, lots of bass drums and cymbals, and I heard the cry of a thousand people reacting to something exciting and spectacular. As my head crested the top of the stairs, I saw the street doors had been propped open, letting in the honk and hiss of traffic, the wail of an approaching siren. Now I was standing in the lobby. From the auditorium came another burst of applause, and a blare of trumpets. The auditorium doors flung open, were doorstopped by ushers in buckskin, and a dozen Indians emerged to repopulate the Indian village. Then hundreds of fresh survivors of the Little Bighorn streamed into the lobby, lighted cigarettes, rushed past me to the washrooms. A lot of them were loud and drunk. I thought I'd be trampled, but they just flowed past me, like I wasn't there. One of the teepees crumpled sideways, as someone stumbled into it. Outside, a dozen policemen on motorcycles roared past, sirens screaming. Out of the melee, Al trotted over to me, his face blue with cotton candy.

"You missed the end!" Al cried.

"I know how it ends," I told him.

After the crowd finally left, and Millie gave me the number of her boardinghouse, we Indians helped break down the teepees and push the buffalo to the loading dock, which wasn't part of the deal, but we were show folk by then and up for anything. We swapped our costumes for street clothes and pocketed our pay. Then we left the theater by the stage door and wandered up the alley to the sidewalk and stood beneath the extinguished marquee, locked out of the shadowed lobby where our village used to stand. The sun was just beginning to rise, but the big hole a half-block north on Broadway, where Hammerstein's theater was going up, made the whole block seem unusually dark. Not many cars passed us, and not many people, either. On the opposite sidewalk was some local oddball, a gaunt old man in a black suit who as he walked was coaxing pigeons out of their roosts by strewing seed corn from a sack. He had skeleton hands, and was cooing something like, "Tica, tica, tica."

"Nasty birds," said the Indian next to me. He mopped his forehead with a handkerchief. "Shit gets in your lungs, you can't breathe." The handkerchief came away red, leaving dark-brown streaks above his eyebrows where the makeup had been. He smiled at me as he swiped his darkening cheeks, and I realized he was a Negro. "The girls did a better job on you," he said.

"I'm Indian already," I said. I scrubbed my fingers back and forth across my chin and held them out for inspection.

"Ah, so I see," the Negro said. "Too bad for you. Those makeup girls were cute."

"I'll ask for a touch-up next time," I said.

He laughed and offered me his hand. "Asa's my name."

"I'm Eddie."

He didn't try to break my fingers in his grip like some big men do, but I could tell I was shaking a strong hand.

"You work steel?" I asked.

"Trains," he said. "Day shift at the BMT yard." He held his palms a foot apart, made the space wider and then closed it. "We pull the cars apart, we fix 'em, we push 'em together again. How about you? You work steel?"

As we talked, a few other Indians stepped from the shadow beneath the dark marquee.

"Yeah," I told Asa, "up there," and pointed.

He shook his big head. "God bless you for it, buddy, but you can *have* that mess. Aunt Hagar's children staying on the *ground* till God lets down a ladder. How you doing, Jacob?"

"How am I?" asked a short Indian with a limp. He clapped Asa on the back. "Hoping Miriam didn't wait up for me, that's how I am. Already she's mad I broke the Sabbath, and now I got such a cramp, she'll say, 'You see? You forsake your people, your own leg should turn against you.'" He turned to me. "You got a wife?"

I shook my head. "Nah. I take girls to a show sometimes."

"Don't kid yourself, that's just how it starts," said Jacob the Indian, slicing the air with his hand. "At least for her I got Jolson's autograph, maybe when I get home she'll *take me to a show*." He winked.

The other Indians who had gathered around picked up the theme of women, at least the ones who knew English. One guy I now sort of recognized: He worked at the Chinese laundry on Mulberry. He nodded at me, and I nodded back, and my stomach growled, wanting breakfast.

The good thing about New York City in those days, though, was that if you stood in one place for fifteen minutes, the food would come to you. In fact, the pushcarts weren't *allowed* to stand still, not in the theater district anyway. So the next vendor to round the corner, a stooped old lady in a babushka pushing a kettle-wagon the size of my forge, found herself surrounded by a band of foraging Indians.

"What have you got, Tia?" the Indians asked. "What's cooking, Babka?"

"Two bits," she said. She held out her cupped right hand as her left hand yanked off the lid, enveloping us in a puff of saltwater steam. The roast-chickpea smell was so good it almost knocked me down. My mouth watered.

"Two bits," said the old lady. She held out a paper cone swollen with roasted peas. "Chi-chi beans. Two bits!"

So I paid her and took hold of the narrow end of the beans. I fisted the cone too hard, and a few chickpeas rained onto the sidewalk. I held it more gently then. I tipped a handful of hot chickpeas into my palm, bounced them around a little, then popped them into my mouth. They were salty and just firm enough as I crushed them into paste between my eyeteeth.

A half-dozen of us were munching happily, those who had beans shaking their cones into the cupped hands of those who had none. The old lady already was trundling away southward toward Bryant Park.

"Damn, these are good," Asa said. "What did she call these?"

"Chi-chis."

"What chi-chis?" Jacob asked. "Arbis, we call this. Whenever a baby is born, we have a dinner, and this is always part of it. After every *Shalom Zachar,* we're picking peas up off the floor for weeks." He carefully selected a single bean and munched it. "No paper cones, though," he added, rattling his. "If the Weinbergs, that's Miriam's people, if they thought we couldn't afford plates, she would die of embarrassment and take me with her."

Another Indian said: "When I was a boy in Livorno, we made a pie of these. *Torta di ceci.* But we mashed 'em up first."

"Mashed?" repeated a mustached Indian, stretching out the "A." "What is this *maaashed?*"

In reply, the Italian Indian, his mouth full, thumped the air downward three times with the heel of his free hand, then spread his fingers, palm up, and repeatedly clenched them.

"Ah, you *crush* them!" said the mustache. "We crush them, *maaash* them, as well. But not for pastry. For dipping." He pinched the air between his fingers and made scooping motions. "Dip bread into the hummus. A little garlic and oil, very good."

Asa laughed. "I don't need 'em mashed. I still got *my* teeth."

Our shadows ran together between the streetlights, and I thought, this won't last, Eddie. We'll all go back to our own neighborhoods, our own jobs, our lives. If we cross paths after tonight, we won't even recognize each other. We'll just see a Negro, or a Greek, or a Jew, and that's all we'll see.

"Why babies?" I asked Jacob.

Jacob was taking longer to eat than the rest of us, plucking out chi-chis one at a time, blowing on each, then chewing methodically. "I don't get you," he said.

"Why, when babies are born, do you eat these peas? I mean, what's the connection?"

"Oh," he said. He looked at nothing, chewed another solitary pea. "Hang on," he said. More chewing. "Wait," he said. "Wait." More chewing. "OK, I got it. I had to think back to what Tateh used to say. Because they're round, and they got no openings. That's what you want at the *Shalom Zachar* table."

"Like a meatball," said one Indian.

"Or a dumpling," said another.

"Or a hardboiled egg."

"Exactly," said Jacob, but he looked unsure.

"But why?" I asked again. "Why, on that occasion, do you need round food with no openings?"

Jacob laughed. "What am I, a rabbi? That's just what we do. You don't ask questions about things like that. You just do 'em, because your parents did 'em, and your grandparents, on back. That's family."

Asa turned to me. "You got any family stories, Eddie?"

"Oh, sure," I said, and there I was, committed. Everyone was looking at me.

"Here's one my grandfather used to tell," I said. "Long, long ago, people didn't live on the Earth. Everyone lived in the sky. They never even looked down here, because, why would they? There was nothing to see, and they were doing just fine in the sky. But parts of the sky were thinner than the rest. These places, they looked just like the rest of the sky, but they had worn thin over time. The Sky People didn't know it, but whoever next put weight there, look out!

"So the Great Chief of the Sky People came walking along, making sure everything was good, because it was his lookout, and he walked right past the thin place on the left, without realizing it. And he said, 'I am content, for the sky is as it should be, and at peace.'

"And later, the medicine man of the Sky People came walking along, looking for signs from the spirit world, and hoping he wouldn't find any, and he just missed that thin place, too, on the right side. And he said, 'I am content, for the spirits are pleased with us.'

"And then later, here came the Great Chief's oldest son, checking up on the things he figured the old man had wrong, and like most young men, he thought his balls were so big, you know, that he had to walk bowlegged, like this. And so he walked right past that thin place on *both* sides, it was amazing how it happened, and he said, 'I am content, for I will be the next Great Chief of my people, and I will be able to fix this.'

"And finally, along came the only daughter of the Great Chief, and she was the only one of the Sky People who looked down a lot, because she thought the world below was beautiful, and she stepped right on that thin place, and broke through, and fell, and as she fell she said nothing but instead sang a song like no one had ever heard, and the birds of the air below, and the beasts of the land below, and the fish of the water below, everybody heard this song, and when Sky Woman landed feet first at the top of the highest hill, the creatures were there to welcome her, except the fish, I guess. And Sky Woman said, 'I am content, for this is a place of beauty, and above me is the sky, always.' And that's how my people say the first person came to live on the Earth."

Nobody said anything. They all just looked at me.

"Huh," Asa said.

"My grandfather told that story so many times," I said, "we kids used to think he was standing there when Sky Woman landed."

A few of them chuckled, not very loudly. Then they all started to move, shuffling from foot to foot or wadding up their empty paper cones or looking at their watches.

"Getting late, fellas."

"Yep, getting late."

None of them seemed impressed by my story. I was plenty impressed, myself, because I had made up the whole thing, on the spot, right there on Broadway under the Colony marquee. My grandfather's actual favorite story was about how he finagled his way into being the last man hired to work steel on the Flatiron Building. I never knew I was so good at lying.

So we all walked away from the Colony. I never saw any of them again, not that I know of, anyway. I walked home, and looked up the whole way at the buildings I had worked, touched by the morning sun, and above me was the sky, always.

Years later, I went by the Museum of Modern Art, where they show the old pictures, including the silents, to see if they were going to show *The Flaming Frontier* anytime soon—since I saw it only the once, and went in late, and left before it was over. I don't think the picture played the Colony long, and Millie had other plans for the next Saturday night, and the next, and the next twenty years. The museum woman had never heard of it but was nice enough to look it up in her big catalogs on the shelves in her office, and she said That's interesting, and she told me *The Flaming Frontier* not only wasn't in the museum's collection, it wasn't in *anyone's* collection, or any distributor's list either. A lot of old movies, she told me, just plain don't exist anymore. The film stock back then was easy to catch fire, or just dissolve, and a lot of studios, when they went bust, threw everything away. But maybe this one will turn up one day, Mister DeLisle. They do turn up, sometimes. That's OK, I told her. The Fred F. French Building is gone, too. But I know it was there.

That Monday morning after the premiere, I was back in the steel. I was early. If I had anything to work out with myself—about being up there again—I wanted to do it alone. As one floor after another dropped past the elevator, I took deep breaths, bounced my lunch sack against my leg in a steady rhythm. Clearing the neighboring buildings, into the light of the sunrise, warmed me, and the higher I went, the better I felt. I felt back to normal when I shoved open the door and stepped off the elevator.

There was no one else on Thirty. Oh, Joe Diabo was waiting for me, all right, as I half expected he would be, but he wasn't on my floor. He was about ten feet west of it, beyond the farthest beam, farther out than anyone in the Fred F. French Building has reached to this day. He was hanging in the air above Fifth Avenue, at eye level with me.

I knew he was standing on nothing, because nothing was out there to stand on, but I still wanted to look down at his feet, see if his toes were pointing toward Fifth, like toes on a crucifix. I fought that urge. I didn't want to look in that direction. I just looked him in the eye.

Joe Diabo spoke to me, but too faintly to hear. Part of me wanted to step closer, to hear him better, but I was already farther toward the edge than I wanted. Somehow I had left behind the platform in front of the elevator, and stepped onto the beam. I kept looking into Joe Diabo's eyes, because I knew if I looked away for a second, when I turned back around he might be closer, a lot closer, and then I'd get in the way of myself for sure. So I held his gaze as I slowly sat down on the beam and hooked my right arm around the nearest support, which was one of the struts of the forge. The sharp edge against my bicep woke me up a little. Joe Diabo's eyes were the saddest I ever saw.

He spoke again, and now the wind was toward me, off the Hudson—I caught a whiff of fish, and the breweries in Union City—and I could hear his voice now, thin and far away. It wasn't English.

"I'm sorry, Joe," I said, though he was still talking. "I can't understand you. I wish I could."

I wanted to say more, to tell him about that Saturday-night Wild West minstrel show, and the foolish story I had made up. But the funny thing was, the longer I listened to Joe's voice, the better I understood it. I'm not sure it ever turned into English, not entirely, but it turned into something I could understand.

"I'm sorry, Eddie. I'm so sorry. Say it's all right, Eddie."

I actually laughed. Well, it wasn't quite a laugh. It was more like the sound Orvis makes when he's punched in the gut, all the air leaving at once. "Sorry for what, Joe? You got nothing to be sorry for."

"I'm sorry I fell," Joe said. "But I was good, wasn't I, Eddie? Except for that? I did a good job before, didn't I?"

He was still out there, but I couldn't see his face anymore, on account of crying. Mohawk men don't cry, but I cried then.

"No one better, Joe," I said. "We all know that. And it don't matter that you . . . It don't matter. You're still the best, Joe. You and I, we'll always know that. I won't forget it, Joe."

The blur in the sky that was Joe Diabo began to fade then, like the fire going out at the end of the day. I swabbed my left sleeve across my eyes to clear them, and Joe Diabo was gone, and I was just sitting there, against a cold forge. Anyone stepping off the elevator would have thought, look at DeLisle, goldbricking. I stood up and got busy.

We had a new guy, of course. He came up with Tom and Orvis. D. B. Lachapelle, his name was. I don't know what the D. B. meant. He was from Caughnawaga village, too. We knew his people. He was young, like a boy. A *large* boy. Short but wide-shouldered, muscled.

"Eddie Two Rivers DeLisle," I said. "Glad to know you."

"Pleased to meet you, Mr. DeLisle," the kid said, wringing my hand. "It's an honor to work with you."

I looked at Tom, who was grinning, and I looked at Orvis, who was handing over the gun. Joe Diabo's gun.

"Just until lunch," Tom said.

So we went to work. Tom plucked out of the coals the reddest rivet he could find, and tossed it into Orvis's bucket. D. B. yanked out the temporary bolt. Orvis stuck the red-hot rivet into the hole, and

D. B. braced the dolly bar and yelled, "OK." I leaned on the hammer until the red tip bloomed flat against the beam, and then I lifted the gun and wiped my forehead and grinned in the high breeze. That one wasn't going noplace.

Beluthahatchie

Everybody else got off the train at Hell, but I figured, it's a free country. So I commenced to make myself a mite more comfortable. I put my feet up and leaned back against the window, laid my guitar across my chest, and settled in with my hat tipped down over my eyes, almost. I didn't know what the next stop was but I knew I'd like it better than Hell.

Whoo! I never saw such a mess. All that crowd of people jammed together on the Hell platform so tight you could faint standing up. One old battle-hammed woman hollering for Jesus, most everybody else just mumbling and crying and hugging their bags and leaning into each other and waiting to be told where to go. And hot? Man, I ain't just beating my gums there. Not as hot as the Delta, but hot enough to keep old John on the train. No, sir, I told myself, no room out there for me.

Fat old conductor man pushed on down the aisle kinda slow, waiting on me to move. I decided I'd wait on that, too.

"Hey, nigger boy." He slapped my foot with a rolled-up newspaper. Felt like the Atlanta paper. "This ain't no sleeping car."

"Git up off me, man. I ain't done nothing."

"Listen at you. Who you think you are, boy? Think you run the railroad? You don't look nothing like Mr. George Pullman." The conductor tried to put his foot up on the seat and lean on his knee, but he gave up with a grunt.

I ran one finger along my guitar strings, not hard enough to make a sound but just hard enough to feel them. "I ain't got a ticket, neither," I bit off, "but it was your railroad's pleasure to bring me this far, and it's my pleasure to ride on a little further, and I don't see what cause you got to be so astorperious about it, Mr. Fat Ass."

He started puffing and blowing. "What? What?" He was teakettle hot. You'd think I'd done something. "What did you call me, boy?" He whipped out a strap, and I saw how it was, and I was ready.

"Let him alone."

Another conductor was standing outside the window across the aisle, stooping over to look in. He must have been right tall and right big too, filling up the window like that. Cut off most of the light. I couldn't make out his face, but I got the notion that pieces of it was sliding around, like there wan't quite a face ready to look at yet. "The Boss will pick him up at the next stop. Let him be."

"The Boss?" Fat Ass was getting whiter all the time.

"The Boss said it would please him to greet this nigger personally."

Fat Ass wan't studying about me anymore. He slunk off, looking back big-eyed at the man outside the window. I let go my razor and let my hand creep up out of my sock, slow and easy, making like I was just shifting cause my leg was asleep.

The man outside hollered: "Board! All aboard! Next stop, Beluthahatchie!"

That old mama still a-going. "Jesus! Save us, Jesus!"

"All aboard for Beluthahatchie!"

"Jesus!"

We started rolling out.

"All aboard!"

"Sweet Je—" And her voice cut off just like that, like the squawk of a hen Meemaw would snatch for Sunday dinner. Wan't my business. I looked out the window as the scenery picked up speed. Wan't nothing to see, just fields and ditches and swaybacked mules and people stooping and picking, stooping and picking, and by and by a porch with old folks sitting on shuck-bottomed chairs looking out at all the years that ever was, and I thought I'd seen enough of all that to last me a while. Wan't any of my business at all.

When I woke up I was lying on a porch bench at another station, and hanging on one chain was a blown-down sign that said Belutha-hatchie. The sign wan't swinging cause there wan't no breath of air. Not a soul else in sight neither. The tracks ran off into the fields on both ends as far as I could see, but they was all weeded up like no train been through since the Surrender. The windows over my head was boarded up like the bank back home. The planks along the porch han't been swept in years by nothing but the wind, and the dust was in whirly patterns all around.

Still lying down, I reached slowly beneath the bench, groping the air, till I heard, more than felt, my fingers pluck a note or two from the strings of my guitar. I grabbed it by the neck and sat up, pulling the guitar into my lap and hugging it, and I felt some better.

Pigeons in the eaves was a-fluttering and a-hooting all mournful-like, but I couldn't see 'em. I reckon they was pigeons. Meemaw used to say that pigeons sometimes was the souls of dead folks let out of Hell. I didn't think those folks back in Hell was flying noplace, but I did feel something was wrong, bad wrong, powerful wrong. I had the same crawly feeling as before I took that fatal swig—when Jar Head Sam, that harp-playing bastard, passed me a poisoned bottle at a Mississippi jook joint and I woke up on that one-way train.

Then a big old hound dog ambled around the corner of the station on my left, and another big old hound dog ambled around the comer of the station on my right. Each one was nearbouts as big as a calf and so fat it could hardly go, swanking along with its belly on the planks and its nose down. When the dogs snuffled up to the bench where I was sitting, their legs give out and they flopped down, yawned, grunted, and went fast to sleep like they'd been poleaxed. I could see the fleas hopping across their big butts. I started laughing.

"Lord, the hellhounds done caught up to me now! I surely must have led them a chase, I surely must. Look how wore out they are!" I hollered and cried, I was laughing so hard. One of them broke wind real long, and that set me off again. "Here come the brimstone! Here come the sulfur! Whoo! Done took my breath. Oh, Lordy." I wiped my eyes.

Then I heard two way-off sounds, one maybe a youngun dragging a stick along a fence, and the other maybe a car motor.

"Well, shit," I said.

Away off down the tracks, I saw a little spot of glare vibrating along in the sun. The flappity racket got louder and louder. Some fool was driving his car along on the tracks, a bumpety-bump, a bumpety-bump. It was a Hudson Terraplane, right sporty, exactly like what Peola June used to percolate around town in, and the chrome on the fender and hood was shining like a conk buster's hair.

The hound dogs was sitting up now, watching the car. They was stiff and still on each side of my bench, like deacons sitting up with the dead.

When the car got nigh the platform it lurched up out of the cut, gravel spitting, gears grinding, and shut off in the yard at the end of the porch where I was sitting. Sheets of dust sailed away. The hot engine ticked. Then the driver's door opened, and out slid the devil. I knew him well. Time I saw him slip down off the seat and hitch up his pants, I knew.

He was a sunburnt, bandy-legged, pussel-gutted li'l peckerwood. He wore braces and khaki pants and a dirty white undershirt and a big derby hat that had white hair flying out all around it like it was attached to the brim, like if he'd tip his hat to the ladies his hair would come off too.

He had a bright-red possum face, with beady, dumb black eyes and a long sharp nose, and no chin at all hardly and a big goozlum in his neck that jumped up and down like he couldn't swallow his spit fast enough. He slammed the car door and scratched himself a little, up one arm and then the other, then up one leg till he got to where he liked it. He hunkered down and spit in the dust and looked all unconcerned like maybe he was waiting on a tornado to come along and blow some victuals his way, and he didn't take any more notice of me than the hound dogs had.

I wan't used to being treated such. "You keep driving on the tracks thataway, hoss," I called, "and that Terraplane gone be butt-sprung for sure."

He didn't even look my way. After a long while, he stood up and leaned on a fender and lifted one leg and looked at the bottom of his muddy clodhopper, then put it down and lifted the other and looked at it too. Then he hitched his pants again and headed across the yard toward me. He favored his right leg a little and hardly picked up his feet at all when he walked. He left ruts in the yard like a plow. When he reached the steps, he didn't so much climb 'em as stand his bantyweight self on each one and look proud, like each step was all his'n now, and then go on to claim the next one too. Once on the porch, he sat down with his shoulders against a post, took off his hat, and fanned himself. His hair had a better hold on his head than I thought, what there was of it. Then he pulled out a stick and a pocketknife and commenced to whittle. But he did all these things so deliberate and thoughtful that it was almost the same as him talking, so I kept quiet and waited for the words to catch up.

"It will be a strange and disgraceful day unto this world," he finally said, "when I ask a gut-bucket nigger guitar player for advice on autoMO-bile mechanics, or for anything else except a tune now and again." He had eyes like he'd been shot twice in the face. "And furthermore, I am the Lord of Darkness and the Father of Lies, and if I want to drive my 1936 Hudson Terraplane, with its six-cylinder seventy-horsepower engine, out into the middle of some loblolly and shoot out its tires and rip up its seats and piss down its radiator hole, why, I will do it and do it again seven more times afore breakfast, and the voice that will stop me will not be yourn. You hearing me, John?"

"Ain't my business," I said. Like always, I was waiting to see how it was.

"That's right, John, it ain't your business," the devil said. "Nothing I do is any of your business, John, but everything you do is mine. I was there the night you took that fatal drink, John. I saw you fold when your gut bent double on you, and I saw the shine of your blood coming up. I saw that whore you and Jar Head was squabbling over doing business at your funeral. It was a sorry-ass death of a sorry-ass man, John, and I had a big old time with it."

The hound dogs had laid back down, so I stretched out and rested my feet on one of them. It rolled its eyes up at me like its feelings was hurt.

"I'd like to see old Jar Head one more time," I said. "If he'll be along directly, I'll wait here and meet his train."

"Jar Head's plumb out of your reach now, John," the devil said, still whittling. "I'd like to show you around your new home this afternoon. Come take a tour with me."

"I had to drive fifteen miles to get to that jook joint in the first place," I said, "and then come I don't know how far on the train to Hell and past it. I've done enough traveling for one day."

"Come with me, John."

"I thank you, but I'll just stay here."

"It would please me no end if you made my rounds with me, John." The stick he was whittling started moving in his hand. He had to grip it a little to hang on, but he just kept smiling. The stick started to bleed along the cuts, welling up black red as the blade skinned it. "I want to show off your new home place. You'd like that, wouldn't you, John?" The blood curled down his arm like a snake.

I stood up and shook my head real slow and disgusted, like I was bored by his conjuring, but I made sure to hold my guitar between us as I walked past him. I walked to the porch steps with my back to the devil, and I was headed down them two at a time when he hollered out behind, "John! Where do you think you're going?"

I said real loud, not looking back: "I done enough nothing for one day. I'm taking me a tour. If your ass has slipped between the planks and got stuck, I'll fetch a couple of mules to pull you free."

I heard him cuss and come scrambling after me with that leg a-dragging, sounding just like a scarecrow out on a stroll. I was holding my guitar closer to me all the time.

I wan't real surprised that he let those two hound dogs ride up on the front seat of the Terraplane like they was Mrs. Roosevelt, while I had to walk in the road alongside, practically in the ditch. The devil drove real slow, talking to me out the window the whole time.

"Whyn't you make me get off the train at Hell, with the rest of those sorry people?"

"Hell's about full," he said. "When I first opened for business out here, John, Hell wan't no more'n a wide spot in the road. It took a long time to get any size on it. When you stole that dime from your poor old Meemaw to buy a French post card and she caught you and flailed you across the yard, even way back then, Hell wan't no bigger'n Baltimore. But it's about near more'n I can handle now, I tell you. Now I'm filling up towns all over these parts. Ginny Gall. Diddy-Wah-Diddy. West Hell—I'd run out of ideas when I named West Hell, John."

A horsefly had got into my face and just hung there. The sun was fierce, and my clothes was sticking to me. My razor slid hot along my ankle. I kept favoring my guitar, trying to keep it out of the dust as best I could.

"Beluthahatchie, well, I'll be frank with you, John, Beluthahatchie ain't much of a place. I won't say it don't have possibilities, but right now it's mostly just that railroad station, and a crossroads, and fields. One long, hot, dirty field after another." He waved out the window at the scenery and grinned. He had yellow needly teeth. "You know your way around a field, I reckon, don't you, John?"

"I know enough to stay out of 'em."

His laugh was like a man cutting tin. "I swear you are a caution, John. It's a wonder you died so young."

We passed a right lot of folks, all of them working in the sun. Pulling tobacco. Picking cotton. Hoeing beans. Old folks scratching in gardens. Even younguns carrying buckets of water with two hands, slopping nearly all of it on the ground afore they'd gone three steps. All the people looked like they had just enough to eat to fill out the sad expression on their faces, and they all watched the devil as he drove slowly past. All those folks stared at me hard, too, and at the guitar like it was a third arm waving at 'em. I turned once to swat that blessed horsefly and saw a group of field hands standing in a knot, looking my way and pointing.

"Where all the white folks at?" I asked.

"They all up in heaven," the devil said. "You think they let niggers into heaven?" We looked at each other a long time. Then the devil laughed again. "You ain't buying that one for a minute, are you, John?"

I was thinking about Meemaw. I knew she was in heaven, if anyone was. When I was a youngun I figured she musta practically built the place, and had been paying off on it all along. But I didn't say nothing.

"No, John, it ain't that simple," the devil said. "Beluthahatchie's different for everybody, just like Hell. But you'll be seeing plenty of white folks. Overseers. Train conductors. Sheriff's deputies. If you get uppity, why, you'll see whole crowds of white folks. Just like home, John. Everything's the same. Why should it be any different?"

"Cause you're the devil," I said. "You could make things a heap worse."

"Now, could I really, John? Could I really?"

In the next field, a big man with hands like gallon jugs and a pink splash across his face was struggling all alone with a spindly mule and a plow made out of slats. "Get on, sir," he was telling the mule.

"Get on with you." He didn't even look around when the devil come chugging up alongside."

The devil gummed two fingers and whistled. "Ezekiel. Ezekiel! Come on over here, boy."

Ezekiel let go the plow and stumbled over the furrows, stepping high and clumsy in the thick dusty earth, trying to catch up to the Terraplane and not mess up the rows too bad. The devil han't slowed down any—in fact, I believe he had speeded up some. Left to his own doin's, the mule headed across the rows, the plow jerking along sideways behind him.

"Yessir?" Ezekiel looked at me sorta curious like, and nodded his head so slight I wondered if he'd done it at all. "What you need with me, boss?"

"I wanted you to meet your new neighbor. This here's John, and you ain't gone believe this, but he used to be a big man in the jook joints in the Delta. Writing songs and playing that dimestore git fiddle."

Ezekiel looked at me and said, "Yessir, I know John's songs." And I could tell he meant more than hearing them.

"Yes, John mighta been famous and saved enough whore money to buy him a decent instrument if he hadn't up and got hisself killed. Yes, John used to be one high-rolling nigger, but you ain't so high now, are you, John?"

I stared at the li'l peckerwood and spit out: "High enough to see where I'm going, Ole Massa."

I heard Ezekiel suck in his breath. The devil looked away from me real casual and back to Ezekiel, like we was chatting on a veranda someplace.

"Well, Ezekiel, this has been a nice long break for you, but I reckon you ought to get on back to work now. Looks like your mule's done got loose." He cackled and speeded up the car. Ezekiel and I both walked a few more steps and stopped. We watched the back of the Terraplane getting smaller, and then I turned to watch his face from the side. I han't seen that look on any of my people since Mississippi.

I said, "Man, why do you all take this shit?"

He wiped his forehead with his wrist and adjusted his hat. "Why do you?" he asked. "Why do you, John?" He was looking at me strange, and when he said my name it was like a one-word sentence all its own.

I shrugged. "I'm just seeing how things are. It's my first day."

"Your first day will be the same as all the others, then. That sure is the story with me. How come you called him Ole Massa just now?"

"Don't know. Just to get a rise out of him, I reckon."

Away off down the road, the Terraplane had stopped, engine still running, and the little cracker was yelling. "John! You best catch up, John. You wouldn't want me to leave you wandering in the dark, now would you?"

I started walking, not in any gracious hurry though, and Ezekiel paced me. "I asked cause it put me in mind of the old stories. You remember those stories, don't you? About Ole Massa and his slave by name of John? And how they played tricks on each other all the time?"

"Meemaw used to tell such when I was a youngun. What about it?"

He was trotting to keep up with me now, but I wan't even looking his way. "And there's older stories than that, even. Stories about High John the Conqueror. The one who could—"

"Get on back to your mule," I said. "I think the sun has done touched you."

"—the one who could set his people free," Ezekiel said, grabbing my shoulder and swinging me around. He stared into my face like a man looking for something he's dropped and has got to find.

"John!" the devil cried.

We stood there in the sun, me and Ezekiel, and then something went out of his eyes, and he let go and walked back across the ditch and trudged after the mule without a word.

I caught up to the Terraplane just in time for it to roll off again. I saw how it was, all right.

A ways up the road, a couple of younguns was fishing off the right side of a plank bridge, and the devil announced he would stop to see had they caught anything, and if they had, to take it for his supper. He slid out of the Terraplane, with it still running, and the dogs fell out after him, a-hoping for a snack, I reckon. When the devil got hunkered down good over there with the younguns, facing the swift-running branch, I sidled up the driver's side of the car, eased my guitar into the back seat, eased myself into the front seat, yanked the thing into gear and drove off. As I went past I saw three round O's—a youngun and the devil and a youngun again.

It was a pure pleasure to sit down, and the breeze coming through the windows felt good too. I commenced to get even more of a breeze going, on that long, straightaway road. I just could hear the devil holler back behind:

"John! Get your handkerchief-headed, free-school Negro ass back here with my auto-MO-bile! Johhhhnnn!"

"Here I come, old hoss," I said, and I jerked the wheel and slewed that car around and barreled off back toward the bridge. The younguns and the dogs was ahead of the devil in figuring things out. The younguns scrambled up a tree as quick as squirrels, and the dogs went loping into a ditch, but the devil was all preoccupied, doing a salty jump and cussing me for a dadblasted blagstagging liver-lipped stormbuzzard, jigging around right there in the middle of the bridge, and he was still cussing when I drove full tilt onto that bridge and he did not cuss any less when he jumped clean out from under his hat and he may even have stepped it up some when he went over the side. I heard a ker-plunk like a big rock chunked into a pond just as I swerved to bust the hat with a front tire, and then I was off the bridge and racing back the way we'd come, and that hat mashed in the road behind me like a possum.

I knew something simply awful was going to happen, but man! I slapped the dashboard and kissed my hand and slicked it back across my hair and said aloud, "Lightly, slightly, and politely." And I meant that thing. But my next move was to whip that razor out of my sock, flip it open, and lay it on the seat beside me, just in case.

I came up the road fast, and from way off I saw Ezekiel and the mule planted in the middle of his field like rocks. As they got bigger I saw both their heads had been turned my way the whole time, like they'd started looking before I even came over the hill. When I got level with them I stopped, engine running, and leaned on the horn until Ezekiel roused himself and walked over. The mule followed behind, like a yard dog, without being cussed or hauled or whipped. I must have been a sight. Ezekiel shook his head the whole way. "Oh, John," he said. "Oh, my goodness. Oh, John."

"Jump in, brother," I said. "Let Ole Massa plow this field his own damn self."

Ezekiel rubbed his hands along the chrome on the side of the car, swiping up and down and up and down. I was scared he'd burn himself. "Oh, John." He kept shaking his head. "John tricks Ole Massa again. High John the Conqueror rides the Terraplane to glory."

"Quit that, now. You worry me."

"John, those songs you wrote been keeping us going down here. Did you know that?"

"I 'preciate it."

"But lemme ask you, John. Lemme ask you something before you ride off. How come you wrote all those songs about hellhounds and the devil and such? How come you was so sure you'd be coming down here when you died?"

I fidgeted and looked in the mirror at the road behind. "Man, I don't know. Couldn't imagine nothing else. Not for me, anyway."

Ezekiel laughed once, loud, boom, like a shotgun going off.

"Don't be doing that, man. I about jumped out of my britches. Come on and let's go."

He shook his head again. "Maybe you knew you was needed down here, John. Maybe you knew we was singing, and telling stories, and waiting." He stepped back into the dirt. "This is your ride,

John. But I'll make sure everybody knows what you done. I'll tell 'em that things has changed in Beluthahatchie." He looked off down the road. "You'd best get on. Shoot—maybe you can find some jook joint and have some fun afore he catches up to you."

"Maybe so, brother, maybe so."

I han't gone two miles afore I got that bad old crawly feeling. I looked over to the passengers' side of the car and saw it was all spattered with blood, the leather and the carpet and the chrome on the door, and both those mangy hound dogs was sprawled across the front seat wallowing in it, both licking my razor like it was something good, and that's where the blood was coming from, welling up from the blade with each pass of their tongues. Time I caught sight of the dogs, they both lifted their heads and went to howling. It wan't no howl like any dog should howl. It was more like a couple of panthers in the night.

"Hush up, you dogs!" I yelled. "Hush up, I say!"

One of the dogs kept on howling, but the other looked me in the eyes and gulped air, his jowls flapping, like he was fixing to bark, but instead of barking said:

"Hush yourself, nigger."

When I looked back at the road, there wan't no road, just a big thicket of bushes and trees a-coming at me. Then came a whole lot of screeching and scraping and banging, with me holding on to the wheel just to keep from flying out of the seat, and then the car went sideways and I heard an awful bang and a crack and then I didn't know anything else. I just opened my eyes later, I don't know how much later, and found me and my guitar lying on the shore of the Lake of the Dead.

I had heard tell of that dreadful place, but I never had expected to see it for myself. Preacher Dodds whispered to us younguns once or twice about it, and said you have to work awful hard and be awful mean to get there, and once you get there, there ain't no coming back. "Don't seek it, my children, don't seek it," he'd say.

As far as I could see, all along the edges of the water, was bones and carcasses and lumps that used to be animals—mules and horses and cows and coons and even little dried-up birds scattered like hickory chips, and some things lying away off that might have been animals and might not have been, oh Lord, I didn't go to look. A couple of buzzards was strolling the edge of the water, not acting hungry nor vicious but just on a tour, I reckon. The sun was setting, but the water didn't cast no shine at all. It had a dim and scummy look, so flat and still that you'd be tempted to try to walk across it, if any human could bear seeing what lay on the other side. "Don't seek it, my children, don't seek it." I han't sought it, but now the devil had sent me there, and all I knew to do was hold my guitar close to me and watch those buzzards a-picking and a-pecking and wait for it to get dark. And Lord, what would this place be like in the dark?

But the guitar did feel good up against me thataway, like it had stored up all the songs I ever wrote or sung to comfort me in a hard time. I thought about those field hands a-pointing my way, and about Ezekiel sweating along behind his mule, and the way he grabbed aholt of my shoulder and swung me around. And I remembered the new song I had been fooling with all day in my head while I was following that li'l peckerwood in the Terraplane.

"Well, boys," I told the buzzards, "if the devil's got some powers I reckon I got some too. I didn't expect to be playing no blues after I was dead. But I guess that's all there is to play now. 'Sides, I've played worse places."

I started humming and strumming, and then just to warm up I played "Rambling on My Mind" cause it was, and "Sweet Home Chicago" cause I figured I wouldn't see that town no more, and "Terraplane Blues" on account of that damn car. Then I sang the song I had just made up that day.

> *I'm down in Beluthahatchie, baby,*
> *Way out where the trains don't run*
> *Yes, I'm down in Beluthahatchie, baby,*
> *Way out where the trains don't run*

Who's gonna take you strolling now
Since your man he is dead and gone

My body's all laid out mama
But my soul can't get no rest
My body's all laid out mama
But my soul can't get no rest
Cause you'll be sportin with another man
Lookin for some old Mr. Second Best

Plain folks got to walk the line
But the Devil he can up and ride
Folks like us we walk the line
But the Devil he can up and ride
And I won't never have blues enough
Ooh, to keep that Devil satisfied.

When I was done it was black dark and the crickets was zinging and everything was changed.

"You can sure get around this country," I said, "just a-sitting on your ass."

I was in a cane-back chair on the porch of a little wooden house, with bugs smacking into an oil lamp over my head. Just an old cropper place, sitting in the middle of a cotton field, but it had been spruced up some. Somebody had swept the yard clean, from what I could see of it, and on a post above the dipper was a couple of yellow flowers in a nailed-up Chase & Sanborn can.

When I looked back down at the yard, though, it wan't clean anymore. There was words written in the dirt, big and scrawly like from someone dragging his foot.

DON'T GET A BIG HEAD JOHN
I'LL BE BACK

Sitting on my name was those two fat old hound dogs. "Get on with your damn stinking talking selves," I yelled, and I shied a rock at them. It didn't go near as far as I expected, just sorta plopped down into the dirt, but the hounds yawned and got up, snuffling each other, and waddled off into the dark.

I stood up and stretched and mumbled. But something was still shifting in the yard, just past where the light was. Didn't sound like no dogs, though.

"Who that? Who that who got business with a wore-out dead man?"

Then they come up toward the porch a little closer where I could see. It was a whole mess of colored folks, men in overalls and women in aprons, granny women in bonnets pecking the ground with walking sticks, younguns with their bellies pookin out and no pants on, an old man with Coke-bottle glasses and his eyes swimming in your face nearly, and every last one of them grinning like they was touched. Why, Preacher Dodds woulda passed the plate and called it a revival. They massed up against the edge of the porch, crowding closer in and bumping up against each other, and reaching their arms out and taking hold of me, my lapels, my shoulders, my hands, my guitar, my face, the little ones aholt of my pants legs—not hauling on me or messing with me, just touching me feather light here and there like Meemaw used to touch her favorite quilt after she'd already folded it to put away. They was talking, too, mumbling and whispering and saying, "Here he is. We heard he was coming and here he is. God bless you, friend, God bless you, brother, God bless you, son." Some of the womenfolks was crying, and there was Ezekiel, blowing his nose on a rag.

"Y'all got the wrong man," I said, directly, but they was already heading back across the yard, which was all churned up now, no words to read and no pattern neither. They was looking back at me and smiling and touching, holding hands and leaning into each other, till they was all gone and it was just me and the crickets and the cotton.

Wan't nowhere else to go, so I opened the screen door and went on in the house. There was a bed all turned down with a feather pillow, and in the middle of the checkered oilcloth on the table was a crock of molasses, a jar of buttermilk, and a plate covered with a rag. The buttermilk was cool like it had been chilling in the well, with water beaded up on the sides of the jar. Under the rag was three hoecakes and a slab of bacon.

When I was done with my supper, I latched the front door, lay down on the bed, and was just about dead to the world when I heard something else out in the yard——swish, swish, swish. Out the window I saw, in the edge of the porch light, one old granny woman with a shuck broom, smoothing out the yard where the folks had been. She was sweeping it as clean as for company on a Sunday. She looked up from under her bonnet and showed me what teeth she had and waved from the wrist like a youngun, and then she backed on out of the light, swish swish swish, rubbing out her tracks as she went.

The Map to the Homes of the Stars

Last night, I heard it again. About eleven, I stood at the kitchen counter, slathered peanut butter onto a stale, cool slice of refrigerated raisin bread, and scanned months-old letters to the editor in an A-section pulled at random from the overflow around the recycling bin. "Reader decries tobacco evils." "Economy sound, says N.C. banker." The little headlines give the otherwise routine letters such urgency, like telegraphed messages from some war-torn front where issues are being decided, where news is happening. "Arts funding called necessary." As I chewed my sandwich, I turned one-handed to the movie listings, just to reassure myself that everything I had skipped in the spring wasn't worth the trouble anyway, and then I heard a slowly approaching car.

We don't get much traffic on my street, a residential loop in a quiet neighborhood, and so even we single guys who don't have kids in the yard unconsciously register the sounds of each passing vehicle. But this was the fifth night in a row, and so I set down my sandwich and listened.

Tom used to identify each passing car, just for practice.

"Fairlane."

"Crown Victoria."

"Super Beetle."

This was back home, when we were as bored as two 17-year-olds could be.

"Even I can tell a Super Beetle," I said. I slugged my Mountain Dew and lowered the bottle to look with admiration at the neon-green foam.

Tom frowned, picked up his feet, and rotated on the bench of the picnic table so that his back was to Highway 1.

Without thinking, I said, "Mind, you'll get splinters." I heard my mother speaking, and winced.

Now Tom looked straight ahead at the middle-school basketball court, where Cathy and her friends, but mostly Cathy (who barely knew us, but whose house was fourth on our daily route), were playing a pick-up game, laughing and sweating and raking their long hair back from their foreheads. As each car passed behind him, he continued the litany.

"Jeep."

"Ford pickup."

"Charger."

I didn't know enough to catch him in an error, of course, but I have no doubt that he was right on the money, every time. I never learned cars; I learned other things, that year and the next fifteen years, to my surprise and exhilaration and shame, but I never learned cars, and so I am ill-equipped to stand in my kitchen and identify a car driving slowly past at eleven o'clock at night.

Not even when, about five minutes later, it gives me another chance, drives past again in the other direction, as if it had gotten as far as the next cul-de-sac, and turned around.

It passes so slowly that I am sure it is about to turn into someone's driveway, someone's, mine, but it hasn't, for five nights now it hasn't. I couldn't tell you if I had to precisely what make of car it is.

I could guess, though.

Maybe tonight, if, when, it passes by, I'll go to the front door and pull back the narrow dusty curtain that never gets pulled back except for Jehovah's Witnesses, and see for myself what make of car it is. See if I recognize it. But all I did last night, and the four nights before, was stand at my kitchen counter, fingertips black with old news, jaws Peter-Panned shut (for I am a creature of habit), stare unseeing at the piled-up sink, and trace in my head every long-gone stop on the map to the homes of the stars.

Even when all we had were bicycles, Tom and I spent most of our time together riding around town. We rode from convenience store to convenience store, Slim Jims in our pockets and folded comic books stuffed into the waistbands of our jeans. We never rode side by side or single file but in loopy serpentine patterns, roughly parallel, that weaved among trees and parked cars and water sprinklers. We had earnest and serious conversations that lasted for hours and were entirely shouted from bike to bike, never less than ten feet. Our paths intersected with hair-raising frequency, but we never ran into each other. At suppertime, we never actually said goodbye, but veered off in different directions, continuing to holler at each other, one more joke that had to be told, one more snappy comeback to make, until the other voice had faded in the distance, and we realized we were riding alone and talking to ourselves. I remember nothing of what we said to each other all those long afternoons, but I remember the rush of the wind past my ears, and the shirttail of my red jersey snapping behind me like a hound, and the slab of sidewalk that a big tree root thrust up beneath me in the last block before home, so that I could steer around it at the last second and feel terribly skillful, or use it as a launching ramp and stand up on the pedals and hang there, suspended, invincible, until the pavement caught up with my tires again.

Then we were sixteen and got our licenses. Tom's bicycle went into the corner of his room, festooned with clothes that weren't quite ready to wash yet; mine was hung on nails inside the garage, in a place of honor beside my older sister's red wagon and my late Uncle Clyde's homemade bamboo fishing poles. Tom had been studying *Consumer Reports* and *Car & Driver* and prowling dealerships for months, and with his father's help, he bought a used '78 Firebird, bright red exterior, black leather upholstery, cassette stereo, and a host of tire and engine features that Tom could rattle off like an auctioneer but that I never quite could remember afterward. Being a fan of old gangster movies, Tom called it his "getaway car." Tom and his dad got a great deal, because the getaway car had a dent in the side and its headlights were slightly cockeyed. "Makes it unique," Tom said. "We'll get those fixed right up," his dad said, and, of course, they never did. I inherited the car my father had driven on his mail route for years, a beige '72 Volkswagen Beetle that was missing its front passenger seat. My father had removed it so that he'd have an open place to put his mail. Now, like so many of my family's other theoretical belongings, the seat was "out there in the garage," a phrase to which my father invariably would add, "somewhere."

We always took Tom's car; Tom always drove.

We went to a lot of movies in Columbia and sometimes went on real trips, following the church van to Lake Junaluska or to Six Flags and enjoying a freedom of movement unique in the Methodist Youth Fellowship. But mostly we rode around town, looking—and only looking—at girls. We found out where they lived, and drove past their houses every day, hoping they might be outside, hoping to get a glimpse of them, but paying tribute in any case to all they had added to what we fancied as our dried-up and wasted and miserable lives.

"We need music," Tom said. "Take the wheel, will you, Jack?"

I reached across and steered while he turned and rummaged among the tapes in the back seat. I knew it was the closest I ever would come to driving Tom's car.

"In Hollywood," I said, "people on street corners sell maps to the stars' homes. Tourists buy the maps and drive around, hoping to see Clint Eastwood mowing his lawn, or something." I had never been to Hollywood, but I had learned about these maps the night before on *PM Magazine.*

"What do you want? You want Stones? You want Beatles? You want Aerosmith? What?"

"Mostly they just see high walls," I said, "and locked gates." I was proud to have detected this irony alone.

"We should go there," Tom said. "Just take off driving one day and go."

"Intersection coming up."

"Red light?"

"Green."

Tom continued to rummage. "Our map," he said, "exists only in our heads."

"That's where the girls exist, too," I said.

"Oh, no," Tom said, turning back around and taking the wheel just in time to drive through the intersection. "They're out there. Maybe not in this dink-ass town, but somewhere. They're real. We'll just never know them. That's all."

I had nothing to add to that, but I fully agreed with him. I had concluded, way back at thirteen, that I was doomed to a monastic life, and I rather wished I were Catholic so that I could take full advantage of it. Monastic Methodists had nowhere to go; they just got gray and pudgy, and lived with their mothers. Tom pushed a tape into the deck; it snapped shut like a trap, and the speakers began to throb.

Lisa lived in a huge Tudor house of gray stone across the street from the fifteenth fairway. To our knowledge she did not play golf, but she was a runner, and on a fortunate evening we could meet her three or four times on the slow easy curves of Country Club Drive. She had a long stride and a steady rhythm and never looked winded, though she did maintain a look of thoughtful concentration and always seemed focused on the patch of asphalt just a few feet ahead, as if it were pacing her. At intersections, she jogged in place, looking around at the world in surprise, and was likely to smile and throw up a hand if we made so bold as to wave.

Tom especially admired Lisa because she took such good care of her car, a plum-colored late-model Corvette that she washed and waxed in her driveway every Saturday afternoon, beginning about one o'clock. For hours, she catered to her car's needs, stroking and rubbing it with hand towels and soft brushes, soaping and then rinsing, so that successive gentle tides foamed down the hood. Eventually, Lisa seemed to be lying face-to-face with herself across the gleaming purple hood, her palm pressed to the other Lisa's palm, hands moving together in lazy circles like the halfhearted sparring of lovers in August.

Crystal's house was low and brick, with a patio that stretched its whole length. From March through October, for hours each day, Crystal lay on this patio, working on her tan—"laying out," she would have called it. She must have tanned successive interior layers of her skin, because even in winter she was a dusky Amazonian bronze, a hue that matched her auburn hair, but made her white teeth a constant surprise. Frequent debates as we passed Crystal's house: Which bikini was best, the white or the yellow? Which position was best, face up or face down? What about the bottles and jars that crowded the dainty wrought-iron table at her elbow? Did those hold mere store-bought lotions, or were they brimful of Crystal's private skin-care recipes, gathered from donors willing and unwilling by the dark of the moon? Tom swore that once, when we drove past, he clearly saw amid the Coppertone jumble a half-stick of butter and a bottle of Wesson oil.

Gabrielle lived out on the edge of town, technically within the city limits but really in the country, in a big old crossroads farmhouse with a deep porch mostly hidden by lattices of honeysuckle and wisteria. She lived with her grandparents, who couldn't get around so good anymore, and so usually it was Gabrielle who climbed the tall ladder and raked out the gutters, cleared the pecan limbs off the roof of the porch, scraped the shutters, and then painted them. She had long black hair that stretched nearly to the ragged hem of her denim shorts. She didn't tie her hair back when she worked, no matter how hot the day, and she was tall even without the ladder.

Natalie lived in a three-story wooden house with cardboard in two windows and with thickets of metal roosters and lightning rods up top. At school, she wore ancient black ankle-length dresses in all weathers, walked with her head down, and spoke to no one, not even when called upon in class, so that the teachers finally gave up. Her hair was an impenetrable mop that covered her face almost entirely. But she always smiled a tiny secret smile, and her chin beneath was sharp and delicate, and when she scampered down the hall, hugging the lockers, her skirts whispered generations of old chants and endearments. Natalie never came outside at all.

Cynthia's was the first house on the tour. Only two blocks from Tom's, it sat on the brink of a small and suspect pond, one that was about fifty feet across at its widest. No visible stream fed this pond or emptied it, and birds, swimmers, and fishes all shunned it. The pond was a failure as a pond, but a marginal success as an investment, an "extra" that made a half-dozen nondescript brick ranch houses cost a bit more than their landlocked neighbors. Cynthia's house was distinguished by a big swing set that sat in the middle of the treeless yard. It was a swaybacked metal A-frame scavenged from the primary school. In all weathers, day and night, since her family moved to town when she was six, Cynthia could be found out there, swinging. The older she got, the higher she swung, the more reckless and joyful her sparkle and grin. When she was sixteen, tanned legs pumping in the afternoon sun, she regularly swung so high the chains went slack for a half-second at the top of the arc before she dropped.

"Zero gee," Tom said as we drove slowly past. Tom and I didn't swing anymore, ourselves; it made us nauseated.

Once a year Cynthia actually came out to the car to say hi. Each Christmas the people who lived on the pond, flush with their wise investment, expressed their communal pride with a brilliant light-ing display. For weeks everyone in town drove slowly, dutifully, and repeatedly around the pond and over its single bridge to see the thou-sands of white firefly lights that the people of the pond draped along porches and bushes and balustrades, and stretched across wire frames to approximate Grinches and Magi. The reflection on the water was striking, undisturbed as it was by current or life. For hours each night, a single line of cars crept bumper-to-bumper across the bridge, past Santa-clad residents who handed out candy canes and filled a wicker basket with donations for the needy and for the electric company. Painted on a weatherbeaten sandwich board at the foot of the bridge was a bright red cursive dismissal: "Thank You / Merry Christmas / Speed Limit 25."

At least once a night, Tom and I drove through this display, hoping to catch Cynthia on Santa duty. At least once a year, we got lucky.

"Hey there, little boys, want some candy?" She dropped a shim-mering fistful into Tom's lap. "No, listen, take them, Dad said when I gave them all out I could come inside. I'm freezing my ass off out here. Oh, hi, Jack. So, where you guys headed?"

"Noplace," we said together.

She walked alongside Tom's Firebird, tugging down her beard to scratch her cheek. "Damn thing must be made of fiberglass. Hey, check out the Thompsons' house. Doesn't that second reindeer look just like he's humping Rudolf? I don't know what they were think-ing. No? Well, it's clear as day from my room. Maybe I've just looked at it too long. When is Christmas, anyway? You guys don't know what it's like, all these goddamn lights, you can see them with your eyes closed. I've been sleeping over at Cheryl's where it's dark. Well, I reckon if I go past the end of the bridge, the trolls will get me. Yeah, right, big laugh there. See you later." Then, ducking her head in again: "You, too, Jack."

With the smoothness of practice, Tom and I snicked our mirrors into place (his the driver's side, mine the overhead) so that we could watch Cynthia's freezing ass walk away. Her Santa pants were baggy and sexless, but we watched until the four-wheel drive behind us honked and flashed its deer lights. By the time we drove down to the traffic circle and made the loop and got back in line again, Cynthia's place had been taken by her neighbor, Mr. Thompson.

"Merry Christmas, Tom, Jack," he said. "Y'all's names came up at choir practice the other day. We'd love to have you young fellas join us in the handbells. It's fun and you don't have to sing and it's a real ministry, too." He apologized for having run out of candy canes, and instead gave us a couple of three-by-five comic books about Hell.

Tina's house always made us feel especially sophisticated, especially daring.

"Can you imagine?" Tom asked. "Can you imagine, just for a moment, what our parents would do?"

"No," I said, shaking my head. "No, I can't imagine."

"I think you should try. I think we both should try to envision this. That way we'll be prepared for anything in life, anything at all."

I cranked down the windowpane until it balked. "I don't even want to think about it," I said. I pressed the pane outward until it was back on track, then I lowered it the rest of the way.

"Oh, but you've *been* thinking about it, haven't you? You're the one that found out where she lived. You're the one that kept wanting me to drive past her house."

"It's the quickest route between Laura's and Kathleen's, that's all," I said. "But if it's such a terrible hardship, then you can go around the world instead, for all I care. You're the driver, I'm just sitting here."

He fidgeted, legs wide, left hand drumming the windowsill, fingertips of his right hand barely nudging the steering wheel. "Don't get me wrong, I think she's a babe. But this neighborhood, I don't know, it makes me nervous. I feel like everybody we pass is looking at us."

"Do what you like. I'm just sitting here," I said. I craned to see Tina's house as we drove around the corner.

Tina lived in what our parents and our friends and every other white person we knew, when they were feeling especially liberal, broadminded, and genteel, called the "colored" part of town. Tina's yard was colored all right: bright yellows, reds, oranges, and purples, bursting from a dozen flowerbeds. As so often when she wasn't at cheerleading practice, Tina knelt in the garden, a huge old beribboned hat—her grandmother's, maybe?—shading her striking, angular face. Her shoulders tightened, loosened, tightened again as she pressed something into place. Without moving her hands, she looked up at us as we passed. She smiled widely, and her lips mouthed the word "Hey."

Once we were around the corner, Tom gunned the engine.

"Uh-uh, no sir, hang it *up*," Tom said. "Not in my family, not in this town. Thousands of miles away, maybe. That might work. Oh, but then they'd want *photos*, wouldn't they? Damn. The other week, all my aunts were sitting around the kitchen table, complaining about their daughters-in-law. My son's wife is snotty, my son's wife is lazy, they aren't good mothers, they aren't treating our boys right, and so on and so on. Just giving 'em down the country, you know?"

"Uh-huh. I hear you."

"And I finally spoke up and said, 'Well, I know I'm never going to introduce y'all to any wife of *mine*, 'cause y'all sure won't like *her*, either."

"What'd they say to that?"

"They all laughed, and Aunt Leda said, 'Tom, don't you worry, 'cause you're the only boy in the family that's got any sense. We know we'll like *any* girl you pick out.' And then Aunt Emily added, 'Long as she isn't a black 'un!' And they all nodded—I mean, they were serious!"

After a long pause, he added, half to himself, "It's not as if I'm bringing *anybody* home, anyway—black or white or lavender."

"You bring me home with you sometimes," I said.

"Yeah, and they don't like *you* either," he said, and immediately cut me a wide-eyed look of mock horror that made me laugh out loud. "I'm kidding. You know they like you."

"Families always like me," I said. "Mamas especially. It's the daughters themselves that aren't real interested. And a mama's approval is the kiss of death. At this moment, I bet you, mamas all over town are saying, 'What about that nice boy *Jack?* He's so respectful, he goes to church, he makes such good grades,' and don't you know that makes those gals so hot they can't stand it."

Tom laughed and laughed.

"Oh, Jack!" I gasped. "Oh, Jack, your SAT score is so—so *big!*"

"Maybe you should forget the girls and date the *mamas,*" Tom said. "You know, eliminate the middleman. Go right to the source."

"Eewww, that's crude." I clawed at the door as if trying to get out. "Help! Help! I'm in the clutches of a crude man!"

"Suppose Kathleen's home from Florida yet?"

"I dunno. Let's go see."

"Now you aren't starting to boss me around, are you?"

"I'm just sitting here."

He poked me repeatedly with his finger, making me giggle and twist around on the seat. "'Cause I'll just put you out by the side of the road, you start bossing me."

"I'm not!" I gasped. "Quit! Uncle! Uncle! I'm not!"

"Well, all right, then."

On September 17, 1981, we turned the corner at the library and headed toward the high school, past the tennis courts. The setting sun made everything golden. Over the engine, we heard doubled and redoubled the muted grunts and soft swats and scuffs of impact: ball on racket, shoe on clay. The various players on the adjoining courts moved with such choreography that I felt a pang to join them.

"Is tennis anything like badminton?" I asked. "I used to be okay at badminton. My father and I would play it over the back fence, and the dogs would go wild."

"It's more expensive," Tom said. "Look, there she is. Right on time."

Anna, her back to us, was up ahead, walking slowly toward the parking lot on the sidewalk nearest me. Her racket was on one shoulder, a towel around her neck. Her skirt swayed as if she were walking much faster.

As we passed, I heard a strange sound: a single Road Runner beep. In the side mirror, tiny retreating Anna raised her free hand and waved. I turned to stare at Tom, who looked straight ahead.

"The *horn?*" I asked. "You honked the horn?"

"Well, you waved," he said. "I saw you."

I yanked my arm inside. The windblown hairs on my forearm tingled. "I wasn't waving. I was holding up my hand to feel the breeze."

"She waved at *you.*"

"Well, I didn't wave at her," I said. "She waved because you honked."

"Okay," he said, turning into the parking lot. "She waved at both of us, then."

"She waved at you. I don't care, it doesn't matter. But she definitely waved at you."

"Are we fighting?" he asked. He re-entered the street, turned back the way we had come. Anna was near, walking toward us.

"Course we're not fighting. Are you going to honk at her again?"

"Are you going to wave at her again?"

Anna looked behind her for traffic, stepped off the sidewalk, and darted across the street, into our lane, racket lifted like an Olympic torch.

"Look out!"

"What the hell?"

Tom hit the brakes. The passenger seat slid forward on its track, and my knees slammed the dash. Dozens of cassettes on the back seat cascaded into the floor. Only a foot or two in front of the stopped car stood Anna, arms folded, one hip thrust out. She regarded us without expression, blew a large pink bubble that reached her nose and then collapsed back into her mouth.

"Hi, guys," she said.

Tom opened his door and stood, one foot on the pavement. "For crying out loud, Anna, are you okay? We could've killed you!"

"I was trying to flag you down," she said.

"What? Why?" Tom asked. "What for? Something wrong with the car?" I saw him swivel, and I knew that, out of sight, he was glancing toward the tires, the hood, the tailpipe.

"Nothing's wrong with the car, Tom," she said, chewing with half her mouth, arms still folded. "It's a really neat car. Whenever I see it I think, 'Damn, Tom must take mighty good care of that car.' I get a *lot* of chances to think that, Tom, 'cause every day you guys drive by my house at least twice, and whenever I leave tennis practice, you drive past me, and turn around in the lot, and drive past me *again*, and every time you do that I think, 'He takes mighty damn good care of that goddamn car just to drive past me all the fucking time.'"

Someone behind us honked and pulled around. A pickup truck driver, who threw us a bird.

"Do you ever *stop?* No. Say hi at school? Either of you? No. *Call* me? Shit." She shifted her weight to the other hip, unfolded her arms, whipped the towel from around her neck, and swatted the hood with it. "So all I want to know is, just what's the *deal?* Tom? Jack? I see you in there, Jack, you can't hide. What's up, Jack? You tell me. Your chauffeur's catching flies out here."

Looking up at Anna, even though I half expected at any moment to be arrested for perversion or struck from behind by a truck or beaten to death with a tennis racket, purple waffle patterns scarring my corpse, I realized I had never felt such crazed exhilaration, not even that night on Bates Hill, when Tom passed a hundred and twenty. My knees didn't even hurt anymore. The moment I realized this, naturally the feeling of exhilaration began to ebb, and so before I lost my resolve I slowly stuck my head out the window, smiled what I hoped was a smile, and called out: "Can we give you a lift, Anna?"

A station wagon swung past us with a honk. Anna looked at me, at Tom, at me again. She plucked her gum from her mouth, tossed it, looked down at the pavement and then up and then down again, much younger and almost shy. In a small voice, she said: "Yeah." She cleared her throat. "Yeah. Yes. That's . . . that's nice of you. Thank you."

I let her have my seat, of course. I got in the back, atop a shifting pile of cassettes and books and plastic boxes of lug nuts, but right behind her, close enough to smell her: not sweat, exactly, but salt and earth, like the smell of the beach before the tide comes in.

"Where to?" Tom asked.

"California," she said, and laughed, hands across her face. "Damn, Anna," she asked, "where did *that* come from? Oh, I don't know. Where are y'all going? I mean, wherever. Whenever. Let's just go, okay? Let's just . . . go."

We talked: School. Movies. Bands. Homework. Everything. Nothing. What else? Drove around. For hours.

Her ponytail was short but full, a single blond twist that she gathered up in one hand and lifted as she tilted her head forward. I thought she was looking at something on the floor, and I wondered for a second whether I had tracked something in.

"Jack?" she asked, head still forward. No one outside my family had made my name a question before. "Would you be a sweetie and rub my neck?"

The hum of tires, the zing of crickets, the shrill stream of air flowing through the crack that the passenger window never quite closed.

"Ma'am?"

"My neck. It's all stove up and tight from tennis. Would you rub the kinks out for me?"

"Sure," I said, too loudly and too quickly. My hands moved as slowly as in a nightmare. Twice I thought I had them nearly to her neck when I realized I was merely rehearsing the action in my head, so that I had it all to do over again. Tom shifted gears, slowed into a turn, sped up, shifted gears again, and I still hadn't touched her. My forearms were lifted; my hands were outstretched, palms down; my fingers were trembling. I must have looked like a mesmerist. You are sleepy, very sleepy. Which movie was it where the person in the front seat knew nothing about the clutching hands in the back? I could picture the driver's face as the hands crept closer: Christopher Lee, maybe? No: Donald Pleasence?

"Jack," she said. "Are you still awake back there?"

The car went into another turn, and I heard a soft murmur of complaint from the tires. Tom was speeding up.

My fingertips brushed the back of her neck. I yanked them back, then moved them forward again. This time I held them there, barely touching. Her neck so smooth, so hot, slightly—damp? And what's *this?* Little hairs! Hairs as soft as a baby's head! No one ever had told me there would be hairs . . .

"You'll have to rub harder than *that,* Jack." Still holding her hair aloft with her right hand, she reached up with her left and pressed my fingers into her neck. "Like that. Right—*there.* And there. Feel how tight that is?" She rotated her hand over mine, and trapped between her damp palm and her searing neck I did feel something both supple and taut. "Oooh, yeah, like that." She pulled her hand away, and I kept up the motions. "Oh, that feels good . . ."

The sun was truly down by now, and lighted houses scudded past. Those distinctive dormer windows—wasn't that Lisa's house? And, in the next block, wasn't that Kim's driveway?

We were following the route. We were passing all the homes of the stars.

Tom said nothing, but drove faster and faster. I kept rubbing, pressing, kneading, not having the faintest idea what I was doing but following the lead of Anna's sighs and murmurs. "Yeah, my shoulder there . . . Oh, this is wonderful. You'll have to stop this in about three hours, you know."

After about five minutes or ten or twenty, without looking up, she raised her left index finger and stabbed the dashboard. A tape came on. I don't remember which tape it was. I do remember that it played through both sides, and started over.

Tom was speeding. Each screeching turn threw us off balance. Where were the cops? Where was all the other traffic? We passed Jane's house, Tina's house. Streetlights strobed the car like an electrical storm. We passed Cynthia's house—hadn't we already? Beneath my hands, Anna's shoulders braced and rolled and braced again. I held on. My arms ached. Past the corner of my eye flashed a stop sign. My fingers kept working. Tom wrenched up the volume on the stereo. The bass line throbbed into my neck and shoulder blades, as if the car were reciprocating.

Gravel churned beneath us. "Damn," Tom muttered, and yanked the wheel, fighting to stay on the road. Anna snapped her head up, looked at him. I saw her profile against the radio dial.

"I want to drive," she said.

Tom put on the brakes, too swiftly. Atop a surging flood of gravel, the car jolted and shuddered to a standstill off the side of the road. The doors flew open, and both Tom and Anna leaped out. My exhilaration long gone, my arms aching, I felt trapped, suffocating. I snatched up the seat latch, levered forward the passenger seat, and stepped humpbacked and out of balance into the surprisingly cool night air. Over there was the Episcopal church, over there the Amoco station. We were only a few blocks from my house. My right hand stung; I had torn a nail on the seat latch. I slung it back and forth as Tom stepped around the car. Anna was already in the driver's seat.

"You want to sit in front?" Tom sounded hoarse.

"No," I said. "No, thanks. Listen, I think I'll, uh, I think I'll just call it a night. I'm nearly home anyway. I can, uh, I can walk from here. Y'know? It's not far. I can walk from here." I called out to Anna, leaning down and looking in: "I can walk from here." Her face was unreadable, but her eyes gleamed.

"Huh?" Tom said. It was like a grunt. He cleared his throat. "What do you mean, *walk?* It's early yet."

The car was still running. The exhaust blew over me in a cloud, made me dizzy. "No, really, you guys go on. I'm serious. I'll be fine. Go on, really. I'll see you later on."

"We could drop you off," Tom said. He spoke politely but awkwardly, as if we had never met. "Let's do that. We'll drop you off in your yard."

Anna revved the motor. It was too dark to see Tom's expression as he looked at her. Her fingers moved across the lighted instrument panel, pulled out the switch that started the emergency flashers, *ka-chink ka-chink ka-chink*, pushed it back again. "Cool," she said.

"I'll see you later," I said. "OK? See you, Anna. Call me tomorrow," I said to Tom.

"OK," he said. "I'll call you tomorrow."

"OK," I said, not looking back. I waved a ridiculous cavalier wave, and stuck my hands in my pockets, trying to look nonchalant as I stumbled along the crumbling asphalt shoulder in the dark.

Behind me two doors slammed. I heard the car lurching back onto the highway, gravel spewing, and I heard it make a U-turn, away from town and toward the west, toward the lake, toward the woods. As the engine gunned, my shoulders twitched and I ducked my head, because I expected the screech of gears, but all I heard was steady and swift acceleration, first into second into third, as the Firebird sped away, into fourth, and then it was just me, walking.

———

They never came back.

Tom's parents got a couple of letters, a few postcards. California. They shared them with Anna's parents but no one else. "Tom wants everyone to know they're doing fine," that's all his mom and dad would say. But they didn't look reassured. Miss Sara down at the paper, who always professed to know a lot more than she wrote up in her column, told my father that she hadn't seen the mail herself, mind you, but she had *heard* from people who should *know* that the letters were strange, rambling things, not one *bit* like Tom, and the cards had postmarks that were simply, somehow, *wrong*. But who could predict, Miss Sara added, *when* postcards might arrive, or in *what* order. Why, sometimes they sit in the post office for *years*, and sometimes they never show up at *all*. Criminal, Miss Sara mourned, criminal.

Anna's parents got no mail at all.

I never did, either, except maybe one thing. I don't know that you could call it *mail*. No stamps, no postmark, no handwriting. It wasn't even in the mailbox. But it felt like mail to me.

It was lying on my front porch one morning—this was years later, not long after I got my own place, thought I was settled. At first I thought it was the paper, but no, as usual the paper was spiked down deep in the hedge. This was lying faceup and foursquare on the welcome mat. It was one of those Hollywood maps, showing where the stars can be found.

I spread it across the kitchen table and anchored it with the sugar bowl and a couple of iron owl-shaped trivets, because it was stiff and new and didn't want to lie flat. You know how maps are. It was bright white paper and mighty thick, too. I didn't know they made maps so thick anymore. I ran my index finger over sharp paper ridges and down straight paper canyons and looked for anyone I knew. No, Clint Eastwood wasn't there. Nor was anyone else whose movies I ever had seen at the mall. A lot of the names I just didn't recognize, but some I knew from cable, from the nostalgia channels.

I was pretty sure most of them were dead.

I searched the index for Tom's name, for Anna's. I didn't see them. I felt relieved. Sort of.

"California," I said aloud. Once it had been four jaunty syllables, up and down and up and down, a kid on a bicycle, going noplace. California. Now it was a series of low and urgent blasts, someone leaning on the horn, saying, come on, saying, hurry up, saying, you're not too late, not yet, not yet. California.

It's nearly eleven. I stand in the cool rush of the refrigerator door, forgetting what I came for, and strain to hear. The train is passing, a bit late, over behind the campus. My windows are open, so the air conditioning is pouring out into the yard and fat bugs are smacking themselves against the screen, but this way I can hear everything clearly. The rattle as my neighbor hauls down the garage door, secures everything for the night. On the other side, another neighbor trundles a trash can out to the curb, then plods back. I am standing at the kitchen counter now. Behind me the refrigerator door is swinging shut, or close enough. I hear a car coming.

The same car.

I move to the living room, to the front door. I part the curtain. The car is coming closer, but even more slowly than before. Nearly stopping. It must be in first gear by now. There was always that slight rattle, just within the threshold of hearing, when you put it in first gear. Yes. And the slightly cockeyed headlights, yes, and the dent in the side. I can't clearly see the interior even under the streetlight but it looks like two people in the front.

Two people? Or just one?

And then it's on the other side of the neighbor's hedge, and gone, but I still can hear the engine, and I know that it's going to turn, and come back.

My hand is on the doorknob. The map is in my pocket. The night air is surprisingly cool. I flip on the porch light as I step out, and I stand illuminated in a cloud of tiny beating wings, waiting for them to come back, come back and see me standing here, waiting, waiting, oh my God how long I've been waiting, I want to walk out there and stand in front of the car and make it stop, really I do, but I can't, I can't move, I'm trapped here, trapped in this place, trapped in this time, don't drive past again, I'm here, I'm ready, I wasn't then but now I am, really I am, please, please stop. Present or past, alive or dead, what does it matter, what did it ever matter? Please. Stop.

Please.

The Pottawatomie Giant

On the afternoon of November 30, 1915, Jess Willard, for seven months the heavyweight champion of the world, crouched, hands on knees, in his Los Angeles hotel window to watch a small figure swaying like a pendulum against the side of the Times building three blocks away.

"Cripes!" Willard said. "How's he keep from fainting, his head down like that, huh, Lou?"

"He trains, Champ," said his manager, one haunch on the sill. "Same's you."

Training had been a dispute between the two men lately, but Willard let it go. "Cripes!" Willard said again, his mouth dry.

The street below was a solid field of hats, with an occasional parasol like a daisy, and here and there a mounted policeman statue-still and gazing up like everyone. Thousands were yelling, as if sound alone would buoy the upside-down figure writhing 150 feet above the pavement.

"Attaboy, Harry!"

"Five minutes, that's too long! Someone bring him down!"

"Five minutes, hell, I seen him do thirty."

"At least he's not underwater this time."

"At least he ain't in a milk can!"

"Look at him go! The straitjacket's not made that can hold that boy, I tell you."

"You can do it, Harry!"

Willard himself hated crowds, but he had been drawing them all his life. One of the farm hands had caught him at age twelve toting a balky calf beneath one arm, and thereafter he couldn't go into town without people egging him on to lift things—livestock, Mr. Olsburg the banker, the log behind the fancy house. When people started offering cash money, he couldn't well refuse, having seen Mama and Papa re-count their jar at the end of every month, the stacks of old coins dull even in lamplight. So Jess Willard, at thirty-three, knew something about what physical feats earned, and what they cost. He watched this midair struggle, lost in jealousy, in sympathy, in professional admiration.

"God damn, will you look at this pop-eyed city," Lou said. "It's lousy with believers. I tell you, Champ, this fella has set a whole new standard for public miracles. When Jesus Christ Almighty comes back to town, he'll have to work his ass off to get in the newspapers at all." Lou tipped back his head, pursed his lips, and jetted cigar smoke upstairs.

"Do you mind?" asked the woman directly above, one of three crowding a ninth-floor window. She screwed up her face and fanned the air with her hands.

"Settle down, sister, smoke'll cure you soon enough," Lou said. He wedged the cigar back into his mouth and craned his neck to peer around Willard. "Have a heart, will you, Champ? It's like looking past Gibraltar."

"Sorry," Willard said, and withdrew a couple of inches, taking care not to bang his head on the sash. He already had banged his head crossing from the corridor to the parlor, and from the bathroom to the bedroom. Not that it hurt—no, to be hurt, Willard's head had to be hit plenty harder than that. But he'd never forgotten how the other children laughed when he hit his head walking in the door, that day the Pottawatomie County sheriff finally made him go to school. All the children but Hattie. So he took precautions outside the ring, and seethed inside each time he forgot he was six foot seven. This usually happened in hotel suites, all designed for Lou-sized men, or less. Since Havana, Willard had lived mostly in hotel suites.

Leaning from the next-door window on the left was a jowly man in a derby hat. He had been looking at Houdini only half the time, Willard the other half. Now he rasped: "Hey, buddy. Hey. Jess Willard."

Willard dreaded autograph-seekers, but Lou said a champ had to make nice. "You're the champ, now, boy," Lou kept saying, "and a champ has gotta be *seen!*"

"Yeah, that's me," Willard said.

His neighbor looked startled. Most people were, when they heard Willard's bass rumble for the first time. "I just wanted to say congratulations, Champ, for putting that nigger on the canvas where he belongs."

"I appreciate it," Willard said. He had learned this response from his father, a man too proud to say *thanks.* He tried to focus again on Houdini. The man seemed to be doing sit-ups in midair, but at a frenzied rate, jackknifing himself repeatedly. The rope above him whipped from side to side. Willard wondered how much of the activity was necessary, how much for effect.

The derby-hatted guy wasn't done. "Twenty-six rounds, damn, you taught Mr. Coon Johnson something about white men, I reckon, hah?"

Ever since Havana. Cripes. Houdini's canvas sleeves, once bound across his chest, were now bound behind him. Somehow he'd worked his arms over his head—was the man double-jointed?

"Say, how come you ain't had nothing but exhibitions since? When you gonna take on Frank Moran, huh? I know that nigger ain't taken the fight out of you. I know you ain't left your balls down in Cuba." He laughed like a bull snorting.

Willard sighed. He'd leave this one to Lou. Lou wouldn't have lasted ten seconds in the ring, but he loved a quarrel better than any boxer Willard knew.

"Balls?" Lou squawked, right on schedule. "Balls? Let me tell you something, fella."

Now Houdini's arms were free, the long canvas strap dangling. The crowd roared.

"When Moran is ready, we'll be ready, you got me?" Lou leaned out to shake his finger and nearly lost his balance. "Whoa," he said, clutching his hat. "Fella, you're, why, you're just lucky there's no ledge here. Yeah. You think he's taking it so easy, well, maybe you want to spar a few rounds with him, huh?"

Now Houdini had looped the canvas strap across the soles of his feet, and was tugging at it like a madman. More and more of his white shirt was visible. Willard resolved that when he started training again—when Lou got tired of parties and banquets and Keys to the City and let Willard go home to the gymnasium, and to Hattie—he would try this upside-down thing, if he could find rope strong enough.

"Well, how about I spar with *you*, buddy? Who the hell are you, Mr. Milksop?"

"I'm his manager, that's who I am! And let me tell you another thing . . ."

Houdini whipped off the last of the jacket and held the husk out, dangling, for all to see. Then he dropped it and flung both arms out to the side, an upside-down T. Amid the pandemonium, the jacket flew into the crowd and vanished like a ghost. Trash rained from the windows, as people dropped whatever they were holding to applaud. Willard stared as a woman's dress fluttered down to drape a lamp-post. It was blue and you could see through it. Even the guy with the derby was cheering, his hands clasped overhead. "Woo hoo!" he said, his quarrel forgotten. "Woo hoo hoo!"

With a smile and a shake of his head, Lou turned his back on it all. "The wizard of ballyhoo," he said. "Too bad they can't string up all the Jews, eh, Champ?" He patted Willard's shoulder and left the window.

As he was winched down, Houdini took inverted bows, and there was much laughter. Willard, who had neither cheered nor applauded, remained motionless at the window, tracking Houdini's descent. Someone's scented handkerchief landed on his head, and he brushed it away. He watched as the little dark-haired man in the ruffled shirt dropped headfirst into the sea that surged forward and engulfed him. His feet went last, bound at the ankles, patent-leather shoes side by side like a soldier's on review. Willard could imagine how they must shine.

That night, as Willard followed Lou up the curving, ever-narrowing, crimson-carpeted stairs leading to the balconies of the Los Angeles Orpheum, the muffled laughter and applause through the interior wall seemed to jeer Willard's every step, his every clumsy negotiation of a chandelier, his every flustered pause while a giggling and feathered bevy of young women flowed around his waist. Hattie didn't need feathers, being framed, in Willard's mind, by the open sky. These women needed plenty. Those going down gaped at him, chins tipping upward, until they passed; those going up turned at the next landing for a backward and downward look of frank appraisal. "We had a whole box in Sacramento," Lou muttered as he squinted from the numbers on the wall to the crumpled paper in his hand. "Shit. I guess these Los Angeles boxes is for the quality." A woman with a powder-white face puckered her lips at Willard and winked. Grunting in triumph, Lou overshot a cuspidor and threw open a door with a brown grin. "Save one of the redheads for me, willya?" Lou hissed, as Willard ducked past him into darkness.

Willard stopped to get his bearings as a dozen seated silhouettes turned to look at him. Beyond, the arched top of the stage was a tangle of golden vines. The balcony ceiling was too low. Willard shuffled forward, head down, as Lou pushed him two-handed in the small of the back. "Hello," Willard said, too loudly, and someone gasped. Then the others began to murmur hellos in return. "So good to meet you," they murmured amid a dozen outstretched hands, the male shapes half-standing, diamond rings and cufflinks sharp in the light from the stage. Willard was able to shake some hands, squeeze others; some merely stroked or patted him as he passed. "A pleasure," he kept saying. "A God's honest pleasure."

Lou made Willard sit in the middle of the front row next to Mrs. Whoever-She-Was, someone important; Lou said her name too fast. She was plump as a guinea hen and reeked of powder. Willard would have preferred the aisle. Here there was little room for his legs, his feet. Plus the seat, as usual, was too narrow. He jammed his buttocks between the slats that passed for armrests, bowing the wood outward like the sides of a firehose. As his hams sank, his jacket rode up in back. Once seated, he tried to work the jacket down, to no avail. Already his face was burning with the certainty that all eyes in the hall were focused not on the stage but on the newly hunchbacked Jess Willard. "Don't worry, he's just now begun," Mrs. Whoever whispered across Willard, to Lou. "You've hardly missed a thing."

His knees cut off the view of the stage below. He parted his knees just a little. Between them, on the varnished planks of the stage far below, Houdini patted the air to quell another round of applause. He was a short, dark, curly-haired man in a tuxedo. At his feet were a dozen scattered roses.

"Thank you, my friends, thank you," the little man said, though it sounded more like "Tank you"—a German, Willard had heard, this Houdini, or was it Austrian? Seen from this unnatural angle, nearly directly above like this, he looked dwarfish, foreshortened. He had broad shoulders, though, and no sign of a paunch beneath his cummerbund. Lou jabbed Willard in the side, glared at Willard's knees, then his face. Sighing, Willard closed his knees again.

"Ladies and gentlemen—are the ushers ready? Thank you. Ladies and gentlemen, I beg your assistance with the following part of the program. I require the services of a committee of ten. Ten good men and true, from the ranks of the audience, who are willing to join me here upon the stage and to watch closely my next performance, that all my claims be verified as accurate, that its every particular be beyond reproach."

The balcony was uncomfortably hot. Sweat rolled down Willard's torso, his neck. Mrs. Whoever opened her fan and worked up a breeze. A woman across the auditorium was staring at Willard and whispering to her husband. He could imagine. *All I can say is, you cannot trust those photographs. Look how they hide that poor man's deformities.*

"Ten good men and true. Yes, thank you, sir, your bravery speaks well for our boys in Haiti, and in Mexico." A spatter of applause. "The ushers will direct you. And you, sir, yes, thank you as well. Ladies, perhaps you could help us identify the more modest of the good men among us?" Laughter. "Yes, madam, your young man looks a likely prospect, indeed. A fine selection you have made—as have you, sir! No, madam, I fear your fair sex disqualifies you for this work. The stage can be a dangerous place."

Willard retreated to his program, to see which acts he missed because dinner with the mayor ran late. Actually, the dinner, a palm-sized chicken breast with withered greens, had been over quickly; you learned to eat fast on the farm. What took a long time was the mayor's after-dinner speech, in which he argued that athletic conditioning was the salvation of America. Willard bribed a waiter for three thick-cut bologna sandwiches, which he munched at the head table with great enjoyment, ignoring Lou. Now, looking at the Orpheum program, Willard found himself more kindly disposed toward the mayor's speech. It had spared him the "Syncopated Funsters" Bernie & Baker, Adelaide Boothby's "Novelty Songs and Travesties" (with Chas. Everdean at the piano), Selma Braatz the "Renowned Lady Juggler," and Comfort & King in "Coontown Diversions," not to mention a trick rider, a slack-wire routine, a mystery titled "Stan Stanley, The Bouncing Fellow, Assisted by His Relatives," and, most happily missed of all, The Alexander Kids, billed as "Cute, Cunning,

Captivating, Clever." And crooked, thought Willard, who once had wasted a nickel on a midget act at the Pottawatomie County Fair.

"Thank you, sir. Welcome. Ladies and gentlemen, these our volunteers have my thanks. Shall they have your thanks as well?"

Without looking up from his program, Willard joined the applause.

"My friends, as I am sure you have noticed, our committee still lacks three men. But if you will indulge me, I have a suggestion. I am told that here in the house with us tonight, we have one man who is easily the equal of any three."

Lou started jabbing Willard again. "G'wan," Willard whispered. "I closed my knees, all right?"

"Knock 'em dead, Champ," Lou hissed, his face shadowed but for his grin.

Willard frowned at him, bewildered. "What?"

"Ladies and gentlemen, will you kindly join me in inviting before the footlights the current heavyweight boxing champion—*our* champion—Mr. Jess Willard!"

Willard opened his mouth to protest just as a spotlight hit him full in the face, its heat like an opened oven.

Willard turned to Lou amid the applause and said, "You didn't!"

Lou ducked his chin and batted his eyes, like a bright child done with his recitation and due a certificate.

"Ladies and gentlemen, if you are in favor of bringing Mr. Willard onto the stage, please signify with your applause."

Now the cheers and applause were deafening. Willard gaped down at the stage. Houdini stood in a semicircle of frenziedly applauding men, his arms outstretched and welcoming. He stared up at Willard with a tiny smile at the corner of his mouth, almost a smirk, his eyes as bright and shallow as the footlights. *Look what I have done for you*, he seemed to be saying. *Come and adore me.*

The hell I will, Willard thought.

No, *felt*, it was nothing so coherent as thought, it was a gut response to Lou, to the mayor, to Mrs. Whoever pressing herself up against Willard's left side in hopes of claiming a bit of the spotlight too, to Hattie more than a thousand miles away whom he should have written today but didn't, to all these row after row of stupid people, most of whom thought Willard hadn't beaten Jack Johnson at all, that Johnson had simply given up, had *floated* to the canvas, the word they kept using, floated, Cripes, Willard had been *standing there*, had heard the *thump* like the first melon dropped into the cart when Johnson's head had bounced against the canvas, *bounced*, for Cripes' sake, spraying sweat and spit and blood, that fat lip flapping as the head went down a second time and stayed, *floated*, they said, Willard wasn't a *real* fighter, they said, he had just *outlasted* Johnson—an hour and forty-four minutes in the Havana sun, a blister on the top of his head like a brand, Hattie still could see the scar when she parted his hair to look—*outlasted*, the papers said! Beneath the applause, Willard heard a distant crunch as he squeezed the armrest, and was dimly aware of a splinter in his palm as he looked down at Houdini's smirking face and realized, clearly, for the first time: *You people don't want me at all, a big shit-kicker from the prairie.*

It's Jack Johnson you want.

And you know what? You can't have him. Because I beat him, you hear? I beat him.

"No, thanks!" Willard shouted, and the applause ebbed fast, like the last grain rushing out of the silo. The sudden silence, and Houdini's startled blink, made Willard's resolve falter. "I appreciate it," he added. He was surprised by how effortlessly his voice filled the auditorium. "Go on with your act, please, sir," Willard said, even more loudly. Ignoring Lou's clutching hand, which threatened to splinter Willard's forearm as Willard had splintered the armrest, he attempted comedy: "I got a good seat for it right here." There was nervous laughter, including someone immediately behind Willard— who must have, Willard realized, an even worse view than he did.

Arms still outstretched, no trace of a smile now, Houdini called up: "Mr. Willard, I am afraid your public must insist?"

Willard shook his head and sat back, arms folded.

"Mr. Willard, these other gentlemen join me in solemnly pledging that no harm will come to you."

This comedy was more successful; guffaws broke out all over the theater. Willard wanted to seek out all the laughers and paste them one. "Turn off that spotlight!" he yelled. "It's hot enough to roast a hog."

To Willard's amazement, the spotlight immediately snapped off, and the balcony suddenly seemed a dark, cold place.

"Come down, Mr. Willard," Houdini said, his arms now folded.

"Jesus Christ, kid," Lou hissed. "What's the idea?"

Willard shook him off and stood, jabbing one thick index finger at the stage. "Pay *me* what you're paying *them*, and I'll come down!"

Gasps and murmurs throughout the crowd. Willard was aware of some commotion behind him, movement toward the exit, the balcony door slamming closed. Fine. Let them run, the cowards.

In indignation, Houdini seemed to have swollen to twice his previous thickness. Must come in handy when you're straitjacketed, Willard thought.

"*Mister* Willard," Houdini retorted, "I am pleased to pay you what I am paying these gentlemen—precisely *nothing.* They are here of their own free will and good sportsmanship. Will you not, upon the same terms, join them?"

"No!" Willard shouted. "I'm leaving." He turned to find his way blocked by Lou, whose slick face gleamed.

"Please, Champ, don't do this to us," Lou whispered, reaching up with both hands in what might have been an attempted embrace. Willard grabbed Lou's wrists, too tightly, and yanked his arms down. "Ah," Lou gasped.

Houdini's drone continued as he paced the stage, his eyes never leaving the balcony. "I see, ladies and gentlemen, that the champ is attempting to retreat to his corner. Mr. Willard, the bell has rung. Will you not answer? Will you not meet the challenge? For challenge it is, Mr. Willard—I, and the good people of this house, challenge you to come forward, and stand before us, like a champion. As Mr. Johnson would have."

Willard froze.

"Or would you have us, sir, doubt the authenticity of your title? Would you have us believe that our champion is unmanned by fear?"

Willard turned and leaned so far over the rail that he nearly fell. "I'll do my job in the ring, you do your job onstage," he yelled. "Go on with your act, your trickery, you faker, you four-flusher!" The audience howled. He shouted louder. "Make it look good, you fake. That's all they want—talk!" He felt his voice breaking. "Tricks and snappy dialogue! Go on, then, give 'em what they want. Talk your worthless talk! Do your lousy fake tricks!" People were standing up and yelling at him all over the theater, but he could see nothing but the little strutting figure on the stage.

"Mr. Willard."

Willard, though committed, now felt himself running out of material. "Everybody knows it's fake!"

"Mr. Willard!"

"Four-flusher!"

"Look here, *Mister* Jess Willard," Houdini intoned, his broad face impassive, silencing Willard with a pointed index finger. "I don't care what your title is or how big you are or what your reputation is or how many men you've beaten to get it. I did you a favor by asking you onto this stage, I paid you a compliment, and so has everyone in the Orpheum." The theater was silent but for the magician. Willard and those in the balcony around him were frozen. "You have the right, sir, to refuse us, to turn your back on your audience, but you have no right, sir, no right whatsoever, to slur my reputation, a reputation, I might add, that will long outlive yours." In the ensuing silence, Houdini seemed to notice his pointed finger for the first time. He blinked, lowered his arm, and straightened his cummerbund as he continued: "If you believe nothing else I do or say on this stage today,

Mr. Willard, believe *this*, for there is no need for special powers of strength or magic when I tell you that *I can foresee your future.* Yes, sir."

Now his tone was almost conversational as he strolled toward center stage, picked up a rose, snapped its stem, and worked at affixing it to his lapel. "Believe me when I say to you that one day soon you no longer will be the heavyweight champion of the world." Satisfied by the rose, he looked up at Willard again.

"And when your name, Mr. Millard, I'm sorry, Mr. *Willard*, has become a mere footnote in the centuries-long history of the ring, everyone—*everyone*—even those who never set *foot* in a theater—will know *my* name and know that *I* never turned my back to my audience, or failed to accomplish *every* task, *every* feat, they set before me. And that, sir, is why champions come and champions go, while I will remain, now and forever, the one and only, Harry Houdini!" He flung his arms out and threw his head back a half-second before the pandemonium.

There had been twenty-five thousand people in that square in Havana, Willard had been told. He had tried not to look at them, not to think about them—that sea of snarling, squinting, sun-peeled, hateful, ugly faces. But at least all those people had been on his side.

"Go to hell, Willard!"

"Willard, you bum!"

"Willard's a willow!"

"Go to hell!"

Something hit Willard a glancing blow on the temple: a paper sack, which exploded as he snatched at it, showering the balcony with peanut shells. Willard felt he was moving slowly, as if underwater. As he registered that Mrs. Whoever, way down there somewhere, was pummeling him with her parasol—shrieking amid the din, "You bad man! You bad, bad man!"—Willard saw a gentleman's silver-handled cane spiraling lazily through the air toward his head. He ducked as the cane clattered into the far corner. Someone yelped. With one final glance at the mob, Willard turned his back on the too-inviting open space and dashed—but oh, so slowly it seemed—toward the door. People got in his way; roaring, he swept them aside, reached the door, fumbled at it. His fingers had become too slow and clumsy—numb, almost paralyzed. Bellowing something, he didn't know what, he kicked the door, which flew into the corridor in a shower of splinters. Roaring wordlessly now, Willard staggered down the staircase. He cracked his forehead on a chandelier, and yanked it one-handed out of the ceiling with a snarl, flinging it aside in a spasm of plaster and dust. His feet slipped on the lobby's marble floor, and he flailed before righting himself in front of an open-mouthed hat-check girl. Beyond the closed auditorium doors Willard could hear the crowd beginning to chant Houdini's name. Willard kicked a cuspidor as hard as he could; it sailed into a potted palm, spraying juice across the marble floor. Already feeling the first pangs of remorse, Willard staggered onto the sidewalk, into the reek of horseshit and automobiles. The doorman stepped back, eyes wide. "I ain't done nothing, Mister," he said. "I ain't done nothing." Willard growled and turned away, only to blunder into someone small and soft just behind him, nearly knocking her down. It was the hat-check girl, who yelped and clutched at his arms for balance.

"What the hell!" he said.

She righted herself, cleared her throat, and, lips pursed with determination, held out a claim ticket and a stubby pencil. "Wouldja please, huh, Mr. Willard? It won't take a sec. My grandpa says you're his favorite white man since Robert E. Lee."

Jess Willard lost the heavyweight title to Jack Dempsey on July 4, 1919, and retired from boxing soon after. When the fight money dried up, the Willards packed up Zella, Frances, Jess Junior, Enid, and Alan, left Kansas for good and settled in Los Angeles, where Willard opened a produce market at Hollywood and Afton. By day he dickered with farmers, weighed oranges, shooed flies, and swept up. Nights, he made extra money as a referee at wrestling matches. He continued to listen to boxing on the radio, and eventually to watch it on television, once the screens grew large enough to decently hold two grown men fighting. He read all the boxing news he could find in the papers, too, until holding the paper too long made his arms tremble like he was punchy, and spreading it out on the kitchen table didn't work so good either because the small print gave him a headache, and there weren't any real boxers left anyway, and thereafter it fell to his grandchildren, or his great-grandchildren, or his neighbors, or anyone else who had the time to spare, to read the sports pages aloud to him. Sometimes he listened quietly, eyes closed but huge behind his eyeglasses, his big mottled fingers drumming the antimacassar at one-second intervals, as if taking a count. Other times he was prompted to laugh, or to make a disgusted sound in the back of his throat, or to sit forward abruptly—which never failed to startle his youngest and, to his mind, prettiest great-granddaughter, whom he called "the Sprout," so that despite herself she always gasped and drew back a little, her beads clattering, her pedicured toes clenching the edge of her platform sandals—and begin telling a story of the old days, which his visitors sometimes paid attention to, and sometimes didn't, though the Sprout paid closer attention than you'd think.

One day in 1968, the Sprout read Jess Willard the latest indignant *Times* sports column about the disputed heavyweight title. Was the champ Jimmy Ellis, who had beaten Jerry Quarry on points, or was it Joe Frazier, who had knocked out Buster Mathis, or was it rightfully Muhammad Ali, who had been stripped of the title for refusing the draft, and now was banned from boxing anywhere in the United States? The columnist offered no answer to the question, but used his space to lament that boxing suddenly had become so political.

"Disputes, hell. I disputed a loss once," Willard told the Sprout.

"To Joe Cox in Springfield Moe in 1911. The referee stopped the fight, then claimed I *wouldn't* fight, give the match to Cox. Said he hadn't stopped nothing. I disputed it, but didn't nothing come of it. Hell. You can't win a fight by disputing."

"I thought a fight *was* a dispute," said the Sprout, whose name was Jennifer. Taking advantage of her great-granddad's near-blindness, she had lifted the hem of her mini to examine the pear-shaped peace symbol her boyfriend had drunkenly drawn on her thigh the night before. She wondered how long it would take to wash off. "Boyfriend" was really the wrong word for Cliff, though he *was* cute, in a scraggly dirty hippie sort of way, and it wasn't like she had a parade of suitors to choose from. The only guy who seemed interested at the coffeehouse last week was some Negro, couldn't you just die, and of course she told him to buzz off. She hoped Jess never found out she'd even said so much as "Buzz off" to a Negro boy— God knows, Jess was a nut on *that* subject. Nigger this and nigger that, and don't even bring up what's his name, that Negro boxer, Johnson? But you couldn't expect better from the old guy. After all, what had they called Jess, back when—the White Hope?

"No, no, honey," Willard said, shifting his buttocks to get comfortable. He fidgeted all the time, even in his specially made chair, since he lost so much weight. "A fight in the ring, it ain't nothing *personal.*"

"You're funny, Jess," Jennifer said. The old man's first name still felt awkward in her mouth, though she was determined to use it—it made her feel quite hip and adult, whereas "Popsy" made her feel three years old.

"You're funny, too," Willard said, sitting back. "Letting boys write on your leg like you was a Blue Horse tablet. Read me some more, if you ain't got nothing else to do."

"I don't," Jennifer lied.

Jess Willard died in his Los Angeles home December 15, 1968— was in that very custom-made chair, as a matter of fact, when he finally

Andy Duncan

closed his eyes. He opened them to find himself in a far more uncomfortable chair, in a balcony at the Los Angeles Orpheum, in the middle of Harry Houdini's opening-night performance, November 30, 1915.

"Where you been, Champ?" Lou asked. "We ain't keeping you up, are we?"

"Ladies and gentlemen, these our volunteers have my thanks. Shall they have your thanks as well?"

Amid the applause, Lou went on: "You ought to *act* interested, at least."

"Sorry, Lou," Willard said, sitting up straight and shaking his head. Cripes, he must have nodded off. He had that nagging waking sensation of clutching to the shreds of a rich and involving dream, but no, too late, it was all gone. "I'm just tired from traveling, is all."

"My friends, as I am sure you have noticed, our committee still lacks three men. But if you will indulge me, I have a suggestion. I am told that here in the house with us tonight, we have one man who is easily the equal of any three."

Lou jabbed Willard in the side. "Knock 'em dead, Champ," he said, grinning.

For an instant, Willard didn't understand. Then he remembered. Oh yeah, an onstage appearance with Houdini—like Jack London had done in Oakland, and President Wilson in Washington. Willard leaned forward to see the stage, the magician, the committee, the scatter of roses. Lou jabbed him again and mouthed the word, "Surprise." What did he mean, surprise? They had talked about this. Hadn't they?

"And so, ladies and gentlemen, will you kindly join me in inviting before the footlights the current heavyweight boxing champion—*our* champion—Mr. Jess Willard!"

In the sudden broil of the spotlight, amid a gratifying burst of cheers and applause, Willard unhesitatingly stood—remembering, just in time, the low ceiling. Grinning, he leaned over the edge and waved to the crowd, first with the right arm, then both arms. Cheered by a capacity crowd, at the biggest Orpheum theater on the West Coast—two dollars a seat, Lou had said! Hattie never would believe this. He bet Jack Johnson never got such a reception. But he wouldn't think of Johnson just now. This was Jess Willard's night. He clasped his hands together and shook them above his head.

Laughing above the cacophony, Houdini waved and cried, "Mr. Willard, please, come down!"

"On my way," Willard called, and was out the balcony door in a flash. He loped down the stairs two at a time. Sprinting through the lobby, he winked and blew a kiss at the hat-check girl, who squealed. The doors of the auditorium opened inward before him, and he entered the arena without slowing down, into the midst of a standing ovation, hundreds of faces turned to him as he ran down the central aisle toward the stage where Houdini waited.

"Mind the stairs in the pit, Mr. Willard," Houdini said. "I don't think they were made for feet your size." Newly energized by the audience's laughter, Willard made a show of capering stiff-legged up the steps, then fairly bounded onto the stage to shake the hand of the magician—who really was a *small* man, my goodness—and then shake the hands of all the other committee members. The applause continued, but the audience began to resettle itself, and Houdini waved his hands for order.

"Please, ladies and gentlemen! Please! Your attention! Thank you. Mr. Willard, gentlemen, if you will please step back, to make room for—The Wall of Mystery!"

The audience oohed as a curtain across the back of the stage lifted to reveal an ordinary brick wall, approximately twenty feet long and ten high. As Willard watched, the wall began to turn. It was built, he saw, on a circular platform flush with the stage. The disc revolved until the wall was perpendicular to the footlights.

"The Wall of Mystery, ladies and gentlemen, is not mysterious whatsoever in its construction. Perhaps from where you are sitting you can smell the mortar freshly laid, as this wall was completed only today, by twenty veteran members, personally selected and hired at double wages by the management of this theater, of Bricklayers' Union Number Thirty-four. Gentlemen, please take a bow!"

On cue, a half-dozen graying, potbellied men in denim work clothes walked into view stage left, to bow and wave their caps and grin. Willard applauded as loudly as anyone, even put both fingers in his mouth to whistle, before the bricklayers shuffled back into their workingmen's obscurity.

"Mr. Willard, gentlemen, please approach the wall and examine it at your leisure, until fully satisfied that the wall is solid and genuine in every particular."

The committee fanned out, first approaching the wall tentatively, as if some part of it might open and swallow them. Gradually they got into the spirit of the act, pushing and kicking the wall, slamming their shoulders into it, running laps around it to make sure it began and ended where it seemed to. To the audience's delight, Willard, by far the tallest of the men, took a running jump and grabbed the top of the wall, then lifted himself so that he could peer over to the other side. The audience cheered. Willard dropped down to join his fellow committeemen, all of whom took the opportunity to shake Willard's hand again.

During all this activity, Houdini's comely attendants had rolled onstage two six-foot circular screens, one from backstage left, one from backstage right. They rolled the screens to center stage, one screen stage left of the wall, one screen stage right. Just before stepping inside the left screen, Houdini said: "Now, gentlemen, please arrange yourselves around the wall so that no part of it escapes your scrutiny." Guessing what was going to happen, Willard trotted to the other side of the wall and stood, arms folded, between the wall and the stage-right screen; he could no longer see Houdini for the wall. The other men found their own positions. Willard heard a *whoosh* that he took to be Houdini dramatically closing the screen around him.

"I raise my hands above the screen like so," Houdini called, "to prove I am here. But now—I am gone!" There was another *whoosh*—the attendants opening the screen? The audience gasped and murmured. Empty, Willard presumed. The attendants trotted downstage into Willard's view, professionally balanced on their high heels, carrying between them the folded screen. At that moment the screen behind Willard went *whoosh*, and he turned to see Houdini stepping out of it, one hand on his hip, the other raised above his head in a flourish.

Surprised and elated despite himself, Willard joined in the crescendo of bravos and huzzahs.

Amid the din, Houdini trotted over to Willard, gestured for him to stoop, and whispered into his ear:

"Your turn."

His breath reeked of mint. Startled, Willard straightened up. The audience continued to cheer. Houdini winked, nodded almost imperceptibly toward the open screen he just had exited. Following Houdini's glance, Willard saw the secret of the trick, was both disappointed and delighted at its simplicity, and saw that he could do it, too. Yet he knew that to accept Houdini's offer, to walk through the wall himself, was something he neither wanted nor needed to do. He was Jess Willard, heavyweight champion of the world, if only for a season, and that was enough. He was content. He'd leave walking through walls to the professionals. He clapped one hand onto Houdini's shoulder, engulfing it, smiled and shook his head. Again almost imperceptibly, Houdini nodded, then turned to the audience, took a deep bow. Standing behind him now, feeling suddenly weary—surely the show wouldn't last much longer—Willard lifted his hands and joined the applause. Backstage to left and right, and in the catwalks directly above, he saw a cobweb of cables and pulleys against stark white brick—ugly, really, but completely invisible from the auditorium. On the highest catwalk two niggers in coveralls stood motionless, not applauding. Looking about, gaping, he was sure, like a hick, Willard told himself: Well, Jess, now you've had a taste of how it feels to be Harry Houdini. The afterthought came unbidden, as a jolt: *And Jack Johnson, too.* Disconcerted, Willard turned to stare at the stage-right screen, as two of the women folded it up and carted it away.

Jennifer barely remembered her Grandma Hattie, but she felt as if she sort of knew her by now, seeing the care she had lavished for decades on these scrapbooks, and reading the neat captions Hattie had typed and placed alongside each item:

FORT WAYNE, 1912—WORKING THE BAG—KO'd J. Young in 6th on May 23 (Go JESS!)

The captions were yellowed and brittle now, tended to flutter out in bits like confetti when the albums were opened too roughly.

"I'm a good typist, Jess," Jennifer said. "I could make you some new ones."

"No, thanks," Jess said. "I like these fine."

"Where's the Johnson book?"

"Hold your horses, it's right here. There you go. I knew you'd want that one."

Jennifer was less interested in Jack Johnson per se than in the fact that one of Hattie's scrapbooks was devoted to one of her husband's most famous opponents, a man whom Jess had beaten for the title, and never met again. Jennifer suspected this scrapbook alone was as much the work of Jess as of Hattie—and the aging Jess at that, since it began with Johnson's obituaries in 1946. Hence the appeal of the Johnson scrapbook; this mysterious and aging Jess, after all, was the only one she knew. The last third of the book had no typewritten captions, and clippings that were crooked beneath their plastic. The last few pages were blank. Stuck into the back were a few torn-out and clumsily folded newspaper clippings about Muhammad Ali.

"Johnson was cool," she said, turning the brittle pages with care. "It is so cool that you got to fight him, Jess. And that you won! You must have been proud."

"I *was* proud," Willard said, reaching for another pillow to slide beneath his bony buttocks. "Still am," he added. "But I wish I had known him, too. He was an interesting man."

"He died in a car wreck, didn't he?"

"Yep."

"That's so sad." Jennifer knew about the car wreck, of course; it was all over the front of the scrapbook. She was just stalling, making noise with her mouth, while pondering whether now was the time to get Jess talking about Johnson's three wives, all of them white women, all of them blonde white women. Jennifer was very interested to know Jess's thoughts about that.

"You fought him in Havana because, what? You weren't allowed to fight in the United States, or something?" She asked this with great casualness, knowing Johnson was a fugitive from U.S. justice at the time, convicted of violating the Mann Act, i.e., transporting women across state lines for "immoral purposes," i.e., white slavery, i.e., sex with a white woman.

"Yeah, something like that," Jess said. He examined the ragged hem of his sweater, obviously uninclined to pursue the conversation further. God, getting an 87-year-old man to talk about sex was *hard*.

"I was trying to tell Carl about it, but I, uh, forgot the uh, details." She kept talking, inanely, flushed with horror. *Massive* slip-up. She never had mentioned Carl in front of Jess before, certainly not by name. Carl was three years older than she was, and worse yet, a dropout. He was also black. Not Negro, he politely insisted: black. He wanted to meet Jess, and Jennifer wanted that to happen, too—but she would have to careful about how she brought it up. Not this way! Sure, Jess might admire Jack Johnson as a fighter, but would he want his teenage great-granddaughter to date him?

"There was some rule against it, I think," Jess said, oblivious, and she closed her eyes for a second in relief. "I be doggoned but this sweater wasn't worth bringing home from the store." He glanced up. "You didn't give me this sweater, did you, Sprout?"

"No, Jess," Jennifer said. She closed the Johnson scrapbook, elated to avoid *that* conversation one more day.

"I wouldn't hurt you for nothing, you know," Jess said. "Wouldn't let no one else hurt you, neither."

She grinned, charmed. "Would you stand up for me, Jess?"

"I sure would, baby. Anybody bothers you, I'll clean his clock." He slowly punched the air with mottled fists, his eyes huge and swimming behind his glasses, and grinned a denture-taut grin. On impulse, Jennifer kissed his forehead. Resettling herself on the floor, she opened one of the safer scrapbooks. Here was her favorite photo of Jess at the produce market, hair gray beneath his paper hat. He held up to the light a Grade A white egg that he smiled at in satisfaction. Grandma Hattie had typed beneath the photo: TWO GOOD EGGS.

"One hundred and thirteen fights," Jess said. Something in his voice made Jennifer glance up. He looked suddenly morose, gazing at nothing, and Jennifer worried that she had said something to upset him; he was so moody, sometimes. "That's how many Johnson fought. More than Tunney, more than Louis. Twice as many as Marciano. Four times as many as Jeffries, as Fitzsimmons, as Gentleman Jim Corbett. And forty-four of them knockouts." He sighed and repeated, almost inaudibly, "Forty-four."

She cleared her throat, determined, and said loudly: "Hey, you want to write another letter?" About once a month, Jess dictated to her a letter to the editor, saying Ali was the champ fair and square whether people liked it or not, same as Jack Johnson had been, same as Jess Willard had been, and if people didn't like it then let them take Ali on in the ring like men. The *Times* had stopped printing the letters after the third one, but she hadn't told Jess that.

He didn't seem to have heard her. After a few seconds, though, his face brightened. "Hey," he said. "Did I ever tell you about the time I got the chance to walk through a wall?"

Relieved, she screwed up her face in mock concentration. "Well, let's see, about a hundred million billion times, but you can tell me again if you want. Do you ever wish you'd done it?"

"Nah," Jess said, leaning into the scrapbook to peer at the two good eggs. "I probably misunderstood him in the first place. He never let anybody *else* get in on the act, that I heard of. He was too big a star for that." He sat back, settled into the armchair with a sigh. "I must have misunderstood him. Anyway." He was quiet again, but smiling. "Too late now, huh?"

"I guess so," Jennifer said, slowly turning the pages, absently stroking her beads so that the strands clicked together. Beside her Jess began, gently, to snore. She suppressed a laugh: Could you believe it? Just like that, down for the count. Without realizing it, she had turned to a clipping from the *Times*, dated December 1, 1915.

TWO CHAMPIONS MEET
RING ARTIST, ESCAPE ARTIST SHAKE ON ORPHEUM STAGE

Young Jess looked pretty spiffy in his evening wear, Jennifer thought. *Spiffy*, she knew from reading the scrapbooks, had been one of Grandma Hattie's favorite words. Jess was crouched to fit into the photograph, which must have been taken from the front row. The two men looked down at the camera; at their feet a couple of footlights were visible. At the bottom edge of the photo was the blurred top of a man's head. Someone had penciled a shaky arrow from this blur and written, "Lou." The background was murky, but Jennifer could imagine a vaulted plaster ceiling, a chandelier, a curtain embroidered with intricate Oriental designs. Beneath the clipping, Grandma Hattie had typed: JESS MEETS EHRICH WEISS a.k.a. HARRY HOUDINI (1874-1926). On the facing page, Houdini's faded signature staggered across a theater program.

Even as a kid, Jennifer had been intrigued by Houdini's eyes. Although the clipping was yellowed and the photo blurred to begin with, Houdini always seemed to look right at her, *into* her. It was the same in the other photos, in the Houdini books she kept checking out of the library. He wasn't Jennifer's type, but he had great eyes.

As she looked at the clipping, she began to daydream. She was on stage, wearing a tuxedo and a top hat and tights cut up to *there*, and she pulled back a screen to reveal—who? Hmm. She wasn't sure. Maybe Carl; maybe not. Daydreaming was a sign, said the goateed guy who taught her comp class, of sensitivity, of creativity. Yeah, right. Sometimes when she was home alone—she told no one this— she put on gym shorts and went out back and boxed the air, for an hour or more at a time, until she was completely out of breath. Why, she couldn't say. Being a pacifist, she couldn't imagine hitting a *person*, no, but she sure beat hell out of the air. She really wanted to be neither a boxer nor a magician. She was a political-science major, and had her heart set on the Peace Corps. And yet, when Carl had walked into the coffeehouse that night alone, fidgeting in the doorway with an out-of-place look, considering, maybe, ducking back outside again, what did she say to him? She walked right up to Carl, bold as brass (that was another of Grandma Hattie's, BOLD as BRASS), stuck out her chin and stuck out her hand and said, "Hi, my name is Jennifer Schumacher, and I'm the great-granddaughter of the ex-heavyweight champion of the world." Carl shook her hand and looked solemn and said, "Ali?" and people stared at them, they laughed so hard, and if *I* ever get a chance to walk through a wall, she vowed to herself as she closed the scrapbook, *I'm* taking it—so *there*.

Senator Bilbo

"It regrettably has become necessary for us now, my friends, to consider seriously and to discuss openly the most pressing question facing our homeland since the War. By that I mean, of course, the race question."

In the hour before dawn, the galleries were empty, and the floor of the Shire-moot was nearly so. Scattered about the chamber, a dozen or so of the Senator's allies—a few more than needed to maintain the quorum, just to be safe—lounged at their writing-desks, feet up, fingers laced, pipes stuffed with the best Bywater leaf, picnic baskets within reach: veterans, all. Only young Appledore from Bridge Inn was snoring and slowly folding in on himself; the chestnut curls atop his head nearly met those atop his feet. The Senator jotted down Appledore's name without pause. He could get a lot of work done while making speeches—even a filibuster nine hours long (and counting).

"There are forces at work today, my friends, without and within our homeland, that are attempting to destroy all boundaries between our proud, noble race and all the mule-gnawing, cave-squatting, light-shunning, pit-spawned scum of the East."

The Senator's voice cracked on "East," so he turned aside for a quaff from his (purely medicinal) pocket flask. His allies did not miss their cue. "Hear, hear," they rumbled, thumping the desktops with their calloused heels. "Hear, hear."

"This latest proposal," the Senator continued, "this so-called immigration bill—which, as I have said, would force even our innocent daughters to suffer the reeking lusts of all the ditch-bred legions of darkness—why, this baldfooted attempt originated where, my friends?"

"Buckland!" came the dutiful cry.

"Why, with the delegation from *Buckland* . . . long known to us all as a hotbed of book-mongers, one-Earthers, elvish sympathizers, and other off-brands of the halfling race."

This last was for the benefit of the newly arrived Fredegar Brace-girdle, the unusually portly junior member of the Buckland delega-tion. He huffed his way down the aisle, having drawn the short straw in the hourly backroom ritual.

"Will the distinguished Senator," Bracegirdle managed to squeak out, before succumbing to a coughing fit. He waved his bladder-like hands in a futile attempt to disperse the thick purplish clouds that hung in the chamber like the vapors of the Eastmarsh. Since a Buck-land-sponsored bill to ban tobacco from the floor had been defeated by the Senator three Shire-moots previous, his allies' pipe-smoking had been indefatigable. Finally Bracegirdle sputtered: "Will the dis-tinguished Senator from the Hill kindly yield the floor?"

In response, the Senator lowered his spectacles and looked across the chamber to the Thain of the Shire, who recited around his tomato sandwich: "Does the distinguished Senator from the Hill so yield?"

"I do not," the Senator replied, cordially.

"The request is denied, and the distinguished Senator from the Hill retains the floor," recited the Thain of the Shire, who then took another hearty bite of his sandwich. The Senator's party had re-writ-ten the rules of order, making this recitation the storied Thain's only remaining duty.

"Oh, hell and hogsheads," Bracegirdle muttered, already trun-dling back up the aisle. As he passed Gorhendad Bolger from the Brockenborings, that Senator's man like his father before him kindly offered Bracegirdle a pickle, which Bracegirdle accepted with ill grace.

"Now that the distinguished gentleman from the Misty Mountains has been heard from," the Senator said, waiting for the laugh, "let me turn now to the evidence—the overwhelming evidence, my friends—that many of the orkish persuasion currently living among us have been, in fact, active agents of the Dark Lord . . ."

As the Senator plowed on, seldom referring to his notes, inventing statistics and other facts as needed, secure that this immigration bill, like so many bills before it, would wither and die once the Bucklanders' patience was exhausted, his self-confidence faltered only once, unnoticed by anyone else in the chamber. A half-hour into his denunciation of the orkish threat, the Senator noticed a movement—no, more a shift of light, a *glimmer*—in the corner of his eye. He instinctively turned his head toward the source, and saw, or *thought* he saw, sitting in the farthest, darkest corner of the otherwise empty gallery, a man-sized figure in a cloak and pointed hat, who held what must have been (*could* have been) a staff; but in the next blink, that corner held only shadows, and the Senator dismissed the whatever-it-was as a fancy born of exhilaration and weariness. Yet he was left with a lingering chill, as if (so his old mother, a Took, used to say) a dragon had hovered over his grave.

At noon, the Bucklanders abandoned their shameful effort to open the High Hay, the Brandywine Bridge, and the other entry gates along the Bounds to every misbegotten so-called "refugee," be he halfling, man, elf, orc, warg, Barrow-wight, or worse. Why, it would mean the end of Shire culture, and the mongrelization of the halfling race! No, sir! Not today—not while the Senator was on the job.

Triumphant but weary, the champion of Shire heritage worked his way, amid a throng of supplicants, aides, well-wishers, reporters, and yes-men, through the maze of tunnels that led to his Hill-side suite of offices. These were the largest and nicest of any senator's, with the most pantries and the most windows facing the Bywater, but they also were the farthest from the Shire-moot floor. The Senator's famous ancestor and namesake had been hale and hearty even in his eleventy-first year; the Senator, pushing ninety, was determined to beat that record. But every time he left the chamber, the office seemed farther away.

"Gogluk carry?" one bodyguard asked.

"Gogluk *not* carry," the Senator retorted. The day he'd let a troll haul him through the corridors like luggage would be the day he sailed oversea for good.

All the Senator's usual tunnels had been enlarged to accommodate the bulk of his two bodyguards, who nevertheless had to stoop, their scaly shoulders scraping the ceiling. Loyal, dim-witted, and huge—more than five feet in height—the Senator's trolls were nearly as well known in the Shire as the Senator himself, thanks partially to the Senator's perennial answer to a perennial question from the press at election time:

"Racist? Me? Why, I love Gogluk and Grishzog, here, as if they were my own flesh and blood, and they love me just the same, don't you, boys? See? Here, boys, have another biscuit."

Later, once the trolls had retired for the evening, the Senator would elaborate. Trolls, now, you could train them, they were teachable; they had their uses, same as those swishy elves, who were so good with numbers. Even considered as a race, the trolls weren't much of a threat—no one had seen a baby troll in ages. But those orcs? They did nothing but breed.

Carry the Senator they certainly did not, but by the time the trolls reached the door of the Senator's outermost office (no mannish rectangular door, but a traditional Shire-door, round and green with a shiny brass knob in the middle), they were virtually holding the weary old halfling upright and propelling him forward, like a child pushed to kiss an ugly aunt. Only the Senator's mouth was tireless. He continued to greet constituents, compliment babies, rap orders to flunkies, and rhapsodize about the glorious inheritance of the Shire as the procession squeezed its way through the increasingly small rooms of the Senator's warren-like suite, shedding followers like snakeskin. The only ones who made it from the innermost outer office to the outermost inner office were the Senator, the trolls, and four reporters, all of whom considered themselves savvy under-Hill insiders for being allowed so far into the great man's sanctum. The Senator further graced these reporters by reciting the usual answers to the usual questions as he looked through his mail, pocketing the fat envelopes and putting the thin ones in a pile for his intern, Miss Boffin. The Senator got almost as much work done during press conferences as during speeches.

"Senator, some members of the Buckland delegation have insinuated, off the record, that you are being investigated for alleged bribe-taking. Do you have a comment?"

"You can tell old Gerontius Brownlock that he needn't hide behind a façade of anonymity, and further that I said he was begotten in an orkish graveyard at midnight, suckled by a warg-bitch and educated by a fool. That's off the record, of course."

"Senator, what do you think of your chances for re-election next fall?"

"The only time I have ever been defeated in a campaign, my dear, was my first one. Back when your grandmother was a whelp, I lost a clerkship to a veteran of the Battle of Bywater. A one-armed veteran. I started to vote for him myself. But unless a one-armed veteran comes forward pretty soon, little lady, I'm in no hurry to pack."

The press loved the Senator. He was quotable, which was all the press required of a public official.

"Now, gentle folk, ladies, the business of the Shire awaits. Time for just one more question."

An unfamiliar voice aged and sharp as Mirkwood cheese rang out:

"They say your ancestor took a fairy wife."

The Senator looked up, his face even rounder and redder than usual. The reporters backed away. "It's a lie!" the Senator cried. "Who said such a thing? Come, come. Who said that?"

"Said what, Senator?" asked the most senior reporter (Bracklebore, of the *Bywater Battle Cry*), his voice piping as if through a reed. "I was just asking about the quarterly sawmill-production report. If I may continue—"

"Goodbye," said the Senator. On cue, the trolls snatched up the reporters, tossed them into the innermost outer office, and slammed and locked the door. Bracklebore, ousted too quickly to notice, finished his question in the next room, voice muffled by the intervening wood. The trolls dusted their hands.

"Goodbye," said Gogluk—or was that Grishzog?

"Goodbye," said Grishzog—or was that Gogluk?

Which meant, of course, "Mission accomplished, Senator," in the pidgin Common Speech customary among trolls.

"No visitors," snapped the Senator, still nettled by that disembodied voice, as he pulled a large brass key from his waistcoat-pocket and unlocked the door to his personal apartments. Behind him, the trolls assumed position, folded their arms, and turned to stone.

"Imagination," the Senator muttered as he entered his private tunnel.

"Hearing things," he added as he locked the door behind.

"Must be tired," he said as he plodded into the sitting-room, yawning and rubbing his hip.

He desired nothing more in all the earth but a draught of ale, a pipe, and a long snooze in his armchair, and so he was all the more taken aback to find that armchair already occupied by a white-bearded Big Person in a tall pointed blue hat, an ankle-length gray cloak, and immense black boots, a thick oaken staff laid across his knees.

"Strewth!" the Senator cried.

The wizard—for wizard he surely was—slowly stood, eyes like lanterns, bristling gray brows knotted in a thunderous scowl, a meteor shower flashing through the weave of his cloak, one gnarled index finger pointed at the Senator—who was, once the element of surprise passed, unimpressed. The meteor effect lasted only a few seconds, and thereafter the intruder was an ordinary old man, though with fingernails longer and more yellow than most.

"Do you remember me?" the wizard asked. His voice crackled like burning husks. The Senator recognized that voice.

"Should I?" he retorted. "What's the meaning of piping insults into my head? And spying on me in the Shire-moot? Don't deny it; I saw you flitting about the galleries like a bad dream. Come on, show me you have a tongue—else I'll have the trolls rummage for it." The Senator was enjoying himself; he hadn't had to eject an intruder since those singing elves occupied the outer office three sessions ago.

"You appointed me, some years back," the wizard said, "to the University, in return for some localized weather effects on Election Day."

So that was all. Another disgruntled officeholder. "I may have done," the Senator snapped. "What of it?" The old-timer showed no inclination to reseat himself, so the Senator plumped down in the armchair. Its cushions now stank of men. The Senator kicked the wizard's staff from underfoot and jerked his leg back; he fancied something had nipped his toe.

The staff rolled to the feet of the wizard. As he picked it up, the wider end flared with an internal blue glow. He commenced shuffling about the room, picking up knickknacks and setting them down again as he spoke.

"These are hard times for wizards," the wizard rasped. "New powers are abroad in the world, and as the powers of wind and rock, water and tree are ebbing, we ebb with them. Still, we taught our handfuls of students respect for the old ways. Alas, no longer!"

The Senator, half-listening, whistled through his eyeteeth and chased a flea across the top of his foot.

"The entire thaumaturgical department—laid off! With the most insulting of pensions! A flock of old men feebler than I, unable even to transport themselves to your chambers, as I have wearily done—to ask you, to demand of you, why?"

The Senator yawned. His administrative purging of the Shire's only university, in Michel Delving, had been a complex business with a complex rationale. In recent years, the faculty had got queer Eastern notions into their heads and their classrooms—muddleheaded claims that all races were close kin, that orcs and trolls had not been separately bred by the Dark Power, that the Dark Power's very existence was mythical. Then the faculty quit paying the campaign contributions required of all public employees, thus threatening the Senator's famed "Deduct Box." Worst of all, the faculty demanded "open admissions for qualified non-halflings," and the battle was joined. After years of bruising politics, the Senator's appointees now controlled the university board, and a long-overdue housecleaning was underway. Not that the Senator needed to recapitulate all this to an unemployed spell-mumbler. All the Senator said was:

"It's the board that's cut the budget, not me." With a cry of triumph, he purpled a fingernail with the flea. "Besides," he added, "they kept all the *popular* departments. Maybe you could pick up a few sections of Heritage 101."

This was a new, mandatory class that drilled students on the unique and superior nature of halfling culture and on the perils of immigration, economic development, and travel. The wizard's response was: "Pah!"

The Senator shrugged. "Suit yourself. I'm told the Anduin gambling-houses are hiring. Know any card tricks?"

The wizard stared at him with rheumy eyes, then shook his head. "Very well," he said. "I see my time is done. Only the Grey Havens are left to me and my kind. We should have gone there long since. But your time, too, is passing. No fence, no border patrol—not even you, Senator—can keep all change from coming to the Shire."

"Oh, we can't, can we?" the Senator retorted. As he got worked up, his Bywater accent got thicker. "We sure did keep those Bucklanders from putting over that so-called Fair Distribution System, taking people's hard-earned crops away and handing 'em over to lazy trash to eat. We sure did keep those ugly up-and-down man houses from being built all over the Hill as shelter for immigrant rabble what ain't fully halfling or fully human or fully anything. Better to be some evil race than no race at all."

"There are no evil races," said the wizard.

The Senator snorted. "I don't know how *you* were raised, but I was raised on the Red Book of Westmarch, chapter and verse, and it says so right there in the Red Book, orcs are mockeries of men, filthy cannibals spawned by the Enemy, bent on overrunning the world . . ."

He went on in this vein, having lapsed, as he often did in conversation, into his tried-and-true stump speech, galvanized by the memories of a thousand cheering halfling crowds. "Oh, there's enemies everywhere to our good solid Shire-life," he finally cried, punching the air, "enemies outside and inside, but we'll keep on beating 'em back and fighting the good fight our ancestors fought at the Battle of Bywater. Remember their cry:

"Awake! Awake! Fear, Fire, Foes! Awake!

"Fire, Foes! Awake!"

The cheers receded, leaving only the echo of his own voice in the Senator's ears. His fists above his head were bloated and mottled— a corpse's fists. Flushed and dazed, the Senator looked around the room, blinking, slightly embarrassed—and, suddenly, exhausted. At some point he had stood up; now his legs gave way and he fell back into the armchair, raising a puff of tobacco. On the rug, just out of reach, was the pipe he must have dropped, lying at one end of a spray of cooling ashes. He did not reach for it; he did not have the energy. With his handkerchief he mopped at his spittle-laced chin.

The wizard regarded him, wrinkled fingers interlaced atop his staff.

"I don't even know why I'm talking to you," the Senator mumbled. He leaned forward, eyes closed, feeling queasy. "You make my head hurt."

"Inhibiting spell," the wizard said. "It prevented your throwing me out. Temporary, of course. One bumps against it, as against a low ceiling."

"Leave me alone," the Senator moaned.

"Such talents," the wizard murmured. "Such energy, and for what?"

"At least I'm a halfling," the Senator said.

"Largely, yes," the wizard said. "Is genealogy one of your interests, Senator? We wizards have a knack for it. We can see bloodlines, just by looking. Do you really want to know how . . . *interesting* . . . your bloodline is?"

The Senator mustered all his energy to shout "Get out!"—but heard nothing. Wizardry kept the words in his mouth, unspoken.

"There are no evil races," the wizard repeated, "however convenient the notion to patriots, and priests, and storytellers. You may summon your trolls now." His gesture was half shrug, half convulsion.

Suddenly the Senator had his voice back. "Boys!" he squawked. "Boys! Come quick! Help!" As he hollered, the wizard seemed to roll up like a windowshade, then become a tubular swarm of fireflies. By the time the trolls knocked the door into flinders, most of the fireflies were gone. The last dying sparks winked out on their scaly shoulders as the trolls halted, uncertain what to pulverize. The Senator could hear their lids scrape their eyeballs as they blinked once, twice. The troll on the left asked:

"Gogluk help?"

"Gogluk too *late* to help, thank you very much!" the Senator snarled. The trolls tried to assist as he struggled out of the armchair, but he slapped them away, hissing, in a fine rage now. "Stone ears or no, did you not hear me shouting? Who did you think I was talking to?"

The trolls exchanged glances. Then Grishzog said, quietly: "Senator talk when alone a lot."

"A lot," Gogluk elaborated.

The Senator might have clouted them both had he not been distracted by the wizard's staff. Dropped amid the fireworks, it had rolled beneath a table. Not knowing why, the Senator reached for it, eyes shining. The smooth oak was warm to the touch: heat-filled, like a living thing. Then, with a yelp, the Senator yanked back his hand. The damn thing *definitely* had bitten him this time; blood trickled down his right palm. As three pairs of eyes stared, the staff sank into the carpet like a melting icicle, and was gone.

"Magic," said the trolls as one, impressed.

"Magic?" the senator cried. "Magic?" He swung his fists and punched the trolls, kicked them, wounding only their dignity; their looming hulks managed to cower, like dogs. "If it's magic you want, I'll give you magic!" He swung one last time, lost his balance, and fell into the trolls' arms in a dead faint.

The Bunce Inn, now in the hands of its founder's great-granddaughter, had been the favored public house of the Shire-moot crowd for generations. The Senator had not been inside the place in months. He pleaded matters of state, the truth being he needed a lot more sleep nowadays. But when he woke from his faint to find the trolls fussing over him, he demanded to be taken to the Bunce Inn for a quick one before retiring. The Senator's right hand smarted a bit beneath its bandage, but otherwise the unpleasant interlude with the wizard seemed a bad dream, was already melting away like the staff. The Senator's little troll-cart jounced through the warm honeysuckle-scented night, along the cobbled streets of the capital, in and out of the warm glows cast by round windows behind which fine happy halfling families settled down to halfling dinners and halfling games and halfling dreams.

The inn itself was as crowded as ever, but the trolls' baleful stares quickly prompted a group of dawdlers to drink up and vacate their table. The trolls retreated to a nearby corner, out of the way but ever-present, as bodyguards should be. The Senator sat back with a sigh and a tankard and a plate of chips and surveyed the frenzy all around, pleased to be a part of none of it. The weight of the brimming pewter tankard in his unaccustomed left hand surprised him, so that he spilled a few drops of Bunce's best en route to his mouth. *Aah.* Just as he remembered. Smacking foam from his lips, he took another deep draught—and promptly choked. Not six feet away, busy cleaning a vacant table, was an orc.

And not just any orc. This one clearly had some man in its bloodline somewhere. The Senator had seen to it that the Shire's laws against miscegenation had stayed on the books, their penalties stiffened, but elsewhere in the world, alas, traditional moral values had declined to the point that such blasphemous commingling had become all too frequent. This creature was no doubt an orc—the hulking torso and bowlegs, the flat nose and flared nostrils, the broad face, the slanting eyes, the coarse hair, the monstrous hooked teeth at the corners of the mouth—but the way the orc's arms moved as it stacked dirty plates was uncomfortably man-like. It had genuine hands as well, with long delicate fingers, and as its head turned, the Senator saw that its pupils were not the catlike slits of a true orc, but rounded, like the pupils of dwarves, and men, and halflings. It was like seeing some poor trapped halfling peering out from a monstrous bestial shell, as in those children's stories where the hero gets swallowed whole by the ogre and cries for help from within. The orc, as it worked, began to whistle.

The Senator shuddered, felt his gorge rise. His injured hand throbbed with each heartbeat. A filthy half-breed orc, working at the Bunce Inn! Old Bunce would turn in his grave. Catching sight of young Miss Bunce bustling through the crowd, the Senator tried to wave her over, to give her a piece of his mind. But she seemed to have eyes only for the orc. She placed her hand on its shoulder and said, in a sparkling gay voice: "Please, sir, don't be tasking yourself, you're too kind. I'll clean the table; you just settle yourself, please, and tell me what you'll have. The lamb stew is very nice today, and no mistake."

"Always pleased to help out, ma'am," said the orc, plopping its foul rump onto the creaking bench. "I can see how busy you are. Seems to me you're busier every time I come through the Shire."

"There's some as say I needs a man about," Miss Bunce said, her arms now laden with plates, "but cor! Then I'd be busier still, wouldn't I?" The orc laughed a horrid burbling mucus-filled laugh as Miss Bunce sashayed away, buttocks swinging, glancing back to twinkle at her grotesque customer, and wink.

At this inauspicious moment, someone gave the Senator a hearty clap on the back. It was Fredegar Bracegirdle, a foaming mug in his hand and a foolish grin on his fat red face. Drink put Bracegirdle in a regrettable bipartisan mood. "Hello, Senator," Bracegirdle chirped as he clapped the Senator's back again and again. "Opponents in the legislature, drinking buddies after hours, eh, Senator, eh, friend, eh, pal?"

"Stop pounding me," the Senator said. "I am not choking. Listen, Bracegirdle. What is that, that . . . *creature* . . . doing here?"

Bracegirdle's bleary gaze slowly followed the Senator's pointing finger, as a dying flame follows a damp fuse. "Why, he's a-looking at the bill of fare, and having himself a pint, same as us."

"You know what I mean! Look at those hands. He talks as if someone, somewhere, has given him schooling. Where'd he come from?"

As he answered, Bracegirdle helped himself to the Senator's chips. "Don't recall his name, but he hails from Dunland, from one of those new, what-do-you-call-'em, investment companies, their hands in a little of everything. Run by orcs and dwarves, mostly, but they're hiring all sorts. My oldest, Bungo, he's put his application in, and I said, you go to it, son, there's no work in the Shire for a smart lad like yourself, and your dear gaffer won't be eating any less in his old age. Young Bunce, she's a wizard at these chips, she is. Could you pass the vinegar?"

The Senator already had risen and stalked over to the orc's table, where the fanged monster, having ordered, was working one of the little pegboard games Miss Bunce left on the tables for patrons' amusement. The orc raised its massive head as it registered the Senator's presence.

"A good evening to you, sir," it said. "You can be my witness. Look at that, will you? Only one peg left, and it in the center. I've never managed *that* before!"

The Senator cleared his throat and spat in the orc's face. A brown gob rolled down its flattened nose. The orc gathered its napkin, wiped its face, and stood, the scrape of the bench audible in the otherwise silent room. The orc was easily twice as wide as the Senator, and twice as tall, yet it did not have to stoop. Since the Senator's last visit, Miss Bunce had had the ceiling raised. Looking up at the unreadable, brutish face, the Senator stood his ground, his own face hot with rage, secure in the knowledge that the trolls were right behind him. Someone across the room coughed. The orc glanced in that direction, blinked, shook its head once, twice, like a horse bedeviled by flies. Then it expelled a breath, its fat upper lip flapping like a child's noisemaker, and sat down. It slid the pegboard closer and re-inserted the pegs, one after the other after the other, then, as the Senator watched, resumed its game.

The Senator, cheated of his fight, was unsure what to do. He could not remember when last he had been so utterly ignored. He opened his mouth to tell the orc a thing or two, but felt a tug at his sleeve so violent that it hushed him. It was Miss Bunce, lips thin, face pale, twin red spots livid on her cheeks. "It's late, Senator," she said, very quietly. "I think you'd best be going home."

Behind her were a hundred staring faces. Most of them were strangers. Not all of them were halflings. The Senator looked for support in the faces in the crowd, and for the first time in his life, did not find it. He found only hostility, curiosity, indifference. He felt his face grow even hotter, but not with rage.

He nearly told the Bunce slut what he thought of her and her orc-loving clientele—but best to leave it for the Shire-moot. Best to turn his back on this pesthole. Glaring at everyone before him, he gestured for the trolls to clear a path and muttered: "Let's go, boys."

Nothing happened.

The Senator slowly turned his head. The trolls weren't there. The trolls were nowhere to be seen. Only more hostile strangers' faces. The Senator felt a single trickle of sweat slide past his shoulder blades. The orc jumped pegs, removed pegs: *snick, snick.*

So. The Senator forced himself to smile, to hold his head high. He nodded, patted Miss Bunce's shoulder (she seemed not to relish the contact), and walked toward the door. The crowd, still silent, parted for him. He smiled at those he knew. Few smiled back. As he moved through the crowd, a murmur of conversation arose. By the time he reached the exit, the normal hubbub had returned to the Bunce Inn, the Senator's once-favorite tavern, where he had been recruited long ago to run for clerk on the Shire First ticket. He would never set foot in the place again. He stood on the threshold, listening to the noise behind, then cut it off by closing the door.

The night air was hot and rank and stifling. Amid the waiting wagons and carriages and mules and two-wheeled pedal devices that the smart set rode nowadays, the Senator's little troll-cart looked foolish in the lamplight. As did his two truant bodyguards, who were leaning against a sagging, creaking carriage, locked in a passionate embrace. The Senator decided he hadn't seen that; he had seen enough today. He cleared his throat, and the trolls leaped apart with much coughing and harrumphing.

"Home," the Senator snapped. Eyeing the uneven pavement, he stepped with care to the cart, sat down in it, and waited. Nothing happened. The trolls just looked at one another, shifted from foot to foot. The Senator sighed and, against his better judgment, asked: "What is it?"

The trolls exchanged another glance. Then the one on the right threw back his shoulders—a startling gesture, given the size of the shoulders involved—and said: "Gogluk quit." He immediately turned to the other troll and said: "There, I said it."

"And you know that goes double for me," said the other troll. "Let's go, hon. Maybe some fine purebred halfling will take this old reprobate home."

Numb but for his dangling right hand, which felt as swollen as a pumpkin, the Senator watched the trolls walk away arm in arm. One told the other: "*Spitting* on people, yet! I thought I would just *die*." As they strolled out of the lamplight, the Senator rubbed his face with his left hand, massaged his wrinkled brow. He had been taught in school, long ago, that the skulls of trolls ossified in childhood, making sophisticated language skills impossible. If it wasn't true, it ought to be. There ought to be a law. He would write one as soon as he got home.

But how was he to *get* home? He'd never make it on foot, and he certainly couldn't creep back into the tavern to ask the egregious Bracegirdle for a ride. Besides, he couldn't see to walk at the moment; his eyes were watering. He wiped them on his sleeve. It wasn't that he would *miss* the trolls, certainly not, no more than he would miss, say, the andirons, were they to rise up, snarl insults, wound him to the heart, the wretches, and abandon him. One could always buy a new set. But at the thought of the andirons, the cozy hearth, the armchair, the Senator's eyes brimmed anew. He was so tired, and so confused; he just wanted to go home. And his hand hurt. He kept his head down as he mopped his eyes, in case of passers-by. There were no passers-by. The streetlamp flared as a buzzing insect flew into it. He wished he had fired those worthless trolls. He certainly would, if he ever saw them again.

"Ungratefulness," the Senator said aloud, "is the curse of this age." A mule whickered in reply.

Across the street, in the black expanse of the Party Field, a lone mallorn-tree was silhouetted against the starlit sky. Enchanted elven dust had caused the mallorn and all the other trees planted after the War to grow full and tall in a single season, so that within the year the Shire was once again green and beautiful—or so went the fable, which the Senator's party had eliminated from the schoolbooks years ago. The Senator blew his nose with vigor. The Shire needed nothing from elves.

When the tavern door banged open, the Senator felt a surge of hope that died quickly as the hulking orc-shape shambled forth. The bastard creature had looked repellent enough inside; now, alone in the lamplit street, it was the stuff of a thousand halfling nightmares, its bristling shoulders as broad as hogsheads, its knuckles nearly scraping the cobbles, a single red eye guttering in the center of its face. No, wait. That was its cigar. The orc reared back on its absurd bowlegs and blew smoke rings at the streetlamp—rings worthy of any halfling, but what of it? Even a dog can be trained, after a fashion, to dance. The orc extended its horrid manlike hand and tapped ashes into the lamp. Then, arm still raised, it swiveled its great jowly head and looked directly at the Senator. Even a half-orc could see in the dark.

The Senator gasped. He was old and alone, no bodyguards. Now the orc was walking toward him! The Senator looked for help, found none. Had the wizard's visit been an omen? Had the confusticated old charm-tosser left a curse behind with his sharp-toothed staff? As the Senator cowered, heard the inexorable click of the orc's claws on the stones, his scream died in his throat—not because of any damned and bebothered wizard's trickery, but because of fear, plain and simple fear. He somehow always had known the orcs would get him in the end. He gasped, shrank back. The orc loomed over him, its pointed head blocking the lamplight. The orc laid one awful hand, oh so gently, on the Senator's right shoulder, the only points of contact the fingertips—rounded, mannish, hellish fingertips. The Senator shuddered as if the orc's arm were a lightning rod. The Senator spasmed and stared and fancied the orc hand and his own injured halfling hand were flickering blue in tandem, like the ends of a wizard's staff. The great mouth cracked the orc's leathered face, blue-lit from below, and a voice rumbled forth like a subterranean river: "Senator? Is that you? Are you all right?"

Sprawled there in the cart, pinned by the creature's gentle hand as by a spear, the Senator began to cry, in great sucking sobs of rage and pain and humiliation, as he realized this damned orc was not going to splinter his limbs and crush his skull and slurp his brains. How far have I fallen, the Senator thought. This morning the four corners of the Shire were my own ten toes, to wiggle as I pleased. Tonight I'm pitied by an orc.

The Big Rock Candy Mountain

A railroad bull was in charge, of course, cane-tapping around the planks till he tripped the trap, feeling two-handed up the post to find the rope-notch, hissing to himself like a slow leak.

Under the planks, six coppers were planted in a circle like fence-posts. One had a bumble drilling into his shin, kicking the sawdust out behind, and another sprouted dandelions from his knobby knees. Everything grows in the Rock Candy country, even a copper's dried-out joints. I once had a toothpick bloom halfway to my mouth, and that is true, as true as the average.

Penned inside the cop-ring, a little leather-faced woman in too-big overalls and a too-small porkpie hat sat in the grass, sharp chin on her knees and skinny arms wrapped around. She cussed a blue streak in a tired, raspy boy-voice, like she had wearied of it. "You withered-up hollowed-out skanktified old shits, old sons."

Me, I'd been down to the lake for a bowl of stew and was feeling belly-warm and prideful. Some miracles get stale with use and others go bad quicker than a Baptist flounder, but friends, a bowl of Big Rock stew—whether scooped from a lake or poured from a falls or welling up out of a crack in the rocks—will stay a miracle till the world looks level. So I was full of stew and full of myself when I stumbled upon the scaffold in the making. I sat beneath a cigarette tree and picked a good one and fired it up by looking at it, and puffing I called from the side of my mouth: "What's happening here, Muckle?"

The bull quit sniffing along the fat rope long enough to yell, "What's it look like?"—not that he knew himself, all the railroad police being blind since birth, if birth they could claim. They were all just alike, but only one came around at any given time, and he always answered to Muckle, so whether Muckle was the full-time name of an individual or a sort of a migrating title like a Cherokee talking stick I'd given up wondering long before.

The setting sun flashed off Muckle's dark glasses as he sniffed his way to just the right spot. "Ahhh," he said, gnawed the rope to mark the place, and started threading it through the notch.

"What has the lady done?" I asked.

"It ain't what Dula's done, Railroad Pete," Muckle replied. "It's what Dula wants to do."

"And that would be?"

"Dula wants to." He shuddered. "Dula's trying to." He spat. "Dula's hankering to, angling to, ootching and boosting to . . . work."

"Work!" snorted the prisoner.

"Work!" groaned the coppers.

"Work!" rumbled the far-off Big Rock Candy, its glittery crystal slopes to the north for a change. The ground shimmied. The air cooled. Mr. Muckle's dickey flew up out of his Sunday vest with a ping. A dark black cloud ate the sun and rained down on us a flock of roasted ducks, burnt on one side and raw on the other.

"I ain't neither," Dula said.

"You see?" Muckle screeched. "You see what the world is coming to? Not a one of them ducks edible!" He shoved his dickey back down and straightened his celluloid collar. The bulls always dressed as if for a railroad owner's ball—I suppose to show up the rest of us stiffs. "Shrimp bushes blooming with razors, chocolate streams hardening up, ice cream turning sour before it's even out of the cow—and it's all the fault of this one, a-using around here, a-using around there, all over Hell's Half Acre, trying to talk perfectly good people into what? Into hitching the Eastbound!"

At that my cigarette lost its taste, and I put it out with a look. Heard screaming in the distance late at night, the Eastbound left your bones rattling like rails; even hearing its name at sunset was enough to give a grown man the greeny ganders. The old-timers said we'd all ridden the Eastbound to get here, and were blessed to have forgotten the details. I looked at Dula again, the set of her jaw. There was something in her face I couldn't name, something I hadn't seen in a long time.

Muckle tied the noose, his face paying no attention to his hands. They were like two crabs fighting. "There ain't no way to ride no Eastbound no how," Muckle went on, addressing the topmost cigarette on the tree, "if you don't scheme and run and sweat and jump and climb and hide and fight and kill and that's work and to hell with it."

"Hell," groaned the coppers.

"Hell," moaned the Big Rock Candy, and blew a little airish fart. A pelter of peanuts came down, skittered off Muckle's hat brim.

"Pah! Poodle dogs," Dula muttered. "Keep on yapping, you pissant poodle dogs."

Muckle laughed like a cat getting cut the long way. No one had been hanged in the Big Rock country since the days of the one-page almanac, and he seemed to be having a high time reintroducing the custom. I'd heard many a tramp say, "Hang me if I ever work again," but I never took it, you know, for law.

I had decided to roll my own, so I snatched a paper from a passing breeze, pinched some loose tobacco off the ground, and set to work. I needed to watch that no more than Muckle needed to look at his rope-ties, so I regarded the prisoner with the edge of my eye. I had identified that long-gone thing in her face. It was need. Everything a human could want lying around for the taking in the Big Rock country, and there was a face full of need. Seeing it was like climbing into a boxcar halfway between Goddamn and Nowhere and being greeted in the cattle-smelling dark by a long-gone friend, or enemy.

"Got it figured full and complete, do you, Muckle?" I asked.

"I do."

"Working is a capital offense, is it?"

"That it is, Railroad Pete."

"*Trying* to work, even?"

"So it is said. So it must be."

"Well, then, Muckle," I said, watching the little fenced-in woman watching me, "who'll be doing the honors next?"

Muckle's hands stopped, but his head swiveled on its wattled neck and trained those eyeless panes at me. I fancied I saw my cigarette reflected in those black squares, but maybe that flame wasn't on my side of the glass at all. "Whazzat?" Muckle snapped. "Honors? What honors?"

"Well, if you yourself hang this gal, then one of the coppers has to hang you next. Because all this time I've been sitting here in the shade taking my ease and smoking freeweed, you've been out there working your ass off and fixing to work even harder, hauling an easily five-stone gal, if she's a day, completely off the ground and holding her there till she's strangled dead. I call that work, and I say more stew for me."

Muckle's jaw worked away, but no sound came out. The coppers gaped, frozen in place like a prairie-dog town. I do not believe the wood in a copper stops at the hips. The Big Rock Candy heaved again, and we all got a nice dusting of powdered sugar. I knocked it off with my hat.

"But what truly gets up between my back teeth," I went on, "is this. However much work it takes you, Muckle, to hang this woman, why, it's going to take two or three times that much to hang you. So whichever copper does that job will just have to take his turn in the noose, and the copper after that, and the copper after that, and before you know it, Muckle, we'll be completely out of coppers in these parts, save one. So I'll have to do the honors on him, and then I'll have to find a passerby to do me, and so on and so forth, and directly, why, this whole country will be put plumb out of business. No, Muckle, I've studied it and studied it, and I frankly see no way out, once you've set that hellish, inexorable vortex in motion."

Coppers never talk much, but after a long quiet time one of them rasped: "You could hang yourself, Muckle, after you do the gal, and break the cycle."

"Shut up!" Muckle said.

"We'd have to work to bury him," another copper said.

"Shut up!"

"Not if the cyclone got him," the first copper said. "The cyclone comes through here every day about five."

"We'd have to throw him in it, though, and we might miss."

"I'll do some throwing, if you don't shut up!"

"Maybe the gal would hang her own self."

"Hey, gal," the first copper called out. "You ain't feeling a mite sad, by any chance?"

Dula looked at me, and I looked back at her. "No, sir," she said, "feeling right as rain," and a little grape spo-de-o-dee spattered down from the sky. Some say the weather is the only thing you *can* do something about in the Big Rock country, just by thinking.

Well, the day got on, as days will, and those coppers jawed and hashed and gnawed the problem so long they took root where they were standing, and Dula just crawled out of the little thicket they had made. Bluebirds landed on their heads and sang a tune. Muckle had a hissy fit, threw down his rope, and stomped down the scaffold stairs, shaking his cane and cussing us both to a fare-thee-well.

"Well, ma'am," I told her. "I'm afraid it's the jailhouse for both of us."

We had a nice get-acquainted visit, she and I, as we led Muckle to the jailhouse, him being blind and all. We got the history out of the way early, since we couldn't remember peaturkey about our lives before we landed in the Big Rock country, and of course by definition nothing had happened since—just eating and sleeping and screwing around, and what is that to talk about? So we helped Muckle over the alky streams and the chocolate rocks and yessired him when he told us we should meditate on our sins, but we otherwise just goofed around. We laughed and laughed when we flushed a little covey of quail with bacon and fennel and buttermilk mashed potatoes, and later I blew her a smoke ring that turned into a spinning pineapple slice. She caught it on her index finger, and when she bit, the juice went everywhere.

It was a nice tin jailhouse, shining in the sun. Muckle shoved us in and slammed the door and felt around for the latch and locked it and threw away the key, which I caught and handed back to him as we came out the other door. "Much obliged," he muttered. "And you can just hush that laughing, Railroad Pete!" he called after us, as we strolled off nudging hips and elbows and meditating on sins yet to come. "Think you're so damn smart. Well, this troublemaker here is your lookout now!" Like I didn't know that already.

Sex in the Big Rock country, like all the other good things in life, is just plumb great, and we'll leave it at that. And when it's done and you roll over, right there at your elbow is a frosty mug of beer or a Cuban cigar or a straight-from-the-oven doughnut with the hot glaze sliding down. The system ain't noways Christian, but it's pretty damn workable all the same, and for a few weeks there Dula and I worked it for all it was worth.

But Dula wouldn't stop talking about the Eastbound and how to catch it, and about that fabulous land we couldn't even remember, but where—if you believed the tales—everything worth having had to be *earned*, was so hard to get, in fact, that no two people had everything the same.

"But Dula, if that's how those poor suckers have it, why, *we're* living the life *they* dream of, right here."

"How do you know *what* they dream of? Do you remember what you dreamed of, when you were there? I don't know about you, Pete, but I damn sure wasn't dreaming about a talking mountain that strolls around firing off cherry jawbreakers."

"Woof!" huffed the Big Rock Candy.

When I woke up at night, Dula might be sitting beside me, framed by stars, stroking my face, or she might be halfway up a licorice tree, hoping to glimpse the Eastbound as it screamed by in the distance.

We fought some.

One night I woke up and sat up at the same time, all a-sweat and chilled. I'd had my first nightmare, maybe the first nightmare ever in the Big Rock country. I turned to tell Dula about it, but she was gone, and so was the memory of the dream. Only it wasn't a dream, I knew; it was my past. It was me.

"Who am I?" I said aloud.

"Who!" said the Big Rock Candy. "Whooo! Whoooooooooooo!"

I got to my feet, mouth dry, and stared off toward the ridge where Dula must have gone. That wasn't the mountain's voice. That was the Eastbound, talking to me.

"I need to pack a bindle," I thought, and here came the memory of what a bindle was, and how I should pack it. I snatched up my blanket and shook it out and started throwing in whatever food was lying about at the time, all B's: Beluga, brie, bologna. Damn that Dula anyway. What other memories would I need before the night was through?

People that want to get around in the Big Rock Country, over to Cockaigne or Lubberland or Hi-Brazil, can just walk up to one of the mail trains and sit down and lift their feet up; that's how slow those rattletraps are. Canoeing's faster, and the river runs both ways. But the Eastbound wasn't one of those trains, and its tracks were off on the far side of the valley, nowhere near the lemonade springs, the crystal fountain, any of the sights. It was just a mile of gleaming rail running from tunnel to tunnel between two hills, with nothing to eat for a good hundred yards on either side.

You heard the whistle when the train was still miles underground, and for a half-hour that sound got louder and shriller and the tunnel mouth got brighter and the gravel started dancing and the rails strummed like guitar strings and yet it was a shock when *Boom*, out of that shotgun barrel in the hill blew a big black gleaming two-header locomotive in a thunderhead of smoke and ash and sparks that burnt your eyebrows, and *Whoosh* the thing seemed to *leap* to the next tunnel where it plunged howling back into the earth for all the world like a sea monster leaving the water long enough to spout and then rolling back into the cold and the dark.

I staggered more than ran through the no-chow zone because the ground was shaking so. The two-header had already gone down, and the cars were zooming by—blinds with one side door, open gondolas, insulated reefers locked up tight. No snatching hold of this train as it passed; only your arm would swing aboard. The only way was from above. And there was Dula just where I feared—a little white smudge in the night perched on the lip of the second tunnel, looking down on the train rushing by. I ran for her and screamed her name just as she let go and dropped into one of the gondolas and not thinking I kept running up the slope into the hanging black cloud that the two-header had vomited and I choked and plunged through to the crumbling brick edge of the mouth and here came three empty gondolas in a row, maybe the last ones I'd get. I took the last big step and couldn't hear myself scream as I hit the moving floor, tumbled, slammed into the oncoming wall. Man hit twice by train, lives. I was crumpled and hurting but I was—what was the phrase—I was *holding her down*. The train hadn't shaken me yet. I rode her, I held her down, as she rolled beneath the surface of the world.

I woke up on hot greasy metal beneath the stars, pine trees whipping past. My arms and legs and fingers and head all felt awful when I moved them, but they moved. I sat up, found my bindle, sipped water, gnawed bologna. Dula had to be twenty, thirty cars up, toward the engine. But how could I know for sure? A drop into the gondola of a speeding train is pure luck. You could drop between the cars or hit the deck of a boxcar instead. And how did I know *that?*

I tied my bindle around my waist, climbed the gondola's forward wall, looked down. Good. Steel bumpers, no need to ride the coupler this time. I eased myself onto the bumper, gauged the rocking of the blind next door, then made the jump easy. Every car has its niches and platforms and handholds, for the sake of the yardmen, but between yards they have their uses, too.

I worked my way forward along the train, up and over when I could, or around the sides. My parts complained, but they did what I asked, started reaching and stepping *before* I asked. I had done this before, many times, and I could do it again and again.

No wonder the Eastbound was so fast. Car after car as I clambered along held no cargo at all. But the train wasn't empty. Not by a long shot. And I recognized just about everybody I came upon—not individual faces, but I knew their types well.

One car was full of fakers, working by lantern light on their little doodads they sucker people with. One punched holes in a sheet of tin with a nail; one pounded two bricks together and scraped the dust into paper packets; the bearded one whittled. I said no to lamp brighteners and love powders and splinters from William Jennings Bryan's church pew, but before I moved on I tossed them a couple of sinkers—as good as money when playing seven-up in a blind at night.

In the corner of another car sat two cripples, one with a pinned-up jacket sleeve, one with a strapped-on peg leg. Like all cripples who meet on the rails, they were swapping tales about the day they didn't move fast enough. They talked at once, stories sliding past each other on parallel tracks.

"I heard it go into the bucket, I did. Made a little clang like a chicken foot."

"There was three swallows of whiskey left in the bottle, and when I woke up, the doc said I could have the rest, and he didn't charge me any more than what I had in my pockets."

"I lifted it, and foot and bucket and all wasn't nearly as heavy as the foot was many a long day."

"I still reach for things with it, and sometimes the candle or bottle falls over, so a ghost hand can do that much, anyway."

"I buried it behind the Kansas City roundhouse where it's soft, cause I was told otherwise it wouldn't rest easy and would itch me forever. It don't itch, but that big toe still aches something fierce when the weather comes up a . . ."

In mid-sentence the two cripples stopped talking and started unwrapping their clothes to compare stumps, and I headed on. Some things, even in a boxcar, are just too private to watch.

Whenever I reached a gondola, I tossed in my bindle and swung over the wall, hoping to raise Dula, but time and again I had no show. All were empty until I tossed my bindle practically on top of a half-dozen tramps sitting in a circle around a mushed candle. As I climbed in, they stared at me and didn't move. One held a jug ready to pour into the glass bottle held by a dough-faced old gal.

"No more!" she squawked, and the whole alky gang tensed to spring.

"I'm not thirsty," I said, quick. "Don't study about me. Just looking for a girl who dropped from a tunnel, that's all."

"No girl here! Not here!"

They stared at me some more. The old gal, satisfied, broke off looking and grunted to the stiff with the jug. He sloshed a little something into her wide-neck bottle, and she swirled it about. Another little slosh and swirl, and he stoppered the jug. They all leaned forward slack-mouthed, watching the old gal take one tee-ninchy sip from the bottle and sigh and pass it on. The water jug would cut it farther and farther around the circle till they were drinking the very memory of gin, and it would be time to go into town and raise another bottle or cup or dreg-drop of the stuff.

As the bottle went round they said a verse, taking turns at that, too.

"Sweet, sweet gin."
"Let us in."
"Sweet, sweet white."
"Light the night."
"Sweet, sweet booze."
"Tell the news."
"Throw my feet to the barroom seat."
"Gin is sweet."

Between that car and the next I crouched on the coupler and took a couple of swigs from my flask, holding the water in my cheeks and letting it seep down my throat slow. I punched the stopper three times with the side of my fist to jam it in good. Many a stiff has gone alky for lack of water.

After that I got more careful about just stepping in without an invite.

Sometimes I couldn't go over, and I couldn't go around. So I went under. It's a decent enough crawlspace down there, only it's deafening loud and the sides are moving and there's nothing to crawl on but trusses and rods. I wasn't proud; I rode the trusses. But then I hit a car with no trusses, so I made like a veteran, and rode the rods.

Beneath the car and running its length was a suspended iron rod, with maybe a foot and a half of space between it and the floor above. Once again, I knew this, and knew the technique. I eased myself onto the rod until I lay full length, hands gripping the rod ahead, legs locked around the rod behind. I inchwormed forward and felt I was flying, like a witch on a broom.

Lying face down, I knew the tracks whipped past a foot away. I couldn't see them in the pitchy black, as dense and solid as a wall. Staring at that wall like a banished child made me want to reach out, to test it with my hand, so to resist the temptation I lifted my head and looked forward, into wind like a hot greasy hand covering my face.

By turning my head to the left and sticking my neck out a little I could snatch enough outside breaths to keep from smothering, but I couldn't keep that up because it hurt my balance and because my eyes naturally focused on the most distant parts of the moonlit landscape, the parts that were moving hardly at all, as if I could just lift my topmost foot and step into them and walk away. That meant time to look down again.

I was face down when the roaring changed tone and the stars came out below me. I gasped and was nearly gone, but my hands and feet remembered. The train was crossing a river, and as the ties of the trestle whipped past I saw through them to the water below. Then all was black and close again.

Halfway down the rod. So far, so good. We plowed through an awful smell, gone before I could gag. Something dead on the tracks. Why in the world, people reading the paper always asked, would even a drunk lie down on the tracks?

My legs and arms ached. The vibration of the rod had roiled my stomach. My teeth hurt from chattering. Not much farther.

Then I heard a new sound up ahead, against the roar of the underside. Nothing regular, just a higgledy-piggledy pinging and clanking, like a youngun tossing pennies into a train.

I had no idea what it was, but it scared me to death. I couldn't move forward, toward that noise. I lay frozen, twined around the rod, staring into the blackness ahead.

The sound getting louder, closer. Pang, ping, thonk. No rhythm at all. It was the sound of someone going mad.

Up ahead, little flickers, like fireflies. No, sparks. Flashing up first here, then there—

Then I remembered.

Back! Back!

I shinnied backward along the rod as fast as I could go. It wasn't very fast.

Someone perched at the front of the car was playing out beneath it a length of rope with a five-pound coupling-pin at the end. The sounds, the sparks—those were the pin ricocheting off the wheels, the ties, the bottom of the car. A one-bullet crossfire. An old brakeman's trick to clear the undercarriage of tramps, if you can call murder a trick.

The pin lunged forward a foot at a time. Backward I inched, and inched, along a rod that was endless, beneath a car that lengthened above me like a telescope.

I inched, gasping. I tasted dust and metal filings. Kicked-up gravel cut my face.

Which would it be?

Wait for the coupling-pin in the teeth?

Or just let go, and let the railbed carry me away?

My foot hit the plate at the end of the rod.

I grabbed the corner strut, one hand at a time. I brought the legs over, one at a time. I squirmed around, got head and shoulders out, grabbed the bottommost outside handhold, hauled myself out and up and onto the bumper. It wasn't easy. I sat on the bumper, worn out, shaking, happy for now to be rocked between the cars. I wasn't alone. Someone sat on the opposite bumper, facing me, rocking left when I rocked right, like a reflection. That car was a gondola, and I now saw there was a light inside it, a glow that got brighter above the wall until it crested, blinding, like the sunrise. Someone holding a lantern. I saw now the figure opposite was Dula, bound and gagged and trussed to the braces. She squirmed and kicked her feet. The man holding the lantern shouted:

"Well, butter my ass and call me a biscuit! It's the one that got away. Swam right off the hook again, eh, Railroad Pete? Proud of you, son. You've proven yourself, you've passed the test. You're home."

They clambered in till the boxcar was packed slam full of stiffs—alkys, fakers, tramps of every shape and description, jostling one another as they rocked with the walls and floor. Even the cripples, who don't do a lot of traveling between cars, were swung down from the deck in a sort of bucket. They lurched straight to the corner and picked up their conversation. Only a few of the stiffs sat near enough the lantern to be seen, but I sure hoped they were the worst of the lot. Each was big and mean and looked like he'd taken a few coupling-pins in the face. They stared at the boss-man like dogs waiting for scraps to fall. I figured that scrap was me.

The boss-man was the highest class of stiff. He was a profesh. He wore a shiny black suit and a black shirt and a black tie and sharp black shoes and a snap-brim black hat with a black band and black horn-rimmed eyeglasses held together with black tape. Instead of sitting directly on the filthy floor, he sat on crumpled newspaper, and the edges floated up and down like slow wings in the gusts from beneath the boxcar door.

"Why, Pete," he said. "Don't tell me you don't know your old pal, your helper in time of trouble. You taught me all the rules of the road, how to ride at the top of the heap."

I sat across the lantern from him. Next to me was Dula, still bound and gagged and watching me like I was supposed to do something. I still had my bindle at my waist, so I could have a snack, I reckon, but I didn't see how that would help.

"I don't know you, mister," I said, just stalling for time. And it was true, though he did look kind of familiar, in the same vague way the others had.

"Why, I'm a profesh, now, Pete, just like you. Aren't you proud?"

"I'm no profesh."

"Not on this train, no," he said. "Only one profesh per train, and that's me."

He made a move with his hand like shooing a fly, and everyone in the boxcar, from the up-front uglies to the shadows in the corners, moved closer, knives and chains and brass knucks clicking and clacking like money, or better than money. A profesh never travels alone; that's how you know he's profesh.

"Meet the guys," he said. "Meet the gals. They climb aboard, they find their way to me, and the survivors, they join up. You know how it is, Pete. Why, it's the best job available on a moving train at night, for a man who knows the score, who knows who he is. The best opportunity and, indeed, the last."

"What sort of job?" I asked. "What do they do?"

The profesh tilted his head, slowly. His voice was velvet. "They mow the lawn," he said. "They park the cars when the Astors come to tea. They do things." He made a two-handed chopping motion in the air.

"Must be hard to get good help," I said.

"Oh, there's no shortage, Pete. Didn't this train strike you as sort of, well, crowded?" He stood and paced in the lantern light. "That's how it is on a train, Pete, when people keep getting on, month after month, every stop on every line, and no one—*practically* no one, Pete—ever escapes. Think of it, Pete. Every bindlestiff, boomchaser, team-skinner, shovel bum and tong bucker, every last ring-tail tooter the whole long rusty length of the Southern P., the Central P., the U.P., the U.T.L., the C.F.T., the C.F.X., everybody and his dog from every blown-away greasewood sagebrush town thinks El Dorado and Hollywood and Daylong Screw, Nevada, are just a toot-toot train ride away." He stopped, too close, looking down at me. "And the Big Rock Candy Mountain is further, even, than those. But not quite out of reach. Is it, Pete?" When I didn't answer, he kept walking. "Last time I saw you, Pete, it was somewhere past midnight, on a fast freight from Ogden to Carson City, and we shared a boxcar, just the two of us. You'd been pretty sick, and when you finally got to sleep, I sat against the door, for fear you'd wake up wild in the night, and step out. I did not sleep, Pete. Instead, I sharpened your brass knucks, hoping to please you when you awoke. I did not sleep, the door did not open, and no one and nothing passed me. Yet when I looked up from my razor and file, I was alone in that boxcar. And I never saw you or heard tell of you again—until tonight."

I didn't remember any of that, but so what? It was no crazier than the truth of where I'd been. I didn't like the way Dula was look-ing at me. I said nothing.

"All these years since, Pete, I have been riding the rails, holding her down in your absence, without your help, sucking smoke and eating skeeter stew, and I have watched. And waited. And stud-ied the scraps of newspaper that blew in during a full moon, and the chalk marks on fences and walls that no one recognizes, and squeezed old-timers for stories of ghost trains and forgotten rail-ways and phantoms on the tracks and crowded boxcars that were empty on arrival. I've done all that, Pete, all that and worse, and never got one station, one division, one rod closer to the Big Rock Candy—until tonight." He crouched, just in the edge of the lantern light. "Now, tell me something, Pete. Tell me one thing—no, two things—and we'll let you both off at the next stop, no hard feel-ings, no more questions asked. Where have you been? And how did you get there?"

"Suppose I don't know?" I asked.

"Then you get out and get under. And she joins us all for the rest of the night, and repeatedly, until we're done. Sort of an employee benefit." He pulled a barber's razor from his jacket, toyed with it in his fingers. "So," he asked, brightly, "how's the Big Rock stew? Good as they say? Cure what ails you?"

I don't know why I did it. Maybe I was just stalling some more. But in the same way it felt right, somehow, to go up and over that first gondola car, it felt right to pull out my bindle, toss it onto the floor, and kick it toward him.

"Taste for yourself," I said.

He sat motionless for so long that I got worried and thought Pete, your time has come. Then he shot out a hand and snatched up the bindle, slit it with one pass of the razor, and dumped everything onto the floor. His face fell.

"There's no stew here," he said, as if to himself. "Bananas . . . beets . . ." He pushed things around with the razor. He pinched and sniffed and opened jars. "Whew! That's some high-smelling cheese. And what the hell is this? *Fish* eggs? Damn." He started to giggle, a high-pitched sound I didn't care for at all. "I'll cut you for this, Pete, I swear I will, and the girl, too. I'll pass my razor to the cripples, they got plenty of experience." He speared the half-stick of bologna, held it up. "Bologna? *This* I couldn't get in any mom-and-pop in Tucum-fucking-cari?"

"Taste it," I repeated, because it still felt right, somehow.

The profesh stared at me, brought the bologna to his nose, sniffed. Sniffed again. He got interested, sawed off a hunk, nibbled it. Everyone strained forward. How long, I wondered, since they'd all eaten? The profesh chewed slowly, then more quickly, began to smile. He stuffed the whole wedge into his mouth, worked it while he cut another. "This isn't bologna," he muttered. "It tastes like . . . like . . ." He dropped the razor, lifted the stick to his face and began to tear into it with his teeth. "The taste! Oh, my God!" He chomped and slurped and slobbered, cheeks and chin smeary with bologna grease.

His followers, excited, stood and yelled and demanded their share. What no one seemed to notice but me was that the train wasn't rocking nearly so much, the racket outside wasn't nearly so loud. This train was rolling to a stop.

While the profesh danced the bologna jig, the braver ones snatched up the other things, began their own slurping and gnawing. Then they danced, too, whooping and carrying on and shouting hallelujah.

"It's true!" the profesh yelled. "It's true!"

Now, stopping a train is a funny thing. An engine starts slowing down miles before the station, and it's going no faster than a walk when it pulls in, but at some point, that engine has got to finally stop dead. And when it does, all those hundreds of tons of steel, in all that rolling stock strung out for miles behind, collide. A fifty-car train stopping is like fifty little train wrecks in the space of a second. And if you're standing on board that train, not expecting the jolt, and you're not braced. . . .

I braced—one hand on the door handle, the other arm around Dula.

Bang!

The profesh and two-thirds of the stiffs in that boxcar went flying, and I lunged forward, grabbed the razor, and cut Dula's ropes before most of them landed. I wrenched the door open and we both rolled out. I landed on hard-packed dirt, and she landed on me, mostly. We scrambled up, and ran.

The place looked like a thousand other deserted rail yards—handcars and crates, sidings and turntables, a wooden-staved water tank with only the H still legible, and all of it gray upon gray upon gray in the hour before dawn. We would never outrun them, once they sorted themselves out, but where could we go? Someone had to be around, however early. But all we passed were closed doors and dark windows. I stumbled once, twice. I started coughing.

Behind us the profesh screamed: "We're finally here!"

The farther I ran, the worse my coughing got. I lagged behind. I stumbled, staggered, leaned against a wall. At eye level, some hobo had chalked weird, unfamiliar signs onto the stone.

"What's wrong?"

I couldn't answer. My throat burned. My mouth tasted of copper. I bent double coughing. My drool was red in the dirt.

The profesh was right. I had been sick, powerful sick, when I landed in the Big Rock Country. And now that I had left it . . .

"Go on," I said. "I'm killed already."

I found myself staring at the hobo signs—stick men, houses, arrows, circles.

"No," she said, and tried to pull me along.

The profesh ran around the corner, whooping and hollering and tearing off his clothes, eyeglasses and all. "I'll beat everybody to the lemonade springs!" he yelled. At the end of a long trail of clothes, he leaped headlong into the dirt and wallowed, barking like a seal.

I could read those signs. Of course I could. I had chalked them there in the first place.

I remembered everything.

"Dula. Those eyeglasses. And his jacket. Get them. Please."

She did. I put them on. They fit fine. For the first time, I could see the wrinkles at the corners of Dula's eyes, and the tears welling up. I plucked the razor out of the dirt where I had dropped it. It had been mine, years ago. It still felt good in my hand.

"There they are!"

The whole pack of stiffs, the uglies in the lead, came charging around the building on both sides. They all pulled up short when they saw my new clothes, my eyes, the look in my face. Swallowing another coughing jag, chest about to split, I stepped away from the wall, braced my feet, tossed the razor from hand to hand, and tried to stare them all down.

"How dare you," I whispered. Louder: "How dare you." With all the air my rattling bloody lungs could muster, I roared: "How dare you abandon me—for that!" I thrust my finger at the poor crazy profesh, then at the writing on the wall. "This is the place I was crowned! I am Railroad Pete, and I am the King of the Tramps!"

Dead silence.

The old alky hag was the first to drop to her knees.

A second. A third.

Then, one by one, the rest. Wails and moans went up. Many lay facedown in the dirt.

"Mercy, Pete!"

"We didn't know you!"

"Help us!"

I felt a wave of dizziness, of weakness. My rattling breath was getting louder. It was like I was drowning inside.

Only the biggest, meanest-looking ugly was left standing. A badly stitched scar split his bald head like a one-track railroad. He stepped forward.

"You weren't so biggedy," he rumbled, "when I went fishing with this." He pulled from his moldy overcoat a rusty coupling-pin.

I couldn't hold back the coughs anymore. I hacked and spat and bent double, lost my balance, dropped to my knees myself.

The ugly showed all the gaps in his teeth and stepped forward, swinging the thick end of the pin like a club.

"Well, this will be easy," he said. "Long live the king."

"No!" Dula screamed.

I gurgled.

Then someone screeched, in a voice like a rusty handcar:

"Alms! Alms, gentlemen! Alms for the poor and blind!"

Coupling-Pin whirled.

Tap-tap-tapping through the crowd was Muckle, cane in one hand, tin cup in the other.

Coupling-Pin raised a hand, as if Muckle could see it through those black lenses. "Back off, you old bastard. Hit the grit, or you'll get what he's getting."

"Oh, a troublemaker, eh?" Muckle said. Ignoring Coupling-Pin, he tapped over to where I lay crumpled and gasping. People in the crowd were getting up. An upside-down giant, Muckle loomed over me. He prodded me with the cane. He ratcheted himself down on one knee, joints popping, and scuttled his fingers over my face. "Oh, my goodness, yes, I know this one. He's from my side of the tracks."

He struggled back up, leaning on his cane. No one offered to help. "Yes, he's a bad one and a hard case, all right," said Muckle, rubbing his hip. "One of our hardest."

"I'll fix him for you, Pops," said Coupling-Pin, stepping forward.

There was a sound like a mosquito, and then Muckle's cane was just *there*, in midair. The ugly stopped just shy of his neck hitting it, eyes big and breath held, like he'd nearly run up on barbed wire at night.

"One of *ours*, I repeat," Muckle said. The cane in his outstretched hand didn't waver a hair. "And he'll be dealt with by us, by me and my kin—and not by a turd like you."

The ugly whipped the coupling-pin around and harder than you'd hit a steer in a slaughterhouse slammed the blind man in the back of the head.

Muckle's glasses flew off. He hunched forward, naked face all squinched up, so many wrinkles between hairline and nose it was hard to find the two closed eyes.

No sign of blood.

No sign of damage.

He hadn't even let go of the cane.

The ugly looked at Muckle, at the pin in his hand, at Muckle again. The ugly's mouth was open.

Everyone's mouth was open.

Muckle slowly stood upright, eyes still closed but face relaxed, no longer looking hurt but just annoyed.

Everyone stepped back with a wordless sound of interest, a sort of *Hmm*, the sound a tramp makes when he sees the chalk for "Get out quick."

Muckle turned to face the crowd, wrinkly eyes still closed.

I told Dula, "Don't look."

Muckle reached up with his free hand, dug his fingers into his face and, hauling on the skin by main force, opened his eyes.

Everyone screamed.

The screams faded away quick, like the whistle of a fast mail.

After a while I figured it was safe to open my eyes, too. The yard was empty except for Muckle and Dula and me, but there was a whole lot of dust in the air, like after a stampede.

Between the chalked wall and a rain barrel, his back to us, knelt Muckle, sliding his hands through the rubbish and weeds. His hands stopped. He grunted. He had found his glasses. He wiped them against his lapel and carefully put them on, hooked each shank over its proper ear. He stood and turned toward us, his face horribly twisted, and Dula and I held each other. His jaw clenched and dropped and clenched again and his eyebrows rode up and down and he squinched his nose.

"God damn things never sit right, once they get bent," Muckle said, and made another adjustment with the side of his mouth.

Next I remember, I hung off a deck, coughing red onto the gravel far below. Something was wrong with the gravel. I could see every little piece of it. It wasn't moving.

Muckle was holding me over the edge while I got it all out. We were on top of a train in the deserted yard. What little air I could squeeze into my curdled liver and lights was being cut off by my collar, knotted like a noose in long bony fingers.

"He'll be all right, won't he?" Dula called up from the yard below.

"Don't you start worrying about him now," Muckle said, "after all the trouble you caused him and the Big Rock Country too. Ever since he hopped the Eastbound. Streams running vinegar. Potatoes you got to dig up. Hens laying eggs what ain't even cooked. Biggest mess I ever heard tell of, on our side of the tracks. Last straw, the Big Rock Candy itself shut down. Wouldn't do nothing but peep like a chicken. Turns out it was saying, 'Pete! Pete!' Why you think we've all been out beating the bushes? Humph! But don't you fret none, he'll be fit as a fiddlehead soon as he gets back to where there ain't no *Mycobacterium tuberculosis* running around. Spit it out, son! There you go. But as for *you*, little missy—you are banished from the Big Rock Country for good!"

"Well, la-de-da," Dula hollered. "That's hard news, considering I just about killed myself getting shut of the place."

I reached down a hand. "I'll miss you, Dula," I croaked out. "I'd stay here with you, really I would, if it wasn't fatal."

She stood on tiptoe and laced her fingers into mine. "Take it easy, Railroad Pete, King of the No-Count Bums. You found out who you are. Now it's my turn." She tugged away her hand. "No, Pete, I ain't gonna watch you go. It's bad luck. Go to hell, Muckle."

"You, too, honey," Muckle said with a wave of his cane.

I plucked at the edge of the roof for purchase, but the slipping was all in my mind. My view of Dula walking away was going black from the outside in, like the last picture in a Chaplin movie, right before "The End."

Muckle hocked and spat a big looey past my head. Where it splatted sprang up a purple orchid. Then Muckle snatched me from the brink and flung me to the middle of the deck like I was made of shucks.

The train jerked forward with a rusty screech. As the couplers pulled taut, a series of slams vibrated along the cars and through my sprawled body on the way to the caboose.

"You're off and rolling now, Pete," Muckle said, as we crawled beneath the water tank. He reached up, grabbed the long spout, and lifted his feet. As the groaning spout slowly swung him away, he called out: "I'll see you later, when you ain't such a mess. Right now, you're a damn sight too much like work."

Nothing special, this train, just a rattletrap old local, cars all mismatched, big letters on the sides that might spell something if hooked up right. I never saw a train you could actually read. The cars screeched and banged, and I held her down, sprawled on top, watching as the yard disappeared. It had been deserted, but as the train picked up speed, tramps sprouted from everywhere, in ones and twos and threes, scrambled from rain barrels and woodpiles and dropped from the water tank and slid down the side of the cut and ran silently alongside, tossing their bindles aboard and then making the leap and clambering on wherever they could. As we went into the cut and around the bend, three dozen shirttail-flapping tramps hung on to the boxes, every one of them my people. Up ahead, against the rising sun, was a pyramid better than 50 feet high, a sight known to every tramp in the West. It was the Ames Monument, the highest point on the U.P., all downhill from here.

Three months, two weeks, and four days after my return—for it was high time *someone* counted the days in the Big Rock country—I was sitting halfway up the slope of the mountain, taking the air and making plans, when a cinnamon-smelling westerly wind sprang up and the photograph sailed into me, *flap!*

I peeled it off my chest. Beneath a neon sign that said "Automat," Dula stood on the corner, hands on hips, dressed like a four-alarmer, from the red silk fascinator with silver webbing that wrapped her head, to the single-seam stockings that must have cost $2.50—look out!—$2.75 a leg. On the back of the picture were a dried, wiped-sideways stain that smelled like spaghetti and a few lines of chicken scratch with a penny pencil.

> Hi Pete The wind seems right today so Im throwing this off the Brooklyn Bridge hoping you get it I hope so Hows the weather Just kidding This aint no Paradise but it's still amazing what you can find just walking around Do you know the trains here got windows and seats too What will they think of next

Take it easy Railroad Pete but take it—Dula—New
York street New York town New York state New
York everything N.Y., N.Y., N.Y., N.Y.

Maybe I'd send a reply one day. Lace it into a shoe and drop it
into the Eastbound at the tunnel, then wait for a how-dee-doo back
to bubble up out of the stew.

I yanked a leg off a turkey bush and said aloud, by way of grace:
"The day I do that will be a no-fooling strange day."

If it was easy to send word back from the Rock Candy country,
why, everyone would do it, wouldn't they? And if I could send word,
who says it wouldn't get all messed up on the way to N.Y., N.Y., N.Y.,
N.Y.? Just hobo signs on a wall. She wouldn't know what she was
reading, what she had.

Mmm. Juicy. With a little cornbread dressing in the middle.

No, there's plenty to keep me busy right here. Got to get this
place organized. Many an opportunity in the Rock Candy country, I
see now, for a profesh who knows who he is.

Looky there on the ground—cranberry sauce. In a little shivery
puddle with a spoon in it, Betty Boop on the handle of the spoon.
All I have to do is reach out my hand.

"Boop!" said the Big Rock Candy, and peppermints peckled
from the barber-striped sky.

Daddy Mention and the Monday Skull

When old Wilmer guarded Block Twelve, there was no radio, because old Wilmer mistrusted people sitting around a box harking at nothing. But one summer the warden made old Wilmer use a month of his hoarded vacation time, for fear he'd cash it all in at retirement and turn out the lights of Tallahassee as he went. The first thing the guards did once old Wilmer was dragged onto the Trailways bus to his mama's in Pensacola was plunk a long-hidden radio onto old Wilmer's desk and get that thing cranking.

Daddy Mention, in Cell A for obvious reasons, was so near the guardroom that he got to listen to the radio, too, whether he wanted to or not. With one part of his mind, though both wood and blade were denied him, he whittled, without medium or tool or external motion, and with the other he listened, at first with resignation and then with sluggish interest, beginning to study how he might put this racket to use.

"And for all you folks who requested it, here's that hot new song from the Prison Airs, 'Just Walkin' in the Rain.'"

Prison Airs?

"Hey, Narvel," called the desk guard to the corridor guard. "It's those jailbirds from Tennessee."

Daddy Mention jerked a little, and in his mind his whittling knife jumped the grain and sliced his thumb. In his cell Daddy Mention sucked his bloodless thumb and listened to the Prison Airs, which sounded to him like a half-dozen colored men trying to sing white.

"They good, ain't they?" Narvel said. "When the governor brought 'em to the mansion to sing for Truman, Truman said, 'Governor, you ought to pardon every damn one of 'em.'"

Now Daddy Mention was two big ears and nothing more.

"Did he pardon 'em?" the desk guard asked.

"Hell, no," Narvel said. "You don't earn no votes in Tennessee by pardoning niggers—just by dressing 'em up and waxing their hair and putting them on the radio."

Amid their laughter, another song started, something about a tiger man who was king of the jungle. Daddy Mention planned never to see a jungle outside a Tarzan movie, but he thought he'd be loose in good honest swampland again before long. If these Prison Airs could go through the wall by singing to white people, Daddy Mention figured he could do that, too. He stopped listening to the radio or to anything except the reasoning inside his head, and an hour past lights-out, he achieved the perfect ironclad silver-dollar plan. For the next hour he turned the plan every which way and saw it shone from all sides, was in fact a plan without flaw, excusing only the technicality, the barely visible chink in the gleaming surface, that Daddy Mention could not sing one blessed lick, sang so bad from the cradle in fact that the mothers of the church had come to the house when Daddy Mention was seven and told his aunt she'd be doing a boon to the Lord if she yanked Daddy Mention out of the children's choir and gave the children a chance. "Well, Daddy Mention," Aunt Ruth said after the mothers left, though she called him not Daddy Mention but his true name, "Well, Daddy Mention, I reckon you and the Lord got to drum you up some other skills." The Lord had been so generous on that score that Daddy Mention, by using only a few of his God-given talents, had earned permanent room and board from the taxpayers of Florida. He knew he had improved his whittling by just thinking about it all this time in Cell A, because whittling was that kind of skill, like robbery and book learning and laying down a woman, but he knew singing was different, like carpentry and conjuring and marriage, a thing you needed a talent for.

Still, as Aunt Ruth said, there's no problem invented that a root somewhere won't cure, or help with, or at least distract from a little.

The next afternoon in the prison yard, Daddy Mention checked with the four-on-four players that it wasn't Monday and then paced the west chain fence and stared at the swamp. He stared through the links until they blurred and thinned and flew apart, and the sound of the game behind got farther away until it was just the basketball bouncing thump, thump, thump, into a wad of cotton, and then just Daddy Mention's heartbeat in rhythm with the bullfrogs. On the five hundredth beat, a rippling V appeared out in the green water. It was like a current around a stick where there was neither, just the V point heading for Daddy Mention. When the point reached the edge of the reeds on the other side of the fence a moss-covered snout lifted streaming, and way down at the far end of it a slitted yellow eye gazed at Daddy Mention. The other socket was a scarred knot like a cypress knee. The gator's head was so wide that Daddy Mention had to move his head, like watching horseshoes, to look from eyeball to eyesocket, which was left to right today. It was to this scaly hole that Daddy Mention spoke, knowing the good eye was only for appearances.

"Hello, Uncle Monday," said Daddy Mention, though no man chained to his ankle could have heard him.

"Hello, Daddy Mention," said a voice like the final suck of quicksand as the head disappears. That chained man would have heard and seen nothing but a swollen green bubble peck the surface. "I'm sorry," the voice went on, "that I can't rise from this water and shake your hand like a man, Daddy Mention, cause you done called me on the wrong day of o'clock. You know you ought to call on a Monday, if you want me at my best."

With the sliver of his mind not holding on and holding off, Daddy Mention vowed he'd sit in Cell A till Judgment before he'd call up Uncle Monday of the second day of a week. But Daddy Mention knew better any day than to flap gums with Uncle Monday, because that just gave him more time to work at you like the Sewanee working its bank. With most of his mind Daddy Mention stuck with the program, and said:

Sunday's dying
And Saturday's dead
Friday's crawling
Into Thursday's bed
Wednesday's drunk
And Tuesday's fled
And Monday's bound
With a piece of—

The vast scaly thing in the water thrashed in place as if speared, roaring and slamming up sheets of water with its railroad-tie tail (and even the guard in the corner tower thought maybe he heard a beaver slide into the shallows, then forgot it before he could turn his head), but it was too late for Uncle Monday, for Daddy Mention already had flung down a three-inch piece of thread, which stretched taut as barbed wire when it hit the ground. Uncle Monday writhed and puked and snarled horrible things, but he finally settled down, his white belly heaving in the murked-up water. He blew a long blubbery breath and said: "Name it, then."

"Make me sing," said Daddy Mention.

"You'll sing," said Uncle Monday, grinding his many teeth, "when I gnaw off your generations."

"Make me sing," said Daddy Mention, sticking to the program. "Make me sing like a mockingbird's mama, like a saint, like a baby, like the springs on a twenty-dollar bed."

"Huh," said Uncle Monday, and the hard-packed dirt at Daddy Mention's feet boiled like an antbed. By the time he jumped back, the dirt had stopped moving around a moss-covered, snaggle-toothed, hang-jawed human skull.

"What devilment is that?" blurted Daddy Mention, and Uncle Monday nearly got his mind. Wrestling it back was a near thing, and Daddy Mention had to bite his own tongue bloody to do it.

"Old bullets well up in my hide," said Uncle Monday, pleasant and dreamy as if crosslegged on a veranda, as Daddy Mention gagged and choked and reeled, "and work their way out as the months pass, and leave a scar. This skull is one of the Earth's old bullets. Rub it, Daddy Mention, and it will smile at you, and while it smiles at you with favor, you will sing."

Daddy Mention spat in the dirt, wiped his mouth with his sleeve, gulped air, and—focused on Uncle Monday all the while—leaned down and rubbed the skull. It was hot and wet and grainy and barked his fingers like an emery board. He stepped back. The skull sat in the dirt, a vacant, crusty hunk of bone with a kick-sized crack in the temple. Daddy Mention stared and stared, and then, before his disbelieving eyes, the skull . . . just kept lying there, deader than dead. It kept on doing that for a long while. And then, just as Daddy Mention was about to lose patience and give that old skull a matching dent with his foot, just as he realized Uncle Monday had made a fool out of him again from age-old habit and cruelty and contempt for all who go two-legged daily, just as he could taste the bitter burn of years climbing his throat to be swallowed again, why, at that precise moment, the old skull that had shown no previous sign of life . . . did not do one goddamn thing. Daddy Mention kicked it across the yard. It rolled nearly to the feet of two blurred prisoners pitching horseshoes in real time, one gray U drifting through the air like a milkweed.

"Damn your evil soul," Daddy Mention said. "You told me this skull would smile on me with favor, and make me sing."

"And so it will," said Uncle Monday, subsiding like an eroded sandbar or a rotten log. "And so it will . . . on Mondays." A smoke curl rose from the string, burnt out like a fuse, and then Uncle Monday was gone.

When they blew the coming-in, Daddy Mention, in real time again, walked back inside with all the others. No one noticed that beneath his shirt, under his arm, Daddy Mention cradled something. No one noticed, either, because Daddy Mention already looked twice as old as Methuselah, that in the exercise yard that afternoon, from going-out to coming-in, he had aged exactly three years, one per minute of Monday's time, one per inch of thread.

The next Monday, an hour before lights-out, Daddy Mention wrinkled his nose, rubbed the nasty skull, hid it beneath the cot behind the bucket, and began to sing.

He had given no thought to material. He'd just sing any of the many songs he picked up in turpentine camps and sawmills and boatyards and boxcars and prison after prison after prison. He decided to start with "Gotta Make a Hundred." He cleared his throat and hummed, *Hmmm,* as preachers sometimes did to launch a song, as if tuning themselves. Then he took a deep breath and began:

> *Lord, I'm running, trying to make a hundred*
> *Ninety-nine and a half won't do . . .*

Except it didn't come out. He thought the words, but his mouth and tongue and lungs and gut didn't cooperate. What came out instead was one of those happy, bouncy, dumbass songs on Narvel's radio all week, a song Daddy Mention didn't know he knew. What came out of his mouth was "If I Knew You Were Coming I'd Have Baked a Cake."

Uncle Monday was having some fun.

Daddy Mention sat dumbfounded. It was his voice, all right, and not the gal's on the radio, but it sounded too damn good to be him. Held a tune and everything. His mouth and equipment were a bellows being worked by other hands, something Daddy Mention sat above and apart from, the balcony looking down on the band. He was about two words ahead of his mouth in knowing the song, as if someone were dictating into his ear.

"What the hell?"

"Pipe down!"

"It's him. It's Daddy Mention."

"Get out."

"Yeah! Look!"

When that song finished, the next one started, then the next. Not work-camp songs. Popular songs. Hit-record songs. White songs. They poured from his gullet like he had taken syrup of Ipecac and couldn't empty himself fast enough. They left a taste like Ipecac, too. The second song was "Rag Mop," then "The Cry of the Wild Goose," then "Bonaparte's Retreat," and Daddy Mention knew them all just in time to sing them, and knew their titles, too. In front of his cell stood the guards of the block, gray-faced, jawstrings popped. The prisoners in their cells whooped and hollered. Daddy Mention sang "April in Portugal" and "A Guy Is a Guy" and "The Little White Cloud That Cried." He had no control over what came up. He was like a nickel jukebox. The whole corridor was full of guards, coming from the four corners to stare like Daddy Mention was an after-hours sideshow. Daddy Mention's face hurt from being worked in strange ways, but still the songs and the guards kept coming. He sang "Glow Worm" and "Tennessee Waltz" and "How Much Is That Doggie in the Window?" Some of the guards barked along, Woof! Woof! He sang "On Top of Old Smokey" and "Sweet Violets" and "How High the Moon" and "Harbor Lights." The guards laughed, whistled, snapped their fingers, danced, cut shines. The guards got louder, the prisoners quieter. Too many guards meant trouble, and so did an obvious hoodoo job. Now the warden was on tiptoe behind the guards like Zacchaeus, come down in his flannels to see for himself that the whole goddamn Hit Parade was indeed venting from the coils and recesses of Daddy Mention—who was now taking requests, things that weren't even English: "Vaya Con Dios" and "Eh Cumpari" and "C'Est Si Bon" and "Auf Wiedersehen Sweetheart" and "Abba Dabba Honeymoon." He had no more control over the singing than a cow the milking, but he had possession of the rest of his body, and so he started to work the crowd a little, add dance steps, hand gestures, a wiggle of the hips, some flash. He high-kicked his way through "Music Music Music," and that was the show-stopper. As the warden led the cheers of "Encore!" Daddy Mention tensed, mouth open, for a next outburst that didn't come. He swallowed; his throat was dry and sore. He waited.

Nothing.

"Show's over," Daddy Mention said, all energy gone.

And he now realized, as the guards and the warden hollered for more, that for quite some time, while playing Mister Bones for the white folks and getting beyond himself, he had not been alone in his mind. That second barely-there presence now ebbed, not before Daddy Mention clearly heard, more as an inner-ear tingle than a sound, someone—some*thing*—chuckle.

The trusties had moved three rows of cafeteria benches into the exercise yard, with folding chairs up front for the warden and the governor and the yes-men. All the prisoners were locked up tight for Daddy Mention's semi-public debut, but the benches were full of invitees—School Board members, Rotarians, preachers, city councilmen, Junior Leaguers, Daughters of the Confederacy, Sons of Confederate Veterans, White Citizen's Council officers, turpentine magnates, all the quality for miles, eating Woolworth's popcorn and drinking pink punch and murmuring in expectation of helping (as the warden had put it) a wayward Negro boy rehabilitate himself through song. Several had shiny pennies to give the performer after the show, if the warden would allow it. Stapled to the benches, leftover Christmas bunting flapped red and green in the rising breeze. The atmosphere was as festive as it gets with a prison in front and a swamp behind.

Up front, the warden, his bald head beginning to sunburn, chatted with the governor, who sat crosslegged and fidgety, wiggling his right foot, exposing a length of shiny new sock with clocks on it. He was technically only the acting governor, because the real governor lay on his deathbed in Tallahassee, watched always by rotating shifts of the acting governor's yes-men. He had lain there for ten months. The governor had hundreds of infant constituents named for him who were not even conceived when he began to die. Month after month the minions of the acting governor sat at the governor's bedside, keen for cessation of breathing. More than one lifted a pillow and punched it and hefted it and checked the door and was tempted, but set it down again because he was a Democrat and had standards.

"Tell me again, Warden," the acting governor said, "why your caged mockingbird sings only on Monday?"

The acting governor encouraged everyone to call him simply "Governor," as a time-saver. "Well, Governor," the warden began, then faltered. His head began to hurt whenever he was asked this question. Daddy Mention had explained this peculiarity at great length—it was something about a family gopher, no, wait, that would be silly, a family goopher, a hex on all his kinfolk that enabled singing only one month per decade, and that on Mondays—but the warden couldn't remember the half of it. And whenever he tried to reconstruct the conversation, which had seemed convincing at the time, he had an unsettling trace memory of Daddy Mention leaning across his desk blotter and blowing dust into his face, but that couldn't have happened. Could it? He tried to tell some of this to the acting governor, who waved him off.

"No, no, never mind, I'm sorry I asked. Do I care what day I'm summoned to take part in a penitentiary minstrel show? It's not as if I have any other claims on my time. I only have a state to run, that's all. Why, I am at the disposal, the utter beck and call of your Grandpa Mumbly, or whatever his name is. Why, he can't even vote. Even if he wasn't in jail."

The circumstances of the acting governor's quasi-administration had left him with an unbecoming streak of self-pity.

"Warden, do you know how many miles of coastline alone I am responsible for, *de facto* if not *de jure?* Do you? Oh, come on, guess. You know you want to guess. Total miles."

The warden squirmed. ". . . A thousand?"

"A thousand, hmm? A thousand. Nice, round figure. Wholly inadequate, but even. Try four, try six, try eight thousand four hundred and twenty-six, hah? Hah, Rand McNally?"

"Here he is!" cried the warden, vastly relieved.

They had come for him at two, Narvel trundling back the cell door.

"Let's go, Daddy Mention," Narvel said.

"Go where?" He glanced at his cot, where the skull lay amid a jumble of sheets, covered by his pillow. "Thought the governor was coming."

"You don't think the governor's coming all the way in here, do you?" Narvel said. "He's waiting in the yard. Come on."

In the yard meant in reach of the swamp, and today was Monday.

Daddy Mention grabbed the bars. "Hold on, now. I got to think about this."

Narvel laughed. "What fool talk is that? Daddy Mention wants to stay *inside* the prison." The others laughed as they took hold of his elbows. "Come on, I said."

Daddy Mention hung onto the bars still, with surprising strength for an old man. He looked at his bedclothes again, for longer this time. "No, Mister Narvel, please," Daddy Mention said, his voice quavering. Those in neighboring cells caught this new note in his voice, and those who could, exchanged glances across the corridor. "Bring the governor in here," Daddy Mention went on, "I'll sing for him just as pretty. Oh, please, Mister Narvel, please don't make me go outside."

"Come forth, Daddy Mention," Narvel said, jaw set. The strong hands on Daddy Mention's arms redoubled their efforts, and a fourth guard grabbed around his waist, pulled backward till he was off his feet, still hanging on. Narvel worked to pry loose Daddy Mention's fingers. "Come forth, Daddy Mention, come forth," Narvel repeated, in a voice not his own, a voice like a cottonmouth gliding into a pool. "Come forth, Daddy Mention, come forth," said the other guards, sounding not like three men but one using three mouths. Narvel, eyes shining faintly yellow, whipped out his pigsticker and went for Daddy Mention's fingers with the blade. Daddy Mention let go of the bars, and the guard at his waist stumbled backward. The skin of the guard's hands looked pebbled-up and scaly. "Come forth, Daddy Mention, come forth."

Daddy Mention looked long and hard over his shoulder at the cot as they hauled him out. What did he have to do, hit these crackers on the head?

"Hey, Narvel!" cried Creflo the bootlegger in Cell B.

Narvel jerked, startled, and blinked the yellow out of his eyes. He shook his head as if to clear it. "What is it, Creflo?"

"I think Daddy Mention's got something hid in there," Creflo said, S-sounds whistling through the gap in his top teeth.

"Is that right?" Narvel was himself again. "Check it out, Dell."

Daddy Mention scowled at Creflo and thought, *Thank you, brother.* Creflo, who lacked the gift for sending, just nodded and grinned. *You're welcome,* that meant, clear to anybody, gift or no gift.

Dell jumped back with a cry, bedclothes in hand. "Damn, Narvel, look at this! Daddy Mention's a body snatcher!"

There sat the skull, the sheet around it stained brown like tobacco juice.

Narvel snatched Daddy Mention close by the collar. "What the hell you up to, boy? Trying to lure the governor down here, work some hoodoo on him?"

"No, sir," Daddy Mention said. He cringed and teared up and trembled, proud and disgusted at pulling the mushmouth so well when he had to. "I don't know where that skeery thing come from.

It's hainted, I swears it is. Oh, please, sir, leave it be. I don't want nothing to do with it."

"Oh, no? Dell, bring Daddy Mention's play-pretty with us. We'll have a talk with the warden later about your witchy ways."

Daddy Mention rolled his eyes and sobbed and pleaded and exulted.

Dell made no move. "Huh-uh. I ain't touching that thing."

Narvel flipped out his pigsticker again and twirled it in his fingers like a little baton. Narvel could be scary even when he wasn't possessed. Dell sidled forward and yanked free the corners of the sheet. He gathered them up and held the sheet, skull and all, away from his body like it was outhouse dirt.

Daddy Mention stumbling in front, Dell creeping behind, the little procession walked down the corridor. The other prisoners listened as one door, a farther door, an even farther door was unlocked and relocked behind. The clanks got fainter, the echoes more ghostly. When they were half memory, Creflo spoke.

"I got a quarter says he won't be back."

There were no takers.

The sight of Daddy Mention disappointed a number of spectators, mostly female, as they had hoped for a younger, more robust specimen of repentant male Negritude.

The warden joined the little party at the single microphone, which he covered with one hand to ask, "What's in the bag?"

"Hoodoo contraband," Narvel said.

"Scary shit," Dell cried, at the same time.

"Tell me later," the warden said. "Just keep it out of sight till they go." He removed his hand and spoke. "Good afternoon, ladies and gentlemen . . ."

As the warden droned, Daddy Mention smelled the air: a whiff of rot, growing stronger. He tasted the breeze: out of the swamp, picking up. He listened past the warden, past the rippling crepe, past the weary sighs of the acting governor, past the cranes hollering in the trees, and heard wet footsteps coming closer, *squelch, squelch.* Then applause drowned them out, and Daddy Mention stood alone.

He figured he was ready. Daddy Mention had nearly worn out the skull rubbing it before Narvel came for him. The wind from the swamp was really whipping now. A popcorn box tumbled to rest, spraying white puffs, at Daddy Mention's feet. He knew Uncle Monday was coming, but he had to speed him up some, for the gift he had fashioned in his mind wouldn't last, and Uncle Monday had to be a whole lot closer when he got it, if this was going to work at all. And so Daddy Mention found himself doing that thing he once vowed never to do: calling Uncle Monday on his very day.

Not that the crowd could hear him, of course. As far as they could tell, he was just standing there, leaning into the breeze, his eyelids half-closed and fluttering.

Someone coughed.

"Well, this is fun," the acting governor told the warden. "Is there no end to the man's talents? He doesn't sing, and he has seizures, too."

"God damn, I'll make him sing," muttered Narvel. He stood and strode forward, fists clenched, only to stop dead with a grunt about three feet from Daddy Mention, as if he had bellied into an electric fence. As the crowd murmured, Narvel slowly turned.

"What's wrong with his eyes?" a woman asked.

Narvel's jaw slowly sagged, dragging his mouth open. Deep inside, something gurgled. Then a voice not Narvel's own emerged, as his jaw worked up and down, not in sync with the words:

"Raw head and bloody bones, rise up and shake yourself. He's halfway here."

Dell jumped to his feet shrieking, because from within the sheeted bundle beneath his bench had come a sound like a cricket chirping: *Rick-de-rick, rick-de-rick, rick-de-rick!*

"Raw head and bloody bones, rise up and shake yourself. He's mostways here."

Dell's bundle slid forward several feet, caught no doubt in a sudden gust from the swamp, though it might have kept moving after the gust died. *Rick-de-rick, rick-de-rick, rick-de-rick!*

Not even the acting governor was joking now. Everyone but Narvel and Daddy Mention sat, frozen. Something yanked up Narvel's right arm, so that it might have been pointing, had the hand not flopped at the wrist like a scarecrow's.

"Raw head and bloody bones, rise up and shake yourself, for Monday's here!"

The wind ripped open the sheet and the skull tumbled out, rolled to a stop at Daddy Mention's feet. *Rick-de-rick, rick-de-rick, rick-de-rick!*

Daddy Mention opened his eyes and smiled. As he squinted into the wind he could make out, in the distance, a tiny dark two-legged figure in a hat, striding ever nearer across the swamp, across the surface of the deep water.

Daddy Mention sometimes wondered why he always took free and bedeviled over locked up and safe, but he couldn't change how he was, any more than Uncle Monday could choose his walking days. There are higher powers in this old world, his Aunt Ruth used to say, and that old woman didn't know the half of it. One day Daddy Mention was going to find those higher powers, and open up a can of whupass. But right now Uncle Monday was laying hold of him. Narvel dropped like an empty sack as Uncle Monday, still a hundred yards distant, pried open Daddy Mention's mouth and began, though him, to sing. It was a song that got amongst the audience like a moccasin in a swimming hole. It carried without need of amplification, without need of eardrums. It was Uncle Monday's song.

Uncle Monday's on his way, better strike a deal
You know he ain't never one to miss a meal
Uncle Monday
Uncle Monday
Uncle Monday Uncle Monday Uncle Monday

Uncle Monday's been dead for many a year
But he keeps hanging round cause he likes it here
Uncle Monday . . .

Uncle Monday likes to crawl up onto the land
Go two-legged dancing like a natural man
Uncle Monday . . .

Uncle Monday goes a-strolling on the second day
He'll let you keep your money, steal your soul away
Uncle Monday . . .

Uncle Monday has so many teeth sharp as a file
Can take you seven days just to watch him smile
Uncle Monday . . .

Uncle Monday walks Okeechobee like it was dry
While bobbin up behind him are the fish that have died
Uncle Monday . . .

His breath blows hot but his blood runs cool
And his nuts swing low like a Georgia bull
Uncle Monday . . .

When Uncle Monday wants a woman he just gives her a shout
She goes skipping into the swamp and never comes out
Uncle Monday . . .

Uncle Monday knows the swamp ain't all that it seems
And you know that wasn't just a panther's scream
Uncle Monday . . .

Uncle Monday made a raw head and bloody bones

Rise up and be a-walkin just to hear it moan
Uncle Monday . . .

Uncle Monday, there's a poor man got no legs
Yes, I swum up beneath him, cut him down a peg
Uncle Monday . . .

Uncle Monday took a trip down to hell and back
Toting seven governors in a croker sack
Uncle Monday . . .

Uncle Monday says have you a drink and a smoke
You'll soon enough be swinging from a cypress oak
Uncle Monday
Uncle Monday
Uncle Monday Uncle Monday Uncle Monday

His walking form now was a dozen yards away and closing, and Daddy Mention could feel him pouring in, opening the skull-door wider, ever wider, in his eagerness to get in. *Rick-de-rick, rick-de-rick, rick-de-rick!* But here's a true thing: a Monday skull is a two-way skull. And while Uncle Monday was sending Daddy Mention his song, Daddy Mention was sending him something in return, something powerful, something he had spent several days whittling with his mind: A little squatty man carved from black oak, with Uncle Monday's true name cut into its stomach; this wrapped with black cloth and tied with black thread around a bundle of blackberry vines.

While Uncle Monday dealt with that, he lost his grip on Daddy Mention, the way a man who steps into a hive has concerns more immediate than honey. In the moment Uncle Monday was distracted, a moment in which Daddy Mention aged more than any human lifespan, Daddy Mention snatched up the microphone stand, swung its weighted base over his head like a hammer, and bashed the Monday skull into graveyard dust.

Then lots of things happened at once.

Daddy Mention, as near as Uncle Monday could tell, ceased to exist—for a few minutes, anyway.

The bad energies Uncle Monday had funneled through the skull sped out in all directions from the impact, like pond water fleeing a chunked-in brick. Snowballs pelted roofs in Key West. A sudden, pervasive hogpen smell emptied the white high school in Tampa. In Orlando, the screens of televisions showing a roller derby telecast flickered and, for just a few seconds, held the grainy silent image of a black man howling. In Tallahassee, the governor in his deathbed sat bolt upright with black orbs for eyes and rasped to the yes-man, "I have come back from where you are going," and fell back dead.

The full brunt of the flood, however, was borne by all those people in the prison yard, who briefly and horribly became aware of Uncle Monday's true nature.

Each reacted after his own fashion. There was moaning and sobbing and puking and tongue-speaking and St. Vitus dancing. Some just sat and moaned, and some ran, knocking their heads into the stone wall or tangling themselves in the fence where they might have been shot had the guards not been jibbering mad at the moment, too.

None of those doused by Uncle Monday that afternoon could remember it afterward, and you could say they all recovered within the hour, none the worse for wear. But the seeds had been planted. And so they found themselves, in the next month or so, for perfectly good everyday reasons (they thought), switching churches or getting saved or writing letters to the editor denouncing Jim Crow or preaching atheism in the town square or taking grocery-store bagboys as lovers or beginning to drink heavily or taking the pledge or buying two-tone Buicks or joining the Klan or the Masons or the Anti-Defamation League or giving all their possessions to colored orphanages or declaring for the fifth congressional seat or burning their hats or crying for two days, all because it's always Monday somewhere.

In the immediate aftermath, as everyone rubbed their heads and picked themselves up off the ground and tried to remember what had happened, it was Dell who first asked:

"Where's Daddy Mention?"

That seemed another uncanny mystery beyond human ken, until they found a cafeteria bench standing on end against the west wall, and discovered the acting governor's limousine was acting gone.

Daddy Mention's latest escape made neither the papers nor the radio, but every inmate in eight states knew about it by Tuesday at 3, when it was the talk of the yard at Tennessee State.

"Picked up Uncle Monday by his tail and slung him right over the wall!" said Marcell, the bass.

"God damn! I'd like to have seen that," said John D., the second tenor.

"Then he dusted the governor with some essence of bend-over and made him hand over the keys to his limousine," said William, the baritone.

"Lord amighty!" said Ed, the third tenor. "Tell it, now."

During all this, Johnny Bragg, lead tenor of the Prisonaires, whom armed guards had escorted to the Sun studio in Memphis to record "Just Walking in the Rain" and then escorted back again, stood in the corner of the yard, facing the wall, practicing a song titled "That Chick's Too Young To Fry." It was a song with meaning for Johnny Bragg, who at 16 had caught his girlfriend half full of another man, her eyes focusing on Johnny Bragg only long enough to wink. The police got there in time to arrest Johnny Bragg, some-how, on a rape charge, and as they had a file drawer of unsolved cases at the stationhouse, Johnny Bragg was now serving six 99-year sentences, which was entirely two many threes for comfort. But Johnny

Bragg knew he had not been delivered from blindness at age 7 just to stare at the walls of a 6-by-8 cell, so he practiced, food bucket over his head for reverb, while his sorry excuse for a vocal group woofed the hour away. Johnny Bragg wondered whether Bill Kenny ever had this trouble with the Ink Spots. He doubted it. He yanked off the bucket, found the outside air just as hot and close as in, and said:

"Daddy Mention this, Daddy Mention that, Daddy Mention shit. How many times Daddy Mention ever got your asses over the wall? Huh? Marcell? Even you can count up to nothing. Are we going to practice today or not?"

The others made no move. "We was just talking," Ed mumbled.

"*Some* of us," said William, his shoulders back, thumbs seeking purchase on absent suspenders, "think a whole lot of Daddy Mention."

"I done time with him," Marcell said. "South Carolina, summer of '52. He whistled down an eagle and flew off over the Congaree. He did! I knew a man who talked to a guard who was in the yard with his back turned and heard it happen."

"Wait, now," William said. "It was Parchman he busted out of that summer. Raised so many sparks gnawing his bars he started a fire that he walked right through and out the door, Shadrach, Meshach, Abednego."

Now all the others chimed in with their own, competing accounts, and Johnny Bragg shook his head.

"My people, my people," he said. "My race, but not my taste. What does it matter how many prisons Daddy Mention got out of at once? Here we sit when Daddy Mention goes in, and here we sit when Daddy Mention goes out. You are four sad gum-beaters."

Johnny Bragg cast down his bucket and tried to walk away, but the effect was spoiled by a guard who made him pick it up. Those damn things cost money, and he didn't want to eat out of his *other* bucket, did he?

That night he woke to find Daddy Mention standing beside his bed, looking down and smiling. He was a lot older than Johnny

Bragg had expected. Johnny Bragg asked, you come to spring me? and Daddy Mention said, hell, no, and Johnny Bragg asked, why you here, then? and Daddy Mention asked, why are you? And then Johnny Bragg—who would never escape, who would serve another three years and be let out and be sent back to serve six more and then be released into a world where even the Ink Spots were forgotten—woke up a second time and woke up mad, that he had fretted his sleep on such useless dreams as that.

Late in the day of Daddy Mention's concert for the governor, old Wilmer, sunburnt and swollen like a boudin sausage, stumped down from the Trailways at the turpentine thicket on the highway, not real close to the prison but as close as the Trailways ran.

Old Wilmer mopped his neck with a scrap of tablecloth as he trudged the shady back road toward the coroner's entrance. Bluebottle flies zummed past. A faraway woodpecker fired off messages, send help send help send help. Old Wilmer set down his case, unhooked his suspenders, and made water in the road, just to watch his stream cut channels in the clay. Old Wilmer was in no hurry, because he knew that in his absence, the prison surely had gone teetotally to hell, and his mind projected Technicolor slides of chaos and ruin.

He stopped on the plank bridge for a cigarette. As he slung his match into the scum, he thought someone was watching beneath the surface of the water, and the sweat beaded cold on the back of his buzz-cut neck. But then it was just a big old gator, still as a cypress log and playing dead. Full of deer, probably, or coon dog. Every time the hounds were let loose in the swamp, one or two didn't come back, and the warden would cry like a woman. They lost a lot more dogs than men. At that moment, old Wilmer heard the hounds baying, as if he had summoned them.

Old Wilmer smoked and stared at the gator, and the gator's one eye stared back. When he was done, old Wilmer felt strangely respectful, did not throw the butt into the water but wedged it into the crack of his shoe between leather and sole, to save for the trusty who collected tobacco and was two-thirds of his way to a Winston by now.

Wilmer found turning his back on the gator surprisingly difficult. He looked back once. Standing stiff-legged on the bridge, arms hanging at his sides, was an old Negro in high-water britches, face shaded by a preacher's hat in the gathering dusk. Wilmer nodded once, the wary acknowledgment one Southern man gives another, and after a pause the figure nodded back—less a nod, really, than a jerk, involuntary, like a flinch from an unseen blow. With the nod was a brief pyrite sparkle in the shadow where the right eye might have been.

Old Wilmer turned and walked on, his fatalism stoked at every step by the baying of hounds and, now, the splashing and cursing of men. The first to stagger into view was that idiot Narvel, now rightly subordinate to the ass end of a hound, Narvel so muck-crusted and bedraggled and snarling that he clearly was on his third or even fourth fruitless sweep through the swamp—and then old Wilmer knew who, of all of them, had got out.

He set down his suitcase till he was done laughing. Then he picked it up and swung it as he walked, and whistled a nasty song his mama's nurse taught him over a Mason jar of coondick. Maybe he could get Cell A for a proper office, once it was cleansed. Surely no prisoner would be moved in there. Who knew what Daddy Mention left behind?

Guards ran in and out the back gate like roaches from a matchbox. Old Wilmer handed his suitcase to one, really just held it out so that the rushing other's pistol arm thrust through the handle and snatched it away as a train snatches mail. Old Wilmer wouldn't need it again for a long, long time. All he needed was here, inside a pair of boots in his locker. Narvel and the other guards might put their faith in locks and walls, muscles and guns, and the color of their skin, but

Old Wilmer kept his eyes open, and believed in whatever worked. If he laid down an X of Draw Back Powder, corner to corner of the cell, and burned a black-over-red candle at the crossroads, that would be a start. Old Wilmer reached into his pants pocket, touched the little nine-knotted bundle of devil's shoestrings, and strode whistling into the prison.

Much that is said about Daddy Mention is not true, and much of the rest is lies. Many of these lies were told by Daddy Mention himself to begin with, and he is always pleased, at a general store or a hog-killing or a shrimp boil, when one he invented is told back to him. They were whoppers to begin with, but my how they grew!

One night beside a campfire beneath a trestle, Daddy Mention held forth to a group of travelers about his many exploits: how he hacked through a prison wall with a single sharp toenail that wasn't even his; how, one August, he swam out of a jailhouse in a river of his own sweat; how he had so many garters from grateful warden's wives and sheriff's daughters that he was paying a granny woman to stitch them into a quilt; how he used a singing skull to reel in Uncle Monday himself like a bream on a line and then threw him on the governor; how he escaped a chain gang by holding his breath till they declared him dead and buried him; and all such tales as that.

Finally a man just beyond the firelight said, "I God, mister. You sound like Daddy Mention himself."

"That's what they call me," Daddy Mention said.

The man stepped forward, flashed a badge, and said: "Well, do you know who I am? I'm the sheriff, I'm the father of two daughters, and you are under arrest."

Daddy Mention replied: "How do, Sheriff. Allow me to introduce myself. I am the lyingest nigger on the face of this Earth."

Zora and the Zombie

"What is the truth?" the houngan shouted over the drums. The mambo, in response, flung open her white dress. She was naked beneath. The drummers quickened their tempo as the mambo danced among the columns in a frenzy. Her loose clothing could not keep pace with her kicks, swings, and swivels. Her belt, shawl, kerchief, dress floated free. The mambo flung herself writhing onto the ground. The first man in line shuffled forward on his knees to kiss the truth that glistened between the mambo's thighs.

Zora's pencil point snapped. Ah, shit. Sweat-damp and jostled on all sides by the crowd, she fumbled for her penknife and burned with futility. Zora had learned just that morning that the Broadway hoofer and self-proclaimed anthropologist Katherine Dunham, on her Rosenwald fellowship to Haiti—the one that rightfully should have been Zora's—not only witnessed this very truth ceremony a year ago, but for good measure underwent the three-day initiation to become Mama Katherine, bride of the serpent god Damballa—the heifer!

Three nights later, another houngan knelt at another altar with a platter full of chicken. People in the back began to scream. A man with a terrible face flung himself through the crowd, careened against people, spread chaos. His eyes rolled. The tongue between his teeth drooled blood. "He is mounted!" the people cried. "A loa has made him his horse." The houngan began to turn. The horse crashed into him. The houngan and the horse fell together, limbs entwined. The chicken was mashed into the dirt. The people moaned and sobbed. Zora sighed. She had read this in Herskovitz, and in Johnson too. Still, maybe poor fictional Tea Cake, rabid, would act like this. In the pandemonium she silently leafed to the novel section of her notebook. "Somethin' got after me in mah sleep, Janie," she had written. "Tried tuh choke me tuh death."

Another night, another compound, another pencil. The dead man sat up, head nodding forward, jaw slack, eyes bulging. Women and men shrieked. The dead man lay back down and was still. The mambo pulled the blanket back over him, tucked it in. Perhaps tomorrow, Zora thought, I will go to Pont Beudet, or to Ville Bonheur. Perhaps something new is happening there.

"Miss Hurston," a woman whispered, her heavy necklace clanking into Zora's shoulder. "Miss Hurston. Have they shared with you what was found a month ago? Walking by daylight in the Ennery road?"

Doctor Legros, chief of staff at the hospital at Gonaives, was a good-looking mulatto of middle years with pomaded hair and a thin mustache. His three-piece suit was all sharp creases and jutting angles, like that of a paper doll, and his handshake left Zora's palm powder dry. He poured her a belt of raw white clairin, minus the nutmeg and peppers that would make it palatable to Guede, the prancing black-clad loa of derision, but breathtaking nonetheless, and as they took dutiful medicinal sips his small talk was all big, all politics—whether Mr. Roosevelt would be true to his word that the Marines would never be back; whether Haiti's good friend Senator King of Utah had larger ambitions; whether America would support

President Vincent if the grateful Haitians were to seek to extend his second term beyond the arbitrary date technically mandated by the Constitution—but his eyes, to Zora who was older than she looked and much older than she claimed, posed an entirely different set of questions. He seemed to view Zora as a sort of plenipotentiary from Washington, and only reluctantly allowed her to steer the conversation to the delicate subject of his unusual patient.

"It is important for your countrymen and your sponsors to understand, Miss Hurston, that the beliefs of which you speak are not the beliefs of civilized men, in Haiti or elsewhere. These are Negro beliefs, embarrassing to the rest of us, and confined to the canaille—to the, what is the phrase, the backwater areas, such as your American South. These beliefs belong to Haiti's past, not her future."

Zora mentally placed the good doctor waistcoat-deep in a backwater area of Eatonville, Florida, and set gators upon him. "I understand, Doctor Legros, but I assure you I'm here for the full picture of your country, not just the Broadway version, the tomtoms and the shouting. But in every ministry, veranda and salon I visit, why, even in the office of the director-general of the Health Service, what is all educated Haiti talking about but your patient, this unfortunate woman Felicia Felix-Mentor? Would you stuff my ears, shelter me from the topic of the day?"

He laughed, his teeth white and perfect and artificial. Zora, self-conscious of her own teeth, smiled with her lips closed, chin down. This often passed for flirtation. Zora wondered what the bright-eyed Doctor Legros thought of the seductive man-eater Erzulie, the most "uncivilized" loa of all. As she slowly crossed her legs, she thought: Huh! What's Erzulie got on Zora, got on me?

"Well, you are right to be interested in the poor creature," the doctor said, pinching a fresh cigarette into his holder while looking neither at it nor at Zora's eyes. "I plan to write a monograph on the subject myself, when the press of duty allows me. Perhaps I should apply for my own Guggenheim, eh? Clement!" He clapped his hands.

"Clement! More clairin for our guest, if you please, and mangoes when we return from the yard."

As the doctor led her down the central corridor of the ginger-bread Victorian hospital, he steered her around patients in creeping wicker wheelchairs, spat volleys of French at cowed black women in white, and told her the story she already knew, raising his voice whenever passing a doorway through which moans were unusually loud.

"In 1907, a young wife and mother in Ennery town died after a brief illness. She had a Christian burial. Her widower and son grieved for a time, then moved on with their lives, as men must do. *Empty this basin immediately! Do you hear me, woman? This is a hospital, not a chickenhouse!* My pardon. Now we come to a month ago. The Haitian Guard received reports of a madwoman accosting travelers near Ennery. She made her way to a farm and refused to leave, became violently agitated by all attempts to dislodge her. The owner of this family farm was summoned. He took one look at this poor creature and said, 'My God, it is my sister, dead and buried nearly 30 years.' Watch your step, please."

He held open a French door and ushered her onto a flagstone veranda, out of the hot, close, blood-smelling hospital into the hot, close outdoors, scented with hibiscus, goats, charcoal, and tobacco in bloom. "And all the other family members, too, including her husband and son, have identified her. And so one mystery was solved, and in the process, another took its place."

In the far corner of the dusty, enclosed yard, in the sallow shade of an hourglass grove, a sexless figure in a white hospital gown stood huddled against the wall, shoulders hunched and back turned, like a child chosen It and counting.

"That's her," said the doctor.

As they approached, one of the hourglass fruits dropped onto the stony ground and burst with a report like a pistol firing, not three feet behind the huddled figure. She didn't budge.

"It is best not to surprise her," the doctor murmured, hot clairin breath in Zora's ear, hand in the small of her back. "Her movements are . . . unpredictable." As yours are not, Zora thought, stepping away.

The doctor began to hum a tune that sounded like

Mama don't want no peas no rice
She don't want no coconut oil
All she wants is brandy
Handy all the time

but wasn't. At the sound of his humming, the woman—for woman she was; Zora would resist labeling her as all Haiti had done—sprang forward into the wall with a fleshy smack, as if trying to fling herself face first through the stones, then sprang backward with a half-turn that set her arms to swinging without volition, like pendulums. Her eyes were beads of clouded glass. The broad lumpish face around them might have been attractive had its muscles displayed any of the tension common to animal life.

In her first brush with theater, years before, Zora had spent months scrubbing bustles and darning epaulets during a tour of that damned *Mikado*, may Gilbert and Sullivan both lose their heads, and there she learned that putty cheeks and false noses slide into grotesquerie by the final act. This woman's face likewise seemed to have been sweated beneath too long.

All this Zora registered in a second, as she would a face from an elevated train. The woman immediately turned away again, snatched down a slim hourglass branch and slashed the ground, back and forth, as a machete slashes through cane. The three attached fruits blew up, *bang bang bang*, seeds clouding outward, as she flailed the branch in the dirt.

"What is she doing?"

"She sweeps," the doctor said. "She fears being caught idle, for idle servants are beaten. In some quarters." He tried to reach around the suddenly nimble woman and take the branch.

"Nnnnn," she said, twisting away, still slashing the dirt.

"Behave yourself, Felicia. This visitor wants to speak with you."

"Please leave her be," Zora said, ashamed because the name Felicia jarred when applied to this wretch. "I didn't mean to disturb her."

Ignoring this, the doctor, eyes shining, stopped the slashing movements by seizing the woman's skinny wrist and holding it aloft. The patient froze, knees bent in a half-crouch, head averted as if awaiting a blow. With his free hand, the doctor, still humming, still watching the woman's face, pried her fingers from the branch one by one, then flung it aside, nearly swatting Zora. The patient continued saying, "Nnnnn, nnnnn, nnnnn," at metronomic intervals. The sound lacked any note of panic or protest, any communicative tonality whatsoever, was instead a simple emission, like the whistle of a turpentine cooker.

"Felicia?" Zora asked.

"Nnnnn, nnnnn, nnnnn."

"My name is Zora, and I come from Florida, in the United States."

"Nnnnn, nnnnn, nnnnn."

"I have heard her make one other noise only," said the doctor, still holding up her arm as if she were Joe Louis, "and that is when she is bathed or touched with water—a sound like a mouse that is trod upon. I will demonstrate. Where is that hose?"

"No need for that!" Zora cried. "Release her, please."

The doctor did so. Felicia scuttled away, clutched and lifted the hem of her gown until her face was covered and her buttocks bared. Zora thought of her mother's wake, where her aunts and cousins had greeted each fresh burst of tears by flipping their aprons over their heads and rushing into the kitchen to mewl together like nestlings. Thank God for aprons, Zora thought. Felicia's legs, to Zora's surprise, were ropy with muscle.

"Such strength," the doctor murmured, "and so untamed. You realize, Miss Hurston, that when she was found squatting in the road, she was as naked as all mankind."

A horsefly droned past.

The doctor cleared his throat, clasped his hands behind his back, and began to orate, as if addressing a medical society at Columbia. "It is interesting to speculate on the drugs used to rob a sentient being of her reason, of her will. The ingredients, even the means of administration, are most jealously guarded secrets."

He paced toward the hospital, not looking at Zora, and did not raise his voice as he spoke of herbs and powders, salves and cucumbers, as if certain she walked alongside him, unbidden. Instead she stooped and hefted the branch Felicia had wielded. It was much heavier than she had assumed, so lightly had Felicia snatched it down. Zora tugged at one of its twigs and found the dense, rubbery wood quite resistant. Lucky for the doctor that anger seemed to be among the emotions cooked away. What emotions were left? Fear remained, certainly. And what else?

Zora dropped the branch next to a gouge in the dirt that, as she glanced at it, seemed to resolve itself into the letter M.

"Miss Hurston?" called the doctor from halfway across the yard. "I beg your pardon. You have seen enough, have you not?"

Zora knelt, her hands outstretched as if to encompass, to contain, the scratches that Felicia Felix-Mentor had slashed with the branch. Yes, that was definitely an M, and that vertical slash could be an I, and that next one—

MI HAUT MI BAS

Half high, half low?

Doctor Boas at Barnard liked to say that one began to understand a people only when one began to think in their language. Now, as she knelt in the hospital yard, staring at the words Felicia Felix-Mentor had left in the dirt, a phrase welled from her lips that she had heard often in Haiti but never felt before, a Creole phrase used to mean "So be it," to mean "Amen," to mean "There you have it," to mean whatever one chose it to mean but always conveying a more or less resigned acquiescence to the world and all its marvels.

"Ah bo bo," Zora said.

"Miss Hurston?" The doctor's dusty wingtips entered her vision, stood on the delicate pattern Zora had teased from the dirt, a pattern that began to disintegrate outward from the shoes, as if they produced a breeze or tidal eddy. "Are you suffering perhaps the digestion? Often the peasant spices can disrupt refined systems. Might I have Clement bring you a soda? Or"—and here his voice took on new excitement—"could this be perhaps a feminine complaint?"

"No, thank you, Doctor," Zora said as she stood, ignoring his outstretched hand. "May I please, do you think, return tomorrow with my camera?"

She intended the request to sound casual but failed. Not in *Dumballa Calls,* not in *The White King of La Gonave,* not in *The Magic Island,* not in any best-seller ever served up to the Haiti-loving American public had anyone ever included a photograph of a Zombie.

As she held her breath, the doctor squinted and glanced from Zora to the patient and back, as if suspecting the two women of collusion. He loudly sucked a tooth. "It is impossible, madame," he said. "Tomorrow I must away to Port-de-Paix, leaving at dawn and not returning for—"

"It must be tomorrow!" Zora blurted, hastily adding, "because the next day I have an appointment in . . . Petionville." To obscure that slightest of pauses, she gushed, "Oh, Doctor Legros," and dimpled his tailored shoulder with her forefinger. "Until we have the pleasure of meeting again, surely you won't deny me this one small token of your regard?"

Since she was a sprat of thirteen sashaying around the gatepost in Eatonville, slowing Yankees aboil for Winter Park or Sunken Gardens or the Weeki Wachee with a wink and a wave, Zora had viewed sexuality, like other talents, as a bank of backstage switches to be flipped separately or together to achieve specific effects—a spotlight glare, a thunderstorm, the slow, seeping warmth of dawn. Few switches were needed for everyday use, and certainly not for Doctor Legros, who was the most everyday of men.

"But of course," the doctor said, his body ready and still. "Doctor Belfong will expect you, and I will ensure that he extend you every courtesy. And then, Miss Hurston, we will compare travel notes on another day, n'est-ce pas?"

As she stepped onto the veranda, Zora looked back. Felicia Felix-Mentor stood in the middle of the yard, arms wrapped across her torso as if chilled, rocking on the balls of her calloused feet. She was looking at Zora, if at anything. Behind her, a dusty flamingo high-stepped across the yard.

Zora found signboards in Haiti fairly easy to understand in French, but the English ones were a different story. As she wedged herself into a seat in the crowded tap-tap that rattled twice a day between Gonaives and Port-au-Prince, Felicia Felix-Mentor an hour planted and taking root in her mind, she found herself facing a stern injunction above the grimy, cracked windshield: "Passengers Are Not Permitted To Stand Forward While the Bus Is Either at a Standstill or Approaching in Motion."

As the bus lurched forward, tires spinning, gears grinding, the driver loudly recited: "Dear clients, let us pray to the Good God and to all the most merciful martyrs in heaven that we may be delivered safely unto our chosen destination. Amen."

Amen, Zora thought despite herself, already jotting in her notebook. The beautiful woman in the window seat beside her shifted sideways to give Zora's elbow more room, and Zora absently flashed her a smile. At the top of the page she wrote, "Felicia Felix-Mentor," the hyphen jagging upward from a pothole. Then she added a question mark and tapped the pencil against her teeth.

Who had Felicia been, and what life had she led? Where was her family? Of these matters, Doctor Legros refused to speak. Maybe the family had abandoned its feeble relative, or worse. The poor woman may have been brutalized into her present state. Such things happened at the hands of family members, Zora knew.

Zora found herself doodling a shambling figure, arms outstretched. Nothing like Felicia, she conceded. More like Mr. Karloff's monster. Several years before, in New York to put together a Broadway production that came to nothing, Zora had wandered, depressed and whimsical, into a Times Square movie theater to see a foolish horror movie titled *White Zombie.* The swaying sugar cane on the poster ("She was not dead . . . She was not alive . . . WHAT WAS SHE?") suggested, however spuriously, Haiti, which even then Zora hoped to visit one day. Bela Lugosi in Mephisophelean whiskers proved about as Haitian as Fannie Hurst, and his Zombies, stalking bug-eyed and stiff-legged around the tatty sets, all looked white to Zora, so she couldn't grasp the urgency of the title, whatever Lugosi's designs on the heroine. Raising Zombies just to staff a sugar mill, moreover, struck her as wasted effort, since many a live Haitian (or Floridian) would work a full Depression day for as little pay as any Zombie and do a better job too. Still, she admired how the movie Zombies walked mindlessly to their doom off the parapet of Lugosi's castle, just as the fanatic soldiers of the mad Haitian King Henri Christophe were supposed to have done from the heights of the Citadel LaFerriéré.

But suppose Felicia *were* a Zombie—in Haitian terms, anyway? Not a supernaturally revived corpse, but a sort of combined kidnap and poisoning victim, released or abandoned by her captor, her bocor, after three decades.

Supposedly, the bocor stole a victim's soul by mounting a horse backward, facing the tail, and riding by night to her house. There he knelt on the doorstep, pressed his face against the crack beneath the door, bared his teeth, and sssssssst! He inhaled the soul of the sleeping woman, breathed her right into his lungs. And then the bocor would have marched Felicia (so the tales went) past her house the next night, her first night as a Zombie, to prevent her ever recognizing it or seeking it again.

Yet Felicia *had* sought out the family farm, however late. Maybe something had gone wrong with the spell. Maybe someone had fed her salt—the hair-of-the-dog remedy for years-long Zombie hang-overs. Where, then, was Felicia's bocor? Why hold her prisoner all this time, but no longer? Had he died, setting his charge free to wander? Had he other charges, other Zombies? How had Felicia become both victim and escapee?

"And how do you like your Zombie, Miss Hurston?"

Zora started. The beautiful passenger beside her had spoken.

"I beg your pardon!" Zora instinctively shut her notebook. "I do not believe we have met, Miss . . . ?"

The wide-mouthed stranger laughed merrily, her opalescent ear-rings shimmering on her high cheekbones. One ringlet of brown hair spilled onto her forehead from beneath her kerchief, which like her tight-fitting, high-necked dress was an ever-swirling riot of color. Her heavy gold necklace was nearly lost in it. Her skin was two parts cream to one part coffee. Antebellum New Orleans would have been at this woman's feet, once the shutters were latched.

"Ah, I knew you did not recognize me, Miss Hurston." Her accent made the first syllable of "Hurston" a prolonged purr. "We met in Archahaie, in the hounfort of Dieu Donnez St. Leger, during the rite of the fishhook of the dead." She bulged her eyes and sat forward slack-jawed, then fell back, clapping her hands with delight, ruby ring flash-ing, at her passable imitation of a dead man. "You may call me Freida. It is I, Miss Hurston, who first told you of the Zombie Felix-Mentor."

Their exchange in the sweltering crowd had been brief and con-fused, but Zora could have sworn that her informant that night had been an older, plainer woman. Still, Zora probably hadn't looked her best, either. The deacons and mothers back home would deny it, but many a worshipper looked better outside church than in.

Zora apologized for her absent-mindedness, thanked this, Freida? for her tip, and told her some of her hospital visit. She left out the message in the dirt, if message it was, but mused aloud:

"Today we lock the poor woman away, but who knows? Once she may have had a place of honor, as a messenger touched by the gods."

"No, no, no, no, no, no, no," said Freida in a forceful singsong. "No! The gods did not take her powers away." She leaned in, became conspiratorial. "Some man, and only a man, did that. You saw. You know."

Zora, teasing, said, "Ah, so you have experience with men."

"None more," Freida stated. Then she smiled. "Ah bo bo. That is night talk. Let us speak instead of daylight things."

The two women chatted happily for a bouncing half-hour, Freida questioning and Zora answering—talking about her Haiti book, turpentine camps, the sights of New York. It was good to be questioned herself for a change, after collecting from others all the time. The tap-tap jolted along, ladling dust equally onto all who shared the road: mounted columns of Haitian Guards, shelf-hipped laundresses, half-dead donkeys laden with guinea-grass. The day's shadows lengthened.

"This is my stop," said Freida at length, though the tap-tap showed no signs of slowing, and no stop was visible through the windows, just dense palm groves to either side. Where a less graceful creature would merely have stood, Freida rose, then turned and edged toward the aisle, facing not the front but, oddly, the back of the bus. Zora swiveled in her seat to give her more room, but Freida pressed against her anyway, thrust her pelvis forward against the older woman's bosom. Zora felt Freida's heat through the thin material. Above, Freida flashed a smile, nipped her own lower lip, and chuckled as the pluck of skin fell back into place.

"I look forward to our next visit, Miss Hurston."

"And where might I call on you?" Zora asked, determined to follow the conventions.

Freida edged past and swayed down the aisle, not reaching for the handgrips. "You'll find me," she said, over her shoulder.

Zora opened her mouth to say something but forgot what. Directly in front of the bus, visible through the windshield past Freida's shoulder, a charcoal truck roared into the roadway at right angles. Zora braced herself for the crash. The tap-tap driver screamed with everyone else, stamped the brakes and spun the wheel. With a hellish screech, the bus slewed about in a cloud of dirt and dust that darkened the sunlight, crusted Zora's tongue, and hid the charcoal truck from view. For one long, delirious, nearly sexual moment the bus tipped sideways. Then it righted itself with a tooth-loosening *slam* that shattered the windshield. In the silence, Zora heard someone sobbing, heard the engine's last faltering cough, heard the front door slide open with its usual clatter. She righted her hat in order to see. The tap-tap and the charcoal truck had come to rest a foot away from one another, side by side and facing opposite directions. Freida, smiling, unscathed, kerchief still angled just so, sauntered down the aisle between the vehicles, one finger trailing along the side of the truck, tracking the dust like a child. She passed Zora's window without looking up, and was gone.

"She pulled in her horizon like a great fish-net. Pulled it from around the waist of the world and draped it over her shoulder. So much of life in its meshes! She called in her soul to come and see."

Mouth dry, head aching from the heat and from the effort of reading her own chicken-scratch, Zora turned the last page of the manuscript, squared the stack, and looked up at her audience. Felicia sat on an hourglass root, a baked yam in each hand, gnawing first one, then the other.

"That's the end," Zora said, in the same soft, non-threatening voice with which she had read her novel thus far. "I'm still unsure of the middle," she continued, setting down the manuscript and picking up the Brownie camera, "but I know this is the end, all right, and that's something."

As yam after yam disappeared, skins and all, Felicia's eyes registered nothing. No matter. Zora always liked to read her work aloud as she was writing, and Felicia was as good an audience as anybody. She was, in fact, the first audience this particular book had had.

While Zora had no concerns whatsoever about sharing her novel with Felicia, she was uncomfortably aware of the narrow Victorian casements above, and felt the attentive eyes of the dying and the mad. On the veranda, a bent old man in a wheelchair mumbled to himself, half-watched by a nurse with a magazine.

In a spasm of experiment, Zora had salted the yams, to no visible effect. This Zombie took salt like an editor took whiskey.

"I'm not in your country to write a novel," Zora told her chewing companion. "Not officially. I'm being paid just to do folklore on this trip. Why, this novel isn't even set in Haiti, ha! So I can't tell the foundation about this quite yet. It's our secret, right, Felicia?"

The hospital matron had refused Zora any of her good china, grudgingly piling bribe-yams onto a scarred gourd-plate instead. Now, only two were left. The plate sat on the ground, just inside Felicia's reach. Chapter by chapter, yam by yam, Zora had been reaching out and dragging the plate just a bit nearer herself, a bit farther away from Felicia. So far, Felicia had not seemed to mind.

Now Zora moved the plate again, just as Felicia was licking the previous two yams off her fingers. Felicia reached for the plate, then froze, when she registered that it was out of reach. She sat there, arm suspended in the air.

"Nnnnn, nnnnn, nnnnn," she said.

Zora sat motionless, cradling her Brownie camera in her lap.

Felicia slid forward on her buttocks and snatched up two yams— choosing to eat them where she now sat, as Zora had hoped, rather than slide backward into the shade once more. Zora took several pictures in the sunlight, though none of them, she later realized, managed to penetrate the shadows beneath Felicia's furrowed brow, where the patient's sightless eyes lurked.

"Zombies!" came an unearthly cry. The old man on the veranda was having a spasm, legs kicking, arms flailing. The nurse moved quickly, propelled his wheelchair toward the hospital door. "I made them all Zombies! Zombies!"

———

"Observe my powers," said the mad Zombie-maker King Henri Christophe, twirling his stage mustache and leering down at the beautiful young(ish) anthropologist who squirmed against her snakeskin bonds. The mad king's broad white face and syrupy accent suggested Budapest. At his languid gesture, black-and-white legions of Zombies both black and white shuffled into view around the papier-mâché cliff and marched single file up the steps of the balsa parapet, and over. None cried out as he fell. Flipping through his captive's notebook, the king laughed maniacally and said, "I never knew you wrote this! Why, this is *good!*" As Zombies toppled behind him like ninepins, their German Expressionist shadows scudding across his face, the mad king began hammily to read aloud the opening passage of *Imitation of Life.*

Zora woke in a sweat.

The rain still sheeted down, a ceremonial drumming on the slate roof. Her manuscript, a white blob in the darkness, was moving sideways along the desktop. She watched as it went over the edge and dashed itself across the floor with a sound like a gust of wind. So the iguana had gotten in again. It loved messing with her manuscript. She should take the iguana to New York, get it a job at Lippincott's. She isolated the iguana's crouching, bowlegged shape in the drumming darkness and lay still, never sure whether iguanas jumped and how far and why.

Gradually she became aware of another sound nearer than the rain: someone crying.

Zora switched on the bedside lamp, found her slippers with her feet, and reached for her robe. The top of her writing desk was empty. The manuscript must have been top-heavy, that's all. Shaking her head at her night fancies, cinching her belt, yawning, Zora walked into the corridor and nearly stepped on the damned iguana as it scuttled just ahead of her, claws clack-clack-clacking on the hardwood. Zora tugged off her left slipper and gripped it by the toe as an unlikely weapon as she followed the iguana into the great room.

Her housekeeper, Lucille, lay on the sofa, crying two-handed into a handkerchief. The window above her was open, curtains billowing, and the iguana escaped as it had arrived, scrambling up the back of the sofa and out into the hissing rain. Lucille was oblivious until Zora closed the sash, when she sat up with a start.

"Oh, Miss! You frightened me! I thought the Sect Rouge had come."

Ah, yes, the Sect Rouge. That secret, invisible mountain-dwelling cannibal cult, their distant nocturnal drums audible only to the doomed, whose blood thirst made the Klan look like the Bethune-Cookman board of visitors, was Lucille's most cherished night terror. Zora had never had a housekeeper before, never wanted one, but Lucille "came with the house," as the agent had put it. It was all a package: mountain-side view, Sect Rouge paranoia, hot and cold running iguanas.

"Lucille, darling, whatever is the matter? Why are you crying?"

A fresh burst of tears. "It is my faithless husband, madame! My Etienne. He has forsaken me . . . for Erzulie!" She fairly spat the name, as a wronged woman in Eatonville would have spat the infamous name of Miss Delpheeny.

Zora had laid eyes on Etienne only once, when he came flushed and hatless to the back door to show off his prize catch, grinning as widely as the dead caiman he held up by the tail. For his giggling wife's benefit, he had tied a pink ribbon around the creature's neck, and Zora had decided then that Lucille was as lucky a woman as any.

"There, there. Come to Zora. Here, blow your nose. That's better. You needn't tell me any more, if you don't want to. Who is this Erzulie?"

Zora had heard much about Erzulie in Haiti, always from other women, in tones of resentment and admiration, but she was keen for more.

"Oh, madame, she is a terrible woman! She has every man she wants, all the men, and . . . and some of the women, too!" This last said in a hush of reverence. "No home in Haiti is safe from her. First she came to my Etienne in his dreams, teasing and tormenting his sleep until he cried out and spent himself in the sheets. Then she troubled his waking life, too, with frets and ill fortune, so that he was angry with himself and with me all the time. Finally I sent him to the houngan, and the houngan said, 'Why do you ask me what this is? Any child could say to you the truth: You have been chosen as a consort of Erzulie.' And then he embraced my Etienne, and said: 'My son, your bed above all beds is now the one for all men to envy.' Ah, madame, religion is a hard thing for women!"

Even as she tried to console the weeping woman, Zora felt a pang of writerly conscience. On the one hand, she genuinely wanted to help; on the other hand, everything was material.

"Whenever Erzulie pleases, she takes the form that a man most desires, to ride him as dry as a bean husk, and to rob his woman of comfort. Oh, madame! My Etienne has not come to my bed in . . . in . . . *twelve days!*" She collapsed into the sofa in a fresh spasm of grief, buried her head beneath a cushion, and began to hiccup. Twelve whole days, Zora thought, my my, as she did dispiriting math, but she said nothing, only patted Lucille's shoulder and cooed.

Later, while frying an egg for her dejected, red-eyed housekeeper, Zora sought to change the subject. "Lucille. Didn't I hear you say the other day, when the postman ran over the rooster, something like, 'Ah, the Zombies eat well tonight!'"

"Yes, madame, I think I did say this thing."

"And last week, when you spotted that big spider web just after putting the ladder away, you said, 'Ah bo bo, the Zombies make extra work for me today.' When you say such things, Lucille, what do you mean? To what Zombies do you refer?"

"Oh, madame, it is just a thing to say when small things go wrong. Oh, the milk is sour, the Zombies have put their feet in it, and so on. My mother always says it, and her mother too."

Soon Lucille was chatting merrily away about the little coffee girls and the ritual baths at Saut-d'Eau, and Zora took notes and drank coffee, and all was well. Ah bo bo!

The sun was still hours from rising when Lucille's chatter shut off mid-sentence. Zora looked up to see Lucille frozen in terror, eyes wide, face ashen.

"Madame . . . Listen!"

"Lucille, I hear nothing but the rain on the roof."

"Madame," Lucille whispered, "the rain has stopped."

Zora set down her pencil and went to the window. Only a few drops pattered from the eaves and the trees. In the distance, far up the mountain, someone was beating the drums—ten drums, a hundred, who could say? The sound was like thunder sustained, never coming closer but never fading either.

Zora closed and latched the shutters and turned back to Lucille with a smile. "Honey, that's just man-noise in the night, like the big-mouthing on the porch at Joe Clarke's store. You mean I never told you about all the lying that men do back home? Break us another egg, Cille honey, and I'll tell *you* some things."

Box 128-B
Port-au-Prince, Haiti
November 20, 1936

Dr. Henry Allen Moe, Sec.
John Simon Guggenheim Memorial Foundation
551 Fifth Avenue
New York, N.Y.

Dear Dr. Moe,

I regret to report that for all my knocking and ringing and dust-raising, I have found no relatives of this unfortunate Felix-Mentor woman. She is both famous and unknown. All have heard of her and

know, or think they know, the two-sentence outline of her "story," and have their own fantasies
about her, but can go no further. She is the Garbo
of Haiti. I would think her a made-up character
had I not seen her myself, and taken her picture as
. . . evidence? A photograph of the Empire State
Building is evidence too, but of what? That is for
the viewer to say.

I am amused of course, as you were, to hear from
some of our friends and colleagues on the Haiti beat
their concerns that poor Zora has "gone native,"
has thrown away the WPA and Jesse Owens and the
travel trailer and all the other achievements of the
motherland to break chickens and become an initi-
ate in the mysteries of the Sect Rouge. Lord knows,
Dr. Moe, I spent twenty-plus years in the Southern
U.S., beneath the constant gaze of every First Abys-
sinian Macedonian African Methodist Episcopal
Presbyterian Pentecostal Free Will Baptist Assembly of God of Christ of Jesus with Signs Following
minister mother and deacon, all so full of the spirit
they look like death eating crackers, and in all that
time I never once came down with even a mild case
of Christianity. I certainly won't catch the local dis-
ease from only six months in Haiti. . . .

Obligations, travel, and illness—"suffering perhaps the digestion,"
thank you, Doctor Legros—kept Zora away from the hospital at
Gonaives for some weeks. When she finally did return, she walked
onto the veranda to see Felicia, as before, standing all alone in the
quiet yard, her face toward the high wall. Today Felicia had chosen to
stand on the sole visible spot of green grass, a plot of soft imprisoned

turf about the diameter of an Easter hat. Zora felt a deep satisfaction upon seeing her, this self-contained, fixed point in her traveler's life.

To reach the steps, she had to walk past the mad old man in the wheelchair, whose nurse was not in sight today. Despite his sunken cheeks, his matted eyelashes, his patchy tufts of white hair, Zora could see he must have been handsome in his day. She smiled as she approached.

He blinked and spoke in a thoughtful voice. "I will be a Zombie soon," he said.

That stopped her. "Excuse me?"

"Death came for me many years ago," said the old man, eyes bright, "and I said, No, not me, take my wife instead. And so I gave her up as a Zombie. That gained me five years, you see. A good bargain. And then, five years later, I gave our oldest son. Then our daughter. Then our youngest. And more loved ones, too, now all Zombies, all. There is no one left. No one but me." His hands plucked at the coverlet that draped his legs. He peered all around the yard. "I will be a Zombie soon," he said, and wept.

Shaking her head, Zora descended the steps. Approaching Felicia from behind, as Doctor Legros had said that first day, was always a delicate maneuver. One had to be loud enough to be heard but quiet enough not to panic her.

"Hello, Felicia," Zora said.

The huddled figure didn't turn, didn't budge, and Zora, emboldened by long absence, repeated the name, reached out, touched Felicia's shoulder with her fingertips. As she made contact, a tingling shiver ran up her arm and down her spine to her feet. Without turning, Felicia emerged from her crouch. She stood up straight, flexed her shoulders, stretched her neck, and spoke.

"Zora, my friend!"

Felicia turned and was not Felicia at all, but a tall, beautiful woman in a brief white gown. Freida registered the look on Zora's face and laughed.

"Did I not tell you that you would find me? Do you not even know your friend Freida?"

Zora's breath returned. "I know you," she retorted, "and I know that was a cruel trick. Where is Felicia? What have you done with her?"

"Whatever do you mean? Felicia was not mine to give you, and she is not mine to take away. No one is owned by anyone."

"Why is Felicia not in the yard? Is she ill? And why are you here? Are you ill as well?"

Freida sighed. "So many questions. Is this how a book gets written? If Felicia were not ill, silly, she would not have been here in the first place. Besides." She squared her shoulders. "Why do you care so about this . . . powerless woman? This woman who let some man lead her soul astray, like a starving cat behind an eel-barrel?" She stepped close, the heat of the day coalescing around. "Tell a woman of power your book. Tell me your book," she murmured. "Tell me of the mule's funeral, and the rising waters, and the buzzing pear-tree, and young Janie's secret sigh."

Zora had two simultaneous thoughts, like a moan and a breath interlaced: *Get out of my book!* and *My God, she's jealous!*

"Why bother?" Zora bit off, flush with anger. "You think you know it by heart already. And besides," Zora continued, stepping forward, nose to nose, "there are powers other than yours."

Freida hissed, stepped back as if pattered with stove-grease.

Zora put her nose in the air and said, airily, "I'll have you know that Felicia is a writer, too."

Her mouth a thin line, Freida turned and strode toward the hospital, thighs long and taut beneath her gown. Without thought, Zora walked, too, and kept pace.

"If you must know," Freida said, "your writer friend is now in the care of her family. Her son came for her. Do you find this so remarkable? Perhaps the son should have notified you, hmm?" She winked at Zora. "He is quite a muscular young man, with a taste for older women. Much, *much* older women. I could show you where he lives. I have been there often. I have been there more than he knows."

"How dependent you are," Zora said, "on men."

As Freida stepped onto the veranda, the old man in the wheel-chair cringed and moaned. "Hush, child," Freida said. She pulled a nurse's cap from her pocket and tugged it on over her chestnut hair.

"Don't let her take me!" the old man howled. "She'll make me a Zombie! She will! A Zombie!"

"Oh, pish," Freida said. She raised one bare foot and used it to push the wheelchair forward a foot or so, revealing a sensible pair of white shoes on the flagstones beneath. These she stepped into as she wheeled the chair around. "Here is your bocor, Miss Hurston. What use have I for a Zombie's cold hands? Au revoir, Miss Hurston. Zora. I hope you find much to write about in my country . . . however you limit your experiences."

Zora stood at the foot of the steps, watched her wheel the old man away over the uneven flagstones.

"Erzulie," Zora said.

The woman stopped. Without turning, she asked, "What name did you call me?"

"I called you a true name, and I'm telling you that if you don't leave Lucille's Etienne alone, so the two of them can go to hell in their own way, then I . . . well, then I will forget all about you, and you will never be in my book."

Freida pealed with laughter. The old man slumped in his chair. The laughter cut off like a radio, and Freida, suddenly grave, looked down. "They do not last any time, do they?" she murmured. With a forefinger, she poked the back of his head. "Poor pretty things." With a sigh, she faced Zora, gave her a look of frank appraisal, up and down. Then she shrugged. "You are mad," she said, "but you are fair." She backed into the door, shoved it open with her behind, and hauled the dead man in after her.

The tap-tap was running late as usual, so Zora, restless, started out on foot. As long as the road kept going downhill and the sun stayed over yonder, she reasoned, she was unlikely to get lost. As she walked through the countryside she sang and picked flowers and worked on her book in the best way she knew to work on a book, in her own head, with no paper and indeed no words, not yet. She enjoyed the caution signs on each curve—"La Route Tue et Blesse," or, literally, "The Road Kills And Injures."

She wondered how it felt, to walk naked along a roadside like Felicia Felix-Mentor. She considered trying the experiment when she realized that night had fallen. (And where was the tap-tap, and all the other traffic, and why was the road so narrow?) But once shed, her dress, her shift, her shoes would be a terrible armful. The only efficient way to carry clothes, really, was to wear them. So thinking, she plodded, footsore, around a sharp curve and nearly ran into several dozen hooded figures in red, proceeding in the opposite direction. Several carried torches, all carried drums, and one had a large, mean-looking dog on a rope.

"Who comes?" asked a deep male voice. Zora couldn't tell which of the hooded figures had spoken, if any.

"Who wants to know?" she asked.

The hoods looked at one another. Without speaking, several reached into their robes. One drew a sword. One drew a machete. The one with the dog drew a pistol, then knelt to murmur into the dog's ear. With one hand he scratched the dog between the shoulder blades, and with the other he gently stroked its head with the moon-gleaming barrel of the pistol. Zora could hear the thump and rustle of the dog's tail wagging in the leaves.

"Give us the words of passage," said the voice, presumably the sword-wielder's, as he was the one who pointed at Zora for emphasis. "Give them to us, woman, or you will die, and we will feast upon you."

"She cannot know the words," said a woman's voice, "unless she too has spoken with the dead. Let us eat her."

Suddenly, as well as she knew anything on the round old world,

Zora knew exactly what the words of passage were. Felicia Felix-Mentor had given them to her. *Mi haut, mi bas.* Half high, half low. She could say them now. But she would not say them. She would believe in Zombies, a little, and in Erzulie, perhaps, a little more. But she would not believe in the Sect Rouge, in blood-oathed societies of men. She walked forward again, of her own free will, and the red-robed figures stood motionless as she passed among them. The dog whimpered. She walked down the hill, hearing nothing behind but a growing chorus of frogs. Around the next bend she saw the distant lights of Port-au-Prince and, much nearer, a tap-tap idling in front of a store. Zora laughed and hung her hat on a caution sign. Between her and the bus, the moonlit road was flecked with tiny frogs, distinguished from bits of gravel and bark only by their leaping, their errands of life. Ah bo bo! She called in her soul to come and see.

Unique Chicken Goes in Reverse

Father Leggett stood on the sidewalk and looked up at the three narrow stories of gray brick that was 207 East Charlton Street. Compared to the other edifices on Lafayette Square—the Colonial Dames fountain, the Low house, the Turner mansion, the cathedral of course—this house was decidedly ordinary, a reminder that even Savannah had buildings that did only what they needed to do, and nothing more.

He looked again at the note the secretary at St. John the Baptist had left on his desk. Wreathed in cigarette smoke, Miss Ingrid fielded dozens of telephone calls in an eight-hour day, none of which were for her, and while she always managed to correctly record addresses and phone numbers on her nicotine-colored note paper, the rest of the message always emerged from her smudged No. 1 pencils as four or five words that seemed relevant at the time but had no apparent grammatical connection, so that reading a stack of Miss Ingrid's messages back to back gave one a deepening sense of mystery and alarm, like intercepted signal fragments from a trawler during a hurricane. This note read:

OCONNORS
MARY
PRIEST?
CHICKEN!

And then the address. Pressed for more information, Miss Ingrid had shrieked with laughter and said, "Lord, Father, that was two hours ago! Why don't you ask me an easy one sometime?" The phone rang, and she snatched it up with a wink. "It's a great day at St. John the Baptist. Ingrid speaking."

Surely, Father Leggett thought as he trotted up the front steps, I wasn't expected to *bring* a chicken?

The bell was inaudible, but the door was opened immediately, by an attractive but austere woman with dark eyebrows. Father Leggett was sure his sidewalk dithering had been patiently observed. "Hello, Father. Please come in. Thank you for coming. I'm Regina O'Connor."

She ushered him into a surprisingly large, bright living room. Hauling himself up from the settee was a rumpled little man in shirtsleeves and high-waisted pants who moved slowly and painfully, as if he were much larger.

"Welcome, Father. Edward O'Connor, Dixie Realty and Construction."

"Mr. O'Connor. Mrs. O'Connor. I'm Father Leggett, assistant at St. John for—oh, my goodness, two months now. Still haven't met half my flock, at least. Bishop keeps me hopping. Pleased to meet you now, though." You're babbling, he told himself.

In the act of shaking hands, Mr. O'Connor lurched sideways with a wince, nearly falling. "Sorry, Father. Bit of arthritis in my knee."

"No need to apologize for the body's frailties, Mr. O'Connor. Why, we would all be apologizing all the time, like Alphonse and Gaston." He chuckled as the O'Connors, apparently not readers of the comics supplement, stared at him. "Ahem. I received a message at the church, something involving . . ." The O'Connors didn't step into the pause to help him. "Involving Mary?"

"We'd like for you to talk to her, Father," said Mrs. O'Connor. "She's in the back yard, playing. Please, follow me."

The back of the house was much shabbier than the front, and the yard was a bare dirt patch bounded on three sides by a high wooden fence of mismatched planks. More brick walls were visible through the gaps. In one corner of the yard was a large chicken coop enclosed by a smaller, more impromptu wire fence, the sort unrolled from a barrel-sized spool at the hardware store and affixed to posts with bent nails. Several dozen chickens roosted, strutted, pecked. Father Leggett's nose wrinkled automatically. He liked chickens when they were fried, baked or, with dumplings, boiled, but he always disliked chickens at their earlier, pre-kitchen stage, as creatures. He conceded them a role in God's creation purely for their utility to man. Father Leggett tended to respect things on the basis of their demonstrated intelligence, and on that universal ladder chickens tended to roost rather low. A farmer once told him that hundreds of chickens could drown during a single rainstorm because they kept gawking at the clouds with their beaks open until they filled with water like jugs. Or maybe that was geese. Father Leggett, who grew up in Baltimore, never liked geese, either.

Lying face up and spread-eagled in the dirt of the yard like a little crime victim was a grimy child in denim overalls with bobbed hair and a pursed mouth too small even for her nutlike head, most of which was clenched in a frown that was thunderous even from 20 feet away. She gave no sign of acknowledgment as the three adults approached, Mr. O'Connor slightly dragging his right foot. Did this constitute *playing*, wondered Father Leggett, who had scarcely more experience with children than with poultry.

"Mary," said Mrs. O'Connor as her shadow fell across the girl. "This is Father Leggett, from St. John the Baptist. Father Leggett, this is Mary, our best and only. She's in first grade at St. Vincent's."

"Ah, one of Sister Consolata's charges. How old are you, Mary?"

Still lying in the dirt, Mary thrashed her arms and legs, as if making snow angels, but said nothing. Dust clouds rose.

Her father said: "Mary, don't be rude. Answer Father's question."

"I just did," said Mary, packing the utterance with at least six syllables. Her voice was surprisingly deep. She did her horizontal jumping jacks again, counting off this time. "One. Two. Three. Five."

"You skipped four," Father Leggett said.

"You would, too," Mary said. "Four was hell."

"Mary."

This one word from her mother, recited in a flat tone free of judgment, was enough to make the child scramble to her feet. "I'm sorry Mother and Father and Father and I beg the Lord's forgiveness." To Father Leggett's surprise, she even curtsied in no particular direction—whether to him or to the Lord, he couldn't tell.

"And well you might, young lady," Mr. O'Connor began, but Mrs. O'Connor, without even raising her voice, easily drowned him out by saying simultaneously:

"Mary, why don't you show Father Leggett your chicken?"

"Yes, Mother." She skipped over to the chicken yard, stood on tiptoe to unlatch the gate, and waded into the squawking riot of beaks and feathers. Father Leggett wondered how she could tell one chicken from all the rest. He caught himself holding his breath, his hands clenched into fists.

"Spirited child," he said.

"Yes," said Mrs. O'Connor. Her unexpected smile was dazzling.

Mary re-latched the gate and trotted over with a truly extraordinary chicken beneath one arm. Its feathers stuck out in all directions, as if it had survived a hurricane. It struggled not at all, but seemed content with, or resigned to, Mary's attentions. The child's ruddy face showed renewed determination, and her mouth looked ever more like the dent a thumb leaves on a bad tomato.

"What an odd-looking specimen," said Father Leggett, silently meaning both of them.

"It's frizzled," Mary said. "That means its feathers grew in backward. It has a hard old time of it, this one."

She set the chicken down and held up a pudgy, soiled index finger, on which the chicken seemed to focus. Mary stepped one step closer to the chicken, and it took one step backward. She and the chicken took another step, and another, the chicken walking backward as Mary advanced.

"Remarkable," said Father Leggett. "And what's your chicken's name, young lady?"

She flung down a handful of seed and said, "Jesus Christ."

Father Leggett sucked in a breath. Behind him, Mrs. O'Connor coughed. Father Leggett tugged at his earlobe, an old habit. "What did you say, young lady?"

"Jesus Christ," she repeated, in the same dispassionate voice. Then she rushed the chicken, which skittered around the yard as Mary chased it, chanting in a singsong, "Jesus Christ Jesus Christ Jesus Christ."

Father Leggett looked at her parents. Mr. O'Connor arched his eyebrows and shrugged. Mrs. O' Connor, arms folded, nodded her head once. She looked grimly satisfied. Father Leggett turned back to see chicken and child engaged in a staring contest. The chicken stood, a-quiver; Mary, in a squat, was still.

"Now, Mary," Father Leggett said. "Why would you go and give a frizzled chicken the name of our Lord and Savior?"

"It's the best name," replied Mary, not breaking eye contact with the chicken. "Sister Consolata says the name of Jesus is to be cherished above all others."

"Well, yes, but—"

The hypnotic bond between child and chicken seemed to break, and Mary began to skip around the yard, raising dust with each stomp of her surprisingly large feet. "And he's different from all the other chickens, and the other chickens peck him but he never pecks back, and he spends a lot of his time looking up in the air, praying, and in Matthew Jesus says he's a chicken, and if I get a stomachache or an earache or a sore throat, I come out here and play with him and it gets all better just like the lame man beside the well."

Father Leggett turned in mute appeal to the child's parents. Mr. O'Connor cleared his throat.

"We haven't been able to talk her out of it, Father."

"So we thought we'd call an expert," finished Mrs. O'Connor.

I wish you had, though Father Leggett. At his feet, the frizzled chicken slurped up an earthworm and clucked with contentment.

The first thing Father Leggett did, once he was safely back at the office, was to reach down Matthew and hunt for the chicken. He found it in the middle of Christ's lecture to the Pharisees, Chapter 23, Verse 37: "O Jerusalem, Jerusalem, thou that killest the prophets, and stonest them which are sent unto thee, how often would I have gathered thy children together, even as a hen gathereth her chickens under her wings, and ye would not!"

Mrs. O'Connor answered the phone on the first ring. "Yes," she breathed, her voice barely audible.

"It's Father Leggett, Mrs. O'Connor. Might I speak to Mary, please?"

"She's napping."

"Oh, I see. Well, I wanted to tell her that I've been reading the Scripture she told me about, and I wanted to thank her. It's really very interesting, the verse she's latched on to. Christ our Lord did indeed liken himself to a hen, yes, but he didn't mean it literally. He was only making a comparison. You see," he said, warming to his subject, to fill the silence, "it's like a little parable, like the story of the man who owned the vineyard. He meant God was *like* the owner of the vineyard, not that God had an actual business interest in the wine industry."

Mrs. O'Connor's voice, when it finally came, was flat and bored.

"No disrespect meant, Father Leggett, but Edward and I did turn to the Scriptures well upstream of our turning to you, and by now everyone in this household is intimately acquainted with

Matthew 23:37, its histories, contexts, and commentaries. And yet our daughter seems to worship a frizzled chicken. Have you thought of anything that could explain it?"

"Well, Mrs. O'Connor—"

"Regina."

"Regina. Could it be that this chicken is just a sort of imaginary playmate for the girl? Well, not the chicken, that's real enough, but I mean the identity she has created for it. Many children have imaginary friends, especially children with no siblings, like Mary."

"Oh, I had one of those," she said. "A little boy named Bar-Lock, who lived in my father's Royal Bar-Lock typewriter."

"There, you see. You know just what I'm talking about."

"But I never thought Bar-Lock was my lord and savior!"

"No, but 'lord and savior' is a difficult idea even for an adult to grasp, isn't it? By projecting it onto a chicken, Mary makes the idea more manageable, something she can hold and understand. She seems happy, doesn't she? Content? No nightmares about her chicken being nailed to a cross? And as she matures, in her body and in her faith, she'll grow out if it, won't need it anymore."

"Well, perhaps," she said, sounding miffed. "Thank you for calling, Father. When Mary wakes up, I'll tell her you were thinking about her, and about her imaginary Jesus."

She broke the connection, leaving Father Leggett with his mouth open. The operator's voice squawked through the earpiece.

"Next connection, please. Hello? Hello?"

That night, Father Leggett dreamed about a frizzled chicken nailed to a cross. He woke with the screech in his ears.

The never-ending crush of church business enabled Father Leggett to keep putting off a return visit to the O'Connors, as the days passed into weeks and into months, but avoiding chickens, and talk of chickens, was not so easy. He began to wince whenever he heard of them coming home to roost, or being counted before they were hatched, of politicians providing them in every pot.

The dreams continued. One night the human Jesus stood on the mount and said, "Blessed are the feedmakers," then squatted and pecked the ground. The mob squatted and pecked the ground, too. Jesus and His followers flapped their elbows and clucked.

Worst of all was the gradual realization that for every clergyman in Georgia, chicken was an occupational hazard. Most families ate chicken only on Sundays, but any day Father Leggett came to visit was de facto Sunday, so he got served chicken all the time—breasts, legs, livers and dumplings, fried, baked, boiled, in salads, soups, broths, and stews, sautéed, fricasseed, marengoed, a la kinged, cacciatored, casse-roled. Of all this chicken, Father Leggett ate ever smaller portions. He doubled up on mustard greens and applesauce. He lost weight.

"Doubtless you've heard the Baptist minister's blessing," the bishop told him one day:

"I've had chicken hot, and I've had chicken cold.

"I've had chicken young, and I've had chicken old.

"I've had chicken tender, and I've had chicken tough.

"And thank you, Lord, I've had chicken enough."

Since the bishop had broached the subject, in a way, Father Leggett took the opportunity to tell him about his visit with the O'Connor child, and the strange theological musings it had inspired in him. The bishop, a keen administrator, got right to the heart of the matter.

"What do you mean, frizzled?"

Father Leggett tried as best he could to explain the concept of frizzled to the bishop, finally raking both hands through his own hair until it stood on end.

"Ah, I see. Sounds like some kind of freak. Best to wring its neck while the child's napping. She might catch the mites."

"Oh, but sir, the girl views this chicken as a manifestation of our Lord."

"Our Lord was no freak," the bishop replied. "He was martyred for our sins, not pecked to death like a runty chicken."

"They seem to have a real bond," Father Leggett said. "Where you and I might see only a walking feather duster, this child sees the face of Jesus."

"People see the face of Jesus all over," the bishop said, "in clouds and stains on the ceiling and the headlamps of Fords. Herbert Hoover and Father Divine show up in the same places, if you look hard enough. It's human nature to see order where there is none."

"She trained it to walk backward on command. That's order from chaos, surely. Like the hand of God on the face of the waters."

"You admire this child," the bishop said.

I envy her, Father Leggett thought, but what he said was, "I do. And I fear for her faith, if something were to happen to this chicken. They don't live long, you know, even if they make it past Sunday dinner. They aren't parrots or turtles, and frizzles are especially susceptible to cold weather. I looked it up."

"Best thing for her," the bishop said. "Get her over this morbid fascination. You, too. Not healthy for a man of the cloth to be combing Scripture for chickens. Got to see the broader picture, you know. Otherwise, you're no better than the snake handlers, fixated on Mark 16: 17-18. 'And these signs shall follow them that believe; in my name shall they cast out devils; they shall speak with new tongues; they shall take up serpents; and if they drink any deadly thing, it shall not hurt them; they shall lay hands on the sick, and they shall recover.'"

"Perhaps this child has taken up a chicken," Father Leggett said, "as another believer would take up a snake."

"Not to worry, son," the bishop said. "Little Mary's belief will outlive this chicken, I reckon. Probably outlive you and me, too. Come in, Ingrid!"

A cloud of cigarette smoke entered the office, followed by Ingrid's head around the door. "Lunch is ready," she said.

"Oh, good. What's today's bill of fare?"

"Roast chicken."

"I'm not hungry," Father Leggett quickly said.

The bishop laughed. "To paraphrase: 'If they eat any deadly thing, it shall not hurt them.'"

"Mark 16:18 wasn't in the original gospel," Ingrid said. "The whole 12-verse ending of the book was added later, by a scribe."

The bishop looked wounded. "An inspired scribe," he said.

"Wash your hands, both of you," Ingrid said, and vanished in a puff.

"She's been raiding the bookcase again," the bishop growled. "It'll only confuse her."

As he picked at his plate, Father Leggett kept trying to think of other things, but couldn't. "They shall lay hands on the sick, and they shall recover." Mary O'Connor had placed her hands upon a frizzled chicken and . . . hadn't healed it, exactly, for it was still a ridiculous, doomed creature, but had given it a sort of mission. A backward purpose, but a purpose nonetheless.

That day Father Leggett had a rare afternoon off, so he went to the movies. The cartoon was ending as he entered the auditorium, and he fumbled to a seat in the glare of the giant crowing rooster that announced the Pathe Sound News. Still out of sorts, he slumped in his seat and stared blankly at the day's doings, reduced to a shrilly narrated comic strip: a ship tossing in a gale, two football teams piling onto one another, Clarence Darrow defending a lynch mob in Hawaii, a glider soaring over the Alps—but the next title took his breath.

UNIQUE CHICKEN GOES IN REVERSE

"In Savannah, Georgia, little Mary O'Connor, age five, trains her pet chicken to walk backward!"

And there on screen, stripped of sound and color and all human shading, like Father Leggett's very thoughts made huge and public, were Mary and her frizzled chicken. As he gaped at the capering giants, he was astonished by the familiarity of the O'Connor backyard, how easily he could fill in the details past the square edges of the frame. One would think he had lived there, as a child. He thought he might weep. The audience had begun cheering so at "Savannah, Georgia" that much of the rest was inaudible, but Father Leggett was pretty sure that Jesus wasn't mentioned. The cameraman had captured only a few seconds of the chicken actually walking backward; the rest was clearly the film cranked in reverse, and the segment ended with more "backward" footage of waddling ducks, trotting horses, grazing cattle. The delighted audience howled and roared. Feeling sick, Father Leggett lurched to his feet, stumbled across his neighbors to the aisle, and fled the theater.

He went straight to the upright house on Lafayette Square, leaned on the bell until Mrs. O'Connor appeared, index finger to her lips.

"Shh! Please, Father, not so loud," she whispered, stepping onto the porch and closing the door behind. "Mr. O'Connor has to rest, afternoons."

"Beg pardon," he whispered. "I didn't realize, when I bought my ticket, that your Mary has become a film star now."

"Oh, yes," she said, with an unexpected laugh, perching herself on the banister. "She's the next Miriam Hopkins, I'm sure. It was the chicken they were here for. Edward called them. Such a bother. Do you know, they were here an hour trying to coax it to walk two steps? Stage fright, I suppose. I could have strangled the wretched thing."

"I've been remiss in not calling sooner. And how is Mary doing?"

"Oh, she's fine." Her voice was approaching its normal volume. "Do you know, from the day the cameramen visited, she seemed to lose interest in Jesus? Jesus the chicken, I mean. It's as if the camera made her feel foolish, somehow."

"May I see her?"

"She's out back, as usual." She glanced at the door, then whispered again. "Best to go around the house, I think."

She led the way down the steps and along a narrow side yard—a glorified alleyway, really, with brick walls at each elbow—to the back yard, where Mary lay in the dirt, having a fit.

"Child!" Father Leggett cried, and rushed to her.

She thrashed and kicked, her face purple, her frown savage. Father Leggett knelt beside her, seized and—with effort—held her flailing arms. Her hands were balled into fists. "Child, calm yourself. What's wrong?"

Suddenly still, she opened her eyes. "Hullo," she said. "I'm fighting."

"Fighting what?"

"My angel," she said.

He caught himself glancing around, as if Saint Michael might be behind him. "Oh, child."

"Sister Consolata says I have an invisible guardian angel that never leaves my side, not even when I'm sleeping, not even when I'm in the *potty*." This last word was whispered. "He's always watching me, and following me, and being a pain, and one day I'm going to turn around and catch him and *knock* his block off." She swung her fists again and pealed with laughter.

Mary's mother stood over them, her thin mouth set, her dark brows lowered, looking suddenly middle-aged and beautiful. Her default expression was severity, but on her severity looked good. How difficult it must be, Father Leggett thought, to have an only child, a precocious child, any child.

"Mary, I've got cookies in the oven."

She sat up. "Oatmeal?"

"Oatmeal."

"With raisins and grease?"

"With raisins and grease." She leaned down, cupped her hands around her mouth, and whispered, "And we won't let that old angel have a one."

Mary giggled.

"You're welcome to join us, Father. Father?"

"Of course, thank you," said Father Leggett, with an abstracted air, not turning around, as he walked slowly toward the chicken yard.

The frizzled one was easy to spot; it stood in its own space, seemingly avoided by the others. It walked a few steps toward the gate as the priest approached.

Father Leggett felt the gaze of mother and child upon him as he lifted the fishhook latch and creaked open the gate. The chickens nearest him fluttered, then stilled, but their flutter was contagious. It passed to the next circle of chickens, then the next, a bit more violent each time. The outermost circle of chickens returned it to the body of the flock, and by the time the ripple of unease had reached Father Leggett, he had begun to realize why so many otherwise brave people were (to use a word he had learned only in his recent weeks of study) alektorophobes. Only the frizzled Jesus seemed calm. Father Leggett stepped inside, his Oxfords crunching corn hulls and pebbles. He had the full attention of the chickens now. Without looking, he closed the gate behind. He walked forward, and the milling chickens made a little space for him, an ever-shifting, downy clearing in which he stood, arms at his sides, holding his breath. The frizzle stepped to the edge of this clearing, clucked at him. The hot air was rich with the smells of grain, bad eggs, and droppings. A crumpled washtub held brackish water. Feathers floated across his smudged reflection. He closed his eyes, slowly lifted his arms. The chickens roiled. Wings beat at his shins. He reached as far aloft as he could and prayed a wordless prayer as the chicken yard erupted around him, a smothering cloud that buffeted his face and chest and legs. He was the center of a tornado of chickens, their cackles rising and falling like speech, a message that he almost felt he understood, and with closed eyes he wept in gratitude, until Jesus pecked him in the balls.

One afternoon years later, during her final semester at the women's college in Milledgeville, Mary O'Connor sat at her desk in the *Corinthian* office, leafing through the Atlanta paper, wondering whether the new copy of the McMurray Hatchery catalog ("All Flocks Blood Tested") would be waiting in the mailbox when she got home. Then an article deep inside the paper arrested her attention.

Datelined Colorado, it was about a headless chicken named Mike. Mike had survived a Sunday-morning beheading two months previous. Each evening Mike's owners plopped pellets of feed down his stumpy neck with an eyedropper and went to bed with few illusions, and each morning Mike once again gurgled up the dawn.

She read and re-read the clipping with the deepest satisfaction. It reminded her of her childhood, and in particular of the day she first learned the nature of grace.

She folded the clipping in half and in half and in half again until it was furled like Aunt Pittypat's fan and sheathed it in an envelope that she addressed to Father Leggett, care of the Cathedral of St. John the Baptist in Savannah. Teaching a *headless* chicken to walk backward: That would be *real* evangelism. On a fresh sheet of the stationery her grandmother had given her two Christmases ago, she crossed out the ornate engraved "M" at the top and wrote in an even more ornate "F," as if she were flunking herself with elegance. Beneath it she wrote:

> Dear Father Leggett,
> I saw this and thought of you.
> Happy Easter,
> Flannery (nee Mary) O'Connor

When Miss Ingrid's successor brought him the letter, Father Leggett was sitting in his office, eating a spinach salad and reading the *Vegetarian News.* He was considered a good priest though an eccentric one, and no longer was invited to so many parishioners' homes at mealtime. He glanced at the note, then at the clipping. The photo alone made him upset his glass of carrot juice. He threw clipping, note, and envelope into the trash can, mopped up the spill with a napkin, fisted the damp cloth, and took deep chest-expanding breaths until he felt calmer. He allowed himself a glance around the room, half-expecting the flutter of wings, the brush of the thing with feathers.

Slow as a Bullet

I ever tell you about the time Cliffert Corbett settled a bet by out-running a bullet?

Oh.

Well, all right, Little Miss Smarty Ass, here it is again, but this time I'll stick to the truth, because I got enough sins to write out on St. Peter's blackboard as it is, thank you, and on the third go-round the truth is easiest to remember. So you just write down what I tell you, just *as* I tell you, and don't put in none of your women's embroidery this time.

You're too young to remember Cliffert Corbett, I reckon, but he was the kind that even if you did remember him, you wouldn't remember him, except for this one thing that I am going to tell you, the one remarkable thing he ever did in his life. It started one lazed-out, dragged-in Florida afternoon outside the gas station, when we were all passing around a sack of boiled peanuts and woofing about who was the fastest.

During all this, Cliffert hadn't said nothing, and he hadn't intended to say nothing, but Cliffert's mouth was just like your mouth and mine. Whenever it was shut it was only biding its time, just waiting for the mind to fall down on the job long enough for the mouth to jump into the gap and raise some hell. So when Cliffert squeezed one boiled peanut right into his eye and blinded himself, his mouth was ready. As he blinked away the juice, his mouth up and blabbed:

"Any of you fast enough to outrun a bullet?"

They all turned and looked at him, and friend, he wasn't much to look at. Cliffert was built like a fence post, and a rickety post, too, maybe that last post standing of the old fence in back of the gas station, the one with the lone snipped rusty barbed-wire curl, the one the bobwhites wouldn't nest in, because the men liked to shoot at it for target practice. And everyone knew that if Cliffert, with his gimpy leg, was to race that fence post, their money would be elsewhere than on Cliffert.

And because what Cliffert had said wasn't joking like, but more angry, sort of a challenge, Isiah Bird asked, "You saying you can do that?"

And just before Cliffert got the last bit of salt out of his eyes, his mouth told Isiah, "I got five dollars says I can, Isiah Bird."

From there it didn't matter how shut Cliffert's mouth was, because before he knew what hit him Isiah had taken that bet, and the others had jumped in and put down money of their own, and they were hollering for other folks on the street to come get in on the action, and Dad Boykin made up a little register that showed enough money was riding on this to have Cliffert set for life if he just could outrun a bullet, which everyone in town knew he couldn't do, including Cliffert, plus he didn't have no five dollars to lose.

"We'll settle this right now," said Pump Jeffries, who ran the gas station. "I got my service pistol locked up in the office there, but it's well greased and ready to go."

"Hold on!" cried Cliffert, and they all studied him unfriendly like, knowing he was about to back out on the deal his mouth had made.

"I got to use my own gun," Cliffert said, "and my own bullets."

They all looked at each other, but when Isiah Bird nodded his head, the others nodded, too. "Fetch 'em, then," Dad Boykin said. "We'll wait right here."

"Now, boys," said Cliffert, thinking faster than he could run, "you got to give me some time to get ready. Because this ain't something you can just up and do, no matter how fast you are. You got to practice at it, work up to it. I need to get in shape."

"Listen at him now. He wants to go into training!"

"How long you need, then?"

"A year," Clifford said. "I'll outrun a bullet one year from this very day, the next twenty-first of July, right here in front of the gas station, at noon."

No one liked this very much, because they were all raring to go right then. But they talked it over and decided that Cliffert wasn't going to be any more able to outrun a bullet in a year than he was now.

"All right, Cliffert," they told him. "One year from today."

So then Cliffert limped on home, tearing his hair and moaning, cursing his fool mouth for getting him into this fix.

He was still moaning when he passed the hoodoo woman's house. You could tell it was the hoodoo woman's house because the holes in the cement blocks that held it up were full of charms, and the raked patterns in the dirt yard would move if you looked at them too hard, and the persimmon trees were heavy with blue bottles to catch spirits, and mainly because the hoodoo woman herself was always sitting on the porch, smoking a corncob pipe, at all hours and in all weathers, because her house was ideally situated to watch all the townsfolk going and coming, and she was afraid if she ever went inside she might miss something.

"What ails you, Cliffert Corbett, that you're carrying on such a way?"

So Cliffert limped into her yard, taking care not to step on any of the wiggly lines, and told her the whole thing.

"So you see, Miz Armetta, I won't be able to hold my head up in this town no more. I'll have to go live in Tallahassee with the rest of the liars."

The hoodoo woman snorted. "Just tell 'em you can't outrun a bullet, that you're sorry you stretched it any such a way. Isiah Bird keeps cattle and hogs both, and he'll let you work off that five dollars you owe him."

When he heard the word "work," Cliffert felt faint, and the sun went behind a cloud, and the dirt pattern in the yard looked like a big spider that crouched and waited.

"Oh, Miz Armetta, work is a harsh thing to say to a man! Ain't you got any other ideas for me than that?"

"Mmmph," she said, drawing on her pipe. "The holes men dig just to have a place to sit." She closed her eyes and rocked in her shuck chair and drummed her fingertips on her wrinkled forehead and asked, "They expecting you to use your own bullet?"

"Yes, and my own gun."

"Well, it's simple then," she said. "You need you some slow bullets."

"What you mean, slow bullets? I never heard tell of such a thing."

"I ain't, either," said the hoodoo woman, "but you got a year to find you some, or make you some."

Cliffert studied on this all the way home. There he lifted his daddy's old service pistol and gun belt out of the cedar chest and rummaged an old box of bullets out of the back corner of the Hoosier cabinet and set them both on the kitchen table and sat down before them. He rested his elbows on the oilcloth and rested his chin on his hands. He wasn't used to thinking, but now that first Isiah Bird and now the hoodoo woman had got him started in that direction, he was sort of beginning to enjoy it. He studied and studied, and by sunset he had his breakthrough.

"The *bullet* is just a lump of metal," he told the three-year-and-two-month-old Martha White calendar that twitched and tapped the wall in the evening breeze. "It's the powder in the cartridge that moves it along. So what I need is *slow* powder. But what would go into slow powder?"

He grabbed a stubby pencil, and on the topmost *Tallahassee Democrat* on a stack bound for the outhouse, he began to make a list of slow things.

For week after week, month after month, Cliffert messed at his kitchen table, and then in his back yard, with his gunpowder recipe, looking for the mix that gave a bullet the slowest start possible while still firing. First he ground up some snail shells and turtle shells and mixed that in. He drizzled a spoonful of molasses over it and made such a jommock that he had to start over, so from then on, he used only a dot of molasses in each batch, like the single roly-poly blob Aunt Berth put in the middle of her biscuit after the doctor told her to mind her sugar. For growing grass he had to visit a neighbor's yard, since his own yard was dirt and unraked dirt at that, but the flecks of dry paint were scraped from his own side porch and in the sun, too, which was one job of work. He tried recipe after recipe, a tad more of this and a teenchy bit less of that, and went through three boxes of bullets test-firing into a propped-up Sears, Roebuck catalog in the back yard, and even though the boxes emptied ever more slowly, he still was dissatisfied. Then one day he went to Fulmer's Hardware and told his problems to the man himself.

"You try any wet paint?" Mr. Fulmer asked.

"No," Cliffert said. "Just the flakings. How come you ask me that?"

"Well, I was just thinking," Mr. Fulmer said. He laid the edge of his left hand down on the counter, like it was slicing bread. "If wet paint is over *here*." He held his left hand still and laid down the edge of his right hand about 10 inches away. "And dry paint is over *here*, and it goes from the one to the other, it stands to reason that the wet paint is slower than the dry, since it ain't caught up yet."

Cliffert studied Mr. Fulmer's hands for a spell. The store was silent, except for the *plip plip plip* from the next aisle. They couldn't see over the shelf but knew it was 6-year-old Louvenia Parler, who liked to wait for her mama in the hardware store so she could play with the nails.

"That stands to reason," Cliffert finally said, "only if the wet paint is as old as the dry paint, so we know they started at the same time."

Mr. Fulmer folded his arms. "Now you talking sense. When you last paint your side porch?"

"I myself ain't never painted it, nor the front porch nor no other part of the house. It don't look like it's been painted since God laid down the dirt to make the mountains."

"That might be the original paint, sure enough, so you're out of luck. I don't stock no seventy-five-year-old paint."

"How old you got?"

Mr. Fulmer blew air between his lips like a noisemaker. "Ohh, let's see. I probably got paint about as old as Louvenia."

"Well, even Mr. Ford started somewhere. Let me have a gallon of the oldest you got."

Mr. Fulmer asked, "What color?" And before he even could regret asking, Cliffert said:

"Whatever color's the slowest, that's the one I want."

Mr. Fulmer laughed. "I know you chasing your tail now. The hell you gone tell what color's slowest? I been pouring paint for thirty years, and it all pours and dries the same."

Cliffert opened his mouth to say he-didn't-know-what, but the sound they heard was a little-girl voice from the next aisle over, stretching out her "I" all sassy like.

"*I-I-I-I* know how," Louvenia said. "*I-I-I-I* know how to tell."

Cliffert looked at Mr. Fulmer, and Mr. Fulmer looked at Cliffert, and when they got tired of looking at each other, they looked over the top edge of the shelf and saw Louvenia sitting on the plank floor, calico skirt spread out like a lilypad, and all around her a briarpatch of nails, tenpenny and twopenny, dozens of them, all standing on their heads and ranged like soldiers.

"Tell us, Louvenia, honey," Cliffert said.

"Watch for when a rainbow comes out," she said, "and see which color comes out the slowest." She scooped up a handful of twopennies and sifted them through her fingers back into the nail keg, *plip plip plip.*

"That's good thinking, Louvenia," Cliffert said. "I thank you kindly."

"You're welcome," she said.

"You put those back when you're done, now, Louvenia," Mr. Fulmer said as he and Cliffert pulled their heads back. "I swear, ever nail in this town will be handled by that child before she's done."

"It *is* a good idea," Cliffert said, "but my eyes ain't good enough to make it a practice."

"Mine, neither," Mr. Fulmer said. "I see a rainbow all at once, or I don't see it."

Cliffert opened his mouth again, but nothing came out. Mr. Fulmer waited. He wasn't in no hurry. If it hadn't been a slow day, he wouldn't have been standing there jawing about dry paint and rainbows. Finally Cliffert turned his hand edgewise and chopped the air seven times.

"They *are* the same order, ever time, in a rainbow," Cliffert said. "Read Out Your Good Book In Verse. Red the first, violet the last."

"Or the other way around," Mr. Fulmer said. "You going left to right or right to left?"

"Has to be one end or the other," Cliffert said. "Gimme a gallon of red and a gallon of violet."

"*I* call it purple," Mr. Fulmer said, "and paint don't come in purple. But I can sure mix you some red and blue to make purple."

"Well, I thank you," Cliffert said.

Mr. Fulmer whistled his way into the storage room, happy because he had helped solve a little hardware problem and because since the Crash he had about given up on ever moving another gallon of paint.

So Cliffert worked through Christmas adding dibs and dabs of paint to his mix, and after New Year's he threw in some January molasses cause those are the slowest, and then he shot off the results back of his house, *bang bang blim bang.* "It's the Battle of Atlanta," his neighbors cried, and beat the younguns who walked too near

Cliffert's fence. He didn't get close to satisfied till the first of June, and only then did he take his gun and his custom-made cartridges over to the hoodoo woman's house to show her what he had.

"Mmmph, mmmph, mmmph," said the hoodoo woman. The second "mmmph" meant she was impressed, and the third meant she was *flat* impressed.

"That's good, Cliffert Corbett," she said, "but hold on here, I got one more idea that might make her better still. Now, where'd I put that thing?" She rummaged her right hand through her apron pockets while holding her left hand out in the air stiff and flat, like she was drying her nails in the breeze, only there was no breeze and the nails were black and broken on her knobbed and ropy hand, and Cliffert didn't like the look of it. Then the hoodoo woman laughed a croupy laugh and pulled forth a corked bottle the size of her thumb, full of a pale green sloshy something. "If it was a snake it woulda bit me," said the hoodoo woman.

"What is it, Miz Armetta?"

"Money Stay With Me Oil. I reckon if it slows down the money, it might slow down your bullet, too. Here, unstop it for me while I reach out my dropper. Don't let none get on you, now! This is for fixing, not anointing."

Cliffert thought the bottle was powerful heavy for such a tee-ninchy dram of liquid, and was glad to hand it back to her when she was done plopping one sallow green blob onto the tip of each cartridge, then wiping them down with a bright red cloth. They should have gleamed brighter then, but instead they looked even duller, like their surface light was being sucked inside to die. "Don't just stand there," she said. "Get to writing. We need some name paper. Write your full name nine times on red ink."

"You got any red ink, Miz Armetta?"

She snorted. "Does Fulmer's have nails?"

Cliffert's hand hurt him by the time he was done—he couldn't make the F's to suit her, and had to keep doing them over—but he had to admit, when they tried out the test bullet, that a little Money Stay With Me oil had gone a long way.

So on the appointed day, everybody in town who was interested in bets or guns or lies, or who was hanging around the gas station on that fateful day the year before, or who was related to any of those, all turned up at the gas station to see whether Cliffert actually would be there to admit to his lie and pay the man. Everyone was half surprised to see Cliffert limping across the lot, about five minutes to noon, and plumb surprised to see him wearing his daddy's gun belt. It was cinched to the last hole and still he had to hold it up with both hands, and the holster went down practically to his knee. But sticking out of the holster was a shiny silver gun butt that suggested Cliffert was open for business.

"Cliffert Corbett, you here to outrun a bullet today?" asked Isiah Bird.

"I will sure do that thing, Isiah Bird," said Cliffert in return.

"Do it, then," said Dad Boykin. "I got corn to shuck and chicken to pluck. I got obligations."

Cliffert planted his feet on the asphalt and looked down the side of the station toward the back of the lot, and hollered at the crowd, "Y'all make way so's a man can work!" But that little bantyweight holding up his belt looked just like a youngun playing gunfighter after a cowboy matinee, and we all just laughed at him. Lord, how we laughed! And didn't nobody budge an inch until he drew that gun—all slow and solemn-like—and pointed it at us with the steadiest hand you ever saw, and then we all found reasons to get behind him and beside him and up against the walls and otherwise out of the man's way. So in a few seconds there was nothing between Cliffert's gun and that shot-up old fence post at the back of the property, the last piece of the fence that separated the gas station from the woods behind. It was right splintered up, though not as much as you'd think, since the men of our town weren't the greatest shots in Florida, not even drunk.

"On three," Cliffert said, and he brought that gun up two-handed and squinted down the barrel, and without his hand on it, his gun belt slipped down to his knees. Nobody laughed, though, because that gun was steady, man, steady.

"One," Cliffert said.

We didn't say nothing.

"Two," Cliffert said.

We didn't breathe.

Then he fired, and we all jumped about a foot in the air. It wasn't just that the shot was three times as loud as any gunshot has any right to be. It also sounded . . . *wrong*. It sounded *interrupted*. It sounded like a scream that lasts only a half-second before someone claps a hand across your mouth. And the smoke coming out of the barrel was wrong, too. Instead of puffing away in an instant, it uncoiled slow in solid gray ropes, like baby snakes first poking their heads from a hidey-hole in springtime. And the fence post looked just the same as before.

"Misfire," someone said.

"Wait for it," Cliffert said, still sighting down the barrel and holding her steady.

The smoke kept on curling. And then, amid the smoke, something dark started pushing forth, like the gun itself was turning wrong side out. Lord have mercy, it was the tip of the bullet sliding into view, and nobody said a word as it eased on out of the barrel. It must have taken a solid minute just for that bullet to clear the gun. And just as we could see daylight between the bullet and the barrel, Cliffert stepped back a pace and raised the gun and blew across the tip. I never saw smoke so loath to be gone. A scrap of it snagged his lip and hung there awhile like a sorry gray mustache before it slid off into nothing.

"Move the gun too quick, you mess up the aim," Cliffert said. "I was days figuring that out."

Then I went back to watching the bullet, which was about a foot away and moving steady but no faster than before. In fact, I reckon it was moving even slower, since all its charge was blown, and from here on gravity takes over—in any normal Christian bullet, that is. You ever craned your neck to look up at an airplane that just seems to be making no progress at all? Watching that bullet was like watching that airplane, one about at the level of the tobacco pouch in my shirt pocket. Even Cliffert just stood there, gun still on his shoulder pointing at the top of the chinaberry tree, staring at the bullet he had made, as hypnotized as anyone.

Someone yelled, "Look at the shadow!"

The bullet's shadow was crawling along the ground, sliding in and out of every chip and crack in the asphalt, in no bigger hurry than the bullet it was tethered to above, and somehow that shadow was even worse than the bullet.

A shudder went through the crowd, and a few folks bust out crying, and they weren't all women neither, while some others started hollering for Jesus.

Cliffert sort of shook himself all over and said, "Look at me! I near forgot the bet." He holstered the gun and ambled forward. He was noways in a hurry, but in only a few steps he'd caught up to that bullet he had loosed, and in a few steps more he had walked past it, and as he walked he pulled a wrinkled paper from his pants pocket. He unfolded it and smoothed it out a little and turned around and held it up as he walked. Drawn on the paper in red ink was a bull's-eye target about six inches across, and Cliffert stumbled a little as he walked backwards, trying to gauge how high the target ought to be for the bullet to hit it square.

Now we had two things of wonderment to look at, Cliffert's bullet and Cliffert himself, and we all was so busy staring at one and then the other that we hadn't paid any mind at all to a third thing: Lou Lou Maddox's toothless mangy old collie dog, the one that was blind in one eye and couldn't see out the other, and had so much arthritis that she wouldn't have been walking if she hadn't been held up and jerked along by the fleas. That old dog had crawled out from under the Maddox porch next door and stood up all rickety and hitched her way across the side yard headed toward the gas station, maybe because she smelled the peanuts boiling, or because she wondered what all the fuss was about, and when we finally noticed her walking into the path of Cliffert's bullet, we all hollered at once—so loud that the damn dog stopped dead in her tracks and blinked at us with milky eyes, and that bullet not six inches from her shackly ribcage and inching closer.

"Salome!" screamed Lou Lou. "Get out of there, Salome!"

The dog blinked and looked sideways and saw that bullet a-coming. Salome yelped and hopped forward twice, so that the bullet just missed her hindquarters as it headed on.

Now Cliffert had finally got his target situated where he wanted it, by jamming it down on a splinter on that highest fence post at the back of the lot. And by the time the bullet was finally about a half-inch from the bull's-eye, everyone had had time to go get some supper and find a few more relations to tell about the marvel and bring them on back to the gas station, so the whole damn town was standing gathered around the target in a half-circle, all watching as the bullet nosed into the paper . . . and dented it a little . . . and then punched through (we all heard it) . . . and then kept on going, through the paper and into the fence post (we all heard a little grinding noise, *eckity eckity eckity eck*, like a mouse in the wall, but all continuous, not afeard of no cat or nothing else in this world, just doing its slow steady job of work) . . . and then the sawdust started sifting out of the back of the post . . . and here came the bullet, out the other side (we had flashlights and lanterns trained on it by then), and we all watched as the bullet went on into the brush and into the woods, and then it was so dark we couldn't see it no more. We thought about following it into the woods with our lights, but then we thought about getting all confused in the dark and getting ahead of it, and how it would be to have that bullet a-nosing into your side, so we decided not to hunt for it but say we did.

"Just imagine," said the hoodoo woman, the only person in town not at the gas station. Still a-sitting on her porch, she struck a match and fired her pipe and told the shapes gathering in the dirt, "Imagine having nothing better to do all day than watch a man shoot a fence post." She pointed her pipestem at a particularly lively patch of ground. "You stay down in that yard, Sonny Jim. I got my eyes on you."

What happened next?

Well, that was about when I left. So I ain't any too clear on the rest of it. I know Cliffert collected him some money, off of me and a lot of the others. It was enough to set him up for life in the style to which he was accustomed, not that he was accustomed to much. Someone told me he took the train to Pensacola that week and tried to sell the U.S. Army on what he had done, but the U.S. Army said thank you just the same, it couldn't see no point, no strategic advantage, in a bullet that even a colicky baby could crawl out of the way of. Not that the U.S. Army had any plans to actually shoot any colicky babies. That was just a for-example. They weren't aware in Pensacola of any immediate colicky baby threat, although they would continue to monitor the situation. So the U.S. Army hustled Cliffert out of the office, and he went on home and lived out his days a richer and more thoughtful man, but if he ever made any more slow bullets, the news ain't reached me yet. So that's more'n I know.

Except no one ever did see that bullet come out of them woods. Maybe it finally come to rest in a tree, and maybe it didn't. Maybe it finally run out of juice, and dropped to the ground and died, and maybe it didn't. Maybe it's still in there someplace, a-looking around for something to shoot. Maybe it found its way out of them woods long ago. Could be anywhere by now. One day you might be going about your business, pestering the life out of some hopeful old man with that notebook of yourn, and his eyes might get wide and he might say, "Hey!" But it's too late, because you can't even get turned 'round good before *eckity, eckity, eck,* Cliffert Corbett's bullet is drilling into the back of your head, and next thing you know, there you is, dead as McKinley on the cooling board.

Why ain't you writing that down?

What? Call yourself educated and can't even spell *eckity, eckity, eck?* Shit. I could spell that myself, if I ever needed it done.

Close Encounters

She knocked on my front door at midday on Holly Eve, so I was in no mood to answer, in that season of tricks. An old man expects more tricks than treats in this world. I let that knocker knock on. *Blim, blam!* Knock, knock! It hurt my concentration, and filling old hulls with powder and shot warn't no easy task to start with, not as palsied as my hands had got, in my eightieth-odd year.

"All right, damn your eyes," I hollered as I hitched up from the table. I knocked against it, and a shaker tipped over: pepper, so I let it go. My maw wouldn't have approved of such language as that, but we all get old doing things our maws wouldn't approve. We can't help it, not in this disposition, on this sphere down below.

I sidled up on the door, trying to see between the edges of the curtain and the pane, but all I saw there was the screen-filtered light of the sun, which wouldn't set in my hollow till nearbouts three in the day. Through the curtains was a shadow-shape like the top of a person's head, but low, like a child. Probably one of those Holton boys toting an orange coin carton with a photo of some spindleshanked African child eating hominy with its fingers. Some said those Holtons was like the Johnny Cash song, so heavenly minded they're no earthly good.

"What you want?" I called, one hand on the deadbolt and one feeling for starving-baby quarters in my pocket.

"Mr. Nelson, right? Mr. Buck Nelson? I'd like to talk a bit, if you don't mind. Inside or on the porch, your call."

A female, and no child, neither. I twitched back the curtain, saw a fair pretty face under a fool hat like a sideways saucer, lips painted the same black-red as her hair. I shot the bolt and opened the wood door but kept the screen latched. When I saw her full length I felt a rush of fool vanity and was sorry I hadn't traded my overalls for fresh that morning. Her boots reached her knees but nowhere near the hem of her tight green dress. She was a little thing, hardly up to my collarbone, but a blind man would know she was full growed. I wondered what my hair was doing in back, and I felt one hand reach around to slick it down, without my really telling it to. Steady on, son.

"I been answering every soul else calling Buck Nelson since 1894, so I reckon I should answer you, too. What you want to talk about, Miss—?"

"Miss Hanes," she said, "and I'm a wire reporter, stringing for Associated Press."

"A reporter," I repeated. My jaw tightened up. My hand reached back for the doorknob as natural as it had fussed my hair. "You must have got the wrong man," I said.

I'd eaten biscuits bigger than her tee-ninchy pocketbook, but she reached out of it a little spiral pad that she flipped open to squint at. Looked to be full of secretary-scratch, not schoolhouse writing at all. "But you, sir, are indeed Buck Nelson, Route One, Mountain View, Missouri? Writer of a book about your travels to the Moon, and Mars, and Venus?"

By the time she fetched up at Venus her voice was muffled by the wood door I had slammed in her face. I bolted it, cursing my rusty slow reflexes. How long had it been, since fool reporters come using around? Not long enough. I limped as quick as I could to the back door, which was right quick, even at my age. It's a small house. I shut that bolt, too, and yanked all the curtains to. I turned on the Zenith and dialed the sound up as far as it would go to drown out her blamed knocking and calling. Ever since the roof aerial blew cockeyed in the last whippoorwill storm, watching my set was like trying to read a road sign in a blizzard, but the sound blared out well enough. One of the stories was on as I settled back at the table with my shotgun hulls. I didn't really follow those women's stories, but I could hear Stu and Jo were having coffee again at the Hartford House and still talking about poor dead Eunice and that crazy gal what shot her because a ghost told her to. That blonde Jennifer was slap crazy, all right, but she was a looker, too, and the story hadn't been half so interesting since she'd been packed off to the sanitarium. I was spilling powder everywhere now, what with all the racket and distraction, and hearing the story was on reminded me it was past my dinnertime anyways, and me hungry. I went into the kitchen, hooked down my grease-pan and set it on the big burner, dug some lard out of the stand I kept in the icebox and threw that in to melt, then fisted some fresh-picked whitefish mushrooms out of their bin, rinjed them off in the sink, and rolled them in a bowl of cornmeal while I half-listened to the TV and half-listened to the city girl banging and hollering, at the back door this time. I could hear her boot heels a-thunking all hollow-like on the back porch, over the old dog bed where Teddy used to lie, where the other dog, Bo, used to try to squeeze, big as he was. She'd probably want to talk about poor old Bo, too, ask to see his grave, as if that would prove something. She had her some stick-to-it-iveness, Miss Associated Press did, I'd give her that much. Now she was sliding something under the door, I could hear it, like a field mouse gnawing its way in: a little card, like the one that Methodist preacher always leaves, only shinier. I didn't bother to pick it up. I didn't need nothing down there on that floor. I slid the whitefish into the hot oil without a splash. My hands had about lost their grip on gun and tool work, but in the kitchen I was as surefingered as an old woman. Well, eating didn't mean shooting anymore, not since the power line come in, and the supermarket down the highway. Once the whitefish got to sizzling good, I didn't hear Miss Press no more.

"This portion of *Search for Tomorrow* has been brought to you by . . . Spic and Span, the all-purpose cleaner. And by . . . Joy dishwashing liquid. From grease to shine in half the time, with Joy. Our story will continue in just a moment."

I was up by times the next morning. Hadn't kept milk cows in years. The last was Molly, she with the wet-weather horn, a funny-looking old gal but as calm and sweet as could be. But if you've milked cows for seventy years, it's hard to give in and let the sun start beating you to the day. By first light I'd had my Cream of Wheat, a child's meal I'd developed a taste for, with a little jerp of honey, and was out in the back field, bee hunting.

I had three sugar-dipped corncobs in a croker sack, and I laid one out on a hickory stump, notched one into the top of a fencepost, and set the third atop the boulder at the start of the path that drops down to the creek, past the old lick-log where the salt still keeps the grass from growing. Then I settled down on an old milkstool to wait. I gave up snuff a while ago because I couldn't taste it no more and the price got so high with taxes that I purely hated putting all that government in my mouth, but I still carry some little brushes to chew on in dipping moments, and I chewed on one while I watched those three corncobs do nothing. I'd set down where I could see all three without moving my head, just by darting my eyes from one to the other. My eyes may not see *Search for Tomorrow* so good anymore, even before the aerial got bent, but they still can sight a honeybee coming in to sip the bait.

The cob on the stump got the first business, but that bee just smelled around and then buzzed off straightaway, so I stayed set where I was. Same thing happened to the post cob and to the rock cob, three bees come and gone. But then a big bastard, one I could hear coming in like an airplane twenty feet away, zoomed down on the fence cob and stayed there a long time, filling his hands. He rose up all lazy-like, just like a man who's lifted the jug too many times in a sitting, and then made one, two, three slow circles in the air, marking the position. When he flew off, I was right behind him, legging it into the woods.

Mister Big Bee led me a ways straight up the slope, toward the well of the old McQuarry place, but then he crossed the bramble patch, and by the time I had worked my way antigodlin around that, I had lost sight of him. So I listened for a spell, holding my breath, and heard a murmur like a branch in a direction where there warn't no branch. Sure enough, over thataway was a big hollow oak with a bee highway a-coming and a-going through a seam in the lowest fork. Tell the truth, I wasn't rightly on my own land any more. The McQuarry place belonged to a bank in Cape Girardeau, if it belonged to anybody. But no one had blazed this tree yet, so my claim would be good enough for any bee hunter. I sidled around to just below the fork and notched an X where any fool could see it, even me, because I had been known to miss my own signs some days, or rummage the bureau for a sock that was already on my foot. Something about the way I'd slunk toward the hive the way I'd slunk toward the door the day before made me remember Miss Press, whom I'd plumb forgotten about. And when I turned back toward home, in the act of folding my pocketknife, there she was sitting on the lumpy leavings of the McQuarry chimney, a-kicking her feet and waving at me, just like I had wished her out of the ground. I'd have to go past her to get home, as I didn't relish turning my back on her and heading around the mountain, down the long way to the macadam and back around. Besides, she'd just follow me anyway, the way she followed me out here. I unfolded my knife again and snatched up a walnut stick to whittle on as I stomped along to where she sat.

"Hello, Mr. Nelson," she said. "Can we start over?"

"I ain't a-talking to *you*," I said as I passed, pointing at her with my blade. "I ain't even *a-walking* with you," I added, as she slid off the rockpile and walked along beside. "I'm taking the directedest path home, is all, and where you choose to walk is your own lookout. Fall in a hole, and I'll just keep a-going, I swear I will. I've done it before, left reporters in the woods to die."

"Aw, I don't believe you have," she said, in a happy singsongy way. At least she was dressed for a tramp through the woods, in denim jeans and mannish boots with no heels to them, but wearing the same face-paint and fool hat, and in a red sweater that fit as close as her dress had. "But I'm not walking with you, either," she went on. "I'm walking alone, just behind you. You can't even see me, without turning your head. We're both walking alone, together."

I didn't say nothing.

"Are we near where it landed?" she asked.

I didn't say nothing.

"You haven't had one of your picnics lately, have you?"

I didn't say nothing.

"You ought to have another one."

I didn't say nothing.

"I'm writing a story," she said, "about *Close Encounters.* You know, the new movie? With Richard Dreyfuss? He was in *The Goodbye Girl,* and *Jaws,* about the shark? Did you see those? Do you go to any movies?" Some critter we had spooked, maybe a turkey, went thrashing off through the brush, and I heard her catch her breath. "I bet you saw *Deliverance,*" she said.

I didn't say nothing.

"My editor thought it'd be interesting to talk to people who really have, you know, claimed their own close encounters, to have met people from outer space. Contactees, that's the word, right? You were one of the first contactees, weren't you, Mr. Nelson? When was it, 1956?"

I didn't say nothing.

"Aw, come on, Mr. Nelson. Don't be so mean. They all talked to me out in California. Mr. Bethurum talked to me."

I bet he did, I thought. Truman Bethurum always was a plumb fool for a skirt.

"I talked to Mr. Fry, and to Mr. King, and Mr. Owens. I talked to Mr. Angelucci."

Orfeo Angelucci, I thought, now there was one of the world's original liars, as bad as Adamski. "Those names don't mean nothing to me," I said.

"They told similar stories to yours, in the fifties and sixties. Meeting the Space Brothers, and being taken up, and shown wonders, and coming back to the Earth, with wisdom and all."

"If you talked to all them folks," I said, "you ought to be brim full of wisdom yourself. Full of something. Why you need to hound an old man through the woods?"

"You're different," she said. "You know lots of things the others don't."

"Lots of things, uh-huh. Like what?"

"You know how to hunt bees, don't you?"

I snorted. "Hunt bees. You won't never need to hunt no bees, Miss Press. Priss. You can buy your honey at the A and the P. Hell, if you don't feel like going to the store, you could just ask, and some damn fool would bring it to you for free on a silver tray."

"Well, thank you," she said.

"That warn't no compliment," I said. "That was a clear-eyed statement of danger, like a sign saying, 'Bridge out,' or a label saying, 'Poison.' Write what you please, Miss Priss, but don't expect me to give you none of the words. You know all the words you need already."

"But you used to be so open about your experiences, Mr. Nelson. I've read that to anyone who found their way here off the highway, you'd tell about the alien Bob Solomon, and how that beam from the saucer cured your lumbago, and all that good pasture land on Mars. Why, you had all those three-day picnics, right here on your farm, for anyone who wanted to come talk about the Space Brothers. You'd even hand out little Baggies with samples of hair from your four-hundred-pound Venusian dog."

I stopped and whirled on her, and she hopped back a step, nearly fell down. "He warn't never no four hundred pounds," I said. "You reporters sure do believe some stretchers. You must swallow whole eggs for practice like a snake. I'll have you know, Miss Priss, that Bo just barely tipped three hundred and eighty-five pounds at his heaviest, and that was on the truck scales behind the Union 76 in June 1960, the day he ate all the sileage, and Clay Rector, who ran all their inspections back then, told me those scales would register the difference if you took the Rand McNally atlas out of the cab, so that figure ain't no guesswork." When I paused for breath, I kinda shook myself, turned away from her gaping face and walked on. "From that day," I said, "I put old Bo on a science diet, one I got from the Extension, and I measured his rations, and I hitched him ever day to a sledge of felled trees and boulders and such, because dogs, you know, they're happier with a little exercise, and he settled down to around, oh, three-ten, three-twenty, and got downright frisky again. He'd romp around and change direction and jerk that sledge around, and that's why those three boulders are a-sitting in the middle of yonder pasture today, right where he slung them out of the sledge. Four hundred pounds, my foot. You don't know much, if that's what you know, and that's a fact."

I was warmed up by the walk and the spreading day and my own strong talk, and I set a smart pace, but she loped along beside me, writing in her notebook with a silver pen that flashed as it caught the sun. "I stand corrected," she said. "So what happened? Why'd you stop the picnics, and start running visitors off with a shotgun, and quit answering your mail?"

"You can see your own self what happened," I said. "Woman, I got old. You'll see what it's like, when you get there. All the people who believed in me died, and then the ones who humored me died, and now even the ones who feel obligated to sort of tolerate me are starting to go. Bo died, and Teddy, that was my Earth-born dog, he died, and them government boys went to the Moon and said they didn't see no mining operations or colony domes or big Space Brother dogs, or nothing else old Buck had seen up there. And in place of my story, what story did they come up with? I ask you. Dust and rocks and craters as far as you can see, and when you walk as far as that, there's another sight of dust and rocks and craters, and so on all around till you're back where you started, and that's it, boys, wash your hands, that's the Moon done. Excepting for some spots where the dust is so deep a body trying to land would just be swallowed up, sink to the bottom, and at the bottom find what? Praise Jesus, more dust, just what we needed. They didn't see nothing that anybody would care about going to see. No floating cars, no lakes of diamonds, no topless Moon gals, just dumb dull nothing. Hell, they might as well a been in Arkansas. You at least can cast a line there, catch you a bream. Besides, my lumbago come back," I said, easing myself down into the rocker, because we was back on my front porch by then. "It always comes back, my doctor says. Doctors plural, I should say. I'm on the third one now. The first two died on me. That's something, ain't it? For a man to outlive two of his own doctors?"

Her pen kept a-scratching as she wrote. She said, "Maybe Bob Solomon's light beam is still doing you some good, even after all this time."

"Least it didn't do me no harm. From what all they say now about the space people, I'm lucky old Bob didn't jamb a post-hole digger up my ass and send me home with the screaming meemies and three hours of my life missing. That's the only aliens anybody cares about nowadays, big-eyed boogers with long cold fingers in your drawers. Doctors from space. Well, if they want to take three hours of my life, they're welcome to my last trip to the urologist. I reckon it was right at three hours, and I wish them joy of it."

"Not so," she said. "What about *Star Wars?* It's already made more money than any other movie ever made, more than *Gone With the Wind,* more than *The Sound of Music.* That shows people are still interested in space, and in friendly aliens. And this new Richard Dreyfuss movie I was telling you about is based on actual UFO case files. Dr. Hynek helped with it. That'll spark more interest in past visits to Earth."

"I been to ever doctor in the country, seems like," I told her, "but I don't recall ever seeing Dr. Hynek."

"How about Dr. Rutledge?"

"Is he the toenail man?"

She swatted me with her notebook. "Now you're just being a pain," she said. "Dr. Harley Rutledge, the scientist, the physicist. Over at Southeast Missouri State. That's no piece from here. He's been doing serious UFO research for years, right here in the Ozarks. You really ought to know him. He's been documenting the spook-lights. Like the one at Hornet, near Neosho?"

"I've heard tell of that light," I told her, "but I didn't know no scientist cared about it."

"See?" she said, almost a squeal, like she'd opened a present, like she'd proved something. "A lot has happened since you went home and locked the door. More people care about UFOs and flying saucers and aliens today than they did in the 1950s, even. You should have you another picnic."

Once I got started talking, I found her right easy to be with, and it was pleasant a-sitting in the sun talking friendly with a pretty gal, or with anyone. It's true, I'd been powerful lonesome, and I had missed those picnics, all those different types of folks on the farm who wouldn't have been brought together no other way, in no other place, by nobody else. I was prideful of them. But I was beginning to notice something funny. To begin with, Miss Priss, whose real name I'd forgot by now, had acted like someone citified and paper-educated and standoffish. Now, the longer she sat on my porch a-jawing with me, the more easeful she got, and the more country she sounded, as if she'd lived in the hollow her whole life. It sorta put me off. Was this how Mike Wallace did it on *60 Minutes*, pretending to be just regular folks, until you forgot yourself, and were found out?

"Where'd you say you were from?" I asked.

"Mars," she told me. Then she laughed. "Don't get excited," she said. "It's a town in Pennsylvania, north of Pittsburgh. I'm based out of Chicago, though." She cocked her head, pulled a frown, stuck out her bottom lip. "You didn't look at my card," she said. "I pushed it under your door yesterday, when you were being so all-fired rude."

"I didn't see it," I said, which warn't quite a lie because I hadn't bothered to pick it up off the floor this morning, either. In fact, I'd plumb forgot to look for it.

"You ought to come out to Clearwater Lake tonight. Dr. Rutledge and his students will be set up all night, ready for whatever. He said I'm welcome. That means you're welcome, too. See? You have friends in high places. They'll be set up at the overlook, off the highway. Do you know it?"

"I know it," I told her.

"Can you drive at night? You need me to come get you?" She blinked and chewed her lip, like a thought had just struck. "That might be difficult," she said.

"Don't exercise yourself," I told her. "I reckon I still can drive as good as I ever did, and my pickup still gets the job done, too. Not that I aim to drive all that ways, just to look at the sky. I can do that right here on my porch."

"Yes," she said, "alone. But there's something to be said for looking up in groups, wouldn't you agree?"

When I didn't say nothing, she stuck her writing-pad back in her pocketbook and stood up, dusting her butt with both hands. You'd think I never swept the porch. "I appreciate the interview, Mr. Nelson."

"Warn't no interview," I told her. "We was just talking, is all."

"I appreciate the talking, then," she said. She set off across the yard, toward the gap in the rhododendron bushes that marked the start of the driveway. "I hope you can make it tonight, Mr. Nelson. I hope you don't miss the show."

I watched her sashay off around the bush, and I heard her boots crunching the gravel for a few steps, and then she was gone, footsteps and all. I went back in the house, latched the screen door and locked the wood, and took one last look through the front curtains, to make sure. Some folks, I had heard, remembered only long afterward they'd been kidnapped by spacemen, a "retrieved memory" they called it, like finding a ball on the roof in the fall that went up there in the spring. Those folks needed a doctor to jog them, but this reporter had jogged me. All that happy talk had loosened something inside me, and things I hadn't thought about in years were welling up like a flash flood, like a sickness. If I was going to be memory-sick, I wanted powerfully to do it alone, as if alone was something new and urgent, and not what I did ever day.

I closed the junk-room door behind me as I yanked the light on. The swaying bulb on its chain rocked the shadows back and forth as I dragged from beneath a shelf a crate of cheap splinter wood, so big it could have held two men if they was dead. Once I drove my pickup to the plant to pick up a bulk of dog food straight off the dock, cheaper that way, and this was one of the crates it come in. It still had that faint high smell. As it slid, one corner snagged and ripped the carpet, laid open the orange shag to show the knotty pine beneath. The shag was threadbare, but why bother now buying a twenty-year rug? Three tackle boxes rattled and jiggled on top of the crate, two yawning open and one rusted shut, and I set all three onto the floor. I lifted the lid of the crate, pushed aside the top layer, a fuzzy blue blanket, and started lifting things out one at a time. I just glanced at some, spent more time with others. I warn't looking for anything in particular, just wanting to touch them and weigh them in my hands, and stack the memories up all around, in a back room under a bare bulb.

A crimpled flier with a dry mud footprint across it and a torn place up top, like someone yanked it off a staple on a bulletin board or a telephone pole:

SPACECRAFT
CONVENTION
Hear speakers who have contacted our Space Brothers
PICNIC
Lots of music—Astronomical telescope, see the craters on the
Moon, etc.
Public invited—Spread the word
Admission—50c and $1.00 donation
Children under school age free
FREE CAMPING
Bring your own tent, house car or camping outfit, folding chairs,
sleeping bags, etc.
CAFETERIA on the grounds—fried chicken, sandwiches, coffee,
cold drinks, etc.
Conventions held every year on the last Saturday, Sunday and
Monday of the month of June at
BUCK'S MOUNTAIN VIEW RANCH
Buck Nelson, Route 1
Mountain View, Missouri

A headline from a local paper: "Spacecraft Picnic at Buck's
Ranch Attracts 2000 People."

An old *Life* magazine in a see-through envelope, Marilyn Monroe
all puckered up to the plastic. April 7, 1952. The headline: "There
Is A Case For Interplanetary Saucers." I slid out the magazine
and flipped through the article. I read: "These objects cannot be
explained by present science as natural phenomena—but solely as
artificial devices created and operated by a high intelligence."

A Baggie of three or four dog hairs, with a sticker showing the
outline of a flying saucer and the words HAIR FROM BUCK'S
ALIEN DOG "BO."

Teddy hadn't minded, when I took the scissors to him to get the
burrs off, and to snip a little extra for the Bo trade. Bo was months

dead by then, but the folks demanded something. Some of my neighbors I do believe would have pulled down my house and barn a-looking for him, if they thought there was a body to be had. Some people won't believe in nothing that ain't a corpse, and I couldn't bear letting the science men get at him with their saws and jars, to jibble him up. Just the thought put me in mind of that old song:

> The old horse died with the whooping cough
> The old cow died in the fork of the branch
> The buzzards had them a public dance.

No, sir. No public dance this time. I hid Bo's body in a shallow cave, and I nearabouts crawled in after him, cause it liked to have killed me, too, even with the tractor's front arms to lift him and push him and drop him. Then I walled him up so good with scree and stones lying around that even I warn't sure any more where it was, along that long rock face.

I didn't let on that he was gone, neither. Already people were getting shirty about me not showing him off like a circus mule, bringing him out where people could gawk at him and poke him and ride him. I told them he was vicious around strangers, and that was a bald lie. He was a sweet old thing for his size, knocking me down with his licking tongue, and what was I but a stranger, at the beginning? We was all strangers. Those Baggies of Teddy hair was a bald lie, too, and so was some of the other parts I told through the years, when my story sort of got away from itself, or when I couldn't exactly remember what had happened in between this and that, so I had to fill in, the same way I filled the chinks between the rocks I stacked between me and Bo, to keep out the buzzards, hoping it'd be strong enough to last forever.

But a story ain't like a wall. The more stuff you add onto a wall, spackle and timber and flat stones, the harder it is to push down. The more stuff you add to a story through the years, the weaker it gets. Add a piece here and add a piece there, and in time you can't remember your own self how the pieces was supposed to fit together, and every piece is a chance for some fool to ask more questions, and confuse you more, and poke another hole or two, to make you wedge in something else, and there is no end to it. So finally you just don't want to tell no part of the story no more, except to yourself, because yourself is the only one who really believes in it. In some of it, anyway. The other folks, the ones who just want to laugh, to make fun, you run off or cuss out or turn your back on, until no one much asks anymore, or remembers, or cares. You're just that tetched old dirt farmer off of Route One, withered and sick and sitting on the floor of his junk room and crying, snot hanging from his nose, sneezing in the dust.

It warn't all a lie, though.

No, sir. Not by a long shot.

And that was the worst thing.

Because the reporters always came, ever year at the end of June, and so did the duck hunters who saw something funny in the sky above the blind one frosty morning and was looking for it ever since, and the retired military fellas who talked about "protocols" and "incident reports" and "security breaches," and the powdery old ladies who said they'd walked around the rosebush one afternoon and found themselves on the rings of Saturn, and the beatniks from the college, and the tourists with their Polaroids and short pants, and the women selling funnel cakes and glow-in-the-dark space Frisbees, and the younguns with the waving antennas on their heads, and the neighbors who just wanted to snoop around and see whether old Buck had finally let the place go to rack and ruin, or whether he was holding it together for one more year, they all showed up on time, just like the mockingbirds. But the one person who never came, not one damn time since the year of our Lord nineteen and fifty-six, was the alien Bob Solomon himself. The whole point of the damn picnics, the Man of the Hour, had never showed his face. And that was the real reason I give up on the picnics, turned sour on the whole fly-ing-saucer industry, and kept close to the willows ever since. It warn't my damn lumbago or the Mothman or Barney and Betty Hill and their Romper Room boogeymen, or those dull dumb rocks hauled back from the Moon and thrown in my face like coal in a Christ-mas stocking. It was Bob Solomon, who said he'd come back, stay in touch, continue to shine down his blue-white healing light, because he loved the Earth people, because he loved me, and who done none of them things.

What had happened, to keep Bob Solomon away? He hadn't died. Death was a stranger, out where Bob Solomon lived. Bo would be frisky yet, if he'd a stayed home. No, something had come between Mountain View and Bob Solomon, to keep him away. What had I done? What had I not done? Was it something I knew, that I wasn't supposed to know? Or was it something I forgot, or cast aside, something I should have held on to, and treasured? And now, if Bob Solomon was to look for Mountain View, could he find it? Would he know me? The Earth goes a far ways in twenty-odd years, and we go with it.

I wiped my nose on my hand and slid Marilyn back in her plas-tic and reached for the chain and clicked off the light and sat in the chilly dark, making like it was the cold clear peace of space.

I knew well the turnoff to the Clearwater Lake overlook, and I still like to have missed it that night, so black dark was the road through the woods. The sign with the arrow had deep-cut letters filled with white reflecting paint, and only the flash of the letters in the head-lights made me stand on the brakes and kept me from missing the left turn. I sat and waited, turn signal on, flashing green against the pine boughs overhead, even though there was no sign of cars a-com-ing from either direction. Ka-chunk, ka-chunk, flashed the pine trees, and then I turned off with a grumble of rubber as the tires left the asphalt and bit into the gravel of the overlook road. The stone-walled overlook had been built by the CCC in the 1930s, and the road the relief campers had built hadn't been improved much since, so I went up the hill slow on that narrow, straight road, away back in the jillikens. Once I saw the eyes of some critter as it dashed across my path, but nary a soul else, and when I reached the pullaround, and that low-slung wall all along the ridgetop, I thought maybe I had the wrong place. But then I saw two cars and a panel truck parked at the far end where younguns park when they go a-sparking, and I could see dark-people shapes a-milling about. I parked a ways away, shut off my engine and cut my lights. This helped me see a little better, and I could make out flashlight beams trained on the ground here and there, as people walked from the cars to where some big black shapes were set up, taller than a man. In the silence after I slammed my door I could hear low voices, too, and as I walked nearer, the murmurs resolved themselves and became words:

"Gravimeter checks out."

"Thank you, Isabel. Wallace, how about that spectrum analyzer?"

"Powering up, Doc. Have to give it a minute."

"We may not have a minute, or we may have ten hours. Who knows?" I steered toward this voice, which was older than the others. "Our visitors are unpredictable," he continued.

"Visitors?" the girl asked.

"No, you're right. I've broken my own rule. We don't know they're sentient, and even if they are, we don't know they're *visitors.* They may be local, native to the place, certainly more so than Wallace here. Georgia-born, aren't you, Wallace?"

"Company, Doc," said the boy.

"Yes, I see him, barely. Hello, sir. May I help you? Wallace, please. Mind your manners." The flashlight beam in my face had blinded me, but the professor grabbed it out of the boy's hand and turned it up to shine beneath his chin, like a youngun making a scary face, so I could see a shadow version of his lumpy jowls, his big nose, his bushy mustache. "I'm Harley Rutledge," he said. "Might you be Mr. Nelson?"

"That's me," I said, and as I stuck out a hand, the flashlight beam moved to locate it. Then a big hand came into view and shook mine. The knuckles were dry and cracked and red-flaked.

"How do you do," Rutledge said, and switched off the flashlight. "Our mutual friend explained what we're doing out here, I presume? Forgive the darkness, but we've learned that too much brightness on our part rather spoils the seeing, skews the experiment."

"Scares 'em off?" I asked.

"Mmm," Rutledge said. "No, not quite that. Besides the lack of evidence for any *them* that *could* be frightened, we have some evidence that these, uh, luminous phenomena are . . . responsive to our lights. If we wave ours around too much, they wave around in response. We shine ours into the water, they descend into the water as well. All fascinating, but it does suggest a possibility of reflection, of visual echo, which we are at some pains to rule out. Besides which, we'd like to observe, insofar as possible, what these lights do when *not* observed. Though they seem difficult to fool. Some, perhaps fancifully, have suggested they can read investigators' minds. Ah, Wallace, are we up and running, then? Very good, very good." Something hard and plastic was nudging my arm, and I thought for a second Rutledge was offering me a drink. "Binoculars, Mr. Nelson? We always carry spares, and you're welcome to help us look."

The girl's voice piped up. "We're told you've seen the spooklights all your life," she said. "Is that true?"

"I reckon you could say that," I said, squinting into the binoculars. Seeing the darkness up close made it even darker.

"That is so cool," Isobel said. "I'm going to write my thesis on low-level nocturnal lights of apparent volition. I call them linnalavs for short. Will-o'-the-wisps, spooklights, treasure lights, corpse lights, ball lightning, fireships, jack-o'-lanterns, the *feu follet*. I'd love to interview you sometime. Just think, if you had been recording your observations all these years."

I did record some, I almost said, but Rutledge interrupted us. "Now, Isobel, don't crowd the man on short acquaintance. Why don't you help Wallace with the tape recorders? Your hands are steadier, and we don't want him cutting himself again." She stomped off, and I found something to focus on with the binoculars: the winking red light atop the Taum Sauk Mountain fire tower. "You'll have to excuse Isobel, Mr. Nelson. She has the enthusiasm of youth, and she's just determined to get ball lightning in there somehow, though I keep explaining that's an entirely separate phenomenon."

"Is that what our friend, that reporter gal, told you?" I asked. "That I seen the spooklights in these parts, since I was a tad?"

"Yes, and that you were curious about our researches, to compare your folk knowledge to our somewhat more scientific investigations. And as I told her, you're welcome to join us tonight, as long as you don't touch any of our equipment, and as long as you stay out of our way should anything, uh, happen. Rather irregular, having an untrained local observer present—but frankly, Mr. Nelson, everything about Project Identification is irregular, at least as far as the U.S. Geological Survey is concerned. So we'll both be irregular together, heh." A round green glow appeared and disappeared at chest level: Rutledge checking his watch. "I frankly thought Miss Rains would be coming with you. She'll be along presently, I take it?"

"Don't ask me," I said, trying to see the tower itself beneath the light. Black metal against black sky. I'd heard her name as *Hanes*, but I let it go. "Maybe she got a better offer."

"Oh, I doubt that, not given her evident interest. Know Miss Rains well, do you, Mr. Nelson?"

"Can't say as I do. Never seen her before this morning. No, wait. Before yesterday."

"Lovely girl," Rutledge said. "And so energized."

"Sort of wears me out," I told him.

"Yes, well, pleased to meet you, again. I'd better see how Isobel and Wallace are getting along. There are drinks and snacks in the truck, and some folding chairs and blankets. We're here all night, so please make yourself at home."

I am home, I thought, fiddling with the focus on the binoculars as Rutledge trotted away, his little steps sounding like a spooked quail. I hadn't let myself look at the night sky for anything but quick glances for so long, just to make sure the Moon and Venus and Old Rion and the Milky Way was still there, that I was feeling sort of giddy to have nothing else to look at. I was like a man who took the cure years ago but now finds himself locked in a saloon. That brighter patch over yonder, was that the lights of Piedmont? And those two, no, three, airplanes, was they heading for St. Louis? I reckon I couldn't blame Miss Priss for not telling the professor the whole truth about me, else he would have had the law out here, to keep that old crazy man away. I wondered where Miss Priss had got to. Rutledge and I both had the inkle she would be joining us out here, but where had I got that? Had she quite said it, or had I just assumed?

I focused again on the tower light, which warn't flashing no more. Instead it was getting stronger and weaker and stronger again, like a heartbeat, and never turning full off. It seemed to be growing, too, taking up more of the view, as if it was coming closer. I was so interested in what the fire watchers might be up to—testing the equipment? signaling rangers on patrol?—that when the light moved sideways toward the north, I turned, too, and swung the binoculars around to keep it in view, and didn't think nothing odd about a fire tower going for a little walk until the boy Wallace said, "There's one now, making its move."

The college folks all talked at once: "Movie camera on." "Tape recorder on." "Gravimeter negative." I heard the click-whirr, click-whirr of someone taking Polaroids just as fast as he could go. For my part, I kept following the spooklight as it bobbled along the far ridge, bouncing like a slow ball or a balloon, and pulsing as it went. After the burst of talking, everyone was silent, watching the light and fooling with the equipment. Then the professor whispered in my ear: "Look familiar to you, Mr. Nelson?"

It sure warn't a patch on Bob Solomon's spaceship, but I knew Rutledge didn't have Bob Solomon in mind. "The spooklights I've seen was down lower," I told him, "below the tops of the trees, most times hugging the ground. This one moves the same, but it must be up fifty feet in the air."

"Maybe," he whispered, "and maybe not. Appearances can be deceiving. Hey!" He cried aloud as the slow bouncy light shot straight up in the air. It hung there, then fell down to the ridgeline again and kept a-going, bobbing down the far slope, between us and the ridge, heading toward the lake and toward us.

The professor asked, "Gravitational field?"

"No change," the girl said.

"Keep monitoring."

The light split in two, then in three. All three lights come toward us.

"Here they come! Here they come!"

I couldn't keep all three in view, so I stuck with the one making the straightest shot downhill. Underneath it, treetops come into view as the light passed over, just as if it was a helicopter with a spotlight. But there warn't no engine sound at all, just the sound of a little zephyr a-stirring the leaves, and the clicks of someone snapping pictures. Even Bob Solomon's craft had made a little racket: It whirred as it moved, and turned on and off with a *whunt* like the fans in a chickenhouse. It was hard to tell the light's shape. It just faded out at the edges, as the pulsing came and went. It was blue-white in motion but flickered red when it paused. I watched the light bounce down to the far shore of the lake. Then it flashed real bright, and was gone. I lowered the binoculars in time to see the other two hit the water and flash out, too—but one sent a smaller fireball rolling across the water toward us. When it slowed down, it sank, just like a rock a child sends a-skipping across a pond. The water didn't kick up at all, but the light could be seen below for a few seconds, until it sank out of sight.

"Awesome!" Isobel said.

"Yeah, that was something," Wallace said. "Wish we had a boat. Can we bring a boat next time, Doc? Hey, why is it so light?"

"Moonrise," Isobel said. "See our moonshadows?"

We did all have long shadows, reaching over the wall and toward the lake. I always heard that to stand in your own moonshadow means good luck, but I didn't get the chance to act on it before the professor said: "That's not the moon."

The professor was facing away from the water, toward the source of light. Behind us a big bright light moved through the trees, big as a house. The beams shined out separately between the trunks but then they closed up together again as the light moved out onto the surface of the gravel pullaround. It was like a giant glowing upside-down bowl, twenty-five feet high, a hundred or more across, sliding across the ground. You could see everything lit up inside, clear as a bell, like in a tabletop aquarium in a dark room. But it warn't attached to nothing. Above the light dome was no spotlight, no aircraft, nothing but the night sky and stars.

"Wallace, get that camera turned around, for God's sake!"

"Instruments read nothing, Doc. It's as if it weren't there."

"Maybe it's not. No, Mr. Nelson! Please, stay back!"

But I'd already stepped forward to meet it, binoculars hanging by their strap at my side, bouncing against my leg as I walked into the light. Inside I didn't feel nothing physical—no tingling, and no warmth, no more than turning on a desk lamp warms a room. But in my mind I felt different, powerful different. Standing there in that light, I felt more calm and easeful than I'd felt in years—like I was someplace I belonged, more so than on my own farm. As the edge of the light crept toward me, about at the speed of a slow walk, I slow-walked in the same direction as it was going, just to keep in the light as long as I could.

The others, outside the light, did the opposite. They scattered back toward the wall of the overlook, trying to stay in the dark ahead of it, but they didn't have no place to go, and in a few seconds they was all in the light, too, the three of them and their standing telescopes and all their equipment on folding tables and sawhorses all around. I got my first good look at the three of them in that crawling glow. Wallace had hippie hair down in his eyes and a beaky nose, and was bowlegged. The professor was older than I expected, but not nearly so old as me, and had a great big belly—what mountain folks would call an *investment,* as he'd been putting into it for years. Isobel had long stringy hair that needed a wash, and a wide butt, and black-rimmed glasses so thick a welder could have worn them, but she was right cute for all that. None of us cast a shadow inside the light.

I looked up and could see the night sky and even pick out the stars, but it was like looking through a soap film or a skiff of snow. Something I couldn't feel or rightly see was in the way, between me and the sky. Still I walked until the thigh-high stone wall stopped me. The dome kept moving, of course, and as I went through its back edge—because it was just that clear-cut, either you was in the light or you warn't—why, I almost swung my legs over the wall to follow it. The hill, though, dropped off steep on the other side, and the undergrowth was all tangled and snaky. So I held up for a few seconds, dithering, and then the light had left me behind, and I was in the dark again, pressed up against that wall like something drowned and found in a drain after a flood. I now could feel the breeze of the lake, so air warn't moving easy through the light dome, neither.

The dome kept moving over the folks from the college, slid over the wall and down the slope, staying about 25 feet tall the whole way. It moved out onto the water—which stayed as still as could be, not roiled at all—then faded, slow at first and then faster, until I warn't sure I was looking at anything anymore, and then it was gone.

The professor slapped himself on the cheeks and neck, like he was putting on aftershave. "No sunburn, thank God," he said. "How do the rest of you feel?"

The other two slapped themselves just the same.

"I'm fine."

"I'm fine, too," Isobel said. "The Geiger counter never triggered, either."

What did I feel like? Like I wanted to dance, to skip and cut capers, to holler out loud. My eyes were full like I might cry. I stared at that dark lake like I could stare a hole in it, like I could will that dome to rise again. I whispered, "Thank you," and it warn't a prayer, not directed at anybody, just an acknowledgment of something that had passed, like tearing off a calendar page, or plowing under a field of cornstalks.

I turned to the others, glad I finally had someone to talk to, someone I could share all these feelings with, but to my surprise they was all running from gadget to gadget, talking at once about phosphorescence and gas eruptions and electromagnetic fields, I couldn't follow half of it. Where had they been? Had they plumb missed it? For the first time in years, I felt I had to tell them what I had seen, what I had felt and known, the whole story. It would help them. It would be a comfort to them.

I walked over to them, my hands held out. I wanted to calm them down, get their attention.

"Oh, thank you, Mr. Nelson," said the professor. He reached out and unhooked from my hand the strap of the binoculars. "I'll take those. Well, I'd say you brought us luck, wouldn't you agree, Isobel, Wallace? Quite a remarkable display, that second one especially. Like the Bahia Kino Light of the Gulf of California, but in motion! Ionization of the air, perhaps, but no Geiger activity, mmm. A lower voltage, perhaps?" He patted his pockets. "Need a shopping list for our next vigil. A portable Curran counter, perhaps—"

I grabbed at his sleeve. "I saw it."

"Yes? Well, we all saw it, Mr. Nelson. Really a tremendous phenomenon—if the distant lights and the close light are related, that is, and their joint appearance cannot be coincidental. I'll have Isobel take your statement before we go, but now, if you'll excuse me."

"I don't mean tonight," I said, "and I don't mean no spooklights. I seen the real thing, an honest-to-God flying saucer, in 1956. At my farm outside Mountain View, west of here. Thataway." I pointed. "It shot out a beam of light, and after I was in that light, I felt better, not so many aches and pains. And listen: I saw it more than once, the saucer. It kept coming back."

He was backing away from me. "Mr. Nelson, really, I must—"

"And I met the crew," I told him. "The pilot stepped out of the saucer to talk with me. That's right, with me. He looked human, just like you and me, only better-looking. He looked like that boy in *Battle Cry*, Tab Hunter. But he said his name was—"

"Mr. Nelson." The early morning light was all around by now, giving everything a gray glow, and I could see Rutledge was frowning. "Please. You've had a very long night, and a stressful one. You're tired, and I'm sorry to say that you're no longer young. What you're saying no longer makes sense."

"Don't make sense!" I cried. "You think what we just saw makes sense?"

"I concede that I have no ready explanations, but what we saw were lights, Mr. Nelson, only lights. No sign of intelligence, nor of aircraft. Certainly not of crew members. No little green men. No grays. No Tab Hunter from the Moon."

"He lived on Mars," I said, "and his name was Bob Solomon."

The professor stared at me. The boy behind him, Wallace, stared at me, too, nearabouts tripping over his own feet as he bustled back and forth toting things to the truck. The girl just shook her head, and turned and walked into the woods.

"I wrote it up in a little book," I told the professor. "Well, I say I wrote it. Really, I talked it out, and I paid a woman at the library to copy it down and type it. I got a copy in the pickup. Let me get it. Won't take a sec."

"Mr. Nelson," he said again. "I'm sorry, I truly am. If you write me at the college, and enclose your address, I'll see you get a copy of our article, should it appear. We welcome interest in our work from the layman. But for now, here, today, I must ask you to leave."

"Leave? But the gal here said I could help."

"That was before you expressed these . . . delusions," Rutledge said. "Please realize what I'm trying to do. Like Hynek, like Vallee and Maccabee, I am trying to establish these researches as a serious scientific discipline. I am trying to create a field where none exists, where Isobel and her peers can work and publish without fear of ridicule. And here you are, spouting nonsense about a hunky spaceman named Bob! You must realize how that sounds. Why, you'd make the poor girl a laughing stock."

"She don't want to interview me?"

"Interview you! My God, man, aren't you listening? It would be career suicide for her to be *seen* with you! Please, before the sun is full up, Mr. Nelson, please, do the decent thing, and get back into your truck, and go."

I felt myself getting madder and madder. My hands had turned into fists. I turned from the professor, pointed at the back-and-forth boy and hollered, "You!"

He froze, like I had pulled a gun on him.

I called: "You take any Polaroids of them things?"

"Some, yes, sir," he said, at the exact same time the professor said, "Don't answer that."

"Where are they?" I asked. "I want to see 'em."

Behind the boy was a card table covered with notebooks and Mountain Dew bottles and the Polaroid camera, too, with a stack of picture squares next to it. I walked toward the table, and the professor stepped into my path, crouched, arms outstretched, like we was gonna wrestle.

"Keep away from the equipment," Rutledge said.

The boy ran back to the table and snatched up the pictures as I feinted sideways, and the professor lunged to block me again.

"I want to see them pictures, boy," I said.

"Mr. Nelson, go home! Wallace, secure those photos."

Wallace looked around like he didn't know what secure meant, in the open air overlooking a mountain lake, then he started stuffing the photos into his pockets, until they poked out all around, sort of comical. Two fell out on the ground. Then Wallace picked up a folding chair and held it out in front of him like a lion tamer. Stenciled across the bottom of the chair was PROP. CUMBEE FUNERAL HOME.

I stooped and picked up a rock and cocked my hand back like I was going to fling it. The boy flinched backward, and I felt right bad about scaring him. I turned and made like to throw it at the professor instead, and when he flinched, I felt some better. Then I turned and made like to throw it at the biggest telescope, and that felt best of all, for both boy and professor hollered then, no words but just a wail from the boy and a bark from the man, so loud that I nearly dropped the rock.

"Pictures, pictures," I said. "All folks want is pictures. People didn't believe nothing I told 'em, because during the first visits I didn't have no camera, and then when I rented a Brownie to take to Venus with me, didn't none of the pictures turn out! All of 'em overexposed, the man at the Rexall said. I ain't fooled with no pictures since, but I'm gonna have one of these, or so help me, I'm gonna bust out the eyes of this here spyglass, you see if I won't. Don't you come no closer with that chair, boy! You set that thing down." I picked up a second rock, so I had one heavy weight in each hand, and felt good. I knocked them together with a *clop* like hooves, and I walked around to the business end of the telescope, where the eyepiece and all those tiny adjustable thingies was, because that looked like the thing's underbelly. I held the rocks up to either side, like I was gonna knock them together and smash the instruments in between. I bared my teeth and tried to look scary, which warn't easy because now that it was good daylight, I suddenly had to pee something fierce. It must have worked, though, because Wallace set down the chair, just about the time the girl Isobel stepped out of the woods.

She was tucking in her shirttail, like she'd answered her own call of nature. She saw us all three standing there froze, and she got still, too, one hand down the back of her britches. Her darting eyes all magnified in her glasses looked quick and smart.

"What's going on?" she asked. Her front teeth stuck out like a chipmunk's.

"I want to see them pictures," I said.

"Isobel," the professor said, "drive down to the bait shop and call the police." He picked up an oak branch, hefted it, and started stripping off the little branches, like that would accomplish anything. "Run along, there's a good girl. Wallace and I have things well in hand."

"The heck we do," Wallace said. "I bring back a wrecked telescope, and I kiss my work-study goodbye."

"Jesus wept," Isobel said, and walked down the slope, tucking in the rest of her shirttail. She rummaged on the table, didn't find them, then saw the two stray pictures lying on the ground at Wallace's feet. She picked one up, walked over to me, held it out.

The professor said, "Isabel, don't! That's university property."

"Here, Mr. Nelson," she said. "Just take it and go, OK?"

I was afraid to move, for fear I'd wet my pants. My eyeballs was swimming already. I finally let fall one of my rocks and took the photo in that free hand, stuck it in my overalls pocket without looking at it. "Preciate it," I said. For no reason, I handed her the other rock, and for no reason, she took it. I turned and walked herky-jerky toward my truck, hoping I could hold it till I got into the woods at least, but no, I gave up halfway there, and with my back to the others I unzipped and groaned and let fly a racehorse stream of pee that spattered the tape-recorder case.

I heard the professor moan behind me, "Oh, Mr. Nelson! This is really too bad!"

"I'm sorry!" I cried. "It ain't on purpose, I swear! I was about to bust." I probably would have tried to aim it, at that, to hit some of that damned equipment square on, but I hadn't had no force nor distance on my pee for years. It just poured out, like pulling a plug. I peed and peed, my eyes rolling back, lost in the good feeling ("You go, Mr. Nelson!" Isobel yelled), and as it puddled and coursed in little rills around the rocks at my feet, I saw a fisherman in a distant rowboat in the middle of the lake, his line in the water just where that corpse light had submerged the night before. I couldn't see him good, but I could tell he was watching us, as his boat drifted along. The sparkling water looked like it was moving fast past him, the way still water in the sun always does, even though the boat hardly moved at all.

"You wouldn't eat no fish from there," I hollered at him, "if you knew what was underneath."

His only answer was a pop and a hiss that carried across the water loud as a firework. He lifted the can he had opened, raised it high toward us as if to say, Cheers, and took a long drink.

Finally done, I didn't even zip up as I shuffled to the pickup. Without all that pee I felt lightheaded and hollow and plumb worn out. I wondered whether I'd make it home before I fell asleep.

"Isobel," the professor said behind me, "I asked you to go call the police."

"Oh, for God's sake, let it go," she said. "You really *would* look like an asshole then. Wallace, give me a hand."

I crawled into the pickup, slammed the door, dropped the window—it didn't crank down anymore, just fell into the door, so that I had to raise it two-handed—cranked the engine and drove off without looking at the bucktoothed girl, the bowlegged boy, the professor holding a club in his bloody-knuckled hands, the fisherman drinking his breakfast over a spook hole. I caught one last sparkle of the morning sun on the surface of the lake as I swung the truck into the shade of the woods, on the road headed down to the highway. Light through the branches dappled my rusty hood, my cracked dashboard, my baggy overalls. Some light is easy to explain. I fished the Polaroid picture out of my pocket and held it up at eye level while I drove. All you could see was a bright white nothing, like the boy had aimed the lens at the glare of a hundred-watt bulb from an inch away. I tossed the picture out the window. Another dud, just like Venus. A funny thing: The cardboard square bounced to a standstill in the middle of the road and caught the light just enough to be visible in my rear-view mirror, like a little bright window in the ground, until I reached the highway, signaled ka-chunk, ka-chunk, and turned to the right, toward home.

Later that morning I sat on the porch, waiting for her. Staring at the lake had done me no good, no more than staring at the night sky over the barn had done, all those years, but staring at the rhododendron called her forth, sure enough. She stepped around the bush with a little wave. She looked sprightly as ever, for all that long walk up the steep driveway, but I didn't blame her for not scraping her car past all those close bushes. One day they'd grow together and intertwine their limbs like clasped hands, and I'd be cut off from the world like in a fairy-tale. But I wasn't cut off yet, because here came Miss Priss, with boots up over her knees and dress hiked up to yonder, practically. Her colors were red and black today, even that fool saucer hat was red with a black button in the center. She was sipping out of a box with a straw in it.

"I purely love orange juice," she told me. "Whenever I'm traveling, I can't get enough of it. Here, I brought you one." I reached out and took the box offered, and she showed me how to peel off the straw and poke a hole with it, and we sat side by side sipping awhile. I didn't say nothing, just sipped and looked into Donald Duck's eyes and sipped some more. Finally she emptied her juice-box with a long low gurgle and turned to me and asked, "Did you make it out to the lake last night?"

"I did that thing, yes, ma'am."

"See anything?"

The juice was brassy-tasting and thin, but it was growing on me, and I kept a-working that straw. "Didn't see a damn thing," I said. I cut my eyes at her. "Didn't see you, neither."

"Yes, well, I'm sorry about that," she said. "My supervisors called me away. When I'm on assignment, my time is not my own." Now she cut her eyes at *me*. "You *sure* you didn't see anything?"

I shook my head, gurgled out the last of my juice. "Nothing Dr. Rutledge can't explain away," I said. "Nothing you could have a conversation with."

"How'd you like Dr. Rutledge?"

"We got along just fine," I said, "when he warn't hunting up a club to beat me with, and I warn't pissing into his machinery. He asked after *you*, though. You was the one he wanted along on his camping trip, out there in the dark."

"I'll try to call on him, before I go."

"Go where?"

She fussed with her hat. "Back home. My assignment's over."

"Got everthing you needed, did you?"

"Yes, I think so. Thanks to you."

"Well, I ain't," I said. I turned and looked her in the face. "I ain't got everthing I need, myself. What I need ain't here on this Earth. It's up yonder, someplace I can't get to no more. Ain't that a bitch? And yet I was right satisfied until two days ago, when you come along and stirred me all up again. I never even went to bed last night, and I ain't sleepy even now. All I can think about is night coming on again, and what I might see up there this time."

"But that's a *good* thing," she said. "You keep your eyes peeled, Mr. Nelson. You've seen things already, and you haven't seen the last of them." She tapped my arm with her juice-box straw. "I have faith in you," she said. "I wasn't sure at first. That's why I came to visit, to see if you were keeping the faith. And I see now that you are—in your own way."

"I ain't got no faith," I said. "I done aged out of it."

She stood up. "Oh, pish tosh," she said. "You proved otherwise last night. The others tried to stay *out* of the light, but not you, Mr. Nelson. Not you." She set her juice box on the step beside mine. "Throw that away for me, will you? I got to be going." She stuck out her hand. It felt hot to the touch, and powerful. Holding it gave me the strength to stand up, look into her eyes, and say:

"I made it all up. The dog Bo, and the trips to Venus and Mars, and the cured lumbago. It was a made-up story, ever single Lord God speck of it."

And I said that sincerely. Bob Solomon forgive me: As I said it, I believed it was true.

She looked at me for a spell, her eyes big. She looked for a few seconds like a child I'd told Santa warn't coming, ever again. Then she grew back up, and with a sad little smile she stepped toward me, pressed her hands flat to the chest bib of my overalls, stood on tip-pytoes, and kissed me on the cheek, the way she would her grandpap, and as she slid something into my side pocket she whispered in my ear, "That's not what I hear on Enceladus." She patted my pocket. "That's how to reach me, if you need me. But you won't need me." She stepped into the yard and walked away, swinging her pocket-book, and called back over her shoulder: "You know what you need, Mr. Nelson? You need a dog. A dog is good help around a farm. A dog will sit up with you, late at night, and lie beside you, and keep you warm. You ought to keep your eye out. You never know when a stray will turn up."

She walked around the bush, and was gone. I picked up the empty Donald Ducks, because it was something to do, and I was turning to go in when a man's voice called:

"Mr. Buck Nelson?"

A young man in a skinny tie and horn-rimmed glasses stood at the edge of the driveway where Miss Priss—no, Miss Rains, she deserved her true name—had stood a few moments before. He walked forward, one hand outstretched and the other reaching into the pocket of his denim jacket. He pulled out a long flat notebook.

"My name's Matt Ketchum," he said, "and I'm pleased to find you, Mr. Nelson. I'm a reporter with the Associated Press, and I'm writing a story on the surviving flying-saucer contactees of the 1950s."

I caught him up short when I said, "Aw, not again! Damn it all, I just told all that to Miss Rains. She works for the A&P, too."

He withdrew his hand, looked blank.

I pointed to the driveway. "Hello, you must have walked past her in the drive, not two minutes ago! Pretty girl in a red-and-black dress, boots up to here. Miss Rains, or Hanes, or something like that."

"Mr. Nelson, I'm not following you. I don't work with anyone named Rains or Hanes, and no one else has been sent out here but me. And that driveway was deserted. No other cars parked down at the highway, either." He cocked his head, gave me a pitying look. "Are you sure you're not thinking of some other day, sir?"

"But she," I said, hand raised toward my bib pocket—but something kept me from saying *gave me her card.* That pocket felt strangely warm, like there was a live coal in it.

"Maybe she worked for someone else, Mr. Nelson, like UPI, or maybe the *Post-Dispatch?* I hope I'm not scooped again. I wouldn't be surprised, with the Spielberg picture coming out and all."

I turned to focus on him for the first time. "Where is Enceladus, anyway?"

"I beg your pardon?"

I said it again, moving my lips all cartoony, like he was deaf.

"I, well, I don't know, sir. I'm not familiar with it."

I thought a spell. "I do believe," I said, half to myself, "it's one a them Saturn moons." To jog my memory, I made a fist of my right hand and held it up—that was Saturn—and held up my left thumb a ways from it, and moved it back and forth, sighting along it. "It's out a ways, where the ring gets sparse. Thirteenth? Fourteenth, maybe?"

He just goggled at me. I gave him a sad look and shook my head and said, "You don't know much, if that's what you know, and that's a fact."

He cleared his throat. "Anyway, Mr. Nelson, as I was saying, I'm interviewing all the contactees I can find, like George Van Tassel, and Orfeo Angelucci—"

"Yes, yes, and Truman Bethurum, and them," I said. "She talked to all them, too."

"Bethurum?" he repeated. He flipped through his notebook. "Wasn't he the asphalt spreader, the one who met the aliens atop a mesa in Nevada?"

"Yeah, that's the one."

He looked worried now. "Um, Mr. Nelson, you must have misunderstood her. Truman Bethurum died in 1969. He's been dead eight years, sir."

I stood there looking at the rhododendron and seeing the pretty face and round hat, hearing the singsong voice, like she had learned English from a book.

I turned and went into the house, let the screen bang shut behind, didn't bother to shut the wood door.

"Mr. Nelson?"

My chest was plumb hot, now. I went straight to the junk room, yanked on the light. Everything was spread out on the floor where I left it. I shoved aside Marilyn, all the newspapers, pawed through the books.

"Mr. Nelson?" The voice was coming closer, moving through the house like a spooklight.

There it was: *Aboard a Flying Saucer*, by Truman Bethurum. I flipped through it, looking only at the pictures, until I found her: dark hair, big dark eyes, sharp chin, round hat. It was old Truman's drawing of Captain Aura Rhanes, the sexy Space Sister from the planet Clarion who visited him eleven times in her little red-and-black uniform, come right into his bedroom, so often that Mrs. Bethurum got jealous and divorced him. I had heard that old Truman, toward the end, went out and hired girl assistants to answer his mail and take messages just because they sort of looked like Aura Rhanes.

"Mr. Nelson?" said young Ketchum, standing in the door. "Are you OK?"

I let drop the book, stood, and said, "Doing just fine, son. If you'll excuse me? I got to be someplace." I closed the door in his face, dragged a bookcase across the doorway to block it, and pulled out Miss Rhanes' card, which was almost too hot to touch. No writing on it, neither, only a shiny silver surface that reflected my face like a mirror—and there was something behind my face, something aways back inside the card, a moving silvery blackness like a field of stars rushing toward me, and as I stared into that card, trying to see, my reflection slid out of the way and the edges of the card flew out and the card was a window, a big window, and now a door that I moved through without stepping, and someone out there was playing a single fiddle, no dance tune but just a-scraping along slow and sad as the stars whirled around me, and a ringed planet was swimming into view, the rings on edge at first but now tilting toward me and thickening as I dived down, the rings getting closer dividing into bands like layers in a rock face, and then into a field of rocks like that no-earthly-good south pasture, only there was so many rocks, so close together, and then I fell between them like an ant between the rocks in a gravel driveway, and now I was speeding toward a pinpoint of light, and as I moved toward it faster and faster, it grew and resolved itself and reshaped into a pear, a bulb, with a long sparkling line extending out, like a space elevator, like a chain, and at the end of the chain the moon became a glowing light bulb. I was staring into the bulb in my junk room, dazzled, my eyes flashing, my head achy, and the card dropped from my fingers with no sound, and my feet were still shuffling though the fiddle had faded away. I couldn't hear nothing over the knocking and the barking and young Ketchum calling: "Hey, Mr. Nelson? Is this your dog?"

Acknowledgments

I am indebted to countless people for their assistance, inspiration and encouragement as I was working on these stories, including: my late parents, who raised me to read; everyone at Clarion West 1994, and all my Clarion and Clarion West students since; my students and teachers at N.C. State University, especially John Kessel, who grew me from a bean; my students and teachers at the University of Alabama; my students and colleagues at Frostburg State University; all the editors who have published my fiction, especially Gardner Dozois, Patrick Nielsen Hayden, and Ellen Datlow; my fellow workshoppers at the Sycamore Hill Writers Conference; everyone at the International Conference on the Fantastic in the Arts; everyone who has read my work, shown up to my readings, and boosted my signal on social media through the years; and, above all, my wife, Sydney.

Publication History

"An Agent of Utopia" and "Joe Diabo's Farewell" are published here for the first time.

"Beluthahatchie," *Asimov's*, 1997

"The Map to the Homes of the Stars," *Dying for It*, 1997

"The Pottawatomie Giant," *SciFiction*, 2000

"Senator Bilbo," *Starlight 3*, 2001

"The Big Rock Candy Mountain," *Conjunctions* 39, 2002

"Daddy Mention and the Monday Skull," *Mojo: Conjure Stories*, 2003

"Zora and the Zombie," *SciFiction*, 2004

"Unique Chicken Goes in Reverse," *Eclipse* One, 2007

"Slow as a Bullet," *Eclipse* Four, 2011

"Close Encounters," *The Pottawatomie Giant*, 2012

About the Author

Andy Duncan's short fiction has been honored with a Nebula Award, a Theodore Sturgeon Memorial Award, and three World Fantasy Awards. A native of Batesburg, S.C., Duncan has been a newspaper reporter, a trucking-magazine editor, a bookseller, a student-media adviser, and, since 2008, a member of the writing faculty at Frostburg State University in the mountains of western Maryland, where he lives with his wife, Sydney.